HELL BAY

Forced to sail from his native Ireland in disgrace, a young doctor is thrust by a stormy sea onto the Scilly Islands, where romance and adventure await him. But his true destiny is many miles beyond—in America, where danger and intrigue test his courage, his strength, and his very will to survive . . .

HELL BAY

Sam Llewellyn

BALLANTINE BOOKS • NEW YORK

*Any resemblance between any character in this book
and any person living is entirely coincidental.*

HELL BAY *first published 1980 by Arlington Books (Publishers) Ltd., 3 Clifford Street, Mayfair, London W.1.*

Copyright © Sam Llewellyn 1980, 1981

Library of Congress Catalog Card Number: 80-70865

ISBN 0-345-9642-7

This edition published by arrangement with
Arlington Books (Publishers) Ltd.

Manufactured in the United States of America

First Ballantine Books Edition: July 1981

Foreword

THIS BOOK is based on material discovered by my builder while dismantling the burnt-out shell of Drumcarty Castle. Found in a sealed niche of the library wall was a tin trunk bearing the name of Nicholas Power. It was marked *New Botallack 1835,* and contained a number of calf-bound journals, both personal and scientific, and a mass of loose papers—letters, bills, newspaper cuttings—much damaged by damp. Surprisingly, the gutting by fire of the library in 1922 had affected them little: so the greater part of the trunk's contents was at least decipherable.

A word of caution: in the course of my writing I have had occasion to check names and dates against the records of the years with which Nicholas Power deals. I fear that his desire to tell a good story sometimes outstrips his scruples in the matter of historical accuracy, as, for instance, in the dates of certain Scillonian wrecks. Equally, some of the characters who walk these pages are by no means as historians would have them. But I have left facts and people as Power represented them. For it is not as if we are assisting at the founding of empires or the intrigues of European palaces, where one fact locks into the next and grows at last into a complex but immutable whole. With Nicholas Power we walk the wild places of the world before the arrival of the chronicler and the legislator.

There is one other thing I should mention. At the bottom of his trunk, I found a miniature, of the kind often commissioned before the popularization of the photographic *carte de visite.* It shows a young man in the roll collar and high gills of the mid-1820's. The brow is broad under straight, black hair carefully disarrayed, the nose

2

straight, with a suggestion of the aquiline. The eyes, set above cheeks still youthfully plump, are long and blue and somehow older than the rest of the face. They are penetrating, doctor's eyes; but they have a restlessness that combines with the full lower lip to throw the whole effect strangely out of balance. On the reverse of the painting, an immature female hand has written, "Papa in 1823." This would make Nicholas Power, if it is indeed a portrait, twenty years old. The identity of the young female scribbler is a mystery. Time has healed over Power without seam or scar.

What follows is all that remains.

Sam Llewellyn, 1980

Prologue

THE WIND had been hammering in from the west all day, piling up the swell rolling down on the islands under the thick, grey blanket of cloud. Sunset was a pale, grim affair, a flash of watery blood between two squalls, then a quick dusk whipped with bursts of rain.

With the nightfall, the growling of the swells in the Western Rocks deepened. The wind faltered, veered north, and gained strength.

The woman had been standing on Castle Down since mid-afternoon, gazing beyond the flower and boom of the black Atlantic in the Kettle Rocks, still as a dolmen on the scrappy turf. As the shadows poured with the rain over the sea, she pushed back her damp hair and looked over the trees of spray at something on the northern horizon. She raised her hand above her head. A coil of the gale twisted inside her cloak, swelling it until she was a grotesque mass against the racing sky. A thread of laughter tumbled away into the solid cairns. Then she turned and walked past the ruins down to the yellow windows of the village.

In the wet street she knocked on a door that poured light and smoke and the fumes of spirits. Men came out, big men with beards. They walked down to the hook of land that sheltered cottages and long, low sheds of thatch and granite. From one of the sheds they drew a slender boat, thirty feet long, with holepins for six oars.

Quietly, they pulled under the end of the ruined quay and across for the dim loom of another island. There were fewer lights on that island; when they landed on the rain-grey beach, there was a dark-lantern and the dim hulks of more men in the dark, and a low murmur of voices.

3

The woman led northwards, through little fields walled with granite pebbles onto hills where the earth was a thin skin punctured by giant molars, and the wind yelled in the black bight below.

In the lee of a rock, a small fire burned. By it they waited. There was no more talk. Wind and sea were too loud. Far to the south, a point of white light came and went behind speeding curtains of rain.

Then there was another light.

Out in the bight, the yellow glimmer of a lantern. The glimmer whitened, became stronger and steadied. It turned bright and constant, glittered on the marching crests. The glow of it cohered into a single beam, and the beam swung northwards.

Now the watchers rose to their feet. They did not look at the light. Their eyes were on the place where the final blade of its beam snipped at the unbroken shoulders of the waves. Five times the spray roared up and masked it; after the fifth, a low groan rumbled under the sounds of the night.

For a moment, the sail was a grey dove's breast straining at the mote of brilliance in the bay. A caged dove, barred with the shadows of shroud and stay, yard and brace. Then the hull rose on a wave, showed gleaming black paint and green copper as the trough came under her, and began to turn ponderously towards the watchers. The wind slammed into her sail and heeled her over until the light showed the streaming planks of her deck, and little dark figures that scurried and toiled. Then a boom like a cannon, and the sail vanished into a hundred flogging streamers at the yard. And after that, only three ragged crucifixes wallowing helplessly into the jaws of Hell Bay.

The light went out. From the sudden blackness came the noise.

It started as a weird humming of stretched cordage that whined up the scale of an Aeolian dirge, rose to a scream and snapped off. Then the shriek of sheared metal and yards thundered to the deck, and the graceful masts bowed wearily down, roaring. A wave pounded in, lifted the hull like a toy boat, receded. Sharp claws of granite reached up from the spume of its passing, drove through double planking and twisted in the great ship's bowels.

Down the wind, harsh and thin and helpless, came the screams of men.

The watchers loosened the coils of rope from their shoulders and began to scramble down the rocks. Grapnels swung and splashed, and more and more they tangled in dark shapes. Once one of the shapes wriggled and whimpered, and the woman called out in a voice like a gull's cry; but a man snarled and a blade bit gristle and something flapped in a granite pool like a mackerel in the box, and became still.

All the night the men worked. Just before dawn, boats began to arrive, and departed again, deep-laden. Then the wind backed to the west again, blowing into the dawn's red face as the sun began to heave itself up over the mines and capes of Cornwall, thirty-five miles to the eastward. The first ray, low and gold, touched the top of Hanjague, a giant granite treestump to the east of the archipelago. The gold flowed down from the top of Hanjague until it touched the water, and behind Hanjague hundreds of islands were infected with light and became solid.

The gilded clouds were torn aside, and blue sky smiled down over the toppling hills of water. Among the hedges of rock to the west they steepened and smashed, throwing up white trees a hundred and fifty feet high that blew away and vanished. The spray damped out the black smear of ashes on Scilly Rock, washed it until only the carbon scars of heat remained. Hell Bay that morning was empty, except for its teeth.

And the flotsam.

It was a bad kind of flotsam. No baulks of timber washed from a deck cargo, no smooth-worn planking planed and moulded by rocks. Fresh planks these were, black with pitch on their outsides, yellow and raw where their ends had splintered across the grain. They spun in the whirlpools behind Gweal until the wind sent them northward round the rugged grey prisms of Shipman's Head toward the Irish Sea. The wind took the flotsam; the floodtide took the bodies northward into the deeps, and the fish got them before they floated. And none of them was found.

Except one.

On the northwestern extremity of Tresco there is a place called Gun Hole. It is a funnel-shaped cave, with

a freshwater spring at its inshore end. It was living up to
its name that morning. As the waves rushed into the funnel, they piled air into its blind breech until it burst out
through the confining water with a thud like a sixty-eight
pound gun. The dull sound of it penetrated even to the
sheltered fields by the Abbey Pool. But it did not wake
the man who lay above it on the hillside scree of rotten
granite. He wore a white shirt, his dark frock-coat being
now draped over a granite ledge eighty fathoms down
and a mile off Shipman's Head. His trousers were of dark
serge, well-cut and of good quality. Low in the right leg
of the trousers a gleaming shard of white bone had torn
a long rent. The ground under the leg was soaked with a
dark liquid, which smelt very attractive, to judge by the
numbers of greater black-backed gulls perched on the
cairns of rock around the body. They did not come too
close; the body, though weak, still breathed. And black-
backs prefer their prey dead, as a result of which they
have developed a keen judgement of matters of life, death
and the frontiers between the two. In this case, they assumed that it was worth waiting. One or two of them even
began to sidle closer.

Book One

I

I OPENED MY EYES. There was light, dull and diffuse, with a brighter patch directly above me. It hurt. I looked away. The movement brought nausea that spread and became pain that ran down my body and settled in my right leg, a hard, aching throb of bone. My tongue was big and gluey in my mouth, and I was thirsty.

The ceiling seemed to be of straw, sloping down steeply on either side of a central ridge. Drab pendants lined the rafters. Bunches of herbs. Now I came to see them I smelt them too, thick and musty. Above me, the bright patch became a skylight, a square of blue. The wind thumped at the thatch, and a seagull slipped and tumbled across my view, clutching at air. Watching it, I became tired. I slept.

"From Greenland's icy mountains to Afric's coral strand," sang the voice.

It was a woman's voice, sweet and husky. By swivelling my eyes far to the right, I could just see a rough table. The timber was worn down so the knots stood out like veins on the back of an old woman's hand. On the table was a pitcher of water and a fat book. The book was bound in worn leather. The tarnished gold blocking on its spine said *Holy Bible.* Beyond the table was something tall and white with diagonal shadows. An apron. A hand came down from a great height and set a pottery mug on the table. The fingers were long and slender, the nails cut short. It looked strong and reassuring, that hand. But the apron drew away, and my eyes were too slow to focus. I caught the impression of broad shoulders and a dark-blue dress, and the ties of the apron knotted above wide hips that swayed. Then a door closed.

The pain in my right leg was losing its dullness. The intervals between the throbs were growing shorter, the pain continuous, shooting up into my groin. I kept my eyes open. The light dug hooks into my retinae, but that was better than the nauseous darkness waiting when I closed them. Beyond the thatch, gulls were shrieking, and there was the rumble of big waves on rock.

The door opened. Warm breath played on my cheek. The woman was tall, with pale golden hair caught into a bun at the nape of her neck. Her eyes were calm and blue. China blue.

"Have you bad pain?" she said.

"No," I croaked. "Quite tolerable, thank you. Who are you?"

"Charity Pender," she said. "And you?"

"I am . . ." I paused. "Doctor Nicholls."

Later, when I was stronger, she let me see the leg.

It was wrapped in rag bandages. I could not move the toes. There was a large, rusty stain in the middle of the shin. The heel arrived just below the ankle-bone of its companion. I knew what that meant. "We'll have to reduce that," I said. "Ridden up badly."

The woman lowered my head back onto the pillow. I tried to resist, but I was weak and her hands were firm. The sweat ran down my forehead, and I was panting.

"Aunt Woodcock set it ten days ago," she said.

Then there was a new kind of darkness.

Carthage Murphy was a small boy, and stupid. He sat in the front row of Carthystown schoolhouse where old Maconochie could keep an eye on him. Old Maconochie did not like Carthage because Carthage's da was poor and a drinker. When Carthage had been inside his ma's belly, Carthage's da had come home drunk and found his dinner not ready and he had kicked her in the belly, so Carthage had come out with a squint and his left leg twisted up and too short. I sat at the back because old Maconochie thought I was clever and my da was the steward at the Castle. Michael Fitzpatrick was my friend and he sat next to me and he was clever too, particularly at cribbing. He used to give Carthage hell. He called him Satan and he used to chase him until he fell down. Michael was a good runner. The only one in Carthystown school who could beat him was me, and running was the only thing I could beat him at. Michael's da was a lawyer and he and

I were the cocks of the school. Michael liked me because
he said I was normal like him, so I liked him too and we
both hated Carthage. Most of the other boys were poor,
and Michael always said that that was not normal, though
I never understood why. But I pretended I did. Carthystown was a tough town, specially if you wore good clothes
and your da was the steward. I went around with Michael
and he called it an alliance. Whatever it was, we could
run like hell.

Carthage died of typhus the second year I was at the
school and Michael said it was a good thing too; how
would he dig his spuds with a leg like that? I was not so
sure but I said yes. It was always a good idea to say yes
to Michael.

Something disturbed the gulls outside. Low women's
voices came through the floor. The smell of the herbs was
pressing me down like a coverlet of warm chain.

Footsteps on the stairs.

Pain in the right side of my groin. Down at the break
the throb, and behind it pressure.

"Aunt Woodcock to see you, Doctor," said the woman's voice.

Aunt Woodcock. Round, red face and forearms like
Hercules' club. "So, pray, how are we going on?"

"Damnable," I said.

She clicked her tongue. "It's hardly surprising. I picked
out twenty bits of splinter, and I doubt there's some there
still. It's a pity you weren't able to help."

I began to feel sick again. "I am glad I was not," I
said. "But thank you for the exercise of your skill. How
long have I been here?"

"Fourteen days." She began to bustle. "Come on, now.
Less chatter. Charity, pail of water. Lie back, and we'll
have a look at you. Oh dear, oh dear. Little bit of a stink.
But it's only the blood. Health will come out of corruption
and healing from the dunghill's fume, eh Doctor? Can you
feel this? Tch, tch. Tender still, is it? Pain stimulates cure,
though, my granny used to say, and 'twas she taught me
the setting of bones. Picked up a bit extra off the surgeon
of an Indiaman as put into St. Helen's Pool. Such a nice
man he was, perhaps you knew him, you'll be Irish by
your voice? He was an Irishman too, name of Molloy,

with a blue coat and a wig powdered still, nice blue eyes
—did that hurt?"

Inside my leg, behind the bone, a monstrous crab, all
angles of claw and shell, twisted sullenly in a fleshy
pocket. "Yes," I said. "I am afraid you have missed a
splinter."

"Dear-o-dear-o-dear," said Aunt Woodcock. "Well to
be sure. What d'you think best, Doctor?"

I looked up at the straw ceiling and the dancing black
spots of agony. "You'll have to cut." My mouth was full
of too much saliva.

Aunt Woodcock looked doubtful. "You're sure?" she
said.

"Sooner the better."

"I'll wait for Johnny," she said. "He'll be back come
tea-time. You get some rest, now. You'll need your
strength."

When Aunt Woodcock had left, Charity sat and
watched me. I was very weak.

"How did I come to be here?" I said after a while. The
fever was scorching my skin.

"Father found you," she said. "Up by Gun Hole, day
after the gale."

"Yes. I remember the gale. The light—" A chill took
me.

"Hush," said Charity quickly. "Don't fret yourself."

"The captain said the light was in the wrong place."

"Not a word." She took the cloth off, re-folded it.
"You're feverish, and you'll be worse if you're not careful. You're only lucky Father was out after wreckwood."

"Bad luck for him."

She frowned. "Why?"

"There he was treasure-hunting, and all he finds is another mouth to feed."

She didn't seem to see it. "The Lord giveth and the
Lord taketh away." Her hand was cool and dry round
mine. "You're welcome here."

I slept.

I was in my familiar consulting room in Merrion
Square. All was as usual. The coal fire in the hearth sending up tongues of blue and red that flickered over the volumes on either side of the chimneypiece. The red velvet
curtains drawn, and through them the sounds of the city,

muffled and dead. Above the chimneypiece, Katie's picture with its odd smile. It was not a good picture. I had met the painter at a card party. His name was Lehane and he was much under the influence of Delacroix and brandy. He had set Katie against the Lady Tower at Drumcarty, a celtic heroine clad in a bizarre mixture of spurious tartan and mothy fur. It was a passable likeness if you ignored the fancy dress, but the smile had undone him. It did not fit into the grandiose perspective of crag and ruin. It was the smile of a self-willed, mischievous child, and Lehane, misunderstanding it, had turned it into the leer of a courtesan racked with self-doubt. But I had won it from him at whist, and it was the only picture of her I possessed. Though I disliked the painter, the picture was useful. Patients with secret doubts about themselves were instantly reassured by the company of one of Dublin's most beautiful heiresses.

The rumble of the city beyond the window changed. There were voices in it now, one of them louder than the others. It was high and reedy and patrician, and it was shouting, "Power! Ungrateful Power! Red-handed Power!" A crowd took up the cry. I began to shake. Walking across to the window, I drew back the curtains. Beyond the panes there was only blackness, like the darkness between star and star. From out of the blackness the voices swelled to a roar that struck me in the chest, sent me staggering back into the room. The lamps glowed and came alight. There was a stickiness on my hands. When I looked down at them, they were red and shining with blood. The picture above the chimneypiece groaned, and a red stream flowed from the false smile. It ran over the mantelshelf and onto the carpet, without soaking in. Like a snake it crept under the sofa.

Behind the sofa was a pool of shadow. It was there that I kept my examination couch, out of the way of the chairs by the fire, so that the chaperones of my female patients would not be offended by too close acquaintance with the details of my prodding of their charges. The Argand lamp above it had a polished tin reflector, but for some reason it had not flared at the same time as the others in the room. The snake of blood was broad now, crawling away under the sofa. I knew what I was going to see. "No!" I yelled. "Stop!" The cries of the mob turned to groans. The lamp above the couch blazed up, casting a livid white light on the thing among the bloody linen, the auburn hair and the cold, dead smile.

"Stop!" I screamed.

"We haven't started yet," said Aunt Woodcock. "Such a roaring!"

The room was full. By the bed, Aunt Woodcock and Charity. Under the peak of the roof two men, full-bearded and long-haired. Behind them, peering between their shoulders, an old man with a soup-strainer moustache and gaunt hollows under the cheekbones.

Aunt Woodcock's voice sounded tinny and distant. "Jimmy Pender," she said. "Him that found you." The old man's eyes were invisible in the deep sockets, but I got the impression of shyness.

"Edward Jenkins." The shorter of the bearded men grinned, tentatively, and looked across at the big man as if for approval.

"My son, Little John," said Aunt Woodcock. Little John had tawny hair. He was very nearly a giant. The roof-tree was a good six feet above the floor, but he seemed bent double under it. He kept his eyes on Charity. Charity was looking at me.

There was silence. I cleared my throat and said, "The looking-glass."

Charity tilted it above my leg.

"The instruments."

Aunt Woodcock brought across a tray. A razor, two probes, and a pair of tweezers, not too rusty. "Excellent," I said. "Extraordinarily well-kept." I laughed. It sounded harsh and false. Edward Jenkins giggled nervously.

"And the blacking."

Using the looking-glass, I guided Charity while she drew a line six inches long on the swollen flesh, three fingers' breadth from the inside of the wound. She drew lightly, but even so I nearly shouted as the wax touched the skin. The fever of the inflammation caught my shoulders. I shuddered.

"Thank you." She tried to smile but her eyes stayed on mine, wide and blue and worried.

There was something else there, too. It made Little John start forward. He banged his head on the rafter and changed his mind. "Shall we proceed?"

Half crouching, Little John and Edward Jenkins came

to the bed. Edward muttered something apologetic and pressed my thigh into the firm pillows. Little John put a hand on each of my shoulders. Above the tawny beard his eyes were remote, as if I were a calf he was branding. Charity sponged my forehead with cool water. "Open," she said. I opened. A strip of leather slid between my teeth.

"Cut," I mumbled.

Aunt Woodcock cut.

I screamed and kept screaming. I was trying to scream my way out of my skull into kind death.

Aunt Woodcock began to probe.

One of my teeth broke.

There was an awful sickness, and God sent the dark to swallow me.

When I awoke my mouth was full of the taste of blood and leather. The light was dim and yellow. The throbbing was gone. I felt feverish and light-headed.

Charity was sitting on an upright chair by the bedside. The lamplight limned her face with a warm glow. The bones of it were strong, the cheekbones wide. Her skin had the bloom of a peach. Red lights glowed in the thick strands of hair pulled back from her forehead. Over her eyes the lids had fallen, and her hands were joined loosely in the lap of her apron. I could not tell if she was sleeping or praying. After a while she looked up, and started when she saw me watching her.

"Water," I said.

"I'll get you some." She went out of the room.

On the wall above my head was a hook. On it there hung my trousers, my shirt, and my waistcoat. I reached out my arm. I was weak, my hand intolerably heavy. By creeping my fingers up the wall like a spider's legs, I found the lap of the waistcoat and squeezed. Sweat ran down my forehead and into my eyes. I moved my hand, squeezed again. Through the thick kerseymere, I felt the slim, round shape of the watch. I let my hand drop. For the time being, I was safe.

Charity came back with water and a bowl of gruel and watched while I ate it. When I finished she said. "You were hungry."

"I was." She was smiling at me. The relief was still bathing my mind. I had never seen anything so beautiful in my life.

"How can I ever pay you?" I said. "All my money . . . went down."

"Pay for what, I beg your pardon?"

"Food. Lodging. Aunt Woodcock . . ."

"There is no need," she said, looking at something on the wall of the room. Following her eyes, I saw it was a gaudy chromolithograph of a gentleman in a cassock preaching to a crowd of angels. "Payment comes from Our Father Which is in Heaven. His will be done."

I became inflamed. I suppurated, and for a week I rolled and tossed with fever. Sometimes I thought I was in Ireland, the hunt raging round my ears. Sometimes I was in America, new and free, moving away from Dublin and chaos on a slow riverboat with drowned trees wobbling in brown water.

But at last I began to improve. I knew I was in Charity's house. And I knew that in this little room with Charity's firm hands feeding me and her soft voice comforting me, I was safe. For the moment.

As soon as I was strong enough I had Charity bring me pen and ink and paper, and I wrote a letter to Michael Fitzpatrick, the only friend I had. I headed it Tresco, Isles of Scilly, Cornwall, and signed it Nicholls. Michael would get it in his chambers, with the law-books round the walls and the smoky Dublin rain drizzling into the grass outside. He would know my writing, but his face would not move. Michael's face never moved unless he wanted it to.

I sealed the letter with a plain wafer, addressed it without return and called Charity. "Could you post this?" I said.

She laughed at me. "You'll have to wait a bit," she said. "There's plenty of ships in the Roads, but not a one of them bound for the Mainland. It's been blowing due west for ten days now, and hard."

"As soon as possible, then?"

"To your lady-love is it?" She blushed.

"No," I said, rather curtly. "A friend."

That morning Aunt Woodcock had brought her particular friend, Aunt Ellis, to visit me. Aunt Ellis was a small, thin woman, wrinkled as a prune under her white lace cap, and at first I expected Aunt Woodcock's barrage of chatter to blow her clean through the thatch. But Aunt

Ellis swiftly showed herself to be a formidable partner in cross-examination; within half an hour of their arrival they had picked my brains of all I had read in the newspapers in the previous six weeks, and in return had given me a good, if rather personal, picture of the islands. By the time they left, I was both exhausted and uncomfortably aware that in the Aunts' minds my antecedents were —to say the least—questionable.

Charity, however, told me that the Aunts had formed a good impression of me; and the way she said it gave me to believe that the Aunts' impressions were not taken lightly. As my strength grew, the pair of them visited me often; and I began to understand something of their lust for fact.

These islands were situated forty miles off Land's End, England's most south-westerly point. Tresco had a population of some five hundred souls, most of whom shared six surnames.

Tresco was the second biggest of the six inhabited islands, the others being St. Mary's, Agnes, St. Martin's, Bryher, and Samson. The Tresco folk did not take their numbers as a sign that they were better than their smaller neighbours; in this they were quite unlike the inhabitants of St. Mary's, which had a population as large as all the other islands put together. St. Mary's was the seat of Government, headquarters of the Preventive service, the centre of commerce; its people tended to grow fat on the pickings of the off-islands, as the rest were called; and as a result the off-islanders were often reduced to a taking of sea beef—their heavily ironical name for limpets, the nastiest and most plentiful of the shellfish tribe—if not actual starvation. Any gleanings of news from outside made a nourishing supplement to so meagre a diet.

I say I was growing stronger; but I was still confined to my bed. By the time I had been at Scilly six weeks, I had never once seen the outside of Jimmy Pender's loft. I had tried, with the aid of Charity's looking-glass, to get a periscopic view from the skylight. All I had managed to collect was a glimpse of white beach bordering a rugged hill of heather, with beyond it the low loom of more islands and the spidery spars and rigging of ships in the distance.

The view I got of myself was even wilder.

Katie used to say sometimes that I looked like the adult size of the late Napoleon Bonaparte. The face that glow-

ered back at me from the glass was that of a Bonaparte
retreating from Moscow in the throes of terminal debauch. The skin was greyish-white, stretched back from
the cheekbones and hanging in dark circles under the
eyes. Over the nose the flesh was pinched and hollow,
showing the bumps where I had smashed it on a gatepost
when my old mare Gráinne had put her foot in a rabbit-
hole. On the thin cheeks and the jawbone sprouted a fine
crop of black stubble, too long to be careless and too short
to be a beard. The whole unpleasant picture was framed
by lank, greasy ropes of hair and lit by a pair of dull eyes
whose blue irises contrasted nastily with yellowish whites.
"Born to be hanged," I said. That was too true to be comfortable. I closed my eyes and tried to drift away from the
pain of it, back into soggy oblivion. There was a lot to
forget. Every itch, every tiny hardening of callosity weld-
ing the two faces of bone, brought me closer to the day
when I would have to hobble out into the world again.
And the world was not going to be a friendly place.

For the last two weeks of September at Carthystown
Michael spent most of the time singing *Croppies lie down*.
October 1st was gale day and I never really knew what
that meant, except that I got into more fights than usual
and if a grown-up saw me getting beaten up in the High
Street he would not stop and interfere. My father would
never let me go to school on the day itself. Instead I
would spend the time at the Steward's House, watching.

First the smart carriages would come rattling down the
hill to the bridge, and I would see the solemn white faces
of the men Michael said were the Dublin lawyers. Then
father would go off, wearing his Sunday coat and towing
one of the stableboys behind him with a wheelbarrow full
of ledgers. And after he had disappeared over the bridge
and through the gatehouse in the curtain-wall, the tenants
would start arriving. Sullivan and Maxwell would come
first, riding stout cobs and dressed in bullet-proof broad-
cloth, as Michael called it. They had six hundred acres
each.

After them came first the smaller tenants, mostly on
foot, but some sidesaddle on donkeys or two by two in
outside cars; and finally, bringing up the rear, the conacre
men. When I was very small I used to hide behind the
wall when they came by. Michael said they were only one

better than tinkers, and the tinkers were the devil's first cousins. Everyone knew that.

Later they would come out again, in reverse order. First the conacre men, slashing at the thistles with their ashplants. Next, later, the small tenants, who got a dinner in the servants' hall. After them Sullivan and Maxwell, slouched on their cobs. They got their dinner with the Earl himself, and Michael said his father had told him that he made them drunk so he could put their rents up every year no matter what.

Finally, my father would come home. He had a big red nose as rough as a cauliflower, and after the rent dinners it glowed as if it had a lamp in it. Usually he locked himself in his study. But this time, he called me in.

There was that horrible old smell of harness and stale coal-smoke. In front of the desk was an old carpet with two holes worn by the shuffling feet of years. I went and put a foot in each, wondering what I had done. My father's breath smelt of whisky. He poured more into a glass and frowned at me. I thought I was probably all right. When he was going to beat me he had his stick out on the table. Today it was not there.

"Now you are nearly thirteen, and entering upon man's estate," he said. "Nominally, you will be wise. In fact, you will be young and callow. So heed well what I say.

"I have brought you up as best I can. You will profit by my example. Consider what it is to be a great lord's steward. The tenantry sees you sitting at the right hand of God, vested with the attributes of the Deity. My Lord of Drumcarty sees you as a majordomo, an upper servant to whom he must entrust a degree of power which might at any minute be turned against him. My Lord is not an . . . easy man."

There was a blob of old ink on the mahogany of the desk. I could never decide whether it was a fish or a hag. I heard the glug-glug of my father drinking.

"Obligations, Nicholas. Provided a man sees his obligations clearly, he cannot go far wrong. Each is obliged to all: the tenant to the steward, the steward to the landlord, the landlord to his creditors' lawyers, his creditors' lawyers to the creditors and the creditors to God. That is the ladder of it, Nicholas. And every time you put someone under an obligation to you, you strengthen that ladder. It is work, Nick. But useful work."

He glowered at me from under the grainy pouches above his eyes. I could not seem to get any words out, so I just nodded and shuffled my feet until he told me I could go. I suppose he drank some more, then.

In the weeks that followed my leg healed well, thanks to the splint I devised with the help of Jimmy Pender, who was a carpenter by trade. Soon I was able to hop about on crutches. But now I was mobile, I had nowhere to go. Not Ireland; not, weak as I was, America. It turned out there was only one doctor in the islands, and he a St. Mary's man who before he prodded patient prodded pocket. Few off-islanders could afford him; many off-islanders were sick. Poor as they were, they had cared for me magnificent y. I decided I would try to reciprocate. So the Nicholls Free Dispensary was instituted in a disused net shed, with a crippled doctor and an old mahogany medicine chest, relic of the failed Mission of 1819.

It was only February yet, but spring was creeping in. In the draughts that insinuated themselves through the slots in the thatch at night, there were occasional whiffs of it, mixed with the tang of salt. In the cottage gardens at the other side of the harbour green spears were bursting into little flecks of colour, and the odd daffodil, arrived God knew how, nodded in the breeze. The roofs of the cottages themselves were developing a greenish tinge, too, as a fur of mosses and lichen drew strength from sun and warmth and reached upwards among the criss-cross of rope that anchored thatch to wall.

The first morning in the dispensary, I diagnosed two cataracts, a double hernia, a rachitic spinal curvature and a cancer of the uterus. These in addition to six or seven cases of general debility through age and poor diet. And that was only the beginning. Day after day they poured in. However ill they looked when they came, they always looked better when they left. It was not medicine; it was faith. I only hoped that their faith had grounds; I said as much to Charity as she labelled the bottles that evening.

"Sure it has," she said. She dipped her brush into the pot carefully, scraped off the surplus, and painted gum onto the back of a label. She seemed improbably absorbed. "You're a fine thing for Tresco, Doctor."

I grunted. I was very tired.

She pressed the label onto the bottle and looked up at me. "You are so," she said. "A gift from on high."

I took her hand. It was hot and slightly sticky from the glue. "It's you they should be thanking. It's you does all the hard work."

She left her hand in mine for a while, without a word, looking into my eyes. A strand of hair had escaped her chignon and hung looped over her ear. Her skin was pink and healthy in the candlelight, her lips a little apart.

At last she drew her hand away and got up. "Time you were in your bed," she said. The disarrangement of her hair made her look a little flustered, and I could see the shadow of her pulse in her throat, rather frequent, I thought.

"You've been very kind," I said. "Thank you, Charity."

"Don't thank me, thank the Lord." She smiled at me. "I do."

She opened her mouth to say something else, but changed her mind and went out of the room.

Next day I had retired early, as was my habit under my regimen of convalescence. I was awakened by sounds below. Jimmy Pender was saying something I could not hear in his usual non-committal rumble. I heard Charity say, "Never," sharply. Then another voice I only half-recognised said, "If that's how ye want it. But never say as I didn't warn ye." The front door of the cottage slammed, and there was silence, broken only by an eerie yelling of curlews. Footsteps shuffled on the stairs. Charity's, but unshod. I lit my candle. Normally she wore her pattens.

She opened the door. Her hair straggled down over her shoulders, and white skin shone through a rent in her dress. She saw my eyes go to it, and brought up a defensive hand. The ends of her fingers were bloody.

"Good God, woman," I said. "What's been going on?"

She did not answer. Her face was flushed. There were the snail-tracks of tears on her cheeks.

"Tell me," I said.

She ran over in a rustle of skirts and fell on her knees by my bed. I could feel her tears wet on the back of my hand.

"Come, now," I said. "Calm yourself. What is it?"

Her shoulders lurched, and she turned her face up at me. There was an angry swelling over her left eye. "Little

John Woodcock," she said, and her shoulders heaved again. "He beat me."

"He beat you?"

"He fetched me a clout. Because of you."

"Because of me? Why should he do that?"

She got up and went and sat on the bed. "He and I . . . were . . . promised. And he said that me looking after you with only Dad for company, weren't right."

"What!"

"He said you was . . .." She cut herself off. "You was finer than him, and you'd use that to get round me. So it weren't right we should be betrothed no more."

"Preposterous," I said. "The man's mad."

She nodded, without conviction, I thought. "Anyway, the end of it was that I told him you was a gentleman, and that he was something else. Then he said that that showed how you'd got round me, and he put a name on me and said he'd see you sorted out. And I said that it would be like him to go for a sick man—which," she added in a sudden burst of fairness—"was a lie, God forgive me. And then he gave me the back of his hand."

"I think I'd better see him," I said.

"No," she said, more like the familiar nurse. "He's not coming in this house again. Not while I live. Besides, he'd mangle you."

"He could try," I said.

"I wouldn't take the chance," she said with finality, and began to fuss with her hair, suddenly much recovered. "You're in my charge now, Doctor. And I'll tell you who your visitors are going to be."

"You—"

"That's enough of that," she said, and began fussing about, tucking the sheets up under my chin.

After she had left, I lay fuming, wishing I had two sound legs. But perhaps it was just as well. This was not the first time I had been at the centre of a misunderstanding which had ended in violence. It was only that I hoped all that had changed.

Perhaps a week later, I was discoursing with the two Aunts on the subject of storms. It was Aunt Ellis who had raised the topic, with a significant glint of her small bright eye and a pointed draught of tea; but at first, I thought nothing of it. Storms brought wrecks, and wrecks were the staff of Scillonian life.

"Ah," said Aunt Woodcock, when the discussion was well under way. " 'Twas a bad one brought you ashore." She rested her massive forearms on the table. "Not the scrap of a ship left, only you. Now what would have been the name of your ship, Doctor?"

I had known that sooner or later someone would ask. I had the answer ready. *"Greylag,"* I said. "Out of Oban."

There was a silence, during which Aunt Ellis held me fixed with her eye, nodding her lace cap encouragingly.

"Ah," said Aunt Woodcock at last, "I knew as the man was wrong."

"What man?" I said, too quickly.

"An Irish feller. He come over from St. Mary's. Insurance, they said. He was after a ship called the—what was it, Aunt?"

"Castletown," said Aunt Ellis, without taking her eye off me. "Never heard of it. Did you, Doctor?"

"Never," I said.

"That's what I thought. Ah, 'twas a terrible storm. Seven ships lost, they say. 'Twas an emigrant ship, the *Castletown.* Most likely rotten. She'll have gone down at sea, no doubt. With all hands. Funny though. The Irishman seemed more interested in a man than a ship. Some doctor fellow."

I must have looked as sick as I felt. Aunt Woodcock said, "Poor man. Wasted journey he had. Went back to Ireland three days ago, none the wiser. Insurance company will pay up, no doubt."

I forced a smile. "Perhaps it was me he was looking for?"

"Oh, no. Wrong ship. We knowed that, didn't we, Aunt Ellis?"

" 'Course we did," said Aunt Ellis, smiling encouragingly. "And even if it had been you, which it wasn't, you're more use to us than you would be to him. We haven't had a doctor on the off-islands for ten years."

"And we thought that even if there was a mistake and it was you, you'd want to tell him yourself. Later. When you're well. But I must say I didn't like his looks. Did you, Aunt Ellis?"

The lace cap shook quickly from side to side. "Nasty,

nosey creature. You'll find a man's business is his own business here, so to speak."

Charity came into the room and curtseyed to the Aunts. "We was just telling the Doctor about the Irish chap looking for the *Castletown*," said Aunt Woodcock. "And the Doctor was saying as he didn't know the ship and how he was going to stay on the island till his leg mended and carry on the dispensary, which was very good of him to be sure and will be a great advantage to us all."

"It will," said Charity, flushing with pleasure.

"Let the dead look after their dead, I say," said Aunt Woodcock, draining her large cup at a draught. "Well, we must be off now. Look at the Doctor. Pale as a sole's belly, poor man. We've tired him."

After they had gone, I had time to think. So the pursuit had gone over me. It was unlikely to come back over the same ground, for the moment. Twice the people of Scilly had saved me, now. That constituted a considerable obligation. I should have to see what I could do to fulfil it.

II

THE PENDERS' HOUSE was built of granite and thatched, like all the others in Palace Row, which was the principal and only thoroughfare of the village of New Grimsby. It faced over a road of white grit onto a beach of silver sand, where pigs and small black cattle and even the occasional sheep picked over piles of weed and household refuse. The beach enclosed a little bay of clear green water, in which three boats, mastless and much in need of painting, rode at moorings of antique rope. To the left, the bay was shut in by a hill with a granite cairn and a flatter neck of land beyond, leading on to more hills and the southern end of the island. To the right was a quay of tumbled boulders, with, at its landward end,

the crazy sprawl of stone and sod and thatch that, Charity
informed me without enthusiasm, was the Palace Inn. To
the southwest, down-channel, was open sea with flecks of
white where the swell surged round reefs and ledges.

In Palace Row, I learned to use my crutches. At first I
went out in the daytime. But after I had twice been
spilled into the road by the mobs of good-natured children, I decided that I would practise at night.

It was perhaps a week after my first outing. The moon
was beginning its last quarter, sliding in and out of ribbons
of silvery cloud. I swung slowly down the road inland,
panting. To the foot of the hill, I thought. No further. I
crunched and swung until I reached the cottage that stood
where the quay road joined another at right angles. There
were no lights in the cottage. I leaned against the wall to
get my breath. Far enough for tonight. Tomorrow further.

On the other side of the harbour a couple of dim yellow lights pricked the dark lump of Bryher. The night was
full of the rustle of water, with beneath it the deeper
grumble and thump of big waves to the North. Peat
smoke drifted at me from time to time from the
banked-up fires of the cottages. The houses were asleep.
Candles were too expensive to waste; on the off-islands
you went to bed with the dusk and got up with the dawn.
Either that, or went to one of the seven inns. Which was
presumably where the crowd coming along the road from
the southward had been, because a couple of them were
singing in parts and the rest were talking animatedly. I
moved back into the shadows of the cottage porch, shy of
being seen at my practising. The crowd came hilariously
on, with a great trampling of nailed leather on grit. The
window above the porch flew open, making me jump.

"Hold your bloody row!" shrieked a female voice.
"Can't a body get a bit of sleep?"

"It aren't sleep you're getting from old Harry," said a
man in the crowd. His companions laughed. "Now get
back to thy bed, blabbermouth, or we'll paint thy windows black."

There was a hiss of breath through teeth, and the window slammed again. As they passed in front of my hiding-
place, I saw a couple of the taller ones silhouetted against
the sky. And one of them had the mane of hair and leo-

nine head of Little John, bent down earnestly as he lectured someone at his side.

I had been wrong. They were not coming back from any public house, not unless they took their horses and carts drinking. There were three carts. As the last of them went off up the hill, something fell sprawling into the road and lay unnoticed. When feet, hooves and the jingling harness had gone off up the hill, I went after it. It was a man's coat, wet with seawater. I picked it up and took it home.

Next morning, I told Charity about it. She said she'd give it back to the owner. I thought no more about it. Until a week later, when four bodies came ashore on Bryher, all naked. And then I began to wonder.

Every morning, I would hop down the road to the netshed and park myself by the examniation couch with my crutches close at hand. Charity would puff some life into the fire, and at nine o'clock the patients would begin to arrive. They tended to come in bunches. On rainy days, and at that time of year there were a good many, they would gather by the door of the shed and watch while they waited their turns. I found it rather disconcerting at first. They kept up a continual barrage of chatter and advice, and seemed as interested in the progress of each individual case as me or the patient. But as the days lengthened and the weather improved, Charity felt it proper to chase them out onto a bench in the sun, and the dignity of practice was to some extent restored.

After a time, it became evident that the patients were not coming to me only because they were sick. It started one afternoon with Susan Odger, an old woman with hands twisted to claws with the rheumatism. I did the best I could for her, which was a bottle of sulphur and oil of turpentine for internal use and a bottle of liniment for external. I then tried to impress on her the danger of swallowing the liniment and the futility of smearing the turpentine oil on her hands. She listened attentively enough, blinking her milky old eyes. When I had finished, she made no move to go and Charity made no move to eject her. This was unusual.

"Anything else I can do?" I said.

She shook her head, but still she stayed.

"Come on, Auntie," said Charity encouragingly. "He won't eat you."

Mrs. Odger looked as if she was not so sure. She fumbled in the pocket of her apron and handed me a paper. "Would ye mind reading this?" she said. "I'd be much obliged, Doctor."

"Delighted," I said, and opened it. The language was lawyer's prose. Even if the old woman had been able to read, I doubt she would have understood it.

A writ of distraint, sworn before the Penwith magistrates, in the sum of three shillings and sixpence. The bailiffs would be arriving by the next packet, to distrain such of Susan Odger's property as would answer the debt.

"When did you get this?" I said.

"Johnny give it to me as I was walking over."

I tried to explain what it meant. She nodded cheerfully, tucked the letter in her apron pocket and hobbled out of the shed.

"What can she do?" I said.

Charity shrugged her shoulders. "She hasn't anything worth three and sixpence. Nothing but the potatoes in her kitchen, maybe."

"And they'll take them?"

"They'll take them, all right. They'll let you run up a debt, knowing you'll never be able to pay it. Then they'll apply to the magistrates and seize your last year's crop in lieu, to about double the value if they can. Year after year, it happens."

"But that's scandalous," I said.

"I suppose so," said Charity. "But what can you do?" She started for the door to let in the next patient.

"I'll see those bailiffs," I said.

"But what can you do?"

"I'll think of something."

The door swung open with a crash. Charity looked around, frowning. "The Doctor's not ready yet," she said, walking round the screen. "Oh. It's you."

"It's me," said Little John Woodcock's voice. "Where's he hiding?"

"He's not hiding," Charity said, with heat. "What do the likes of you want with him anyway?"

"Mail's in."

I struggled to my feet. Suddenly my heart was thumping. Charity and Little John were glaring at each other, but I did not pause to think about that. My eyes were fixed on the white oblong of folded paper the big man was tapping against his thigh.

"Look at him hop," said John.

"The letter," I said.

"And not so much as an 'if you please'," said John. He handed it over. "Try to teach him some manners, would you, Charity? Seeing as you're with him all the time." He turned and walked out the shed.

"Brass nerve," said Charity. I paid no attention. My fingers were shaking so much I couldn't break the seal.

"I'll go, then," said Charity.

I had the seal broken. There were two pages, crackling with the trembling of my hands. The door banged angrily. I dragged myself over to my chair and sat down.

The address at the top of the page said Moyle, Bevan. Attorneys-at-Law. Dublin.

Dear Nick, I read. *I was much gratified to receive your letter and learn you are still alive. But that is about all. The matter between you and Katie is still the talk of the town, and certain parties (whom it would be needless to name) are hunting you like a pack of furies. In answer to your questions: Yes, it is true that the universal belief about it is, as you put it, 'the worst.' And no, under no circumstances should you contemplate a return to Ireland, whether to Dublin, Carthystown or any other place, now or in the foreseeable future. Your likeness has, I am told, been circulated to all stations. There is a reward offered for your apprehension.*

The only consolation is that since the Castletown *disappeared without trace between Kingstown and the Cove, you are presumed dead. My advice to you is to profit by this lucky accident and start a new life somewhere you will not be recognised. They will be looking for you in England as well as this side of the water.*

Please keep me informed as to your progress. But be discreet: sign your letters George Sullivan, and use no return address. I enclose a small token of the fact that while others may have deserted you I am still your friend, Michael Fitzpatrick.

P.S. Burn this letter.

To the top right-hand corner of the second page was pasted a ten-pound Treasury note.

When I was fourteen, my face looked five years older. Maconochie at the school said it was a mask of villainy. I was extremely proud of my low voice. I spent huge sums on oil of macassar in attempts to persuade my whiskers down to the turn of my jawbone, like Michael. The village girls said they loved them.

I hoped that they would be as successful with Katie.

Katie was the Earl's daughter. Her real name was Lady Katherine Elizabeth Constantia Villiers Browne-Ormonde. Her mother was dead, she had no brothers or sisters, and her father spoilt her rotten. He had sent her away from Drumcarty when she was eight, to acquire the benefits of an English upbringing. When she was fourteen she returned because, it was said in the Steward's House, they had taught her all they could in England. I later discovered that while this was true in a sense, the real reason was that her English cousins refused to have her one more second in the house.

The day she came back, it had been raining. I was walking down the avenue with Michael, bored, kicking dirty water from the puddles at his breeches. He was reciprocating; and as I stopped to wipe off a clod of mud, I heard the drum of hooves and the crash of carriage-springs and the distant tootling of a key-bugle. Michael had gone on ahead, and was just passing a particularly foul pool at the side of the gravel. I said, "Stop a minute," and ran after him. He turned and looked round, and just as he turned round I caught the muck with my boot and sent a great fan of it across his shirt-front.

"Oh damn you," he said. "That's me new stock." He was all pimples and vanity then, was Michael. I saw the old mean look come into his eyes, and I knew he was plotting devastating revenge.

The carriage came out of the trees and down the hill towards the bridge at a good fifteen miles an hour. It was one of His Lordship's, and the groom was drunk on the box beside the coachman. But the groom was always drunk; it was not him that caught my attention. What had me gaping was the young lady among the cushions, straight-backed in a pelisse of emerald-green silk that perfectly matched the pair of eyes with which she was looking straight through me. Her face was pale and long and wore a half-smile, as if she found something amusing on a plane not accessible to mere mortals.

A shoulder slammed into my back, and as I pitched forward a boot swept my feet from under me, and I went face-down into the puddle. I had forgotten about Michael. When I picked myself up, he was grinning his self-satisfied grin. "Tit for tat," he said mincingly.

I seethed with rage. In the rear window of the coach a white face looked down at me, and I heard a musical tinkle of laughter.

"Oh, that was a good one," said Michael. He had heard the laughter, too, and it doubled his pleasure.

I walked home filled with real hatred. Normally, I would not have worried; if you were a friend of Michael's you took the consequences. But this time it was different. For as I floundered absurdly in that filthy puddle I had fallen in love. And I knew I had made a damned bad beginning.

I took up the pen and ink-bottle Charity used for making labels and trimmed a sheet of paper to size with a scalpel. When I had finished writing, I stumped back to the cottage. I kicked open the door and sat down at the kitchen table and poured a lot of brandy into a mug. Charity glided in and began blowing up the fire. Turf-smoke billowed into the room, stinging my eyes.

"I'll put the soup to heat up," she said. "I must go to Meeting. Father's over to Agnes till morning. You'll be all right on your own?"

"I always have been," I said. "One night more or less won't make much difference." I picked up the tankard and looked at the brandy slopping as I turned it in my hand. Her eyes were on me. "Well?" I said. "What are you waiting for? Go."

Her eyes were too bright. "Poor Doctor," she said softly. "It must be lonely for you. You weren't made for this."

"How the hell do you know what I was made for?" I snarled. She half-ran into her room.

By the time she came out again, her hair brushed and wearing a clean apron, I still had not touched the brandy. She pulled a long cloak round her shoulders. The wind caught it when she opened the door. She said, "It's blowing up." The door closed.

I itched, a deep itch that started at the break in my leg and spread from there up my body and into my stomach,

and stopped me breathing properly. The rising wind
shoved down the chimney and blew smoke and yellow
peat-dust into the room. I picked up the tankard and
flung its contents into the fire. There was a blue *whoomp*
of flame. Dragging my crutches towards me, I heaved myself to my feet and swung myself into the road.

There was a puddle of water outside the door. My
crutches splashed in it as I went out. The wind was up
even since Charity had gone. Ragged gusts eddied round
the headland and beat rain into my face.

Once I was in the road I stopped. Then I limped to the
dark porch of the gossip's cottage. I had never gone any
further. I meditated on this. There was no reason. I was
strong enough now. But I needed a sign.

The sign came.

A woman walked past me. She did not see me. She
could not have seen me. But as she passed, she turned her
head into the porch where I stood. She wore a dark cloak,
hooded. I could not see her face but I knew she was smiling. Then she passed on, flitting up the hill, gliding like a
ghost. But no ghost smelt of verbena. Particularly a Scillonian ghost.

I paused, like a diver on a high cliff. It was not as dark
as I had expected; there was something of a moon, and
from time to time it lit up thin places in the cloud.

The road was made of the silvery grit the islanders call
ram, and it shone before me like a steep-rising river. I
began to climb, panting. My shoulders ached where the
crutches dug in. The woman blended into shadow ahead,
vanished. I went on. At the top, the road curved to the
right. There was no sign of the woman. I paused to catch
my breath. Below me was Dolphin Town, and beyond
that Old Grimsby. It was the most thickly-populated part
of the island, with the church and the meeting-house and
several taverns, and the rain-softened glow of lighted windows. Up here, the wind was stronger, still broken by
rocks but steadier. I could just distinguish a path leading
off between tumbledown granite walls through the fields
on the crest of the ridge. On the path was the flit of a
shadow. A cloaked figure, walking.

I went after her. After the walls there was an eerie
plain of bare rock splashed with white quartz where nothing moved but the wind, unbaffled, flat and hard from the
east. I panted on, the crutches biting my armpits, until the

rock gave way to heather, with a straight line marking the transition from one to the other. I had seen it before, in the starving West of Ireland where the turf lies so thinly on the rock that the cutters flense the land to its bones in a couple of seasons. There was no sign of the woman.

I paused to catch my breath in the lee of a cairn like heaped skulls in the moonlight. A pall of cloud moved across the sky, and the darkness became absolute. There was the wet salt smell of shattered waves in my nostrils and the thudding of blood in my ears. I had the sensation that the air was still and that I and the cairn were bulleting through the inky void. Then the bluster of the wind faded. And I smelt verbena again.

The cloud passed away, and the moon swam in a black ravine of stars. The shape of the woman grew from the ground like the rocks, the cloak and hood catching the same silver as the lichen.

She said, "Come with me." Her voice was clear as falling water. The wind huffed up and roared. "Take my shoulder."

There was bone and firm muscle under the cloak, and a round of hip pushed against my upper thigh. We walked down into the wind, heading into the darkness to the left of the lights of Old Grimsby, skirting the loom of a watchhouse. I wanted to ask her who she was and where she was taking me, but I needed all my breath for the slope of tussocky heather diving towards the sea.

The heather gave way to little fields, and my crutch sank in tilled earth. After that, a beach. I blinked the sweat out of my eyes. There were two boats, one long and predatory, the other a punt of the kind I had seen in New Grimsby harbour. The Penders' house and Charity and the gossip of the dispensary seemed a long way away. From the rocks there came the dark shapes of men. One of them said something to the woman, and she laughed, and said something that sounded like, "He'll learn." Then she turned to me, the moon shining on white teeth in the hood's shadows, and said, "Can you row?"

I said, "Yes." I would have said the same if I had never touched a pair of oars.

The men dragged the punt down to the water and I struggled in, feeling the cold salt water on my splints. There was a point sheltering the beach from the wind. The woman sat on the stern thwart and said, "Row, then."

As we came abreast of the point, the wind hit us. After that, we crossed a stretch of water where the wind howled and the boat pitched and the woman put her hands on mine and pushed as I pulled. I remember being surprised at the strength in her, for her hands were slender and she was slight. We came at last to the lee of an island. Then there was more open water, this time with the moon on it, glowing in a dark stone on one of her fingers. After that another island, the sweat stinging my eyes so I could hardly see, my arms empty of strength and aching.

The next open water we crossed downwind, and that was almost pleasant, even if the spray did come sousing over the stern out of the black eye of the gale, and I recovered enough to look over my shoulder and see the high sway of three masts against the stars. The woman said, "Put her alongside," and threw her hood back. A dark banner of hair streamed out into the wind. "Thank you. You did very well. I'll be back soon," she said. A rope-ladder came down from the deck above, and she went up into the lanternlight, carrying a bundle. I sat in the boat with my head down, panting, with her thanks ringing in my ears, feeling inordinately proud.

Laughter floated down to me, the woman's voice, chaffing, men answering her. I looked up to see if I could catch her face in the light, but there was only the reel of the high spars against the scud. I began to get my bearings. We must have come in a wide circle, in under the shoulders of the islands that rose beyond the ship's pitching bowsprit. Astern, lights half-hidden by spray might be Old Grimsby.

The night was loud with the groan of timbers and the crash of water. The laughter on the deck took on a wild, almost erotic note, and I felt a twinge of jealousy. I wanted to talk to the woman and find out how she had mesmerised me, a cripple, into this bucketing punt alongside a strange ship in an icy gale. I wanted to see her face. And I wanted to thank her for making me feel human again, after all that time talking to old women, closeted in the warm house with Charity clucking round me.

A cloud covered the moon, and there was a new sound. It did not come from the deck. It was a dull *chunk* of oars in tholepins, and it came down the wind from the dark spray forward. I peered into the noisy blackness, shielding my eyes with my palm. Nothing. Until about five minutes later, when I thought I saw a long, low shape pull away and vanish in the black loom of the islands.

There was a final crash of laughter from above, and the woman came down the ladder and said, "Go," in a strange, breathless voice.

We went down the wind and through a narrow gap of black water between two streaks of silver foam that jumped and barked at us. The moon edged out again. I caught a last glimpse of the ship's masts; I thought I saw them swing out of line, as if she had turned beam-on. Then the black gap closed behind us and the waves were smaller, and five minutes later the punt's bow grounded on a beach of white sand where a bonfire burned.

The woman helped me out of the boat and put my crutch under me. There were a lot of men on the beach, most of them bearded, cheekbones and brow-ridges lit from below by the red of the fire. Lanterns bobbed along the foreshore, glowing on granite and turf and thatch. The woman came back and gave me a tin mug. The brandy glowed down into my stomach. I said, "Old Grimsby."

The woman brushed her hood back impatiently. She was looking back the way we had come, where jagged glints from the bonfire danced in the waves. "Out there," she said, pointing.

But I was watching her face, in stark profile against the fire.

It had the cold perfection of something chiselled from hard stone. The nose was proud and aquiline, the set of the lips firm above the clean chin. Her hair streamed in the wind like the banners of a cruel army. She was laughing.

A boat shot out of the night with that *chunk* of oars I had heard while I waited in the punt. I stared at it, hard. It was long and lean, very like the one that had waited on the little beach where we had embarked. The shapes of the men spilling onto the sand were familiar, I thought. But I could not be sure.

When I turned back to the woman, she had gone. Everyone was looking out into the wind.

The squall rolled off the moon. For a moment I saw the three masts of the ship. My breath caught in my throat. She was beam-on to the wind, canvas sprouting from her mainyard, much closer. She seemed to be moving sideways, as if her captain was trying to fight her back upwind. As well he might; for close under her lee was the growl and suck of the ledges.

A new squall blotted out the light. The wind howled in my ears. From the sea there came a sharp crash, as of a crate being dropped. Then a deeper sound and a long, terrible grinding. The moon drew a flood of silver across the sea and I saw the ridge of rocks black and jagged, the channel through which we had passed. Just to the left of the channel lay the ship, canvas flogging at its spars. As I watched, the foremast went, and the mainmast with it, toppling. Finally the mizzen, bent by the weight of its fallen companions, snapped at the cro'jack with a crack like a pistol. The ship lay a dead hulk, and the moonlight burned evil in the lace of spray sweeping her decks. From the beach the boats began to pull off like beetles to a corpse.

"She be well set," said a satisfied voice at my side. It was Edward Jenkins, his beard fluttering in the wind. I was surprised he had volunteered a comment; I had him down as a tentative creature, much under the thumb of Little John Woodcock. "They'll not get 'er off there in a hurry."

"Anchors must have dragged, I suppose," I said.

"Ay, ay," said Edward. "Must of." He winked. "You was out with Mary, I seed."

The long boat was standing off the beach now, the oarsmen holding water. The big man standing at the tiller roared, "All right, Eddie!" It was Little John Woodcock. Eddie gave me an apologetic grin, waded into the chop and clambered aboard.

I looked around for the woman. The beach was filling up with people, and there were more lanterns bobbing down the road. My clothes were soaked, my teeth chattering. I could not see her. I clambered up the beach towards a house with an open door and a sign creaking in the wind. There was a fire blazing in the hearth and a woman filling mugs from a tap. I got more brandy and put myself on a settle, acknowledging greetings from people I knew from the dispensary. The brandy warmed me, and my coat and trousers began to steam. Who was the woman? Why had she taken me out in the boat? How had the ship dragged its anchors? There were no answers. But my mind went back to another storm, the poop-deck of the emigrant ship *Castletown* and the captain barging the helmsman off the wheel, screaming at him to sheer off as the white light glittered on black rocks and booming towers of spray.

A group of men came through the door. At their head was a thick-set individual in a pea-jacket. His teeth were clenched so the muscles knotted under his ears, and his eyes flicked round the room like a caged bear's. From behind the crowd, Eddie Jenkins' voice said, "Here you are, then. Missis'll take care of you." The landlady bustled over from her barrels. "It's the captain and the crew off the wreck, pore fellows," said Eddie, very solicitous.

"Oh dear, oh dear, come by the fire now," said the landlady, her red cheeks shining with sympathy. I got up. The men filed to the settle and sat down. Their faces were shocked and vague.

"Anyone hurt?" I said.

The man in the pea-jacket snapped, "Who wants to know?"

"I'm a doctor."

"I ain't paying no damned croaker," he growled.

"There will be no charge," I said.

"Then you can look at Mister Jones' hand and be damned to you." He glared round the room. "It ain't your fault you're not murderers."

Mr. Jones' hand was badly bruised, but not broken. I said, "We'll be getting over to the dispensary, then."

"No you will not, by God," said the man in the pea-jacket. I deduced that he must be the captain. "We'll watch these vultures. We'll account for every last nail of her to the owners, split me if we don't."

"Watch your tongue," I said. "There's no call for that kind of talk. Those people turned out in half a gale to pick you off the rocks. Just you watch who you're blackguarding." As I said it, I knew it was the gig I had heard, while the woman distracted the crew. They had cut the cables and put the ship ashore. And the woman had made certain I was part of it. The worst of it was that I was glad she had made me come.

When I hobbled back onto the beach there were two more bonfires, and the sand was black with human figures in the moonlight. By the waterline, piles of boxes and barrels rose against the sea. As I pushed through the crowd a man barged into me, reeled and went sprawling. There was a powerful smell of spirits. A woman stood by a stove-in hogshead with a mug, dealing it out to all comers. Before, the noise had been an expectant mumble. Now the voices were higher and louder, and there was a good deal of laughing, but the laughter had a harsh, quarrelsome edge to it. Then one voice cut above the rest. "You bloody thief!" it roared. Silence fell under the crash of waves and the howl of wind. I elbowed my way through the crowd surrounding one of the bonfires. A space had cleared. In its middle stood the captain, stooping forward like a baited bear. Opposite him, three feet away, ands loosely at his side and fire reddening his mat of beard, Little John.

"I'll see you hang," said the captain. "I'll see you hang for this. You send your hell-bitch aboard my ship and while we ain't looking you cut my cables and put us on your bloody stones, and then you pick us clean . . . Piracy," said the captain. "Damned corsairing piracy."

Little John spread his hands. "Wine is a mocker and strong drink is raging," he said. Then he turned his back and said, "Eddie. We'd best start getting yon stuff up to the sheds."

The captain's hands started to move up from his waist, very slowly, until they were like claws. A sound suggestive of strangulation came from his throat. He leaped at John's back.

Little John did not even turn round. The captain must have weighed fifteen stone, and he was not soft. He landed on John like a cartload of bricks, and his forearm went round under the beard. A gust of wind swept off the sea, and the bonfire roared low and yellow in the draught. Then the captain was a big bat sailing through the air and down to the flames. There was a crash and a yell and shower of sparks. John said, "The carts." A couple of women were pouring sand over the captain's smouldering coat. I heard one of them say, "You poor man. 'Tis a terrible thing, to be ship-wrecked." I went after Little John. He was at one of the piles, heaving barrels onto a cart. I said, "I want a word with you."

His eyes were quite impassive "You do."

"Is it true that you cut his anchor-cables?"

"What if it was?"

"Then you'd be nothing short of a thief."

He nodded, slowly. Then he said, "You're new on the islands. So you listen. 'Tis my business in the Lord to save human souls as come ashore. 'Tain't none of my busines to worry how they gets here." He heaved another barrel onto the cart.

"One thing," I said. "How did I come to be here?"

"You was washed ashore."

"There was a light," I said. "The night my ship went down."

"Agnes," said John, impassive.

"It can't have been Agnes," I said. "We were sailing due south. We would have had to sail slap through Bryher to be that close to Agnes. It must have been—"

John heaved the last barrel onto the cart and said, "You must have bin seeing things. Giddap, there." The cart rolled away up the beach to the road.

Someone took me by the arm. It was the woman, her hood pulled over her face. "Come and take a drop, Doctor," she said. Her voice was soft, without the dangerous hint of laughter. "I want to meet you." We went back across the island, leaving the crowded beach roaring now almost as loud as the gale. She said, "Best of it's over now. Receiver'll be along in the morning."

"Who's the Receiver?"

"He has charge of wrecks. Takes possession in the name of the King, doles out a proportion of the value to the salvors."

"He won't find much here."

"We're only poor islanders," she said. "Fortune's cruel oftener than she's kind, so we don't trifle with her."

We went down Palace Row to the sprawl of buildings above the quay. "The Palace Inn," said the woman. The place was almost empty. We got brandy and sat at a dirty table.

On Scilly you judged by the lines of suffering, the roughnesses and incongruities left by hard living and hard weather. She showed nothing of that. The skin was deep and smooth, slightly creamy in colour, with a delicate flush at the cheekbones. When I had seen her profile against the bonfire's glare, I had thought of her as carved from hard stone. I had been wrong. What I had seen as stateliness was in fact a complete composure, a self-sufficiency as absolute as that of a Byzantine saint. The set of the mouth was as much humorous as regal, the eyes set at a slant, hinting at deep ambiguities. The irises were huge, of a blue so deep that I expected to see constellations swim over the horizons of the pupils. As they looked at me I had the sense of enormous space, as if I was lying on my back gazing at the night sky.

She said, "So you are Doctor . . . Nicholls." She smiled. There was mockery in the shadows under her cheekbones, and I knew the pause had been deliberate.

"And you are Mary," I said. "The dark angel. Mary who?"

"Mary Prideaux. But why do you call me the dark angel? Should I be flattered?"

"I think so."

She laughed. "Well, how gallant, Doctor. But Mary from now on, if you please. We all have different names for different times, do we not?" They seemed to look straight through me, those eyes.

"What was the purpose of our little jaunt tonight?" I said. "Did it have anything to do with the manner of my coming ashore?"

She made a dismissive gesture with a long hand. The red stone flashed on the first finger. "I thought you needed cheering up," she said. "As to the rest, whatever I was to say would make no difference."

I did not answer. I did feel vastly cheered, it was true, though I was not entirely sure why. And it was she who had cheered me. But as to the wreck. . . . There was no doubt in my mind that the ship's cables had been cut. Naturally, I should inform the authorities. But that might have all manner of unpleasant consequences. And not only for Mary Prideaux and the rest of the islanders. While I sympathised with the captain's fury, the cargo would be useful on the island. The ship was doubtless insured.

"Yes," said Mary, as if she had been watching the thoughts go by in my mind. "You're beginning to think the way we think here."

I felt myself flush, and tried to put words to the vague ideas of obligation. "It's that the island's been very kind to me. I had a notion I would stay here and . . . see what I could do in return."

"Noble," she said. "But it's not the island that's kind to you. It's the sainted Charity." I had the impression that she was not talking about people when she said "the island." It was as if she saw the place, granite and gorse and sand and sea, as something more than the sum of its parts. Something with a life of its own, independent of humans.

A door opened somewhere in the house. A little man with a sly landlord's eye and bushy brown whiskers and an air of raffish respectability, not much enhanced by the ruins of a frock-coat, scuttled over to the table and said, "Little John's coming in."

Miss Prideaux got up. "Well, we wouldn't want to meet him, would we, Harry? Good night to you, Doctor. I hope you clear up your mysteries." She pulled up the hood of her cloak. The door closed behind her. Straight away, I found myself missing her.

Little John came in a moment later. He said, "Brandy." Then he looked at me and said, "Oh. You," and came and sat down and combed at his beard with his vast fingers. He did not look friendly. But there were things I wanted to say to him, after tonight.

"Landlord," I said. The bushy-whiskered individual cocked an eyebrow at me, very self-possessed. "Have you a chart of the islands?"

"I have," he said, and threw a much-folded wad of paper across the room. I spread it on the table. "Mr. Woodcock," I said. "A small demonstration. Given that on the night my ship went down, we were sailing due south. You will observe that between us and St. Agnes there lies the island of Bryher, with to the west of it a lot of rocks and islets. How then could I have seen the Agnes light not a quarter of a mile away just before we hit?"

"Powerful 'magination," said Little John.

"I am not a very imaginative man. My rational faculties, however, have been well trained. And they lead me to believe that the light I saw would have been considerably to the north of Agnes. Here, for example." I stabbed my finger at a disc of rock split roughly across its diameter. To the east of it, the little figures of the soundings dwindled rapidly. "On Scilly Rock. Which would put the unwary mariner on the stones in Hell Bay."

"It would," said John. "If there had been a light, which there wouldn't have been. Strikes me you've enough to be grateful for, with your deliverance by the hand of God."

"I am duly grateful," I said. "But when I hear stories about cut cables I begin to wonder. That's all."

"You don't want to believe all you hear," said John. "We've our own ways here. You'll see. We don't ask too many questions." He stroked his beard. "Now how would you like if it I started asking questions of you? Why should a fine gentleman like yourself be content here? Perhaps there's some would like to know, somewhere?"

I held his eye. "Perhaps there are," I said. Honour among thieves, I was thinking. Or as Aunt Ellis had put it, "a man's business is his own business." They had asked no questions of me. After tonight, what right had I to ask questions of them?

"Oh, yes," said John. "You're part of it now."

When Mary had said the same thing, it had been almost comforting. In Little John's burred growl it had quite the opposite effect. My leg suddenly ached in its splints. "I'll be going."

"There is one other thing," said John. "Charity Pender. She thinks a lot of you. I wouldn't like to see her disappointed."

"What the hell do you mean by that?"

"You know," said John. The pint pot was made of thick pewter. In his hand, it looked like a rummer. The huge sinews of his knuckles whitened. The pot creaked, became oval, and collapsed in on itself. "I think a lot of Charity Pender. If you're going to stay here, you'll do right by her. Otherwise . . ." He sent the crushed tankard spinning into the fireplace.

I left, feeling that a golden age had simultaneously begun and ended.

Charity was sitting bolt upright at the kitchen table, the Bible open in front of her, her lips pressed tightly together. She was not reading. At the sight of the china on the mantel, the fire wheezing in the grate, shame gripped me. I said, "I'm sorry if you were worried. I was at the wreck."

"I know," she said, without raising her eyes. "It doesn't signify."

"Would you mind if I took my coat off?"

She looked up. Her eyes kindled in the lamplight. "But you're wet," she said. She sat me down in a chair and began to bustle round me, pulling off my boots and my coat and my shirt.

"Good meeting?"

"Oh, fine, fine," she said, in her nurse's voice. "But I was worried sick when I came back and found you had gone. The idea! You're mad. You scarce out of bed, trampling round in the sea."

"Not exactly in the sea—"

"And you'll be lucky if you don't get an inflammation of the lungs." She clashed the kettle on to the hearth and yanked out her father's black bottle and tugged a blanket over my knees, nailing back the comfortable web I had ripped down. I sat in the middle of it, thinking my own thoughts. Mary Prideaux featured in them strongly. I was angry with the woman because she had sneered at Charity. But not as angry as I should have been. As I watched Charity pour water into a mug of brandy and spoon in precisely the amount of sugar she knew I liked, I was conscious of a very small lapse into claustrophobia.

The Cooneen horse fair always brought the tinkers through Carthystown. When they came they would be towing their endless strings of skewbald ponies. When they left the strings would have shrunk after the selling of colts and fillies and the acquisition of new breeding-stock. On the way to the fair, so Carthystown lore declared, they were too busy with the horses to think of larceny. On their return, flush with money and light on stock, the village got ready for trouble, and the tinkers seldom disappointed them.

We rode down the drive, keeping safely out of range of the big house at the end of the High Street where Michael's parents lived. His father was an attorney in Waterford, and moving up in the world since the Act of Union. His mother was small and fat and full of bitterness that her husband had failed to secure one of the baronetcies handed out so liberally by the British to bribe Parliament out of Ireland and back to London. Now Michael was half-full of whisky, his parents held few terrors for him. Still, he kept well clear.

On the wide strip of common land beyond the village, the tinkers had set up booths. The front line dealt in commodities like Nostradamus' Universal Curative Oil, baskets, clothes-pegs and trinkets. Round at the back of the brightly-painted waggons were tents devoted to a less legitimate but to me and Michael more interesting trade. A surprising number of the village's menfolk seemed to share our preferences. The tent was small. One end of it was filled with a row of barrels, out of which a gentleman in a red and white neckerchief was dispensing a clear liquid into tankards. There were quite a few surly looks and a lull in the talk as we pushed through to the barrels. Michael's face was red and jolly as ever, but his eyes kept darting to and fro. Nobody greeted us. Popularity is largely hereditary in Carthystown.

The man in the neckerchief sized up our clothes and became very polite. "Fine young gents," he said. "Greatly honoured." There was a wry twist to his mouth. Michael drank and went purple trying to stop the coughing.

"Grand stuff," I said, and drained mine with what I hoped was a practised flick of the wrist. I did not choke, and as I waited for the fire in my belly to put itself out I felt quietly thankful.

Michael nudged me in the arm and jerked his head to the back of the tent. Two women had come in. They had black hair and brilliant blouses and full skirts. Their feet and ankles were bare and brown. "Will ya look at that," said Michael.

The potheen was making me feel warm and brave. "Come on," I said.

"Whatcha doin'?" said Michael.

"Whatcha think?" I said. When we got closer I saw that the women were not really women. They were girls, about the same age as us except around the eyes, where they were centuries older. "May I present His Grace the Duke of Wellington?" I said. "I am Daniel O'Connell. We are here enquiring into the natural beauties of Hibernia."

"Stop it," hissed Michael. The girls giggled. One of them, the prettier, said something to her companion in Irish.

"Shall we go?" I said. Without waiting for an answer, I grabbed her by the hand and dived for the flap of the tent. When I looked back I saw Michael was following, only it was the girl that was doing the dragging. It was about the first time I had ever seen him at a loss.

I put my arm around the girl's waist and pointed to a thicket of rhododendrons. She grinned at me, a most inflammatory grin, and off we ran. I was feeling a bit nervous myself by this time. Those eyes. . . .

From the concealment of the shrubbery I took another glance back. Michael and his consort were panting close behind. And behind him, the skeletal figure of Maconochie, dour as dry oatmeal, turned round and directed his lethal schoolmaster's gaze on the fleeing Fitzpatrick. It might have been the potheen or it might have been the mischievous fingers fumbling at my breeches; one way and another, it clean slipped my mind to tell Michael he had been overlooked.

Now that his scruples were being tampered with by lust Michael lost his reserve and bore his wench to the ground. I moved discreetly away, deep into the thicket. For a while I could hear his grunts and the muffled squeaks of his playmate. Then I was on the ground too, and the tinker's skirts were around her ears and my breeches were round my knees and a hot tongue was making hay with my carefully-rehearsed procedures. For the first time I felt myself drawn down between a pair of fine thighs and connected to something like a warm, wet thrashing-machine. I consigned Michael to the devil and concentrated on giving as good as I got.

Matters were becoming critical when there was a huge crashing in the bushes far behind. I stopped what I was doing. 'Oh,' said my partner. "Go on. Don't stop now."

"Minute," I said, lowering my head onto her breast. "More coming." I lay watching one pink nipple pointing at the sky six inches away, waiting.

The voices started. First, a woman. An old woman. "Eeee!" she said, like pigs being killed. "Eeee!"

Then Michael. "Mother," he said, terror and astonishment all at once. "Oh my God."

Then Michael's tinker girl. "Go on," she was saying. "Yer was nearly at the good part." I buried my face in soft flesh to quell the gales of laughter.

Then a walking stick. *Thwack,* it went. "Ow!" said Michael. "Will ye not do that!"

Michael's mother again, shivering on the brink. "All these years," she said. Her voice rose slowly to the full banshee effect. "All these years I *scrimp* and save and *ruin* my life chasin' after you, clearin' up your mess, trying to give you a *dacent* start and the first thing I know is I turn my back and there you are *fornicatin'* with a damned poxy tinker's whore in front of the whole VIL-LAGE." On the word 'village' her voice cracked, and the hysterics arrived. Maconochie took over. "You're expelled," he said. "Your poor mother. Your father'll beat hell out of you, or I will. Home with you now. Support your poor mother."

"DON'T LET HIM TOUCH ME!" roared the mother. "HE'S NO SON OF MINE GOD KNOWS!"

The last thing I heard was Michael's tinker wench, saying "Ain't you goin to pay me? Not even a shillin'?"

"No," said Maconochie. "Get along we' ye."

"I'll scream," said the tinker's wench. "I will so."

Brief pause. Then Maconochie's voice, saying "Pay her. Sixpence will do."

Under my loins the thrashing-machine started up again.

When it was over, we sneaked out of the far side of the laurels. The tinker girl bit the guinea I gave her and kissed me on the mouth, long and wet, running her hand down the front of my breeches.

A voice behind me said, "Oh!" I jumped back.

A pair of green eyes was watching me from under the fringe of a parasol. They belonged to a long white face set above a smart frogged walking costume.

"Lady Katherine," I said, and stuck.

The tinker girl said, "Tell your cards, Ladyship?" leaning on my arm. Her body was suddenly thick, the sensuous mouth sluttish, the pores of the skin wide and dirty.

"Oh, no thank you," said Katie. "I am sure Mister Power has more profitable ideas." She walked away, chin high, smiling a scornful little smile.

At that moment, I almost wished that I had a mother to catch me in the act. Anything but to be despised by Katie Drumcarty.

About three weeks after the wreck the sheriffs arrived to distrain Susan Odger's goods. I was in the dispensary, working. The first warning I had was when her reedy little voice sounded round the shed door. I had had a conference with her already. The whole thing seemed to have passed over her head, whether because she didn't know what a writ of distraint was or because she'd had so many served on her that she accepted them as she accepted a shower of rain, I couldn't tell.

The sheriffs were brought to the quay in a smartish two-oared boat. They were both stout men. One of them was bald and red and the other brown-haired and greasy. The bald one did most of the talking.

"Could someone direct me to the Widow Odger's house?" he asked as he stepped ashore. The arrival of a strange boat being an event of some moment, there was a goodish crowd of my patients and assorted idlers grouped on the rough stones. Ten voices immediately started giving directions, some accurate but most entirely misleading. The sheriff gave his understudy a God-help-us twitch of the eyebrows. "One at a time, please," he said.

"Bugger off the island, you fat old bugger," shouted an uninventive urchin at the rear of the crowd.

"Here's Mrs. Odger," I said, grasping her by her frail arm and propelling her forward.

He looked me up and down, and so did his understudy, "You her son?" he said, wrinkling his nose at my now dense beard, three-quarter-length trousers, ragged shirt and thread-bare jacket.

"No," I said, rather pleased at the effect I had produced. "A friend." Susan looked up at me with a flattered if toothless grin.

"Writ of distraint," said the sheriff, as if the word was entirely foreign to him. He pulled a paper from the breast of his rusty frock-coat. "Three and sixpence is the sum," he intoned. "Plus costs, seven shillings. Total, half a guinea."

"Seven shillings costs?" I said.

"The Law, my man, is impartial but not free."

"Oh," I said. "Well, can the Law change a ten-pound note?"

"Ten pound?" said the sheriff, astonished. "How did you come by ten pound?"

"Mind your own business," I said. "We'll try the Palace Inn."

The sheriff nodded sourly. His colleague, who had been standing all the while as if badly stuffed and mounted, ran a greyish tongue round his lips.

The taproom was empty but for a couple of my patients sitting over a game of dominoes and a couple of mugs of something by the unenthusiastic turf fire. The potboy clanked around the inner regions, calling for Harry Jack. I chatted with Susan Odger about the potato harvest. It had been good, she said. Very good. Why, she wouldn't be surprised if there wasn't twenty shillings' worth of taties in her shed. The sheriff began to look surly at these tidings, but the potboy's return with an assortment of coin seemed to take the sting out of it. "Harry Jack says here's two pound and he'll keep the rest on account, if you'll trust 'un, Doctor."

"Thank you," I said, and counted out ten and six, which I gave to Susan Odger. She in her turn handed it over to the sheriff, who was looking at me with curiosity not unmixed with suspicion.

"Doctor who?" he said.

"Nicholls is the name."

"How did you come to be here, now?" Confidential smile. "You're not the sort as usually brings up on Tresco."

"Just blew in," I said, with the unpleasant feeling that my only disguise was the Aunts' conspiracy of silence. "Well, you'll want to be getting along."

"Ah," said the sheriff. "Yes. They'll be pleased on St. Mary's, I should think. To know that there's a man of eddication and substance on the off-islands, I mean."

"Can but hope," I said. "Well, back to the consulting-rooms, I'm afraid."

As the dispensary door closed behind us, Susan Odger became incoherent with gratitude. I prescribed something or other, probably turpentine, and told her to be off home. Then I asked Charity to call me in the next patient. She hung back.

"They'll know you now," she said. "They'll be on the lookout for you."

"Who?"

"Them on St. Mary's."

"It'll take more than a sheriff to bring us down," said I.

Charity shrugged—bravado never seemed to have much effect on her calm—and summoned the next victim, and I worked on, telling myself again that the hunt had gone over me. But I wished there was some way of being certain.

After a silent dinner I got up and decided to go and distract myself at the Palace. I suggested to Charity that she come with me. She refused, and off I hopped.

The taproom was crowded. There was a buzz of talk that spilled out into the road and died as I hopped in. Perhaps forty pairs of eyes swivelled onto me. One or two voices said, "Good evening," but the majority just stared, that cold blue Tresco stare that is neither friendly nor unfriendly. I found a place on a bench near the fire and sat down. The tapboy brought me sixpennorth of brandy without my asking him, and said, "Compliments of Harry Jack."

"And my compliments to him," I said.

Five minutes later the potboy returned and said, "Harry Jack's respects, and would you join him in the parlour?"

"With pleasure," I said. I hopped after the potboy through a door and into a small chamber, fierce hot from the turf fire glowing in the hearth, with a table and a couple of settles.

"Ah ha, the Doctor," said the little man with the bushy brown whiskers. His air was distinctly proprietary. He would be Harold Jenkins, known as Harry Jack to distinguish him from the island's three other Harold Jenkinses. He introduced me to the select company, which consisted of Captain Bolitho, a square-shouldered merchant skipper with a bullet head and iron grey hair; and a gentleman in a rusty black frock coat with the appearance and manner of a middle-aged weasel, who rejoiced in the name of Adolphus Dumas. Captain Bolitho's schooner *Jane and Emily* was anchored in New Grimsby harbour; I was unable to discover what Mr. Dumas did for a living, though he appeared familiar with the wine and spirit trade on both sides of the Channel.

After an exchange of civilities, conversation became general. Harry Jack passed a few remarks unflattering to the Receiver of Wrecks, Mr. Dumas spoke of the excellence of the brandy, and Captain Bolitho, a taciturn man, damned the Preventives. For my part, I expressed my gratitude for so select an invitation and stuck my nose in my tankard. The bottle circulated freely and often. One was flung empty through the window. Another appeared, emptied and followed. A third sprang up in its place.

Harry Jack, who had been discussing the weather as if he owned it, addressed himself to me with some formality and said, "I hear there aren't no more news about the leases."

"The leases," I said. "What leases?"

He looked shocked. "Why the leases of the island holdings," he said. "You didn't know? We has our leases from the Duke of Leeds, as is the landlord. And lately we can't get Mr. Johns, his agent as lives on St. Mary's, to tell us whether he means to renew or not. Seems that the Duke's lease from the Duchy of Cornwall is coming to an end, and he don't know whether or not to renew. I don't care if he do or he don't. All I want is to be able to build without I be told to raze 'er down straight away."

"Happening all over the world nowadays," said Bolitho. "What ain't profitable goes by the board. Reasonable enough. And you can't say as the Duke has had much profit out of these islands. Practical man of business would let 'em all slide."

"Ah," said Harry Jack, with no conviction at all. " 'Course he would."

"Strikes me his profit depends on his investment," I said. "Short leases and squeezery don't sound particularly business-like to me."

Bolitho shook his bullet head. "Wrong, wrong," he said. Harry Jack winked at me from behind his back. "No reason for muddling a landlord with a philanthropist. Duke can dispose of his lands as he sees fit."

Dumas looked at me with his shifty eyes. "Ah yes," he said. "Doctor Nicholls. Now I remember. I've heard of you in Hugh Town. Your fine philanthropical schemes. If I may make a suggestion? You be careful, young man. You may think you've nothing to lose. They will invent something."

"Hold your bloody jaw, Dumas," said Bolitho unexpectedly. "You're filled with pusillanimosity." He turned to me. " 'Pologise for Dumas," he said. "Used to cringing. Does it for a living."

At this, Dumas became enraged and started to demand retractions or blood. I realised that all of them, with the possible exception of Harry Jack, were far gone in liquor. I was not exactly sober myself. While Harry Jack got more booze to oil down this nasty chop of controversy, Dumas and Bolitho glared at each other and I sat looking at the dirty cracks in the table. My fingers caressed the watch in the secret pocket of my waistcoat. It had been three long months. I was getting too well known. Something would have to be done. But what?

The tempers of our little company improved with further libations, though Dumas, as insulted party, was still rather brisk and snappish.

"Thing about the off-islanders," said Dumas, burying his nose in his tankard. "They're like children. Look at the fish-cellar."

"The fish-cellar was a damned imposition," said Bolitho.

"The fish-cellar," said Dumas, having trouble with the
sibilants, "was an excellent thing. An excellent thing. The
Relief Committee built that fish-cellar to give employment
to the needy of the islands. Through the charity of the
good subscribers of England. And to let it fall into ruin
and disuse is rank ingratitude. Rank."

"Rubbish," said Bolitho. "Poppycock. The fish-cellar
was built to give employment to the merchants of St.
Mary's. And having milked the Fund for every penny
they could get, they abandoned the islanders to their fate.
Charity won't work. There's pride in these islands."

"Can't eat pride," said Dumas, "Pride's for the rich.
Anyway, where's their pride when they bring their diseases to the Doctor here?"

"Fair exchange," I said. "They looked after me when I
came ashore. I'll do the best I can for them as long as
they need me."

Dumas shrugged his shoulders. "I wouldn't get too
many ideas if I were you. Scilly's a small place, and there
are some on St. Mary's won't like it if they're interfered
with."

"I wasn't intending to interfere with anyone."

"Naturally not," said Dumas. He got up and went outside.

"Look out for him," said Harry Jack. "He's a tricky
one."

"He is."

Bolitho laughed. "You're doing a bit of a stir-up round
here, Doctor. You may not realise. But beside Harry here
and the parson, there's few with a mind to it. And Harry
Jack likes to keep himself to himself, and the parson—
well, he's a foreigner and nobody pays much attention to
him. So you just look out that you don't get yerself nipped
in the bud. I like you, Doctor. You're a live one." He rose
to go. "If you need any help, you can count on me."

"Thank you," I said. Dumas came back into the firelight, buttoning his trousers.

"That goes for me, too," said Harry Jack, winking
knowledgeably.

"What does?" said Dumas sharply.

"Ah, nothing. Drop more, gentlemen?"

Dumas' mind was instantly diverted from his suspicions. "Gladly," he said.

I refused and followed Bolitho out onto the quay, where I bade him goodnight. Then I hopped back up the Row to Charity's house. There was a glow of candlelight through the Penders' kitchen curtains. It occurred to me that this was unusual. Charity was not much given to sitting up late. I took a last look at the night, which was clear and full of stars. I had my hand on the latch when I heard a man's voice.

"It is your duty, woman," it said. Little John's voice.

"John!" said Charity sharply. "You're mad."

"Ask him," said John. "He'll tell you."

I opened the door and went in. Charity was in a chair by the fire, back very straight, spinning. Little John was standing over her, head bowed under the low plank ceiling. As my crutch ground on the door-step he swung round.

"Tell her what?" I said.

"Where her duty lies."

"What business is that of yours?"

"I told you. In the Palace." His hands rested on the back of a chair. Again I saw the tankard crushing in his crane-hook grip.

"You were talking rubbish then, and you're talking more now. I suggest you go away."

He stepped forward and glared down at me from on high. "Duty is the Lord's burden, Doctor. You have no fear of the Lord, so you bear not the burden. It may be my task to make sure you take it on your shoulders." He brushed past me and strode out into the night.

III

WHEN THE SPLINTS came off my leg, I knew I had to be moving on. It was only a matter of time before someone began asking awkward questions and following them up. But I was curiously reluctant to move; and besides, there were few ships in the roads. Aunt Ellis, who made no secret of the fact that she and Aunt Woodcock thought I should stay, told me that one Amor Odger had a horse he would rent me; so a couple of days after my white, shrunken shin emerged into the daylight, I went for a walk.

There were fields sloping away on my left, green over black, peaty soil. On my right was the Abbey Pool, a sheet of water of perhaps fifty acres. Knots of wildfowl bobbed out of shot. I limped up to my left, pausing on top of the ridge to get my breath. Stretched out before me was the sea, blue and wrinkled. It was low tide. There were the shadows of sunken rocks, brown on turquoise, and here and there a knob of granite shaggy with weed. Beyond the sound were islands crowned with bracken and heather, the biggest of them with geometric fields in its sheltered places. I hobbled down to the low thatched house that stood under the brow of the ridge.

House and yard looked neat and clean, but as I hobbled nearer I saw the thatch was old and black and the roof-timbers showed through at the ridges. The Aunts had said that Amor was one of the bigger farmers on Tresco. That meant five acres, scattered over the island in the usual pocket-handkerchief sized lots.

"Hello!" I called.

Nobody moved. I walked round to the yard. There was a tumbledown barn and a sty where a rangy sow rooted disconsolately. The tell-tale pile of limpet shells rose by the midden. Not as big as some I had seen, but big enough.

A man came out of the barn, large and bent and gaunt, wearing boots and a stocking cap, carrying a fork. " 'Pologies," he said, in the flat voice of the very deaf. "Didn't hear ye come. You'll be the Doctor."

His face was pitted with smallpox scars. I supposed it had got to his ears. "You have a horse," I said loudly.

He frowned a moment, working out half-heard sounds. His brow cleared. "Ah," he said. "Aunt Susan said as you wanted a horse. Good horse, too. Bugger to eat, though." He looked at my withered leg, and tactfully shifted his eyes away. "Aunt Susan said as you was very good to her," he blared as he led me into the mottled darkness of the barn. "Thankee, thankee. Times is hard and they'll be harder."

At the far end of the barn stood a dirty grey pony, gazing listlessly at the wall to which its headstall was tied. In another corner of the barn were a couple of bales. I wondered if they were off the wreck. I felt the pony's legs and looked at her teeth.

She seemed healthy enough, considering that her diet that winter would have consisted almost exc'usively of seaweed. So the bargaining started, complicated by Amor's deafness. Eventually we closed, and Amor spat in his palm and we shook. I put oats in a bucket and we talked noisily while the horse ate. The story he told was becoming familiar. The farm was falling down round his ears, but he would do nothing about it. Why not? Because there was no way for him to tell whether the Duke's agent would renew his lease or not. So why spend a lot of time patching his buildings if he might have to start again in a couple of years? They were all the same, the Scilly farms. Crops were thin and rank. The land looked good enough, but there was no richness in it, even in the best fields. It was like the mare, thin and listless and dull. A man with money could feed a horse. The land was a different matter.

Amor helped me saddle up the mare and boosted me onto her back, and I set off down the track that led through the dunes to the shore.

When I came to the beach I struck off towards the north end of the island. The mare settled into a slow amble, which was as much as either of us could manage. At first I felt curiously lopsided. My right stirrup was two holes higher than the left, and I had to sho.e down with my sound leg to stop myself sliding off. After a while I got the hang of it, and I began to look about me.

The tide was rising. Little groups of dunlin and turn-stone rooted in the sand by the edge of the sea. Oyster-catchers skimmed the wavelets, piping. The sun beat down out of a clear blue sky, and the heat of it warmed my bones. For about a mile I saw no-one but a tow-headed youth rummaging under a boulder with a pole. I said "Good morning" to him. He did not answer, but darted a suspicious glance from pale blue eyes and stepped quickly in front of a pile of wreckwood. I shrugged my shoulders and went on, round a headland crowned with the ruins of a fort. Part of the ruin still held a roof, and a thread of blue smoke issued from the chim-ney. Below the walls was the inevitable pile of limpet shells.

The headland sheltered a bay of white sand. There were one or two boats drawn up on the beach, and on the foreshore were the thatched roofs of a considerable vil-lage. Old Grimsby, where the wreck had come ashore. I walked the mare along the beach and up onto the road that separated the houses from the shore. She jerked her head at a black pig picking over a pile of rubbish on the beach and I kicked her on, waving at a tired-looking woman who came out of a cottage and tipped a pail of dirty water into the road. She curtsied and said, "Good morning, Doctor." She was one of my patients. Charity had told me she had twelve children. She had a growth on her womb and a husband who had drowned the pre-vious year, fishing in a rotten boat.

Seven or eight men were sitting on a low wall in front of the Ship Inn. The sign showed a red brig on a crudely-painted green sea. A couple of them nodded at me, but the others looked and looked away again and resumed their low-voiced conversation. The road turned to the left but I kept straight on over the hill and parallel to the shore, which trended to the left, with tiny fields running down to a scoop of bay. A moth-eaten man weeding be-tween black ridges of potatoes leaned on his hoe and watched me pass, the bulge of his quid moving in his lower jaw. After a while the fields gave way to rock and patches of heather squared by turf-cutting. The beach where it ran up to the point was a tumble of granite boulders, lined on the foreshore with little piles of timber, each surmounted by a stone as a token of ownership. The bay was full of gulls, wheeling and swooping against the backdrop of granite islands and heaving aquamarine sea. The screaming of the gulls grew louder, more quarrelsome. There was a focus to the pack of them. Something in the water, forty feet off the shore. Something at which they dived and tore until they were chased away by others, diving and tearing in their turn. For a moment I thought it was a dead seal. But it was too clumsy for a seal. The black stuff that covered it wrinkled and billowed with the lapping of the waves, and something white flopped at the extremity of its articulations. The mare saw it too. She flung up her head and danced away, rolling her eyes and whickering.

I looked back at the man with the hoe. He was still leaning, chewing at his quid, watching me. I shouted something and slid off the mare and stumbled down onto the boulders. He dropped his hoe and started to run towards me, clumsy in his laceless boots, looking at the gulls now, and the thing in the water.

By the time I had grovelled my way over the slippery rocks, I could smell it. The gulls soared away, shrieking. I lay looking at it, at the soggy black cloth and the swollen hands and the gross blob of flesh that had once been the head and the holes of the eyes.

Something clattered on the rock beside me. "Get it in," shouted a voice. "I'll fetch help." The man with the hoe began to pound back towards Old Grimsby. I groped in a crevice and pulled out the coil of twine with the barbed lead at its end. My fingers shook as I untangled the line. I took a deep breath and threw, missed, and threw again. The lead bit with a wet thump, and I took up the slack, feeling the barbs bite. A bow-wave of water grew under the thing's side. The disgusting sweetness in the air grew. It was the sweetness of the bins in the dirty yard behind the Anatomy House at Trinity. I got it up on the rocks and caught hold of one of the lapels of the coat and held it there. Out of the grey balloon of face the eyeholes stared raggedly at the sky. The gulls' shadows flicked across it like random thoughts.

The clothes had once been good. What was left of the hair, floating like weed away from the ruined scalp, was black. That and the eyeholes were the only features that remained. Three months ago, but for a miracle, that might have been me. I turned my head away.

Perhaps it could still be me.

Clenching my teeth, I began to go through the pockets. They were empty. Hanging onto the lapel with one hand, I fumbled in the secret pocket in my waistcoat. The sun glinted cheerily off the slim gold half-hunter, picking out the engraving on its back. *"Nick Power, with fond remembrance. K."* The corpse's waistcoat was drawn tight over the bloated stomach. I tucked the watch into the right-hand fob. Nailed boots ground on the boulders behind me. I waited until they had dragged the thing out of the water and onto the hurdle and hidden it with a tarpaulin. Then I began to stagger back towards the clean-smelling green shore.

Bees were humming in the gorse of the hedges, and birds were singing. But the thing on the hurdle spread a grim circle of silence which covered the bearers and blanketed my thoughts.

They took it to a shed nearby, at the back of the house of the man with the hoe, and there what laying-out was possible was done, and done fast. The smell of it spread down the row of houses, and we sat upwind, the pall-bearers and I, and tried to forget the closeness of it by drowning it in words. Jimmy Pender, as carpenter, had been summoned back from Agnes, and the parson informed. The burial was to be that night. To wait longer would be unhealthy.

The man with the hoe introduced himself as John Sinclair. He had taken it upon himself to go through the pockets. Now he sat on the wall, swinging the watch by its chain, the breeze fluttering the rags of his shirt.

At last he looked at me. "It's yours," he said. "You found him."

"I don't want it," I said. "Put it to the cost of the funeral." Wood was rare on Scilly, and coffins expensive.

"You'd bury ten for that," said Sinclair. "Besides, I gets the clothes." He stuck a finger into one of the myriad holes in his breeches.

"All right," I said, repressing a shudder. "I'll buy it off you." Sinclair looked at me as if I was mad.

"How much?"

"Three pound."

Sinclair rocked slightly. "Done," he said quickly. "Funeral extry."

"Good enough," I said. "Harry Jack's holding the money, over at the Palace."

He handed me the watch. I took it, looking down at the engraving.

"What do it say?" said Sinclair.

"Nicholas Power," I said levelly. "Wonder who he was."

"Don't matter now," said Sinclair, hacking off a new quid from his plug.

And it didn't.

It was surprising, the independence I felt when they shipped Michael off to Dublin to take articles with a firm of attorneys. I suppose that since Katie had come into my life I did not believe in him so unquestioningly.

The day before he left I stole a bottle or two from my father's cellar and we took them down to the river. After the second glass, he told me magnanimously that he bore me no grudge for my not warning him about Maconochie. He still showed a tendency to sulk, however; but that passed as I began to draw him a picture of the possibilities of Dublin. He frowned and looked unpleasantly pompous and said, "I'm going to take my articles seriously. Lay a firm foundation for life." And having promised to write, he left on the Bianconi stage-coach.

It must have been obvious to everyone except my father that pretty soon Carthystown would be too small to hold me, or anyway too hot; but my father stayed glued to the Drumcarty estates and paid me no attention from one month to the next. So I cruised the countryside on Gráinne, hunting, drinking and whoring with rips of similar inclinations but maturer years. By the time my fifteenth birthday was well in view I knew how to conduct myself at a debauch or a cockfight, or in a haystack with a tenant's daughter. By and large, I thought myself a pretty fine fellow.

But not when I was anywhere near Katie.

A more self-confident lover would have profited from her physical closeness. Since her return from England, she came to the Castle quite often. But even though I knew that she was a mere hundred yards away from the Factor's House, I could not bring myself to confront her. When she was in residence I sulked and mooned and wrote her passionate letters that I subsequently burned. When she was in Dublin, I told myself that next time she came down, I would . . . well, I would do something. But always I saw the white scornful smile in the carriage window, and when her carriage rolled over the bridge I would be cringing in my room.

In the end, it was she who made the advance.

A couple of miles upstream from the Castle the river takes a big bend. On the outside of the bend is a deep hole in which running salmon like to rest. It was my habit to set off in that direction on summer afternoons when I knew the bailiffs were elsewhere. There was a big dead tree overhanging the hole, and with a long-handled gaff and a little daring it was not difficult to hoist the aforementioned salmon out of the river. I was walking up the bank one fine June day, limping a bit from the sections of gaff stuck down my trouser leg, when I heard a voice calling my name. Ditching the deadly weapon in a handy bush, I turned round. It was Katie, cool in white muslin, with a little frilly parasol hung over her arm and a Pomeranian in tow. My heart jumped into my throat and stuck. She smiled prettily and said, "Nick Power, is it not?" She knew perfectly well who I was. I felt a strong urge to tell her to go to hell but the green eyes were savaging me. So I said, "Yes, indeed, Your Ladyship," and grinned at her like an oaf.

"What are you doing?" she said, with that teasing half-smile of hers.

"Taking the air," I said, finding some composure "Looking for a poem to write. A picture to paint."

"Oh no you're not," she said. "You're going poaching."

I goggled at her.

"Yes," she said. "I know you are, because I watched you yesterday. From the Lady Tower. With Papa's telescope. I saw you quite clearly."

I said, "No. Never."

She tossed her auburn curls. "I want to come with you," she said.

"But—"

"And if you don't take me I'll tell Papa."

I took her.

All the way she told me how bored she was at the Castle with nothing to do, how she was planning to go back to Dublin as soon as possible, how everyone was fighting duels over her in the great city. I trudged along beside her taking furtive kicks at the Pomeranian, sneaking looks at her pale, lovely profile.

When we got to the hole I shinned elegantly out along the tree. There was an eddy in the brown water, a little mud-coloured dimple. I screwed the gaff-handle together and let the hook sink slow and gentle. When I felt it touch the rock I moved it back and drew up, sharply. The handle began to throb angrily. I scrambled to my feet and ran like hell over the slippery moss-grown trunk, making the leap for the bank, hauling in. I got a foot under the six-pound peal flapping on the mud beach and heaved it into the bushes. Then I stood back.

"That's how it's done," I said.

Katie's eyes were like fiery emeralds. "But that's *wonderful*," she cried. "Oh but you must be so *strong*."

I mumbled something, feeling my face heating up. The fish was crashing around in the laurels hotly pursued by the Pomeranian, and I dived in after it. I did feel remarkably strong and clever. It was the eyes that did it.

When I returned, Katie was creeping along the mossy trunk with the gaff in her hand. The breath froze in my chest.

"For God's sake," I said. "Come back! You'll fall!"

"Shut up," she said. Her white skirts trailed in the water.

"I'll have to come and get you," I said.

"Not unless you want Papa to hear." She turned around and gave me her grin, waving her hand. When she put her hand down again, it hit a patch of mud my boot had left on the trunk. She said, "Oh!" and slipped and fell in the river.

She came up spluttering and choking. I was standing like a statue, mouth open. "I can't swim?" she shrieked. Then she sank again, her skirts billowing round her head like a big white waterlily. I dived in after her.

When I surfaced, she had moved. Her head was above water again, her arms flailing. "Oh help!" she cried. "Oh save me!" She was in the tide now, moving swiftly downstream.

I went after her. I was a good swimmer, and I caught her quickly. I got my hands under her arms and turned her on her back, feeling the swell of her breasts, oh joy! through the wet muslin. She said, "Mr. Power! What can you be thinking of?" Then she turned over and began swimming down the river like an otter, me following, the Pomeranian yapping like a mad thing from the bank.

When she tired of the game and went ashore we were well in sight of the Castle. I crawled up the mud beach after her and said, "What did you do that for?" knowing that I sounded like a whipped dog. Her dress clung to her body. I could not take my eyes off her nipples.

"It's your fault," she said, drawing herself up.

I lost my temper. "First you tag along and ruin an afternoon's fishing in your damn silly white dress. Then you go behaving like a silly bitch—"

"Come, Toto," she said to the Pomeranian, freezing cold. "Mummy is returning to the Castle."

"Not until you apologise, you slut!" I roared. "By God, I ought to smack your pretty little bum until you tell me you're sorry—"

I had not seen the welcoming committee approaching across the park. They heard every word. Katie was wrapped in blankets and half-carried back to the Castle. I was taken by the ear and dragged to the nearest ash-copse, where half the hide was taken off me by two strong men, working in relays.

A couple of days later, a Castle footman brought me a small package. When I opened it I found a wafer-thin, gold half-hunter, inscribed. There was a note, on white paper with the mastiff crest. It said, *"I watched them larrup the ticking off you. This is to put it back in."* Outside the window, the black Drumcarty coach rattled past. Two green eyes looked out of the window, and a white-gloved hand blew me a kiss. I sat there staring at the watch, not knowing whether to laugh or cry.

From that day onward, everywhere I went the watch went with me.

There were a lot of people at the funeral. I went too, ostensibly because I had found the man but actually because I wanted to hear myself buried.

I stood near the back of the crowd, leaning on my stick. As the parson rattled earth on the coffin-lid I saw Charity's head, veiled in black, bow, and felt a vague guilt at having deceived her. Beside her was Little John's mane of tawny hair and tangled beard. I looked away quickly, letting my eyes stray over the tombstones beyond. They fixed on a slim figure standing high on a spire of rock. I thought I knew who it was. The long cloak blowing in the wind, the waving banner of night-black hair. Behind her the clouds hung low, and dark over islands and sea. Higher, they were white and fleecy, tips gilded with the last gold of the sun. The little figure moved down the rock, light as a deer, and I knew I had been right. It was Mary Prideaux.

The parson stopped talking and the crowd flooded out of the churchyard. I found myself much greeted as I pushed my way against the stream, even by people who had avoided my eye before. John Sinclair and the men who had carried the hurdle were working briskly with shovels at the pile of fresh earth by the black mouth of the grave.

"Doctor . . . Nicholls?" said a soft, cultured voice. I turned. It was the parson, his cassock flapping. I did not want to talk to him or anyone else at that moment.

"Could I have a word?" he said. He had a thin face with sandy hair and large, pale eyebrows which rose as he talked. "A glass of wine, perhaps?"

"With pleasure," I said, without pleasure.

"Good," he said, beaming. We walked slowly back onto the road and up the hill, the professional class of Tresco, the mare clopping behind. He turned into a gateway and up through a wildly overgrown patch of garden to a square, solid-looking house. His housekeeper met us at the door, and the parson asked her to have my horse seen to and to bring us wine in his study. Then he waved me in. I went, gingerly. It seemed a long time since a servant had opened a door for me.

The study was a big room, full of books. The parson fussed about, lifting piles of volumes from chairs onto other chairs and waving away the clouds of dust he raised. He lit a couple of candles, sat me down, and took a chair himself. It was very cold, but he did not seem to notice. "A bad business, that of poor Mr. Power. It will be my melancholy duty to inform the newspapers. Sad task, sad task."

"Yes indeed," I said. "Poor fellow," and took a relieved draught of wine.

"Sad, sad," said the parson again, his eyebrows near his hair-line. "But all too frequent an occurrence, I fear."

"Mmm," I said. The housekeeper came in with a decanter and a couple of glasses. As he poured, I wondered what he was driving at.

"You yourself had a lucky escape," said the parson. "Very lucky."

"It was that."

"Lucky for the islanders as well as yourself. Though yours was not what they would call, um, a *good* wreck. The ship was too badly smashed and scattered."

"You sound as if you're a connoisseur," I said, smiling.

"Not a *connoisseur,* exactly, but, um, rather against my inclinations I have come to see these wrecks as not a bad thing. For the islands. They are on the whole beneficial."

"Even when people get killed?"

Horror covered his face. "No, no, you misunderstand me," he said. *"Humans* must be saved. The islanders will go to any length to make sure of that, even to putting their own lives in the most appalling danger. But the wrecks themselves make a great *contribution*—I suppose you could say that, um, the sea is an instrument of Providence in that respect."

"An interesting separation of humans from their chattels," I said, thinking of Little John at the Old Grimsby wreck. "I have heard it so expressed before. But how does the Law see it?"

"Oh, the Law," said the parson. "Well, you cannot have failed to notice the searches since the last wreck. But the islanders see no reason why the Law should have all the rewards with none of the labour. Once I thought that iniquitous. Now, I am by no means so sure."

"No," I said, sipping. "I am inclined to agree with you."

"One has to be very accommodating. This I have learnt. A bitter lesson." The parson sighed. "God knows, on an island this size one might expect some uniformity. But no. The more I know about it, the more astonished I become at its diversity. The schisms! The dissimulation! Do you know that my flock will attend Evensong in my church, having spent the morning in the Wesleyan meeting-house? To avoid showing partiality, I suppose. And then there are the Bryanite meetings. To listen to a woman preaching. A woman!" He took a horrified gulp from his glass. The wine seemed to restore some of his former meekness. "But I am sorry. I am forgetting myself. To the point. Yes, the point." He stopped, why I could not tell.

"Go on," I said.

"Really it is most embarrassing," said the parson, his eyebrows struggling. "But here it is. I have been approached by a *deputation*, Doctor. About your inhabiting the house of James Pender."

"You have?"

"They were all good *church folk*, you understand," said the parson. "They felt strongly that you were alone too much with Charity for, ah, propriety's sake."

"And was Little John Woodcock one of the church folk?"

"Goodness me, no," said the parson, looking shocked. "If he is anything he is a Bryanite. He considers himself —well, a man of principle. But his principles are—"

"Idiosyncratic," I said. "I had noticed. So what apart from deploring my cohabitation with Charity Pender, did your deputation have in mind?"

"They merely felt that you should take lodings elsewhere. Lodgings that were suitable for a, a gentleman. It is because you are a gentleman that they did not like to make a more direct approach."

"How discreet," I said, "And you. You are sure I am a gentleman?"

He looked surprised. "Of course," he said. "I have heard of your works on the island, Doctor. And I must say that they show a selflessness, a nobility of spirit, which I find most laudable."

That jarred. Power, the noble fugitive. The noble wrecker.

"Yes," said the parson, taking my hesitation as polite demurral. "It is evident to me that you could have a flourishing practice in any of the great cities of the world. Yet you make no effort to retrace your past. None at all. Instead, you busy yourself as a Samaritan, without reward, for the benefit of the poor inhabitants of these derelict isles."

I finished my wine at a gulp and levered myself painfully to my feet. "You are quite wrong," I said. "You do not know—"

He held up his hands. "Your diffidence does you enormous credit," he said. "But you may rest assured that I shall make every effort to join you to your past. Stay among us if you will: but I think the world should know of your work, if only as a shining example in the gathering darkness."

"Please," I said. Oh, my God, I thought. He was standing, his eyes shining with honest enthusiasm. "Do this much for me. Let me work here without the world and without my past." I forced into it all the treacly sincerity I could summon up.

"Hide not your light under a bushel," he said solemnly. "That men may see your good works and glorify your Father which is in heaven."

"No," I said, with disgusting hypocrisy. "Ignore the man. Let the works speak for themselves."

"Perhaps you are right," he said. "If you wish it so. You are a man in a million, Doctor Nicholls. I shall be silent. But there will be others—"

"I shall rely on you as a man of like mind to persuade them to share your silence," I said solemnly. "And now. You spoke of lodgings?"

"There is a house for you in Old Grimsby."

"And how will I pay?"

"The house is empty, and has been so for a while."

"And the housekeeper?"

"I suppose the best thing would be for me to send down Mrs. Clitheroe from time to time. She is much underemployed here."

I agreed. Mrs. Clitheroe, consulted, expressed willingness. We walked down to Old Grimsby to inspect the house, which was poor enough but not as bad as I had expected. Now all I had to do was tell Charity that I intended to leave her.

Charity was sitting at the table, spinning with Ursula Evans, Jemima Odger, and a couple of other young women I didn't recognise. They all put aside their skeins and spindles, rose and curtsied and smiled, and Jemima, who was pretty, though not as pretty as Charity, blushed. "Good evening, Doctor," she said. "Terrible day, has it not been?"

"Terrible." I looked at Charity, who was rolling her skein rather too busily. "Don't let me interrupt."

"Ah, we were just going," said Jemima. "You'll be tired out, I'm sure. It must have been dreadful, seeing him floating like that."

I mumbled something about doctors becoming accustomed to such sights, and the young women shuddered. Then they said their goodbyes to Charity, wrapped their cloaks about them, and filed out of the door.

There was a silence while Charity gathered up the tea-cups. I said, "I saw you in the churchyard. I had to stay behind."

"And the priest caught a hold of you," she said. "I heard."

"News travels fast," I said.

"It didn't need to. The brethren have been at me for a month now."

"Why didn't you tell me?"

Her eyes were as calm and frank as ever. "I was afraid you'd go."

"Afraid I'd go?" I couldn't think of anything else to say, so I stood there, leaning on the back of a chair, wishing I could look away.

"Sit down," said Charity quietly. I sat. "I want to tell you something, if you haven't guessed it already. When my Dad found you lying up by Gun Hole with your leg in two halves, he wanted to put you over to St. Mary's and have done with you." She smiled, very slightly. "But I told him no, and he gave in. He always does give in. And the reason I asked him was because of something I saw in your face, even before you came back to yourself. I knew you weren't like the rest of us on these islands. And when I saw you so helpless and like to die, I thought how fine it would be to have a gentleman of my own. Like a doll, I suppose. To look after you and see you get well or die. I didn't care, God forgive me. Just as long as you were in the house. Because I've always wanted to know what went on away on the mainland. Do you know I've never seen a carriage? A real gentleman's carriage, I mean. Well, when you began to mend I thought that if I nursed you, you might take me away and show me, one day." She paused, sighed and began again. "God punished me. I started thinking of me in fine clothes and the rest of it, and somehow I couldn't stick to it. I kept seeing you, all thin and white and sad. And after a bit I'd forgotten all about wanting to be a lady, and all I could think about was you and about keeping you near me here." A tear swelled at the corner of each eye, ran down her cheeks and fell on the table. "All I wanted was you. And now you're well and you're taking yourself away. And you're right to do it. It was vanity in me to expect anything else, and God has punished me for my vanity."

"No, not vanity."

"I'd rather you left it at that," she said in a very small voice. Then she ran upstairs.

The birds on the *famille rose* vase on the mantelpiece jeered at me with their laughing beaks. I clambered aboard the mare and went across the island to my new home and Mrs. Clitheroe, with a face like lemon-juice, presiding.

In the next six weeks, as the days lengthened and then began to grow short again, I found out more about the island than I had in the past three months.

Most of the time I spent behind my screen at the dispensary. Charity was always very correct and discreet. Her duties now included receiving the eggs, chickens and vegetables which, with the occasional bottle of spirits, were left me by grateful patients. It was a measure of the Scillonian sense of what was fitting that these contributions started of their own accord, after I had moved away from the Penders'. No doubt it was felt that I needed consolation, away in my half-ruined house to norrard.

Actually, I did not. I spent my few leisure hours collecting the molluscs and arthropods with which Scilly abounded, and in time I began to consider attempting a catalogue. As word spread that there was a doctor on Tresco, I was frequently summoned to the other off-islands, where there was a burden of disease and illness at least as bad. And I had a constant stream of visitors. Principal among these was Mrs. Clitheroe, who had not deviated by one grain of sugar from her acidity of temperament, and whom I strongly suspected of having been on the vigilante committee which had expelled me from the Penders' in the first instance; and the parson, something of a naturalist himself, who lent me books and discussed my work. Neither of them was exactly stimulating. Mrs. Clitheroe seemed convinced that, having been torn from the arms of the Penders, I was on the verge of hurling myself at her; the parson, sure I was a saint, always led the conversation from the beauties of Nature to his Doubts. These were plentiful but abstruse, brought on by the long island winter and the absence of society.

My other callers were mostly passers-by pausing to relay the latest episodes in the net of news and gossip that held the island together. One thing I noticed. There were the Church lot and Chapel lot and the farmers and the fishers and the drinkers and those with no visible means of support. They were all disrespectful about each other; but nobody was ever disrespectful about Mary Prideaux. When they spoke of her, which was seldom, it was always with a kind of reverence, tinged with dislike or incomprehension. I found this surprising, because Scillonians were quite remarkably open-minded, as well as open-mouthed.

I was musing on this and other subjects late one night in my house, looking out of the window at the full moon heaving itself up over St. Martin's and a black metal sea. The houses of my neighbours were dark, and behind them the treeless hills rose smooth as a whale's back. It was hot, and the window was open. (Actually the window was always open, having no glass in it: but tonight I was glad of it, and was therefore pretending that it was so by design.) There was a smell of heather and crushed bracken and salt, with a whiff of honeysuckle. A little breeze rustled the grasses.

There was no breeze tonight.

The door opened, slowly, pushed by the same nonexistent zephyr that had blown through the garden. And mingled with the smell of the sea and the heather was a sweet, sharp scent. Last time I had smelt it was on Castle Downs, in the storm.

"Good evening, Mistress Prideaux," I said, and lit the candle.

She laid down her bundle and I drew her up a chair. For a while we sat in silence, looking out of the window at the moon. Finally she said, "I thought I would come and see how you were getting on." In profile, her face was innocent and delicate, calm as a statue's. The moon turned her flesh to white marble. Orange lights from the candle flickered in her black hair.

I said, "I am glad you came," and meant it.

She turned, her skin warming in the candle-light. "Everyone comes to the Doctor," she said.

"You look very well to me."

She smiled. "I am, thank you kindly. But so are a lot of your patients."

"Yes." Since the business of Susan Odger and the bailiffs, my patients had been bringing me more than their bodily ills. There were quarrels and lawsuits and debts on the off-islands which had lain unsettled for years. The island court, the Council of Twelve on St. Mary's, was supposed to deal with such questions. But six or seven years ago the court had ground to a messy halt, torn by the bickering of its members; since then it only reconvened to consider serious threats to its independence. I was impartial, and I was the Doctor. So the cases came to me, and I did what I could. "It seems to be useful."

"And the doctoring takes all your time," said Mary.

"No. Not all of it."

"You must be lonely." The great blue-black eyes made me feel like a moth on a pin.

"I have my diversions," I said. "Natural philosophy and my journals to keep up."

"Been taking any more night walks?"

"Some. But none as . . . interesting as when I met you."

"Not even when you meet Charity Pender?" I felt the blood rise to my face, and she laughed. "I'm sorry, Doctor. I didn't mean to touch you on the raw."

"There's nothing raw about it," I said. "Charity helps me with my work. That's all."

"That's not what Johnny Woodcock's saying."

"As far as I am concerned, Little John Woodcock is under a sad misapprehension. I have told him as much."

"I know. I was only teasing. He's a hard man to tell he's wrong."

"You know this from personal experience?"

Her laughter had a curious quality of secrecy to it. "He wouldn't come near me," she said. "Not to say I was wrong."

"Why would that be?" I said, intrigued.

She got up and went to the table and said, "You collecting shells?"

"Among other things. Why wouldn't Little John come near you?"

"Hermit-crabs, too," she said. "Poor little limping things. Can't face life on their own, so they have to pull another animal's shell around them." She smiled. "You'll find out, if you come out of your shell."

Abuse I could take. But I was beginning to discover that Mary Prideaux made me want to justify myself. "I'll ask him, then."

"Ask away," she said. "You're a puzzle, Doctor. Where do you fit? You're not shipwrecked on your way somewhere, or you'd be off the island by now. You're not

one of God's soldiers like the parson or the mission surgeon they sent a while back. What the hell are you? What
makes you stay?"

"I like it here," I said. "That's all."

She shook her head. "That's a hermit-crab's answer.
He puts on his shell because it's simpler like that. He
doesn't ask what made the shapes or the colours of it. All
he cares about is that it fits. No, Doctor. I don't believe
you're like that. I wonder what you're really like?"

I was torn between admiration of her beauty and wanting her to go away and leave me in peace. "Like most
other people," I said.

"Well, that's a start," she said. "At least you're telling
lies now."

"You're very sure of yourself."

"Tell me." The voice was mesmeric. I had not talked
about it for a very long time. I could not stop myself.

"Yes, there was a woman, and I lost her. I lost it all.
And now I am trying to start clean." My hands were
shaking. I could not tell her any more. "So go and spread
that round the island."

"I wouldn't do that," she said. "Even if I did, they
wouldn't listen. You're the Doctor, and I'm only Mary
Prideaux."

"Only Mary Prideaux?" I said. "Why 'only'? It strikes
me—"

"Have you ever heard them talk about me?"

"No," I said. "They don't."

"Doesn't that tell you something? They'll talk about
anyone else, but me, I'm invisible. There are whispers,
but you or the parson, you'd never hear them. Too foul
for the gentry."

"I was never much of a one to listen to what other people said."

"That's what I hoped."

"So tell me, why do you say you're invisible?"

She picked up her bundle, hesitated. Finally she said,
"On a clear day, you can see the mainland from the dunes
above Pentle Bay. But there's not many on the island will
go and look. Why should they? They've nothing to do with
it, so they ignore it. You might say there were parts of me
that are nothing to do with the island, not the way they
understand it. So they don't talk about those parts. But
they know they're there, and that makes them scared."

"Tell me about them."

She brushed her hair back from her face, smile gleaming. "If you want to know, you can seek me out. Ask at the Abbey. They'll tell you." She reached out a slim, brown hand. I took it. "I'd be pleased if you came," she said quietly. The breeze rustled in the rank grasses of the lawn again, and she was gone.

I had the sensation that a spell had somehow lifted. What remained was a lingering hint of verbena, and my curiosity.

I went back to my table and the odorous remains of the hermit-crab. But I could not concentrate. My thoughts kept straying to the soft, mocking voice. I even thought I might go after her, talk more. It would be good to talk. . . .

Fool, I told myself. An easy mark for clear skin and bright eyes. But it was after midnight when I went to bed, and even then I did not sleep.

Soon after my acquisition of the gold watch I was removed from the village school. For the next few months I was put out to a variety of long-suffering tutors, mainly poor clergymen in need of the money. Most of these expressed great respect for my abilities and utter disgust at my personal habits; as a result of which, the burden of my company frequently outweighed the pecuniary advantage I represented. I left a trail of frazzled pedants in my wake until I met Doctor Connolly of New Ross. I thought I was something of a rake until the day I knocked on his front door. He disabused me of this idea by leading me into his dining-room, summing me up with one sweep of his yellowish eyes, and drinking me under the table. This naturally filled me with a deep respect for his learning, and soon we were fast friends.

He was an excellent teacher, a moderately good physician, and a fierce critic of the Union. In the catastrophes of 1798, he had escaped with his neck only because of his quite impartial sympathy for human suffering. His escape had in no way moderated his disgust at the atrocities of the far-off Parliament, and he expressed himself still with nerve-racking frankness on any subject that excited his attention.

With me, he kept away from politics as far as he could, which was not very far. He kept up my Latin and Greek, brow-beat a timid little Abbé into teaching me French, and dragged my not unwilling mind through the natural sciences. In this he was helped by the fact that, despite my reputation, Drumcarty Castle remained open to me. In my schooldays, I had been allowed into the library under suprvision. Now, I spent most of the time not occupied in massacring the local fauna and chasing the daughters of the tenantry closeted there.

Katie had departed for the Continent amid whispers of scandal narrowly escaped in Dublin. At first, my visits to the Castle were a painful reminder of her. But as I fell more to my studies, she came less and less into my mind. And after I had been six months with Connolly, I was surprised to find that I could think of her without any of the old palpitations. I had a pretty high estimation of myself, now I was no longer a schoolboy. Soon, I came to see her as part of my childhood. And at the age of fifteen and a half, childhood is still too close to be a comfortable subject for recollection.

The library occupied the whole of the ground floor at the western end of the long Jacobean house by the circular keep. The windows looked out on a formal garden running up to the grey curtain wall. I seldom looked out of the windows. Unlike many of the libraries of the great houses of Ireland, Drumcarty possessed an enormous number of books not related to politics or the chase. Plays and novels were well represented, as were the philosophers. At an early stage I decided to waste no more time than was necessary with the Ancients, turning instead to the seventy-volume Voltaire bound in mottled calf with Morocco labels and the Drumcarty arms, Rousseau and Bentham and others whose free thinking would certainly have shocked the little Abbé.

Most of the books dated from before the turn of the century, though after I went to Doctor Connolly I noticed that recent books on medicine and physical science began to appear. This I put down to the Doctor's influence. He seemed to be a friend of His Lordship's, and he certainly had a way of getting round him, at least as far as my education was concerned. One day as I was wondering with Voltaire whether the cockleshells found in the summits of the Alps had really fallen from the hats of pilgrims, I heard the library door open. I got hastily to my feet.

"Sit down," said the Earl of Drumcarty. "I am sorry to have disturbed you at your studies."

I mumbled something about it being an honour, not an interruption.

"No, no," he said. "I expect great things of you. I shall leave you. What are you reading?"

"Voltaire."

He frowned. "Salutary. But never confuse freedom of thought with rebellion."

"No," I said. "I shan't."

After he had gone, I wondered what he had been talking about. While I listened to Connolly on politics, I had no views of my own, except some hazy ideas about the rights of the individual that I tended to ignore because they did not fit the conditions of the Drumcarty tenantry. Besides, I had no need of politics. Reading was a good diversion; but what I really wanted was a commission in the Dragoons.

IV

NEXT MORNING on my way to the dispensary I passed Little John, squatting by the shore at New Grimsby weaving a long twig of tamarisk into a lobster-pot, his tangled mane hanging over his face. He looked up at the sound of the mare's hooves, and I felt his eyes following me as I turned her out on the beach to forage. Charity was waiting, and so were the patients; the day's business started, and I forgot about him. I sewed up a Bryher cut, lanced a St. Martin's abscess, and doled out some medicine to Samson. Then Abram Hicks and Fat Charles Mortimer came in together, Agnesmen both, and I spent the rest of the afternoon trying to unravel the latest in their endless succession of squabbles. When they had gone Charity told me that there was nobody else waiting. I offered her the pollack they had left me, which she refused, and tried to draw her into conversation. As usual now, she mumbled something about getting her Dad's tea and fled for home.

I stayed in the dispensary a while, composing a new letter to Michael Fitzpatrick. He had not answered my last, so I supposed it had gone astray. Curiously enough, this had not worried me too much. Since my funeral, Scilly was occupying so much of my time that I seldom even thought of Ireland.

I finished the letter and closed the dispensary door behind me, wondering if I would go and have a chat with Harry Jack at the Palace. I could hear voices raised in the inn, voices I recognised: Fat Charles was giving tongue in tones of high indignation, Abram having doubtless suggested to him that he should contribute to the Hicks's share monies equivalent to half the pollack with which he had presented me. If I went into the inn, I would get sucked into the shouting match. Experience suggested that like boils, such matters were best dealt with when they had come to a head. I whistled up the mare, slung the pollack behind the saddle, and climbed aboard. Little John was still by the shore, splicing tail-lines now. I waved to him. He did not wave back. Grinning, I went on to the junction where I had hidden in the porch on my first midnight outing. The summer was well in and the evening was fine, with the magical clearness of light that is unique to Scilly. It seemed almost as if I could have counted the bracken-fronds sprouting pale green on the north end of Samson, a mile and a half away. Smoke from the kelp-fires rose in snow-white pillars to the sky. And for a wonder the wind was from the east, just strong eough to blow away the stink of them without flattening the smoke over the islands. Too good an evening to go back to my solitary splendour in Old Grimsby. Reining the mare's head round to the right, I set off for the southern end of the island.

The Abbey Pool was blue with the reflection of the sky. The road passes round its squared-off north-western end, then along its south side under the ridge of land, known as Abbey Hill, that stands between it and the sea. South of Abbey Hill the road sinks down onto a flat space of marshy grazing that stretches to the rock and heather of the uncultivated southern end of the island. On the slope there are a couple of ruined arches, built of a red sandstone not found elsewhere on the islands. These are all that remain of the ancient Abbey of St. Nicholas, from which hill and pool draw their names. Round the arches sagged a cluster of black-thatched hovels. There were a few tiny fields, bearing rank crops of barley and millet-like pillars. The piles of limpet-shells were nearly as tall as the cottages. I rode up to the nearest, where a couple of rachitic children were scrounging in the midden in competition with a long-legged Scilly pig.

"Where will I find Mary Prideaux?" I said to the larger of the two children, a boy. He shot me a green look of horror, grabbed his little sister by the arm, and bolted for the dark doorway of the cottage. I heard shouting. A woman came to the door, lean and ragged, with black hair that might once have been thick and glossy as Mary's.

"Who wants her?" she said, scowling. From the look and smell of the cottage, the broom in her hand was used solely for maintaining discipline and repelling boarders.

"Doctor Nicholls."

She went back into the cottage. A man's face appeared, at the door, blinking and pale. He started to say something, but a fit of coughing took him and he lurched back into the darkness. The woman came out again. "Over to the cairn there," she said. "Round house."

"Thank you," I replied. "Come down to the dispensary tomorrow. I'll give you something for the children."

She squinted at me, suspicious. "Ain't got no money for doctors."

"You won't need it," I said. "Bring them."

"P'raps," she said, and went back into the hovel.

I rode on, glad to get upwind. The houses round the Abbey were a byword for squalor, even by Scillonian standards. I had not been so close before.

I rode past a mangy trio of the inevitable black cattle, round the margin of a small pool and over a heather-covered hillock topped with a mass of weathered granite. The walls of Mary's house were so crusted with lichen that I had to look twice before I realised it was there. Then I pulled up the mare and sat gaping.

The house was round, thirty feet in diameter, built of huge granite pebbles chinked with white mortar. The conical roof was perhaps twenty feet high at its apex, sloping to five feet at the eaves. The thatch was golden and good, and there was no heap of limpet-shells. At first I could not understand why I had never seen the place on any of my rides. Looking around me, I realised that it was closed in on all sides by the rise of the ground. It would be well sheltered from the westerly gales that whip across this end of the island, but at the same time it had a degree of privacy unique on Tresco.

"Well, well, Doctor," said a voice. "So soon, too."

Mary came out of the door and stood there, smiling. I realised it was the first time I had seen her close to in full daylight. She was wearing a dress of some dark blue stuff. Her eyes shone against the honey-brown of her skin like lakes in winter bracken. The planes of her face were fine and smooth. Her teeth were white, and showing in a smile that asked me what the hell I was doing. Which was sitting on the pony, staring like a stuffed owl. I felt my face grow hot and slid out of the saddle.

"Come in," said Mary. "Let her forage. She'll come to no harm."

I followed her, watching the movement of her slim body beneath the loose cloth of her dress, aware of the ridiculous lurching of my walk. Now I came to meet her on her own ground, I felt as if my hands and my feet were the size of whale's flippers. The interior of the house rather reinforced that impression. The place was a pool of soft colour. There was a central fireplace with a chimney of granite blocks that supported the thatch. In it there burned a fire of peat. The floor was of flagstones covered with salt-bleached Oriental rugs. There was a kitchen table and a few wooden chairs on the far side from the door. On the other was a good sofa, a writing-desk and a high-backed, cane-seated chair upon which Charles the first might have sat without shame.

"Tea?" said Mary. "Or something stronger?"

"Stronger."

On the wall by the sofa were two six-foot shelves, and the shelves were full of books. Raffles' *History of Java*, bound in salt-stained calf, rubbed shoulders with Strabo, Garcilaso de la Vega, De Foe, a blue Admiralty Almanac, various books of history and demonology. At the end of one of the rows stood a pottery vase bearing Greek-looking figures in white on a black ground.

"Herculaneum," I said, and sat with my mouth hanging open.

Mary put a jug and two glasses on the low table and smiled. "Very perceptive, Doctor. Not what you expected?"

I had myself under control. "On the contrary," I said. "I cannot think how I could ever have expected anything else."

"Oh, prettily done," she said.

"From wrecks?" I said.

"The vase and some of the books from the *Colossus,* Sir William Hamilton's ship, sunk off the south end of Samson with His Lordship's loot and library. The furniture, some of it, from the *Queen Charlotte* ashore on Scilly Rock and subsequently sunk, ten years ago. The rest of it from various other wrecks, except the brandy, which comes from Jeannot Drenec of Roscoff, direct. Any further questions?"

I shook my head. Then I said, "Yes. How did you come by it all? You and nobody else, I mean."

She led me to a pair of pictures hanging in a shaft of light from a recessed window. They showed a rocky coastline, the same in each picture. In the first, there was a crowd of ragged men looking out over a calm sea at a full-rigged ship, sails glowing in a patch of sun on the horizon. Standing on the rock was a woman, also looking out to sea. She wore a crescent moon in her hair, and in her right hand was a staff of some white wood or bone.

In the second picture, the sky was black and heavy, the sea raging. The crowd of men was engaged in tearing apart the hulk of a ship impaled on the rocks of the shore. It was quite obviously the same ship as in the first painting. The woman had turned. The staff in her right hand was raised to the threatening sky, and lightning played from its tip into the cloud-wrack. The crescent moon played in the night-black hair, and the red mouth was laughing in triumph. The face was the face of Mary Prideaux. I had seen her laugh like that on Old Grimsby beach, in the hard east wind.

"A shipwreck," I said. "Very good. Very fantastical."

Mary laughed her ironic laugh. "Quite fantastical," she said. "Sancta Warna. The patron saint of the islanders. Some islanders."

"And the artist?"

"Oh, a man I used to know. Conrad Alexander was his name."

Something up near the thatch squawked, "Con, Con, my beauty." I looked up, startled. A parrot's beak clacked at the bars of a cage high in the rafters.

"And he gave you his parrot," I said, because the pang of jealousy that attacked me made it impossible to be anything but banal.

"I took it," said Mary. "Should I tell you how?"

I shrugged, affecting casualness, knowing she could see through me.

"Conrad came to Tresco when I was twelve. He was a painter from Bristol. My mother always told me my father was drowned before I was born. He was a pilot. Conrad came to like my mother, or so he said, and she believed him. He stayed here and painted, built this house. Then he got bored and he took us off to Bristol. Mother was pleased to go; I wasn't, but I had no option. She wasn't well liked. Too fast for the island. In Bristol we were gay enough, until Conrad started on the drink and my mother with him. He forgot how to paint, with the drink. Then she died, and Conrad turned his mind on me." Her eyes lost focus, remembering. "I hated him. He made sure he was going to educate me. His friends took me in hand as a curiosity and drilled me in reading. He cultured me like a prize rose. I was fifteen when he plucked me. It was Waterloo year, 1815. They had just won the battle, I remember. People were running wild in the streets. Conrad got up out of the bed and went out and straight under a coach and six. I took those paintings and his parrot and came back here. That's all." She laughed. "Except that the stories followed me. They said I had ill-wished him, still do. Do you believe that, Doctor?"

I tried not to, but I did not quite succeed. I said, "Did you?"

She laughed.

I watched her. There was something about her smile that gnawed at the roots of logic. The Mainland might have educated her, but it had not touched her. Her beauty and mystery were Scilly, and only Scilly. "Did you ill-wish my ship?" I said.

Her focus shifted until she seemed to look clear through me, at something lost in a place beyond time.

"Not me," she said. "At least, not the me you see now. It was history."

"History?" I said. "History doesn't light bonfires on rocks and murder innocent sailors."

"Not the kind you know about, perhaps," she said. "An island is a strange place, Doctor. It . . . teaches people. It needs people, and the people need it. It tells its people what to do when things are . . . difficult. Its ground embraces the old kings in the barrows on the downs. Its harbours shelter fishermen, its hills protect farmers. Its teeth bite ships for the benefit of men who have no boats or fields. It looks after its own." Her eyes shifted back to me. "You will tell me that islands are only rock and soil and sand. You're right, by your lights. It was history killed your innocent sailors. History and blind chance."

"So there was a false light."

"I didn't say that. You're a very literal man."

I thought of the *Castletown*'s crew. I thought of my own ruined leg. I said, "Don't chop logic with me. You set a false light."

"History wrecked you," said Mary. "You might as well go out and flog the sea, hang the rocks. It wouldn't get you anywhere if I told you. Would it?"

"I want to know what happened," I said. "Can't you understand? I want to know who I can trust."

"O ho," said Mary. "Is that it? Is it Doctor Nicholls worrying about himself? Or is it the poor dead sailors?" Her voice was almost a purr.

I could not answer. The *Castletown* and the captain and the men were transparent, like phantoms. They linked the Dublin road with Palace Row, that was all. "They were human," I said.

"And so are you. I don't want you to be angry. Look at me now. And believe me. I do not know why your ship came ashore. It may have been a false light or a cannon, for all I know. It may have been an accident. I tell you frankly, though; I was glad it came ashore, for my sake and the island's sake. If I hear anything about it, I'll tell you."

"That will be good of you," I said guardedly.

"Do you trust me now?"

"I don't know," I said. She was all enamel and ivory. Only the huge midnight eyes were alive, glittering.

"Try," she said. "See where it gets you."

We talked on for a long time after that. When I started home, it was as if I was walking in a new world. The stars were brighter, the smells of the night sweeter, the air warmer than they should have been. When I thought of Charity I saw her as through the wrong end of a telescope, tiny and unreal. She was no longer breathing the same atmosphere as me, I thought as I walked the mare down the road under the ridge of Abbey Hill. She was a figment of my imaginary past. The present was Mary, beautiful Mary.

"Stop there," said a voice like gravel in a bucket. A hand took the reins. The figure before me was an enormous black hole in the night sky.

"Who's that?" I said, impatient at the interruption of my train of thought.

"Your conscience," said the voice. "And lo I say unto you my hand is as the hand of the Lord, and in my vengeance I will strike your ox and your ass and your flocks and your herds—"

"Little John," I said. "You will kindly remove yourself from my light. I am on my way home."

"Ay, ay," he growled. "From the arms of the harlot Prideaux. I know. I have seen you."

"Mind your own business," I said, and drove my heels into the mare's sides. But he held tight to the reins. She stepped sideways and I heard him grunt with pain as she stood on his toe.

"Fonicator," he said. "I warned you."

"I am by no means interested in your judgments on my habits or my conscience," I said. "Would you be so good as to get out of my way?"

He did not move.

"I would point out that I am a cripple," I said. "But I also have in my hand a stout stick. With this I shall be forced to smite you unless you remove yourself before I have counted three. One. Two . . ." I was sincerely hoping that he would not take me at my word. ". . . Three." I raised the stick.

John's shoulders seemed to lurch. There was a sound like an axe chopping a hollow log. The mare's spine slackened. She crumped at the knees and lay down. Little John stepped away, fondling his right fist with his left hand. "God blast you," I said. "You've killed my horse." I was filled with rage. "You damned idiot." John was doing more grunting. At first I thought it was anger; then I realised he had smashed his hand. "Get along with you." I gave him a cut across the shoulders with my stick. He roared like a bull and came at me. If the punch had connected, it would have been the end. I ducked, and it hummed through the air over my head. I poked him in the stomach with the stick, hard, heard the whoosh of his breath. The mare stirred at the road with mazy hooves. I realised that I had to hurt him, badly, before he hurt me.

The mare staggered to her feet and stood with her head hanging. Little John came in again, head down, bellowing. His arms clawed at me. As he blundered by, I saw the back of his neck exposed; it seemed too good to miss. I brought the stick down sharply just south of his nape. He fell flat on his face and stayed there. I led the mare away, slowly. By the time I got home I was shaking hard. From now on, I was going to have to keep out of corners when Little John was around.

Exactly a week later, the Preventives came with a strong force from St. Mary's, arrested Mordecai Ellis, Harry Ellis, and Jane Ellis and, on searching the premises and purlieus, did find divers kegs and tubs of spirits hid. It was reported that they did not find the best of it, which was hidden in the jakes, the Ellis household having made use of the rocks for the past few weeks. But nonetheless, Mordecai, Harry and Jane were hauled off to St. Mary's and, not possessing the money for bail, clapped in the Bridewell. The charges were: possessing spirits on which His Majesty's duties had not been paid; and transporting such spirits with intent to avoid such payment. The latter of the two was the gravest, since it would entail not only a long spell in Bodmin Jail but also confiscation of the Ellis boat, on which the Ellis livelihood depended.

This news reached me on the morning of the seventh day after Little John's concussing of the mare. The mare had recovered well, and I had had the moral satisfaction as well as the security of seeing John walking past the dispensary with eyes averted and his right hand in a sling. My patients told me the Ellis story, each embroidering its events as far as they thought my gullibility would allow, so that when I went homeward that night I had arrived at a pretty fair lowest common denominator of what would have happened. I had just put away my books, and was preparing to dig into a cold pie of seal-meat that Mrs. Clitheroe had left, when a knock came on the door.

"Come in," I said, hoping it would be Mary.

The parson's eyebrows appeared, hotly pursued by the rest of him. I covered the pie with a pile of books and asked him to sit down. This he did, humming and hawing a good deal. At first I thought I was in for more Doubts. But he quickly came to the point. "You've heard about the Ellis business, I suppose," he said.

"I have." My stomach rumbled, and I tried not to think about the pie.

"Shocking," he said, watching me narrowly. "Shocking."

"Oh, I don't know," I said. "I can't see His Majesty bankrupted over a little bit of duty like that."

"True," said the parson. "But the principle . . ."

"It ain't the principle," I said. "It's the people."

"Of course," he said, nodding hard. "But the Preventives always like to make a mountain out of a molehill. It looks so well to the Inspecting Officers."

"Yes," I said. "And what are the chances of the Court showing clemency?"

"Slim," said the parson. "They are inclined to view the off-islanders as hardened liars. Not always without reason, alas. And there are no witnesses who are not off-islanders."

"What about you?"

The parson looked down, improbably interested in his fingernails. "The Chaplain of the Isles—" he said. "Ah, the Chaplain of the Isles has told me that he wishes me to limit my contact with my flock to matters . . . ah, spiritual. Apparently some of my predecessors sought consolation with the young women of the islands, and even in ardent spirits. I fear that if I appeared for the Ellises the Chaplain might draw the wrong conclusions." He looked up at me, miserable. "It is a great hardship," he said. "I have prayed about it much. And I was hoping—"

"Yes?" I said.

"I was hoping you would speak for them. I know they have every confidence in you. And I think a man of your bearing . . . a correct presentation of the defence . . ."

"I'm no lawyer," I said. Someone on metropolitan St. Mary's might recognise me. Tresco was tiny, but Tresco was wild and safe. "I don't think I would be of any use."

"Oh," said the parson, looking sad. "Well, then I suppose we shall just have to hope for the best. Perhaps the court won't commit them for trial, after all. But Bodmin Jail—Bodmin Jail is no joke. Full of fever, and damp. Very damp. Poor Aunt Ellis is not strong. Perhaps you could give her some sort of tonic before she is taken away. If she is taken away, I mean."

Before my eyes there rose the picture of Aunt Ellis' prune-like face, framed in its spotless cap of lace. Behind her was a dark wall, green with slime, and a tiny window pierced in thick masonry.

Which was why I found myself ten days later hobbling up the principal town of Hugh Town, tricked out in one of the Parson's cleaner shirts, his second-best frock-coat, and a pair of shiny black boots. The *tout ensemble* was a good deal too small, but it was certainly more respectable than my usual rusty rags. Behind me walked the Ellises, clad in their Sunday best.

Aunt Ellis was in a high good humour. It was not every day she got taken to St. Mary's, and she looked as if she meant to enjoy herself no matter what. She kept drawing her son's attention to new-painted wood, new goods in shop windows, and island worthies, and I could almost hear her making mental notes to pass on to her cronies on Tresco. I wished I shared her confidence. Her sons seemed properly aware of the gravity of their situation. Mordecai, a big, bumbling, good-natured fellow full of clumsy enthusiasms, had been fortifying himself at the Palace. His elder brother, Harry, whom some claimed to be half-witted, walked along staring at his feet and kicking stray stones into the gutters.

We turned onto Garrison Hill, on which Star Castle stands. I did not like the look of the place. It is one of those no-nonsense fortifications put up by Elizabeth of England's vassals, a practical machine designed for the sheltering of friends and the systematic slaughter of foes. The masonry looked uncomfortably solid. Once you were well inside there, there would be little chance of getting out. I said as much to Mordecai, who laughed.

"No bother," he said. "All they've got to guard you is a handful of old sojers. All for show, since the war."

Still, as we walked under the gatehouse itself, I fingered my beard and hoped it had grown thick enough.

The courtroom consisted of a long table with twelve

chairs for the members of the council. Eight of them were
occupied by prosperous-looking citizens who looked as if
they would have been more at home behind ploughs or
the counters of shops. The two in the middle, facing out
at three more chairs—set, I presumed, for the defendants
—were empty. "That be where Johns sits," Mordecai
hissed. "Him and the clerk." The members of the court
looked up from their scribblings to see where the noise
was coming from, and looked away. "Sit down, Mother,"
he said to Aunt Ellis. " 'Twill be all over, soon."

"Better or worse," said the Aunt, smiling brightly if
toothlessly. "Better I hopes, eh Doctor?"

"I hope so too," I said.

Aunt Ellis folded her hands in her lap and stared
brightly at the members of the court, nodding and winking
as she caught their eyes. I looked over at the wad of paper
before the nearest of them. *"Norway Spruce, 5000 ft. Oak
Hamshire 14 doz knees as ordered,"* it said.

The double doors flew open with a bang that bounced
round the bare stone vaulting, and a voice roared something, mostly lost in the echoes, about being upstanding
for the President, John Johns Esquire, Steward to His
Grace the Duke of Leeds and a string of other titles. Into
the room there struggled with the aid of a stick an elderly
citizen with a face the colour of a loganberry, dressed in
the style of fifteen years ago. With him was a sallow individual in a wig, carrying a vellum-bound ledger, and a
stiff-backed gentleman in a coat of faded blue with tarnished braid at neck and wrists. Under his arm he carried
a cocked hat, which had once been black but which was
now the universal Scillonian shade of rusty green. The
face he turned on the defendants was weatherbeaten, with
heavy cheeks and a grim slit of a mouth.

"Well, now!" cried Aunt Ellis cheerily. "It's the Preventive man!"

The officer scowled. Mr. Johns and his clerk proceeded
round the table with much puffing and wheezing. Mr.
Johns, with the clerk's assistance, lowered himself into his
chair. The clerk sat down, opened his ledger, snapped
back the top of his inkwell, looked at a quill, discarded it,
cut another, blotted, cut again, made himself comfortable,
and said, "The court will be seated."

The court was. The proceeding began.

They were simple enough. First the Preventive man

made the Prosecution's case. "Acting on information received," he said, glowering, "on 12th July I took a party of His Majesty's Preventive Force to the house of the widow Jane Ellis at Borough on the Island of Tresco, Scilly. There I found the defendants, Jane, Mordecai and Harry Ellis. Upon my informing them of my reasons for wishing to search the house, defendant Jane Ellis did use on me defamatory and indecent language and did assault me with contents of a household utensil."

"Wha'?" said President Johns, cupping a veiny hand to his ear.

"Chamber pot, 'twas," said Aunt Ellis, laughing merrily. "Desprit flux on him had our Mordy."

"Silence, woman," said the Clerk, frowning. "Pray continue, Captain Maltby."

"On searching the house my men discovered run goods, to wit: in the waterbutt, an anker with 1 ½ gallons brandy—"

"Keepin' it cool, we was," said Harry, aggrieved.

"Silence in court," roared the clerk, dreaming no doubt of the Old Bailey.

"And in the cairn of rocks behind the house, fifteen further ankers, with two gallons brandy in each, to a total of thirty gallons brandy. Also one tub negro head tobacco, twelve pound weight. Defendants, asked where they had got goods, deponed they knew nothing of goods in cairn, and were keeping the spirits in the waterbutt—" ferocious glare at Harry Ellis—"cool. Defendants were then apprehended under powers vested in His Majesty's Preventive Force and conveyed to Hugh Town Lockup."

"Hrumph," said Johns. "That all?"

"That's all," said Maltby.

" 'Nough to hang a saint," mumbled Johns, apparently under the impression that he was inaudible to any but himself. "No defence, I suppose?"

"Yes," I said. "I am appearing on behalf of Mrs. Ellis and her sons."

Johns turned on me a pair of eyes like rose bonbons, boiled. "And who, pray, are you?"

"Doctor Nicholls of Tresco. I went bail for the defendants."

"Never heard of you," said Johns, reaching across and pulling the court record away from the clerk. He turned back the pages, deaf to the clerk's protests that he was smudging the ink. "So you did," he said. "Sworn by the Tresco constables. Bloody fools. Damned Irishman, by the sound of him. Very well," he said, in a louder voice. "What is it?"

I stepped forward, fingering my beard. Twenty-two eyes looked at me from behind the table. None of them was friendly. The Ellises, however, exuded a confidence I was far from sharing. "Gentlemen of the Council," I began. "First, I should explain why I am here, since the well-known impartiality of the Council makes advocacy needless." There was a general settling of impartial backsides into chairs. The atmosphere grew perceptibly less hostile. "I have come not so much to plead the case of the Ellises, as to render them something of a testimonial and make some observations. Since my unfortunate shipwreck on Tresco, the people of that island have shown me every care and tenderness. They do not, as you do, benefit from the advantages of the age. They are simple folk—yes, and feckless, you may say—but I think they are entitled to the sort of mercy and justice that they meted out to me." A restlessness was beginning to spread. Time to switch to the offensive.

"Frankly, Gentlemen of the Council, it is a case that to the simple would appear damaging. To the more sophisticated, however, to those whose wits are sharpened by daily traffic with the noble sciences of stewardship—" I bowed to John Johns—"and Commerce"—I bowed to the gentleman with the timber lists—"and all the other arts of civilisation"—here a general sweep of the hand from end to end of the table—"it presents rather different aspect. Let me analyse it, piece by piece.

"It falls, like post-Caesarian Gaul, into three parts. First, the assault with the . . . household utensil. Second, the anker in the waterbutt. Third, the tubs in the cairn. Taking these in reverse order: the cairn is, I believe, part of the commonage of Tresco. It is no part of the Ellis lease, and goods found on it are *prima facie* no responsibility of the Ellises. As for the anker in the waterbutt—well, the weather has been warm of late. I, myself, having some small skill in the medical arts, have on occasion prescribed cool spirits against the flux." I paused, frowning heavily. "The last offence is the most serious." I turned on my good heel and glared at Aunt Ellis, who was looking more beady than contrite. "That this woman should besmirch with ordure the uniform of an officer in the service of His Majesty King George is an affront before God and the Nation. Let us hope that she is cognisant of this, and having received condign punishment will in future mend her ways." I paused to let the thundering echoes die away, and got a look at the Preventive man. Not encouraging. "As to the other charges: we are not, thank God, under the code of Bonaparte. In England, a man is innocent until proven guilty. There is insufficient proof. The court, in its wisdom, will I am sure see where its duty lies." I sat down, fast.

There was a silence, in which Johns could be heard muttering to himself. "Glib, very," he was saying. "Do believe the feller's right. Can't send 'em to the Assize for that. Duke's man would have me head. Fine the old 'ooman for assault, leave the rest be." He leaned over and whispered in the clerk's ear. The clerk started writing in his book. "Common assault, three and six to parish funds. Other charges, not guilty," he said. "Court's costs, four shillings. Defendants to pay."

Outside Star Castle the sun was hot. Over the yards of the ships anchored in St. Mary's Pool, I thought I could see the roof of Mary's house against the purple and green of Tresco.

A hand fell on my shoulder and spun me round. The Preventive officer's face was the colour of underdone beef, and he was breathing hard. "Damn you, Nicholls," he said. "Damn you for a villain. I run the Force on these islands and I run it well. I'll have no interference from Johnny-come-latelies like you."

"Your manners," I said. "Improve them. Fast."

"You bloody—" He noticed that the crowd had gone silent and was listening with interest. "I'll catch you at it," he puffed. "Damme if I don't. Then we'll see who talks his way out of what."

"For the moment you can talk yourself out of my sight," I said.

He stood looking at me for a moment. I did not like his eyes. They were too cool, and they gave me the impression they were used to committing faces to memory. At last, he turned on his heel and stumped down the hill and into the warren of grimy thatch. And I turned away too, and laughed with the rest of them. But I confess I did not feel altogether easy in my mind.

A month before gale-day the year after Michael left, the housekeeper caught me as I came in to breakfast. I had been out with a few choice spirits drinking in the duck-shooting, and I had a couple of brace slung over my back. "Your father wants to see you," she said, sniffing. Once she had been all over me, considering herself a mother to poor motherless Nicky. Nowadays she kept her distance, but she was a kindly old thing and a good friend.

"Christ," I said. "Is he savage?" I ran hastily over my recent misdeeds, but could think of none he would know of. Unless O'Brien had been up about his daughter. . . .

"Not very," she said. "But he will be if you keep him waiting."

I scraped some of the mud off and introduced myself into the Presence.

The old man was drinking whiskey. The big clock on the wall said ten past nine. "Sit down," he said.

That was unsual. Over the years the deep-worn footmarks in front of the desk had become old friends. I plumped myself down in one of the smelly horsehair armchairs. The old man took a pull at his glass and looked at the papers under his thick, red hands.

"I have received a . . . letter," he said at last. There was a curious quality in his voice. Normally he spoke in a harsh growl. Now it was lighter. Almost respectful. "It has to do with a trust I accepted from your dear Mother. She had some money of her own. She put it aside for the continuance of your education. You are to go to Dublin and enter Trinity College. There they will try to teach you to become a doctor."

"Devil take it," I said, without thinking, "I'm going into the Army."

"No you aren't," growled my father. "You're going to be a doctor, like it or not. And count yourself lucky, you ungrateful pup. You'll travel outside on His Lordship's carriage, day after tomorrow. While you're at the University you'll be allowed a thousand a year. Now get out."

I reeled out of the room. A thousand a year was a lot of money. About five times what my father saw. I went and got some sleep. When I woke up I went for a long ride which landed me in New Ross at the house of Doctor Connolly.

By the time I got there my head was clear. A thousand a year in Dublin would be as good as the Army any day.

I knew nothing at all about Universities, though. Connolly fed me whiskey punch and enthusiasm, told me I would be crazy not to jump at the chance of getting away from what he referred to as the Mausoleum, and that as far as he was concerned I was as good as most doctors already. He sent me off with a tumbler of punch that made my eyes bulge and a letter to an acquaintance of his in Dublin who would give me lodging. The man was a doctor himself, he said, and a fashionable one. His name was Duquesne and he was of a fine, open disposition. I might find him old-fashioned in some ways, but he had been fond of a wench and a bottle himself, once.

A week later I was standing on the step of a good-sized house in Merrion Square, not the least fashionable quarter of the capital, reading a brass plate that said *Hippolyte Duquesne*. No qualifications. Only an elegant hand with the graving-iron and a couple of windowboxes chock-full of pink geraniums. I rang the bell. A footman let me in, with a glance at my wool breeches and thick stockings. I was presented to the great man.

Duquesne was a French doctor of the old school, who had migrated to Dublin thirty years before, after the Terror. He had once been a favourite with Marie Antoinette's courtiers, and he retained the foppish manners and dress of Versailles. He read Connolly's letter, showed me a room, and told me where the School of Anatomy kept itself. Then he looked me up and down, took a large pinch of snuff, and asked me if I wanted to be his apprentice. When I said I would, he gave me the name of his tailor. "You are quite pretty," he said. "Perhaps a little too like the Corsican pig, but your size saves you. But your clothes!" And spinning on one red wooden heel, he minced off to his consulting room.

Having visited bootmaker, hosier, tailor, shirtmaker, haberdasher, barber and hatter, I settled into my tasks with a will. The School of Medicine was then under Doctor Macartney, who had made it one of the best-regarded in Europe. I watched the good doctor chopping up cadavers and demonstrating on wax models tolerantly enough; but my real education in the Hippocratic science came from Duquesne. Duquesne made me his assistant apothecary (he was too mean to use one in the town) and foil. He professed a total belief in the power of fertilised eggs as a cure for all ills. His patients were mostly women; he would pay grave attention to their complaints, soothe with a few preciously-turned compliments, and send them packing with their jar of eggnog, for which he never charged less than a guinea. On the rare occasions he bled, I held the bowl.

After a month of this, I was exhausted, and I told him so.

"Ah, Nicholas," he said. *"Il faut souffrir pour être sage.* It is not painless, the acquisition of wisdom. Now I tell you. In a week's time, you tell me what you think is the essential quality of a doctor. *Un maxime.* When I think you have got this right, we shall revise your duties. *Entendu?"*

That week I watched him very closely. On the Saturday morning at breakfast he said, "Well, Nicholas? *Le maxime?* But perhaps it is too early days, yes?"

"By no means," I said. "It seems to me that the answer is to tell your patients the worst at all times, but if they are dying, to reassure them that they are dying of nothing serious."

Duquesne's pencilled eyebrows shot up his white forehead. He dosed up with snuff. Then he said, "Well, well. Doctor Connolly said you were quick. I think you have earned the revision of your duties. We shall discuss it soon. My congratulations." Bowing, he minced from the room.

After the trial, life went on much as usual. It was high summer, and the islands had on their holiday clothes. The sun shone down day after day from a deep blue sky, the winds were light and from the south-west, and the sea was calm as glass. In the fields, the corn started to whiten towards harvest. Apart from the hours I spent in the dispensary or visiting, I spent little time on the island. There was no news from Michael Fitzpatrick, and the idea of him sank further and further into the past until the present began to heal over my life in Ireland as the flesh had healed over the bare bone of my leg. Most of the days I spent at sea or on the uninhabited islands, fishing or merely botanizing, usually accompanied by Mary. After my first visit to her house, she did not speak of her past, and I did not attempt to bring it up. There seemed no need. Charity hardly spoke to me now, and Little John I avoided as best I could, which was not very well, in view of the size of the island. He kept his distance, I think, because of something Mary said to him. So bound up was I in the present that I enquired no further. My self-esteem was enormously swelled by the success of the Ellis trial. The off-islands were able to look after themselves when it came to farming, fishing, and business. But when it was a matter of law, or, as happened more frequently, a tenant-landlord dispute, it was to me they turned. I had seen the other side of the coin in Ireland; the Duke and his agents and their corruption and callousness I had come to understand with my father's whiskey, if not my mother's milk.

So it was a cheerful and complacent Doctor Nicholls who sat over the oars of Mary's punt by Crebawethan in the Western Rocks on the afternoon of the twelfth of August. The sea was a liquid green mirror. Terns and kittiwakes screamed and dived in endless loops. The rocks stood calm and serene, druids' stones smoothed by kindly sacrifice of cream and sweet water. And on the after thwart, head thrown back at the sun, shoulders bare, a soft swell of breast rising above her faded blue bodice, sat Mary.

"Tide's turning," I said. "We'd better get back."

"Wait," she said. "Listen."

I listened. Small gurglings at the waterline, endless keening of the birds. "I can't hear anything," I said at last.

"Look, then." She pointed to something floating a couple of hundred feet away. It looked like a buoy, until it turned, showing a huge, liquid eye.

"A seal," I said. "Atlantic grey."

Mary laughed. "What a poet," she said. "Put your books away, Doctor Nicholls. And keep yourself still." She turned toward the seal and began to sing. There was no scale to the singing. It was a sound as harsh and wild as the cries of the gulls. The seal's head turned, inspected us narrowly, sank from view.

"Frightened him off," I said.

"Her," said Mary. "Look over the side, Doubting Thomas."

The green of the water darkened to sapphire with depth, lanced with the rays of the hot, lazy sun. Just as I was beginning to feel ridiculous, something long and silver glided out of the dark and rose balloonlike toward me.

"Keep still," said Mary.

The seal's head broke the water a foot from my eyes. I heard a faint, disdainful hiss, and smelt fish. Mary leaned over and scratched the sleek, neckless head.

"Sing to her," she said. "Go on."

The seal waited politely, like a fat alderman at a ceremonial dinner. I cleared my throat and began singing *SlievenaMón* in an embarrassed undertone. One verse was enough. The seal submerged, without applauding. "I don't think she liked that," I said.

"She loved it," said Mary, getting up. "She wants to play, is all." She began taking her clothes off. "You come, too." She pulled her dress over her head. I had a glimpse of her body, high-breasted, slim-flanked, and then she was over the side. Pulling my shirt over my head, I followed.

It was icy cold. I trod water, looking over the oiled satin of the surface at Mary, laughing ten feet away. The seal's head came up, so close I felt the brush of her whiskers, the powerful turbulence of her flippers. She looked at me and said, "Hargh."

"Put your arms around her neck," said Mary.

The seal seemed used to the procedure. I locked my hands under her chin, if seals have chins, and she swam sedately across to Mary. Mary gripped my shoulders. I felt the hardness of her nipples against my back. "Take a deep breath," she said.

The seal dived, and we went with her, down into the dark, water rushing past my ears, powerful muscles working against my belly. At last we came up, a hundred yards away from the boat, panting. I found myself grinning with pure delight, Mary too, the seal treading water and watching us like a diffident aunt who has just given her nephew and niece a treat.

"Try to catch her," said Mary.

I lunged forward. The seal leaned back, and I missed. On the third attempt she let me, and started to pursue Mary playfully. We played catch-as-catch-can all the way back to the boat and clung to the gunwale, panting, beginning to feel the mid-Atlantic chill of the sea. I heaved myself aboard, gave Mary my hand. She came up wet and glistening, honey-coloured in the glaring sun. We sat down, I on the rower's thwart, she in the stern.

She put her head forward and kissed me, salt and cold, lips hard and puckered. It was a sister's kiss. The seal watched, said "Hargh," and sank. Next time she surfaced, she was three hundred yards away.

As I dressed, I had the sense that I was moving out of magic back into the real world. A world where I wanted Mary's kiss to be more than sisterly.

"How did you do it?" I said. "Learn the language?"

She was combing her wet hair with her fingers. "There's no language," she said. "They like music. I knew her when she was a pup, approached her quiet, took it slow. She became a friend. She's nice, isn't she?"

"Very." The laughing Mary in the water had been the real Mary, shorn of her enigmas. The Mary I now knew I desired. Who had given me that sisterly kiss.

I shoved out the oars and began to pull through the gaps in the rock ledges, north of the pyramidal Haycocks and towards the silver and green whaleback of Tresco. After a while we caught a little breeze, so I hauled up the ancient gunter sail and we ghosted home with the flood, just clearing Tresco Flats under a triumphal arch of white kelp-smoke. The wind dropped as I put the punt's head in towards the beach under the fish cellar, and Eddie Jenkins came down and helped me push her out on the tripping-line. We walked back up the beach together, talking. Away from Little John Woodcock, Eddie was less tongue-tied than usual. Still, he addressed his remarks to me, rather than Mary. Little John's faction had been steering noticeably clear of her in the past months. As we parted, Mary and I for her house and Eddie in the opposite direction for his, he cleared his throat.

"What is it?" said I.

"We was wondering . . . Pa and I . . . if you'd come to the last kiln this night? At Appletree beach, there. She's been fired up since noon."

"Early for it," I said.

"Early or late, the price is all the same," said Eddie. "Could be the last year, I reckon. We'd be honoured if you'd come." He reddened, made his farewells and went his way.

The kelp, the soda-ash derived from the burning of the ore-weed that grows on the rocks and in the shallow waters round Scilly, had long been one of the mainstays of Island trade. It was exported in quantities to Waterford and London and other manufacturing centres, where it was used in the making of soap and glass. But Scillonian kelp, made by a rough-and-ready process of incredible antiquity, was not of the quality demanded by modern factories. New methods of manufacture had been found, and the price had fallen from seven pounds a ton in 1800 to twenty-five shillings a ton in the present year. All through the summer I had been hearing gloomy tales of the prospects. It would be a hard winter; the kelp provided almost the only source of ready cash on the off-islands, and ready cash was vital to supplement the produce of the tiny and exhausted Island farms. But there was a saw which I heard at least five times a day from my patients. "Feast or famine on Scilly," they always said. Whatever the prospects for the harvest, it was summer, and tonight there would be a fine old time by the last of the Jenkins' kilns.

At Mary's house I sat writing up my journal by the light of the westering sun pouring in through the deeply-recessed windows. Mary was at her embroidery, a huge frame on which half-heraldic figures moved over island rocks against an apocalyptic sunset. She had been working at it for ten years, she said; by the look of it she would be at least another ten finishing it. I closed my journal, went across and looked over her shoulder.

"You're changing it again," I said. In the foreground, by a cairn of rocks, there had been a man bent over the ribs of a half-finished boat. Now he had been ripped out, and in his place was a figure in a dark frock-coat, strangely bent over to the right. In the hand was the outline of something that might have been a walking-stick.

"I am," she said, tightening a stitch at the figure's shoulder. "Who do you think this is?"

"No idea," I said.

"Con," said the parrot, irritatingly.

"You," said Mary.

"Me? Well, this is a great honour."

"Any more preening and I'll rip you out," said Mary. "I put you in because you're part of it now."

"And the rest of them," I said, pointing at the other figures that lined the foreground. "Who are they?"

"Oh, other people," said Mary vaguely.

I wasn't sure I liked that. There was a man with brushes and an easel and a green parrot on his shoulder, who would be Conrad. Beside him was a bearded individual with a hammer on which was inscribed in tiny stitches

FAITH. A woman with a huge belly occupied the middle, a little set back. She had the look of Mary, but she was not Mary. "Who's she?" I said.

"My mother," said Mary. Abruptly, she shoved her needle into the linen, threw a cloth over the frame, and stood up. "It's not interesting."

Later, when we walked over the paths to the beach, the sun was falling behind the north hill of Samson. Curtains of golden fire blazed across the sky. On the summit of the hill, barrows stood out black against the light beyond. Far to the westward a purple wall hung low above the sea. The air was hot, dead quiet. Mary said, "It's too still."

We stopped on the crest of the line of dunes above the beach. Out on Tresco Flats oyster catchers whistled. The sand glowed in the low light, clear of weed for the first time since June. The ebb-tide was black in the shadow of the rocks, and on it swam wobbling medallions of gold where the ripples caught the sky. The kelp-kiln was a kernel of molten white below us and to the right. There was laughter and the wheezy scrap of a fiddle being tuned. As we walked down the path in the dunes the heavy air parted on either side of my face like warm water before a boat's stem. The heat and stillness were unnatural. Sea and sky seemed to be holding their breath. Mary looked into my eyes and smiled at me. She pressed my hand below the rise of her left breast. "The heart is the loudest thing," she said. "Feel how it beats." I nodded, swallowing, the dull thunder of blood in my own ears. We stood for a long moment like that. Then the fiddler scraped a tentative chord and loped into *Old Hag you have killed me*, and we walked arm-in-arm towards the group by the kiln.

Bottles appeared suddenly from cool nests in the wet sand, and before I knew what was happening I had a glass in my hand and was locked in a contest of innuendo-packed badinage with Aunt Ellis and another old woman, who had warts. Out of the corner of my eye I saw Mary dancing, floating over the sand as if on air, and I dug savagely at the sand with my stick. Then the talk seized me and I was off and away as the sun plunged below the horizon and a big yellow moon heaved up and hung dropsical above the hill. And on we talked, of kelp and fish and old wrecks and new wrecks and Mr. Canning and the Duke of Wellington and the Preventives and good times and hard times and this time, perhaps the last time, and the brandy flowed hot and sweet over the tongue and burned the good burn in the throat, until heads were singing with it and then voices were singing too, ballads with the lift and surge of the swell in them, and death and coming home, and the sweat gleamed on the faces of the women and Mary was by my side with her soft breast against my arm, pushing the hair from her eyes and laughing and panting, and the fiddler toiled on and round and down and into an expectant minor chord and stopped.

In the silence four men walked towards the circular pit. The fire burnished the shining skin of their chests and arms. They carried long forks, which they thrust into the pit, turning and folding the molten mass until the hot sparks leaped at the cool, hazy stars, and what was in the pit ran like white-hot water under the tines. One of the shining giants shouted in a voice hoarse with smoke, and the piles of sand fell in on the fire, and the moonlight struck without competition through the quiet watchers, slapping their shadows stark on the ghostly sand. The fire wheezed and popped. A bottle ran on pewter, and out there burst a roar of talk that skated across the metal water to the westward and lost itself among the far rocks. The fiddler played an arpeggio, bottom to top, and launched into *The wind that shakes the barley,* and one of the shining giants plucked Mary from my side and pulled her into the whirling circle of dancers. But the dancing was slacker now, without the focus of the fire. The main group broke up into smaller ones. The fiddler stopped his reels and jigs and embarked on a long, twisting improvisation. Mary came to me. We stood listening for a moment, then turned up into the darkness. She leaned her head against my chest, and I smelt her perfume, that sharp, sweet stuff. So still was the air that it hung about us in a cloud. I was saturated in it, surrounded, swamped. My heart was thumping, driving the rich mixture of blood and brandy round my veins so my head rang with it. But it was not the brandy that opened every pore in my skin to the warm power of the night. It was Mary, lithe and pliant under my hand. Mary, who lifted her head so I could see her eyes white in the darkness and said, "We'll go back to the house. Won't we?"

"We will," I said, and hastened across the hills as best I could. She paused on the crest of the path down into the dell, and I paused with her. The stars had gone out, and the furnace air hung dead. There was a dumb cracking of thunder far away. The horizon flicked blue, lightning on the underside of heavy black cloud.

My memories of what came next are hazy. I can see only a series of disjointed pictures. Mary, standing naked with the candlelight gleaming from the curves and hollows of her body, her dark-tipped breasts kissed by her silky black hair. Mary's face, the lids low over the great dark-blue eyes, mouth gasping, twisted back on the pillow as she cried out at me, pain or joy or both. Mary astride, a statue of flesh gilded with the sweat of passion, moving with the slow power of waves of the sea, mounting and surging. And finally, Mary leaning over me on one elbow, the silky hair falling away from her cheek, smiling. For the first time since I had known her, it was a smile entirely without mockery.

"Sleep well," she said. "And stay."

"Yes," I said. "I'll stay."

The next thing I knew, someone was shaking me by the shoulder and my head was aching and my mouth was dry. I opened my eyes and put out a hand and felt warm skin, round and soft.

"Hush," she said, pushing my hand away. "Listen."

The night was no longer quiet. There was a dull roar at the bottom of it now. "Ground sea," said Mary. "There's something been blowing, out there. I thought I felt . . ."

A gust of wind tumbled across the rise of ground and bumped the thatch. "Come here," I said. "Don't you mind the wind." The inside of her thigh was like silk.

Again she pushed me away, this time more reluctantly. "There's a ship out there," she said. "Get dressed. Quick, now."

I was incredulous. "How do you know?" I said. "And what if there is?" I dragged my trousers over my feet and began buttoning my shirt. "The sea's full of them." We went for the door.

On top of the rise we stopped to look. There was nothing to see until the lightning flickered again, far out to sea, and the blue light of it caught white on the roaring foam of the Western Rocks. The air was stagnant as a rainwater tank in August. "To the gig shed," said Mary. "Here's the mare."

Up I got, and off we set. As the pony jogged and stumbled along the path through the heather, I wondered why we were doing this. There was certainly nothing happening at sea. Nothing unusual, that is. We ought to be in bed. Three hot gusts of wind buffeted out of the black quiet, boxing the compass.

"Starting," said Mary.

A lagoon of calm air, during which we climbed the south face of Abbey Hill and started down the spine of the ridge towards the fish-cellar. The sound of the swell in the rocks took on a new quality. Over the roar there was a hissing, sharp and edgy, that grew and rounded itself until the world was full of it, a giant sheet of canvas stretched drum-tight and torn in two. The rain thrashed down in rods, wavered, and held. Then the wind came, and suddenly the water was not falling but driving horizontally, like bullets, from the north-west. The mare shied and stepped sideways, recovered, and plodded on. My left ear was completely numb, and I could feel water running down inside my collar. "Bloody madness!" I yelled. I could hardly hear my own voice. Mary plodded on, gripping the pony's reins at its curb, a dark shape bent for shelter behind the animal's neck.

The wind howled up and faltered. "Wait," I felt her say. We waited, staring out to westward. There was nothing there, of course. I screwed my eyes up against the lumps of water smacking at them. All of a sudden, the wind dropped and the rain faded to drizzle and stopped. It was still as black as the inside of a cow.

"There," said Mary.

Far away to the west, a spark of red flame pricked the darkness. A second or two later, the report of the signal gun came, a tiny *thump* at my tympanum.

"Quick," said Mary, and began to run down the last slope of the ridge, dragging the pony behind her. The wind whirled, roared and began again. With it came the rain. The night was full of it, hissing in the water and drumming and clattering in the fields.

Thunder split and rumbled as we went across the green at the end of the Abbey Pool. Lightning flashed again, and its glare shone in the streaming oilskins of the men running for the long, low shed at the top of the beach. I slid off the pony, leaning on Mary's shoulder. Someone had lit a lantern in the shed, and the doors stood open. The light danced over the faces of the men arranging themselves round the long, slender gig like pallbearers round a coffin.

"Heave," cried a voice.

"*Heave,*" they answered, and the gig slid head-first on its rollers and eased out of the doors into the black and the blast of the wind. Little John was at the stern, grinning a tight grin of strain. His eye caught mine, swivelled to Mary, and returned. "Bear a hand there!" he yelled.

I put my shoulder to the boat's quarter and shoved with my good leg. Underfoot, the coarse grass of the foreshore gave way to sand. A wave came up out of nowhere and broke against the wooden side, showering me with cold water. I looked round for Mary, but I was still dazzled from the lamplight and if she had been a couple of feet away I wouldn't have seen her. I heard the knock of oars going out through tholepins, and began to step back, ashore. A hand grabbed my collar and I found myself lifted up like a feather, my legs banging at the gunwale, and dropped in the stern of the gig. "We might need ye," roared Little John in my ear. "Even if we don't, we'll see if ye can deal with stronger stuff than women." A wave burst under the gig's bow.

"*Giiive* way, all!" shouted Little John, legs braced, standing at the tiller like a Colossus. Oar-blades bit and the gig shot smoothly forward into the channel.

My eyes were getting used to the dark. The dim ghost of a sail climbed, slatted, and filled on the starboard tack. Little John balanced the tiller against his mighty thigh and hauled in the sheet. The gig heeled sharply to port, the oarsmen scrambling to windward. I slid helplessly on the bottom-boards, braced myself, struggled up and perched my buttocks precariously on the starboard gunwale. Little John was staring into the darkness ahead, the hair and beard whipping in the wind. I tried to pick out the landmarks, but I could see none. The wind backed and fell, and the sea flattened. We must be in the shelter of Bryher, I thought, in the gap between Russia Bay and Bollard Point, the northernmost extremity of Samson.

"We have 'em beat," roared John. "Bryher gigs aren't off yet, and they'll not pull up from Agnes against this." The wind curved down and round at us through Gerwick neck and he paid off a little to keep the sails full. Under my feet the gig lifted, caught by the tail-end of one of the rollers marching down from the north-west. The wind stif-

fened at the nape of my neck, and white spray fizzed from
the stem. A patch of foam slid rapidly by to starboard,
then another, larger. I caught a huge black shadow and
the *boom* as Mincarlo flung tons of Atlantic at the sky,
and then we were climbing an endless slope of wave in
open water, with nothing between us and Ireland but a
hundred miles of tearing wind and leaping seas; nothing
between us and America but Carntop and the Crim, and
a ship that had fired a gun.

Little John made the mainsheet fast, hooked the tiller
behind his knee, and stared stolidly ahead. I kept thinking about what would happen if we took a gust with a
cleated sheet. The gig would knock down and the next
wave would have her right over. . . . It seemed incredible
that only an hour ago I had been in Mary's bed with
Mary's silky body lying against me, warm and smooth.
Wave after wave rolled under us. The wind was blowing
straight at our starboard gunwale, working at the swell,
sharpening it until the foam spilled dancing down the hills
of water. Whenever he saw a break, Little John would
luff up a little, meeting the falling water with the gig's
starboard bow rather than her broadside. On dry land he
might be a stubborn oaf. Here at sea, he was in his element. Quite against my will, I began to feel something
like respect for him.

And on and on she surged, the gig, half-skating, her
lee gunwale buried in foam, riding the waves as a gannet
rides the air.

I do not know how long it was that we tore to the westward. It cannot have been much more than an hour, for
we were making a good six knots. But as far as I was concerned it might have been a week of blackness and roaring water. Once I heard John curse and saw him pull in
more mainsheet, and the wind moved from my neck and
butted at my right cheek. Soon after that, I thought I saw
a lightening on the port bow. It vanished, then returned.
Hard, irregular sounds came under the night's cacophony,
a rumble and boom. John shouted and shoved the tiller
away from him. The gig came head to wind, pitching
nose-up, then standing on her head. The sail came down
and the oars came out, and slowly, holding water, we
moved stern-first down on Zantman's Rocks. I watched
the lightness increase. My mouth was dry and I kept swallowing, though there was nothing to swallow. The sea

licked with creamy tongues round something black and solid and long, with stubs of mast jabbed over the boil of surf. The masts faded into a sheet of grey water. John nodded abruptly and roared again. The gig slid astern faster, past the rock, just beyond the orbit of its suction, and edged into the patch of turbulence in its lee. Here the sea boiled and flung the gig from side to side like a twig. The shadowy oarsmen pulled and held water, pulled and held water, moving forward three feet, slipping back two as a wave swept under them, then inching forward again. I sat with my fingers clamped on the gunwale, watching the black emptiness that showed in gaps in the white water, and the loom of the masts caught like fibres of straw in a giant tooth. The rain had stopped, and the sky was grey instead of black. The wind still bore down like flying houses, but it had backed to the westward, whipping up a short sea across the swell. The mast stumps, I saw as we came closer, were tangled with cordage and clots of splintered wood and blocks. There was no sign of life.

One of the clots of darkness raised an arm, let it flop down again. A scroll of water snarled over the ship. When it had gone, the clot was still there. I heard Little John shout. The oars dipped and pulled, dipped and pulled and the gig edged up, reluctantly, towards the rock. The oars pulled harder, and a wave burst over the gig's bow, twisting her up corkscrew-wise. The spray slammed aft so fast that it caught me with my eyes open, and I clapped my hands to my face, trying to shield the bruised orbs. When I could see again there was wet black going past my face like a cliff I had fallen over. The gig fell thirty feet, fast, ten feet off the sheer of the rock. The trough bottomed out, and water roared into the rock's lee as if into a lock. We started to rise, the speed of it compressing the knee-joint of my left leg, the wet black whizzing past. The noise grew, a tongue sucking at a giant tooth, and we came to the crest in the middle of an ear-splitting shower of spray. In the middle of which, Little John, catching me by my soaking coat-collar, stepped overboard.

For a moment, everything stopped, including my heart. Five miles off the most westerly outpost of England, in a full Atlantic gale surging round the last tooth of granite before America. *He's murdering me. And himself, too,* I thought. But then I felt his boot grate on dry land, and he was running across a fragment of rock towards the pale, wet deck of the stranded ship, and I was dragged after him like a sack of potatoes.

Zantman's is a rugged wall of rock running north-east to south-west. The ship was wedged across it, nose to the east, with a strong list to starboard. She was lucky, if you could call it that. She was tilted away from the waves, so the man at the foremast had some protection. We scrambled up the tangle of cordage at her side. The white ghost of a wave lifted its mane over the rail as John's nailed boots tore wet splinters on the hill of deck under the lip of the forehatch. He threw me into the dark hole and jumped himself. I landed in a pool of water. It was very cold and I could feel no bottom to it: John splashed down beside me and the hatch-square went black and a deluge of water came down on me. The ship shivered. There was the grinding of wood on rock.

"Coming low water," said John. "Let's get on deck."

One of the companion ladders was still there, and up it we climbed, out onto the wreck's soggy planking, groping our way forward among the snares of timber and rope to the stub of foremast. The waves seemed smaller now. It was raining again, pitch black.

"Halloooo," cried Little John, in the break between two inundations.

There was a weak sound forward, like the mewing of a cat. We crept on, dragging ourselves along the web of wreckage. The stub of the foremast was blacker than the rest of the night. I put out my hand, feeling rope, varnish, and then the roughness of a serge coat, soaking wet. The serge coat screamed, and I jumped halfway out of my skin. "It's all right," I lied, when I had swallowed my heart again. "You're safe now."

The serge coat whimpered. Little John said, "I'll go aft. Look in the cabin." A wave boomed at the base of the rock. The wreck shivered under my feet. There was a long, loud scraping, and she started to slide backwards. I shut my eyes. She stopped sliding. "Nasty," said Little John, and disappeared aft.

It was very lonely, up here with the serge coat. Be systematic, I said to myself. Rush nothing.

"Arm," said the serge coat. "Caught."

I found the shoulder, followed the left arm down to

the elbow and past the elbow, to the place where it went between two spars, or broken ends of spars. Thin screams tore the wind at the touch of my hands. "Easy," I said. The foreyard had fallen parallel to the mast, and had become lashed snugly against it. Then the whole lot had broken off about ten feet in the air. The man in the serge coat must have been hugging the mast with his arm when it had come down. The gap between the two spars was too narrow for me to put a finger in. He might have been better off if the foreyard had landed on his head. From the size of the spars and the position of the forearm, radius and ulna were both crushed. I fingered the fisherman's knife I wore at my belt. The ship lifted, crashed down with a jolt that knocked me full-length on the deck. When I got back to the serge coat, his head lolled on his shoulder. I slit the coat sleeve with my knife, whipped off my neck-cloth and twisted it round the arm. Little John materialised at my side. "She's sliding. She'll go any minute now. We'd best be off."

"Hold this," I said, giving him the neck-cloth. "Twist it up tight. Anyone below?"

"No," said John. "Come on."

I hardly heard him, tracking down the bicep, over the ligament, down the forearm to the place where the swelling began. "Hold him," said I, traced the place on the skin with finger, and cut. The knife was sharp. I made a circular incision, taking care to sever the muscles between radius and ulna. The smashed ends of the bones came free. Warm blood ran over my hand, but not much. "Get him aft," I said. "To the cabin."

"Will I bloody hell," said Little John, with unusual profanity. "We're getting off here."

"Frightened, is it?" I said. I suppose I should have been, very, but at that moment I only wanted to tie off the arteries before this man emptied his blood on the deck.

"Come on," said John. But he did not let go of the tourniquet.

The ship gave another of its lurches. Under my feet I could feel the deck tremble.

"She's going!" shouted John. "Will you—"

Something tore deep below. The ship began to move. It gathered speed, plunging. The deck heaved and twisted to

a wave, slanted steeply to starboard. The bows came off
the rock with a crash and flume of spray.

It was not like the *Castletown*. There, one moment I
was staring out over the after-rail, and the next I was
struggling in dark water. Now, there was no abruptness to
it: only the sensation that I was somehow too heavy for
the deck, and that it was wearily leaving my feet to fend
for themselves while it sought rest on the seabed.

The hull rolled to port, into the face of a wave, moved
back to starboard. I clung to the cordage round the foot of
the mast, hanging like a pendulum as the deck became a
cliff of wet wood. Below, there was rumbling and a crashing. I did not hear it, I *felt* the sounds, like a tooth twisted
free of its socket. She rolled back to port perhaps fifteen
degrees. And there she stayed.

"Cargo's shifted!" shouted John's voice close to my ear.
"Have you up." For the third time that night, his hand
gripped my collar and lifted me. The difference this time
was that I wanted to be lifted.

We climbed along the tangled cordage like a pair of
spiders carrying a trussed fly from web to den. There was
the black loom of a deckhouse amidships. John wedged
the patient on the ledge formed by the house's port side. I
scrambled after him, and he leaned down and bellowed in
my ear. "Hold the bandage. I'm going to see to the gig."

"I don't understand," I said stupidly.

"Bubble of air in the hold," said John. "Pray." He
scrambled forward into the darkness.

With a stern effort of will I turned my attention back to
my patient. The tourniquet was tight. As far as I could tell
without looking, the man would not have lost much blood.
But we could not keep it there, or there would be mortification and gangrene. Every now and then a wave flooded
clear over us. I hacked up some bits of rope with my
knife, secured myself to a ringbolt, and did the same for
the man in the serge coat. Then I felt with my fingers for
the arteries of the arm. When I found them I applied
pressure, releasing the tourniquet with my free hand. I felt
the pump of blood under my fingers, weak and fast.

Little John came back. "Any sign?" I said.

"No," said John. "Wind's back sou'west. They'll think
we was sunk, shouldn't wonder. Hold on!" Another wave
sluiced over us, battering me down into the angle of deck

and deckhouse bulkhead. "Tide's turned. If that bubble holds, we might still be afloat come daylight."

"How long's daylight?"

"Hour and a half."

The seas were longer and smoother now that the wind was no longer fighting the tide. But every time we rolled to port, my mind went to that fragile bubble of air hanging under the timbers on which I lay. All it needed was for her to come on an even keel for a second; then out it would hiss and in the water would pour and down we would go. . . . I tried not to think about it, concentrating on the fluttering heartbeat under my fingers. At first the strain on the muscles of my hands made them ache so I had to re-fasten the tourniquet, change hands, unfasten. But after about an hour I could comfortably hold it with my right hand. I hung my eyes on where I thought the horizon might be, looking for the first gleam of light.

When it finally came, I had given up looking for it long ago. Against my will I had been thinking about the bubble of air again. I thought I could feel the deck bulging up against my ribs with the pressure. Little John lay lashed down behind me. From time to time I heard him muttering words I assumed were prayers. The first I knew of the dawn was when I saw dark streaks running away from me forward. I blinked. When I opened my eyes they were still there. I reached out and rubbed them with my fingers. I felt wet planking and the hard lines of pitch caulking, bulging up in ridges from the deck.

"Daylight!" I said. "Thank the Lord!"

But John only grunted. And as the light grew and the sea turned from black to grey and the islands lifted dreary backs from the drizzle ahead, I saw why. The south hill of Samson was about half a mile away, its skirts trimmed with a beach of boulders. There was not much sea breaking on the beach itself. The brunt of it was being borne by the scattering of rock ledges which lay between us and the beach. There was a lot of white water.

"Great Minalto Ledges," said John. "Can you swim?"

Looking at the crunching break of water on granite, I realised that Little John had a sense of humour.

My patient opened his eyes and said something in a blurred voice. It sounded like "Catherine."

"Yes, old fellow," I said. The pulse in the stump was very weak.

"Catherine," he said, with surprising strength. His eyes focused. "What . . . How . . . I thought I was dead."

"You're quite safe," I said, the smile stretching my face disagreeably. "You'll be ashore soon."

He frowned. "Ashore? Ah. You might tell Catherine—"

The pulse in the arm stopped. He looked surprised. Then he was dead. It was as simple as that. I watched him for a moment, stupidly. He had a broad, workmanlike face. I hoped that whatever he had had to tell Catherine hadn't been important.

"The gig," said Little John. "There she be."

I looked round. South and west of the high granite fin of Minalto, a lugsail dipped into a trough. When the gig rose to the crest I could just see a tiny figure waving.

"Saying goodbye," said Little John. "God be merciful unto me, a sinner."

A grey ridge of water rolled past us. I watched it forward. As it went under our bow, it steepened. The crest of it turned from grey to a clear green. Roaring, it collapsed in ruins. I shut my eyes. The roaring came up forward until it was all around us. I put my hands over my ears. My knees came up under my chin, and I started to pray. Or tried; but the pictures in my mind elbowed the prayers aside, pictures of Kingstown Harbour slipping away in the drizzle over a ship's rail, and the long road from Dublin and the consulting-rooms and the waxy corpse on the consulting-room couch.

There was a *bang* on my left. I clenched my teeth, waiting. But after the bang there was nothing, only a gradual shrinking of the roar. And the sound of laughing. I opened my eyes. Little John was standing there, feet spread on the deckhouse bulkhead. He was looking astern at the grey waves pounding the Ledges. And roaring, bellowing, squeaking with laughter.

"You bugger!" he shouted, rounding on me, his beard dripping and his eyes full of water or tears. "We come through! The Devil looks after his own. God willing we'll walk ashore after all."

I looked at Samson, now only a cable's length away. I did not share John's optimism. Ledges or no ledges, a man would smash like an eggshell on that beach. But John had other ideas. He ran aft. A minute later he came back with an axe. He raised it above his head, and waited. The waves steepened as the water shallowed. There was a ridge of rocks to our right, creamy with foam. I saw the veins in his neck stand out like ropes. The axehead came over in a rusty blur and bit deep into the ragged scar left on the side by the Ledges. Nothing happened. He tugged at the handle. The axe stayed firm, but little bubbles appeared in the film of water where blade met side. Then the axe leaped into the air, spun up into the grey drizzle and splashed into the sea. The air rushed up through the hole with a tearing *whoosh* that widened the axe-slot into a jagged mouth of planking as the ship's side burst like a balloon and we dropped with a crunch onto the boulders below low-water mark.

"Praise be," said John.

The gig was coming round the south side of Great Minalto Ledges. He ran astern, to the wreck's poop, three-quarters submerged. I looked down at the dead man. He wouldn't go anywhere. So I followed John, stumbling as the waves washed over the near-vertical deck. When I went through the door he was up to his waist in water, going through the drawers of a desk. He looked up at me. "Hurry, hurry," he said. "Afore them in the gig gets here." He weighed a string of pearls in his hand. "Won't be needing them no more," he said. "See what you can find."

John seemed to have forgotten his quarrel with me as he divided the spoils of the aftercabin into two halves. Not that there was much: some fragments of jewellery, a bag of twenty-eight golden guineas, a chronometer with the glass smashed and a pint of seawater in the works, some books and letters and a couple of other bits and pieces which were portable and worth money. When we again struggled out on deck, the gig was alongside. All I wanted to do was feel the dry land under my feet again. I crossed with my patient's corpse to Samson, where I sat on a rock —a fine, solid rock, well set in the earth—and felt glad to be alive. I thought about the man in the serge coat. He would probably have a wife and children, who would get some sort of news by some roundabout means, and they would wonder how it had all happened, where were the Isles of Scilly. And in time it would all heal over. It would have made little difference if no-one had heard the signal gun. He would have gone down quiet, him and his mates, and nobody any the wiser. Perhaps that was how it should be. That was how it had been with me.

I sat there as the sun came out and the tide turned and began to ebb. The salt in my clothes dried stiff, and still I sat. The Bryher gigs were out, and the other two from Tresco, and a couple from Agnes and St. Mary's flocking round the beached wreck. First went the brass fittings and the cordage from the deck. As the tide exposed the hatchways, the islanders tore at the hulk like gulls at a corpse.

The Widow Webber, one of the few remaining folk scratching a precarious living from the steep flanks of Samson's hills, brought me a mug of tea and brandy. There was quite a crowd on the shore. They were not talkative; a wreck was too serious for that. Too much hung on the richness of the spoils. Boats hurried away, laden with boxes and barrels, to the out-of-the-way beaches and the ancient hiding-places.

I saw them go, and vaguely wondered why. The explanation was vouchsafed me at eight o'clock, when a smart white boat came bowling over from St. Mary's Pool. I trained the telescope that had been part of my booty on it. In the stern-sheets, face red and puffy, the early sun glittering off the braid at neck and wrists, was Captain Maltby of the Preventives.

"Customs," I said to the Widow Webber, pointing.

She stuck her chin out at the boat, screwing up her old eyes. "Aar," she said. Then she stood up and screamed something at the men around the wreck. Oars went out, sails went up, and the whole crazy fleet, from fishing-smacks to rotten dinghies smaller than a bathtub, broad-reached away for White Island and the neck between Samson and Bryher. By the time the Preventive men arrived, the sea round the broken curve of the wreck's side was empty. I could see the scowl on Maltby's face from where I sat. He jumped stiffly from his boat, skidding on the weedy rocks, scrambled up the foreshore and confronted me.

"Good morning, Doctor," he said. "Surprised to see you here."

"Really?" I said. "It is part of my duty as I see it, to succour the afflicted." I pointed down at the tarpaulin-wrapped bundle that was the man in the serge coat.

"And mine is to make certain that the Receiver of

Wrecks does justice to the owners of this unhappy ship, as well as the Excise and her salvors."

"There she lies," I said. "All yours."

"Stripped bare, I have no doubt." He made harrumphing sounds in his throat. "It behoves you, Doctor, to give me an entire account of all those islanders you saw removing goods, wreck or flotsam from yonder vessel."

"It's been a long night," I said. "I was asleep since she came ashore. Not so, Mrs. Webber?"

"Aar," said the Widow. "Like a baby." She bared her single tooth at Maltby. "You dint ought to be hard on him, he having brought her in."

Maltby looked unimpressed. "You and who else?" he said.

"Little John Woodcock. Crew of the Tresco gig *Emperor*."

Maltby wrote on his ivory tablets with a pencil. "All right," he said. "A word of advice, Doctor." He leaned over towards me, the eyes cold and a little yellow at the pupils. "You're on the wrong side. Be careful. Very careful. The law of the land applies here, you know. No matter what the off-islanders may tell you. Frankly, you are beginning to excite my suspicions."

I got up and began to hobble towards the eastern shore, ignoring him. But I could feel his eyes on my back. It was almost a comfort to see Little John's enormous figure standing by a small boat drawn up on the white sand, looking over at Tresco. A plume of smoke was rising behind the jumbled rocks of the Long Crow. Mary's chimney. All at once I was very tired. I wanted to get close to her, take off my stiff clothes and warm myself with her body. And sleep.

"You going across?" I said to John.

He jumped, as if I had surprised him. Then he nodded and began to haul the boat down the beach. I waded out and struggled into the stern. He took the oars and started to row up towards New Grimsby. His hair and beard were matted into tacky strands, and dried salt crusted his face. He rowed for a while in silence, looking past me at the little mob of people on the strip of rocks at Samson's south end. Finally, he said, "Doctor?"

I grunted at him. All I wanted was to see Mary, then sleep for a week.

"I wanted to thank you," he said. "I was trying to get you off that ship."

"Makes no difference," I said, thinking of the dead man in his tarpaulin.

"Not to the wreck," he said. "But to me. You wouldn't know what we did. The luck of it. Last night we come straight through Gunners and Minalto Ledges. That's impossible."

"Luck," I said. "It's always been good."

He rowed a few strokes in silence, pulling across under Plump Island to get out of the tide. "It has," he said. "You're lucky I haven't tore your head off before now."

I laughed, light-headed. "You've got too much sense. I'm useful."

"I wouldn't put too much faith in that," said John. "I put my trust in the Lord. All flesh is as grass, the Book says. There's them as will talk you along if it suits them. After that. . . ." His voice trailed away. He looked at me, detached and musing. I thought back to the day he held me down while they gouged at my leg. "No," he said. "Don't put your trust in me. You cut up with Charity Pender, and I was resolved you'd do right by her. Still am. But I owe you something for this night. You showed me I was wrong, and I respect that. Even so, my duty is clear. It tells me two things. First, I'll keep away from you. You brought me luck, so that's what I must do. And second, it is my task before God to see that you do right by Charity Pender, as nursed you from death's door."

"Well, well," I said, encouraged to frankness by his withdrawing of threats to life and limb. "It'll take you long enough. Charity Pender is her own woman, and she wants no part of me."

"I shall try to bring her to her duty," said John, fending off from the quay with an oar. "Get you ashore before I drop you overboard."

I climbed ashore, feeling as usual with John that I had been talking to a hurtling boulder, and stumbled up towards the dispensary, my share of the loot banging against my thigh. I was tired, my vision blurred. A tall woman in a white apron and a dark dress was standing by the door. As I drew nearer, I saw that it was Charity, and that she was smiling, her face alight at the sight of me. She ran forward. "Oh, Doctor," she cried. "I heard, and I'm so glad you're safe."

"Safe as houses," I said. Then I stopped, not knowing what to say to her. And she stopped too.

"Come on," said Mary's voice. "Let's get you home." She was coming down the hill from the Palace, leading the mare. "Your stick," she said. "Oh. I'm sorry. Was I interrupting?"

Charity's face was quite blank. She mumbled, "No," shoved the dispensary door open, and slammed it behind her.

"I saw you rowing up-channel with Little John," said Mary. "You brought the ship in, I hear."

"Yes," I said. There was coldness in my belly. Charity was watching us from the dispensary, I knew. *Damn her,* I thought. *Just because she was my nurse. What kind of hold does that give her?*

"You'd best forget about it," said Mary.

I looked at her sharply. "Forget about what?"

"The man on the ship. The one that died."

"Forget," I said. "Yes. I will."

And thanks to Mary, during the next four weeks I did.

V

AARON HICKS AND JOSHUA LEGG ROSE, shook me by the hand, clapped their hats on their heads and marched off to the Palace. It had been a hard afternoon. The heat and the wreck had brought the Agnes feuds to boiling-point and me close to the end of my tact. These two seemed satisfied, however, a rare and miraculous state. But it would not last. Harry Jack's brandy would start it up all over again, sure as shooting. I lay back in my chair feeling like a wet rag. The summer had reduced the flow of patients to a trickle, but I was not sure that I wouldn't have preferred a hip amputation to the litigious Agnesmen.

I heard Charity's voice outside the door. It was higher than usual, curiously excited. The latch clicked and a voice said, "Afternoon, Doctor."

I was out of my chair so fast that I stumbled and had to clutch at the table for support. The man was tall, red-faced, with black hair and whiskers. He was dressed with an elegance quite un-Scillonian, his trousers white, his coat blue with brass buttons.

"Michael," I said, barely able to get my breath. "Michael bloody Fitzpatrick."

"Nicko," he said. "By God you took some finding." He laughed that deep, hearty laugh that always brought the blood to his florid face.

"Come up to the house," I said. "Charity! No more patients. Mr. Fitzpatrick and I will be leaving for the night."

We walked out and onto the road. A sleek black schooner with a gold line at her strake lay in the road-stead. "That yours?" I said.

"Larry O'Keefe's, said Michael. "I persuaded him to let me bring it over. Picquet, y'know."

"Not changed, then, Michael."

"Life goes on," he said. "Hand of cards keeps it interesting." He looked down at my leg, swinging in the air in its crazy loop. "Pity about the pin."

"Oh, that. I don't notice it any more," I said, lying.

As we walked over the spine of the island and started back down towards Old Grimsby, Michael said, "Wild sort of place."

"Yes, I suppose it is."

He eyed a pig suspiciously. "Don't understand why you're still here. Hardly safe, is it?"

"You'd be surprised. I mind my own business."

He shook his head. "That wouldn't be like you." He grinned the sly Michael grin. "It's a woman, ain't it?"

"Part of it."

"And the rest of it?"

"They're poor people with a bad landlord. I do what I can."

He laughed. "Guilty conscience." He jingled money in his pocket. "It'll be hard to mind your own business if you get tangled up with the landlord. Look, Nick. I know you and trouble. You're like two peas in a pod. If you had any sense you'd get the hell away from here. Don't you understand? They're after your guts. Drumcarty in particular. He never forgets."

"You're sure?"

"Wasn't I with him only last week? Sure, the man's crazy and getting crazier. But he's crazy after you, Nick. You'd do well to get right away."

We went up the path and into my house. Michael ducked his black mat of hair under the lintel, looked around him with the air of one trying not to wrinkle his nose, sat down and accepted a glass.

"Good brandy," he said. "Look, Nick. In your last letter you told me you wanted to know when the uproar died down. I came to try to make you understand. It'll never die down. In Dublin they think you're a murderer. It's not only Drumcarty."

"You came to tell me that?"

Michael turned the top of his head to me and threw up his chin so he was looking me full in the eye. "You wouldn't have believed me if I'd written. You're a friend. That's why I'm doing this."

"So you think I'm a murderer?"

"Christ, Nick. I don't know," he said. "You may be or you may not be. It doesn't matter. Forget about Ireland. Go to America, China, anywhere you want. But if you come back to Ireland they'll tear you to pieces. And if you stay here they'll find you."

"But if I had a chance to defend myself?"

"How?" he said. He sat down and ripped bread and cut cheese. He looked as if he ate more than was good for him. I took a drink of beer. My stomach felt shrunk like a walnut. "What defence have you?" he said with his mouth full.

I watched him chew. Then I said, "You must know. You must believe me. You're an attorney. You'd know a barrister—"

"Be reasonable," he said wearily. "A woman is found in your consulting-rooms, having bled to death. You are nowhere to be found. Enquiries reveal that you took passage on an emigrant ship, in haste, a couple of hours after the time of the operation. The woman is a known intimate of yours, and damned well-connected to boot. No." He shook his head. "You wouldn't last five minutes. Anyone who took your part would go down with you."

"So that's it."

"That's it," said Michael. "You were popular, but you had no bloody tact. You're tried and convicted before you get into court." He drank beer and wiped his mouth with his large linen handkerchief. "You're dead, Nick. Count your blessings. Don't resurrect." He put his hands on his knees and got up.

"So that's it," I said again.

"I'm afraid so."

"And you wouldn't speak out for me."

"There'd be no point."

"I wouldn't want to drag you down," I said, with bitterness.

Michael squared his shoulders. "You won't get the chance," he said. "You're a good friend, though. You always will be." He stood up. "We sail for Plymouth on the tide."

I followed him to the door. He pulled an envelope from his pocket. "I brought you some money," he said.

The envelope was fat between my fingers. "No," I said. "Keep it. I'll look after myself."

He shrugged. "If that's how you want it. Stay in touch, for old times' sake."

"For old times' sake," I said, turning back into the room.

I felt his eyes on me for a moment. Then the door banged and he was gone.

My first outing in Dublin took place under the auspices of Michael Fitzpatrick. He had left his card the day of my arrival, but it was not for six weeks that I found time to see him, and then only because I pleaded a sick friend with Duquesne.

He took me down to the Quays, to an establishment with the high-sounding title of the Mauritius Rooms. Its connection with the island in the Indian Ocean was at best tenuous, but I wasted no time on geographical enquiries. This was Dublin at last, the Dublin of which Michael had written from his masters' chambers, fast and glittering. Actually, glitter was conspicuous by its absence in the Mauritius Rooms. The place was no more than a tavern, filled with a cloud of smoke that stung the eyes, and peopled with a curiously mixed clientele. Perhaps three quarters of them were young gentlemen like Michael and myself, or gownless Trinity men in brown coats and Belcher handkerchiefs, drinking deep of whiskey-punch. The remaining quarter were older, hard-bitten citizens of sporting appearance. From the back of the room came a muffled barking, as of kennelled dogs.

Michael introduced me to a fat-faced undergraduate by the name of McGinchy, and we fell into conversation. It was Michael who did most of the talking. I was rather awed by his new polish, and McGinchy, though well up in matters sporting, was well down in intellect. After about an hour, during which I drank considerably more than I could take, Michael said, "I'll book us in ringside," and left.

McGinchy said, "Capital fellow, Fitzpatrick. Known him long?"

I said he was an old friend, which seemed to increase my stock. McGinchy took me familiarly by the arm and we went after Michael.

In the back room a circle of floor had been closed off with a wooden fence. We worked our way through the crowd to Michael's side at the rails. A hatch in the wooden wall opposite me opened, and for a moment the room hushed. Then the talk rose again, loud and high. The badger walked round the ring with the rolling gait of its kind, sniffing. McGinchy said, "Dashed old. Murphy's Billy will eat him raw."

I didn't answer. The badger looked up at me with short-sighted little eyes in the black and white stripes running down his face. I had watched his cousins playing in the moonlight by the setts in Drumcarty woods.

The hatch opened again, and two dogs, Roman-nosed, muscular-chested, trotted in. The bigger of the two was white, with little prick ears and scars on his flanks. "Look at the muscles on him," said McGinchy, squeaking with excitement. "Now you'll see old shaving-brush go—oh, stout work, sir!"

The larger dog, without so much as a growl, launched himself at the badger's throat. I wanted to leave. Both the dogs were on the badger's neck now. Brock had his head down, plodding across the boards, dragging his tormentors behind him. McGinchy said something to me. I said, "Yes," hoping the badger would kill those damned murdering dogs and have done with the whole beastly business.

"Good," said McGinchy. "A hundred to two hundred against the shaving-brush. In eighs."

"Done," I said, looking at his wet white jowls, the silly eyes on his betting-book. I had no idea what an eigh was, but I was damned if I was going to show greenness by asking. All I wanted, drunkenly, was to do what I could for the badger.

Michael cast me a strange look, then went back to talking money with the man on his right. I watched the proceedings in the ring, McGinchy baying at my shoulder.

The badger smashed the smaller dog's foreleg with one crunch of its axe teeth. The brute ran away to the trapdoor, yelping in agony. The door stayed closed. Billy continued his attack. For ten minutes he was dragged growling and worrying round the ring, his injured partner screaming with pain by the trap. There was blood on the boards now, and the badger was looking tired. He had a right; he had done all the work. McGinchy was beside himself. The circle of red faces shone with sweat, eyes bulged, hair matted on foreheads, and the sounds that howled from the drunken mouths were quite as animal as the sounds from the ring.

When the end came, it came quickly. The badger stopped dead. Billy, seeing his chance, loosened his grip and went for the throat. McGinchy screamed like a woman. Brock's head moved. I turned away. The roar that went up rattled the rafters. When I looked back, the white dog was lying in a pool of its own blood, the badger crouching against the wall, silent, weaving its long head from side to side.

McGinchy pushed a piece of paper into my hand. His mouth had a sullen cast, and he said, "There you are. Fitzpatrick will do the needful." Then he turned and pushed out of the room. I waited for Michael and said, "Let's go."

"Not like it, Nicko?" We went out onto the quays. I was finding it difficult to walk straight. After the Mauritius Rooms, even Dublin air smelt good. We walked back to Michael's rooms in York Street for some supper. He made punch and said, "Well, now. You certainly took McGinchy."

I remembered the paper in my pocket. "Did I?"

Michael took it out of my hand. "I'd be glad if next

time you didn't bet so high. Your man's father's a client of mine, and I have expectations of him." He winked.

"Bet high?"

"I heard you. Look there." He stabbed the paper with his blunt red forefinger. The writing ran and twisted. I was past focusing.

"What does it say?"

"You should know better than bettin' eighs," said Michael. "You've none yourself."

"I have a thousand a year," I said. "And would someone tell me for God's sake what is an eigh?"

He gave me a strange look. "A is for acre," he said. "One hundred acres good Antrim bottom land."

I stared at him. Then I began to laugh. When the laughing was over, I said. "We'll give it to the badger. You'll be the badger's attorney. Go and buy him tomorrow, and have him turned loose on the land."

He did not laugh. He said, "You're crazy. You don't mean it."

"I do."

"Will you not grow up?" He gave his head a very tired old shake.

"Are you or are you not my attorney?" I said, a little angry.

"Yes," he said. "Very well. I suppose I am. But you'll have to learn. Look out for number one."

"I'll leave that to you," I said.

That seemed to cheer him up, all right. I was too drunk to wonder why.

As I rode down into the hollow by Great Rocks I could hear her singing. There was a warm smell of heather and salt from the sea. The stink of the kelp-fires was gone now, buried with the kilns. The singing stopped, and a shaft of lamplight fell across the patch of white sand before the door.

"It's the Doctor," she said, smiling. "Come in, love. I was thinking of you."

Shadows lapped the eaves of the round room beyond the pool of lamplight over the embroidery frame.

"That yacht just sailed," said Mary. "I saw her lights in Crow Sound. Friends of yours?"

I thought for a moment, said, "No," and sat down.

Mary watched me, pushing the black hair back from her brown cheek. "Come here," I said.

She sat beside me, took my hand and turned it palm-up in her lap. "Trouble," she said. "A lot of it. Change is coming."

"Change has come," I said.

"It was that big black-haired lump with the red face. Wasn't it?"

"How the hell did you know that?" I said.

She patted the telescope case, slung on its hooks in the wall. "I saw him by the lantern at the boat's counter. Walking up and down as if he had St. Vitus's dance. He looks a funny one."

"He is." But I had not come up to Mary's house to talk about Michael Fitzpatrick. I put my arm around her waist, watching the curve of her eyelash over her cheek and wondering what I had done to deserve her.

"Mary," I said.

The eyelash flew up and the eye, huge, the colour of a midsummer night, looked at me.

"There is something I want to talk to you about." I took a deep breath. "I want to marry you," I said.

The pupil suddenly dilated, then contracted. Still she said nothing.

"Will you marry me?" I repeated. "I've decided I want to live at Scilly. With you."

A brightness spread over the eye, magnifying the iris. The lens in the corner thickened and spilled down the flawless brown skin. "Don't ask me that," she said. "Please. Ever."

Up in the rafters, the parrot squawked, "Con."

"No," I said. "Mary. Why?"

"Why should I?"

"Con," said the parrot infuriatingly.

At last, she said, "All right. Because I don't think you mean it. That's why. Or part of it."

"Of course I mean it," I said. "I wouldn't ask otherwise."

"You come up here shaking like a leaf, pale as paper. You've just had a rich visitor who stayed precisely three hours. What does that mean, I ask myself? You've had a shock, your visitor brought bad news."

"What's that got to do with it?"

"I don't believe you'll stay on the island. That's all.

And if you married me, you'd be regretting it in a year."
She laughed. "Why marry anyway? We've got each other,
haven't we?"

"Yes," I said. 'I suppose so." I felt cold and empty.
Curious, how a friend visiting could make me feel so utterly lonely. She pulled me up and pushed me down on
the bed. And soon, everything was as usual again.

It was Sunday, so the dispensary was closed. The
church bell hammered the air over Old Grimsby. I spent
the morning trying to read. But Mary kept on getting between me and the page, so after a while I gave up and
went out to the fields running down to Gimble Bay on the
north-eastern side of the island.

The barley looked ready for harvest, the little fields
rippling with white gold between their high walls. I said
as much to John Sinclair, who was leaning on the rotten
gate of one of his fields, staring down the rows, the dead
man's coat hanging from his spare shoulders like a ragged
tent.

"Little while yet," said John. "Still a lot of wet in 'er."
He looked with dislike at the sky, where white seventy-
four-gun clouds sailed down the cool wind. "If we ever
gets to cut it. I reckon she'll blow tonight, and who the
hell knows what'll happen then." He stuck a bit of grass
between the black stumps in his rotten jaw, and resumed
his watch.

When I got back to the house at about noon, I lugged a
chair outside and sat in the sun writing my journal, trying
to work out the thoughts that crowded my head but succeeding only in making them more complicated.

The wind was rising steadily, backing north. I closed
the book and took my chair into the house and went out
again, down to the beach. The colour of the clouds had
changed. They were dirty grey now, streaming down the
wind in squally strips, spreading and thickening, hiding
the sun. It was getting cold. The overcast sucked the colour from the islands and turned the sea a dull stone-grey.

I heard a voice calling my name. It was Mary. She
said, "Hurry." I went up over the granite and took the
sack she was carrying. We began to walk quickly down
the road and over the hill to New Grimsby. She said,
"We're going west."

"In this?"

"I want you to see something."

We walked down Palace Row to the quay: Charity was shaking out a mat in the garden of her house. She gave us a half-glance and went inside. I could feel her watching us through the window as we rowed out into the anchorage and Mary let go her punt's moorings and I heaved on the lugsail halyards. The wind funnelled down through Oliver's Tower and Hangman's Island, and the shrouds began to sing. It was very cold. Mary said, "Two hours to high water." We sailed on until we were off Russia Bay.

Then Mary said, "Look there."

Far to the south and west, a blue-and-white mote lifted under a tiny chip of lugsail. Beyond the mote was a tower of canvas, foresail, topsail, topgallants, with an elegant heel. *"Emperor,"* I said. "Bringing a ship in."

"Maybe," said Mary. "Put up your helm."

I pushed the tiller away from me and heaved in on the sheet. The punt's gunwale dug bubbles from the water.

"Will he be taking her into St. Mary's Roads?" I said.

"Maybe. Maybe not," said Mary. "It's looking thick out there."

To the north and west the clouds lay heavy on the sea. The loom of the islands merged into the grey murk.

"What are we doing?" I said.

"I want to see where they're going to take that ship," said Mary.

"Into St. Mary's Roads," I said.

"Little John's in *Emperor*. He's got Eddie Jenkins and five more. They asked me to go too."

"What's wrong with that?"

"You remember the paintings?" I nodded. "They wanted me as a mascot."

"That's absurd," I said, with an involuntary clutch at the tiller.

"Stop behaving like a scientist and watch your sail," she said. I put us back on course. "I've decided to change my ways. That's why I didn't go with them." Her hair was clinging to her cheek in damp strands. "I don't want that ship on the rocks, God forgive me."

"Do you mean they'll deliberately put her ashore?"

She laughed at the horror on my face. "Why not?" she said. "They've done it before. You've made me soft, that's all."

"How's that?"

"In an hour's time you won't be able to see your hand before your face. The gig'll get lost. The pilot they have aboard will go over the side or faint, or God knows what. The last course he gave her'll put her on the stones."

"Why'd she be coming in on a night like this?"

She laughed again. "Scilly pilots are famous from Jamaica to Archangel. It's only that there's a bad apple in the barrel."

Emperor was blazing along on a broad reach, lee gunwale under. I counted six heads in her. One man on the ship already. Brown faces looked across as we passed, and a hail floated across the vicious chop. A couple of cables' lengths ahead, the brig's towering bow hacked the waves. Mary scrambled into the punt's bow and coiled a long painter with a monkey's fist tied at its end. I could see the feathers in the gold eagle's wings at the knees where the great bowsprit spouted, the gold letters saying *Montezuma*. Then she was on us, a wet black wall of wood the height of a house, with a couple of heads peering over the rail, silhouetted against her colossal tower of canvas. Mary yelled, *"Huevos!* Cabbage! Potatoes!"* Her arm swung and the heaving-line snaked up at the ship's deck as I shoved the tiller away from me and we came tightly about and alongside. There was a sharp jerk as the painter came taut, dragging the punt onto her fenders. Mary pulled her bundle from under the thwart. A rope ladder came down, and up we went.

It was very dark now. The *Emperor* was a light smudge ahead. The islands had disappeared, but to port there was the hard rumble of breaking water.

Two grinning sailors helped Mary over the rail. One of them said, *"O la guapa,"* and gave me the wary look reserved for the husbands of beautiful women. Mary untied her bundle as if she had no care in the world and began to bargain over her couple of dozen eggs and five cabbages.

The brig was flush-decked. The red and yellow of Spain blew stiff at her ensign-staff, but I was not looking at flags. I was watching the knot of men at her wheel. There was the helmsman, a dark-bearded individual in a stocking cap; on his left a broad-shouldered man with a dark watch-coat and a braided peaked cap, who I presumed was the captain; on his right, Little John. As I watched them, Little John was looking out to port. His eyes came down the deck, met mine, strayed and returned. His mouth made a black 'O' in his beard. I picked my way aft.

Little John's mouth was still open. I said to the captain, "Would you give us a tow into the roads? It's a dirty night."

He frowned at me and said something in Spanish and waved a dismissive hand. I could understand how he felt. Pilot or no pilot, it was a bad time to be moving down the North-west Channel with a storm at your heels. If he had known just how bad, it would have turned his face white. I said, "John'll get us home safe. Won't you, John?"

Little John looked at me for what seemed like ten minutes. Then he said, "What else did you expect?"

I said, "Oh, I don't know. Thought you might be thinking of popping ashore. Or asking the captain here to follow you down-channel in the gig. Terribly hard to see, sometimes, those gigs."

He nodded, his eyes travelling down the deck to where Mary Prideaux was chaffering with the cook. "I might still ask the captain to do that," he said. "He'll keep you aboard."

"Terrible thing if you lost your mascot," I said.

"Looks like she's changed sides."

"You might as well earn your fee. If you don't bring the ship in, Mary will."

John said, "Starboard two." He paused. "Might as well."

"I don't understand," said the captain. *"Qué pasa?"*

"Saludando a un amigo," I said, giving him the big smile. *"Ahora le dejo a navegar."*

"'Sta bien," said the captain, relieved to be shot of me. I went to join Mary, much to the cook's disgust. The roar of breakers was very loud to port. The mate began shouting in Spanish, and hands swarmed into the dark web of the rigging to take off sail. On deck, hands eased braces. The roar began to grow quieter. Mary said, "Five more minutes and he'd have had her on Castinicks," and squeezed my hand. Suddenly I began to feel very weak.

About an hour later, *Montezuma* sent her anchors plunging to the bottom five cables off the lights of Hugh Town. It was raining hard. Mary and I were long gone.

It was black as ink, that night, or what I could see of it

from the window of my house. The rain came flying in from the north, riding the chops of the gale. The house sighed and moaned, and once I heard the crash of a chimney-pot from the village. I sat up late with Mary. I had no wish to be asleep if Little John came calling.

Tiny rivers began trickling through rock and heather, rushing with pygmy violence towards the bursting sea. It got colder and colder. Sometime after midnight I dozed with Mary's head on my chest.

Early in the morning, the rain turned to hail.

When I woke up I was stiff and sore. Mary was making coffee, singing. It was good to see her in the house. I said, "You're ruined."

"What do I care?"

"You'll not be able to show your face on the island."

She laughed. It was the last laugh I heard that day.

Later, we went out after wreckwood.

The fields by Gimble Bay were dotted with human figures. They stood staring woodenly at the brown, flat, sodden mass of what had once been waving barley, staple food for the long winter ahead. The wind had started the work, beating the rain into the corn and laying it over like thatch. Then the hail had finished it off, threshing it so that the ears were broken and empty, the kernels driven irretrievably into the soft, black loam.

John Sinclair was leaning on his stick as I rode past. I stopped and said, "I'm sorry about the corn, John."

He looked up at me, his eyes light blue, the dark skin stretched back in the fans of wrinkles at their corners. The rags of his coat billowed in the wind. Inside the cloth his body seemed to have shrunk in on itself. "And so am I," he said quietly.

"If there's anything I can do . . ."

He shook his head. "Not a lot anyone can. 'Less you can send us a nice wreck. Or money'd do, but St. Mary's'd steal it all."

Unless you can send us a nice wreck. I repeated his words to myself thoughtfully. If it was like this everywhere, the off-islands would starve. Later that day I watched *Montezuma* sail for the Mainland, white and tall. I did not feel as proud as I should have.

I waited until the full extent of the damage was apparent. It rained more, and the kernels in the ground sprouted through the flattened stalks. The fields wore a haze of green once more, but it was disease-green, not the green of growth. I went down to the Palace to see Harry Jack. He listened to what I had to say, whistled, stared, shook his head and finally looked very sly. Then he put the word about the island, and on the Friday night about forty of the island farmers packed into the dispensary. Harry Jack started the proceedings off, dressed in a fine rusty black coat, his whiskers bristling with enthusiasm. The parson was there too, and Little John glowering at the head of a deputation consisting of Eddie Jenkins and a couple of fishermen. I had not seen Little John since the *Montezuma,* or wanted to. The feeling, by his looks to-night, was mutual. Eddie kept casting me apologetic glances, then doing the same to Little John, jockeying to keep some sort of neutral ground and failing.

"Gentlemen," said Harry Jack, heaving himself up on the examination couch and sweeping his hand across his audience. "Gentlemen, we all know of the shocking state of affairs brought on by the hailstorms of the Twelfth. We are gathered here to make a resolution as to how best to save ourselves. It is not long since we were last in famine. The memory of it will be lively in most minds. It is something we would wish to avoid." Harry Jack was losing steam. He wiped his forehead with a big bandana and said, "As chairman of this meeting I now call for suggestions from the floor."

Several of the farmers looked down at their feet, as if expecting solutions to this insoluble problem to spring out of the earth. One of them got up, an old man with a fountain of grey-white beard and a knitted cap. He cleared his throat and said, "WELL I DON'T KNOW WHY WE ALL COME HERE, WE GOT BY WELL ENOUGH AFORE NOW BY OURSELVES, WHY'D WE HAVE TO ALL COME AND BLATHER LIKE HENS IN A BLOODY HENHOUSE. THE LORD WILL PROVIDE." And sat down quickly, leaving the ears of his audience ringing like Bow Bells.

His invocation of the Lord stung the parson into action. Raising his sandy eyebrows high on his forehead, he used them to pull the rest of his body into an upright position, and said, "Um, yes. Yes, the Lord will provide. But I *do* feel, Mr. Ashford, that our voice would be more easily heard if we all asked together. Concerted action . . . um, the lack of it did make it *rather more difficult* during the last hard times." There was a general murmur of agreement. Mr. Ashford frowned and shook his head, the great gush of beard wagging ferociously. "So I suggest that we call on the Society to come among us in their charity, as they have before now, and relieve the distress of the islands in their wisdom and bounty."

There was a gloomy silence, during which the parson sat down, looking earnestly to left and right, as if trying to hammer his points home with blows of his eyebrows. Eventually, Little John got up. "That'll not work," he said. "They'd never give us nothing after what happened last time."

"What happened last time?" I whispered to Harry Jack.

"Mission bought boats, seed-corn, nets," he whispered back. "Sold the boats, ate the corn, lost the nets. Great time, while it lasted."

"And even if we did get them to come," Little John continued, "what would they do? They'd have an appeal on the mainland and we'd get the proceeds in about March or April next year. And by that time. . . ."

There was no need for him to carry on. Every eye in the room was turned inward, to the horrors of the last famine, when the corn and potatoes had given out in February, with no hope of a new crop because the seed potatoes had gone the way of the rest.

"And anyway," said the loud deaf voice of Amor Odger, who had rented me the horse. "Even if they did raise a fund, how much of it would we see after them on St. Mary's had their hands in it?" He sat down, nodding to himself, darting his eyes round the room to read the meeting's lips.

There was a silence. Then Little John said, "There's them as knows what to do about it." Eddie Jenkins looked suitably grim, caught my eye and looked sharply at the ceiling. "The Lord will provide, Mr. Ashford says. Well I'll give him a hand."

There was a murmur of approval. Everyone but the parson knew what he meant.

"Anyone else?" said Harry Jack.

A pause. Then John Sinclair got up, grinning nervously. He had put on a new coat, with fewer holes than usual. "I ain't got no answers," he said, shuffling his big laceless boots. "But I thought I'd say how we got into this state here, when a storm of wind knocks us out for the winter. 'Twasn't always like this, now. It's since the kelp went down; so to earn a bit of money now we has to sell the potatoes, 'stead of eat 'em. And the fish, with the salt tax—"

"What's he talking about?"

Harry Jack reapplied his hoarse whisper to my ear. "They needs money to buy salt to salt the fish. Foreign salt's cheap and easy to get but there's duty on it, so they has to buy English salt dear. So they're buggered every way," he concluded succinctly.

"So," said John Sinclair. "We've got no corn to speak of. There are a few potatoes, but not many. If we want fish for the winter we'll have to sell the potatoes to buy the salt, and we all know about eating scad without taties and taties without scad—"

"And sea beef for Easter," said Harry Jack. "You'll get no price for taties this time of year. I was talking to Mumford t'other evening. He won't give you more than half what he gets. Says he's got more freight than he knows what to do with without a lot of spuds nobody wants."

"And that's a bloody lie," said Amor Odger in a flat burst of words. "He'll take the taties easy enough. He knows we've no ship big enough on Tresco, that's all, so there's no option."

"Surely you could beat him down?" I said.

"Wouldn't even try," said John Sinclair, his boots drumming indignant thunder. "Before you'd know what, we'd all have had our leases took away."

"I hold no lease," I said. "I'll go and see Mumford, if you want me to."

There was another silence. Several men were frowning. Mr. Ashford was shaking his head. "Well," said John Sinclair nervously. "I don't know. You ain't been on the island too long, Doctor. You don't know our ways. . . . Fact is, Scilly don't combine too easily. We likes to keep ourselves to ourselves, and. . . ." He trailed off into embarrassed silence, plucking at a thread on his frayed cuff.

The fire flared up in Harry Jack, and he jumped onto the bench. "God damn you all," he roared, " 'scuse me, Parson. Course it's the only way. Starve alone if you want. Any man as likes can say he don't want the Doctor to speak for him. But I say the Doctor has patched you all up, and he never ask you for money. You know damned well he's got a good head on him. More'n one of you's asked him to hold money or settle a difference with a neighbour. So if he offers to go to see old Croesus Mumford, you'd be bloody mad not to thank him for it and let him." He paused, glaring round the weatherbeaten faces of his audience. "Anyone who'll let the Doctor speak for him, put his flipper in the air. And anyone who doesn't can starve and keep quiet about it." He thrust his rusty black arm at the ceiling.

John Sinclair's hand came to his shoulder, hesitated, and rose above his head. Others followed, and others, until only five or six remained in their owners' laps. "A'right," said Harry Jack. "Motion carried. If you'll each tell me how much you got to sell, I'll draw up a bill of lading for the Doctor to take."

After the meeting, I walked up towards the Palace. A man stepped out of the shadows and caught me by the sleeve. The moon shone on a cloud of white beard. "Word with you, Doctor," said Mr. Ashford, looking about him nervously. "I'm sorry I didn't up my hand for ye. But I changed my view. I'd be happy if you'd speak for me, too."

"Course I will," I said. "Tell Harry Jack what you want to sell."

And I walked on, feeling very pleased with myself.

Next morning I borrowed some decent clothes from the parson, had myself rowed over to St. Mary's in the *Emperor*, and limped up to Mr. Johns' house, a grey granite building rather bigger than the parsonage on Tresco.

I gave the bell a hearty pull. A pretty maidservant in a starched white apron opened the door.

"Doctor Nicholls of Tresco to see Mr. Johns," I said.

The maidservant ran her eyes up from my boots to my face, looked me boldly in the eye for a moment, and said, "Master's in the garden. If you would come this way?" She turned and went down the hall, rolling her hips at me. The house was cool and dark, its gloom deepened by solid mahogany furniture and oil-paintings crusted with tobacco-smoke. We passed through a little conservatory and out into the hard Scilly sunlight on a lawn of coarse grass. Over the lawn arched three or four mulberry-trees. The breeze whispered softly in their leaves and discs of green-filtered sun swam over the table and chairs that stood in their shade. In one of the chairs sat the purple Johns, whiffing at a long churchwarden pipe with a ledger in front of him. The mulberry trees were the first plants higher than gorse-bushes I had seen for eight months. I had forgotten the coolness and the green smell of a tree's shade, and I stood breathing it all in for what must have been an indecently long time.

"Doctor Nicholls," said the maid to Johns. "Will there be anything else?"

Johns' pink eye turned on me. "No," he said. "Nothing else." The maid fluttered her lashes and left. "Doctor feller from Tresco," he said to himself in his low, phlegmy voice. "Wonder what the deuce he wants. What can I do for you?" he said, for public consumption.

"I've come to ask a favour," I said. "Because you know better than anyone else how these islands work."

"Oily cove," said Johns to himself. "Quite right, though. Ask away."

"It concerns the Tresco potato crop," I said. "Since the corn was ruined by the gale a couple of weeks ago, your Tresco tenants find themselves compelled to sell their potatoes on the mainland."

"Quite right too," said Johns. "I won't stand in their way." His voice dropped. "Who does he think he is? Why can't the idle beggars do their own asking?"

"But the freight charges are very high. In my opinion, absurdly high. If the Tresco men have to pay what Mr. Mumford is asking there will be considerable hardship. Indeed, I doubt that many of them will be able to find the Duchy's rent. So I came to ask you to use your considerable influence with Mr. Mumford to persuade him to reduce his charges."

"Good God," said Johns to himself. His face darkened a couple of shades. "Now let me tell you something, Doctor. I have been here man and boy for more than sixty years. And I think I know the off-islanders pretty well by now. A good deal better than you." He poked a thick blue-black finger into his palm. "And a worse lot of damned rascals you would not meet. Not if they were Chinamen. They'll steal the coat off your back, the bread from your mouth, and give you their blether and grin at you while they do it. Do you hear me, Doctor? So my answer to you is this. They have made their bed and they will damned well lie in it. It is not my business to pamper them. Mr. Mumford can set what rates he pleases, and if the Tresco people don't like them, well, they needn't sell their potatoes. They can eat them. And one more thing, Doctor. I don't know who you are or where you come from. But I do know that these islands are held from the Crown by the Duchy of Cornwall and from the Duchy of Cornwall by His Grace the Duke of Leeds. I am the next in the chain of command, and it is my job to see that it is not interfered with by a lot of mealy-mouthed charity-boys with ideas above their station. So mind your own business, Doctor."

"You are quite unreasonable," I said. I pivoted on my cane and limped back towards the house.

Behind me, Johns was muttering, "Insolent scoundrel. Damned radical no doubt. Duchy *shall* hear, by God."

The maid took me back through the hall without a wink or a sway of her posterior, from which I deduced that she had been listening throughout. And thirty seconds later, I was standing in the street of Hugh Town with the door's slam still ringing in my ears. But not at all disheartened; it was, indeed, no more than I had expected. Now there was the second part. Walking on up the street, I turned into a door by a window with hand-bills stuck against the glass. Over it there was a sign that said Jas. Mumford Indian Merchant Grocer. The shop smelt of cheese and coffee. There were a couple of poke-bonneted women at the counter, talking to a cadaverous individual in shirt-sleeves, mutton-chop whiskers and a green baize apron. The women looked round at me curiously, curtsied, and said, "Good day." I raised my hat, returned the greeting, and said, "Mr. Mumford?"

"Yes, sir," said the character in the apron, rubbing his hands. "Can I be of any assistance? Some little article perhaps?"

"I was wanting to discuss your freight rates."

"Certainly, sir," he said. "If you will forgive me while I attend to these ladies—"

"Oh, don't mind us," said the taller of the two. "If the gentleman is perhaps moving his establishment to the Island, he must make all despatch." Meaning that they wanted to hear the sum of my notional household goods, whether I was married, where I lived. . . .

"Wait a minute," said Mumford, frowning. "Have I the honour of your acquaintance already? Your face is strangely familiar—Goodness me! You're that doctor from Tresco!"

"I am," I said. "And it is your very high rates for transporting the Tresco potato crop that I wish to discuss with you."

"No discussion," said Mumford, losing his charm. "Rates are fixed. They stand. You don't like 'em, find another carrier."

"Thank you," I said. "Perhaps I shall."

"And perhaps you won't," said Mumford.

"Good day, ladies," I said. The two noses, disillusioned, rose as one nose towards the hams hung in the joists.

As I let the door swing to behind me, I heard Mumford say, "He'll be back."

I grinned to myself. If the likes of Johns and Mumford thought they could make their own laws, they could hardly expect me not to make mine. Whistling *Drowsy Maggie*, I stepped and tapped my way down to the quay, where the gig lay waiting.

Captain Bolitho's ship was lying in New Grimsby harbour, rocking as much as her broad beam allowed in the remains of the long swell pounding the rocks at Gun Hole. I heaved myself onto the quay, thanked the gig's crew, and made my way up to the Palace. I went through the taproom into the parlour with its big window looking back over the quay and away down past Plump Island and Rag Ledges to St. Mary's Roads. Bolitho was sitting by the fire clutching a large pewter mug and staring at the masts of the shipping in the Roads.

"You saw 'em," he said. "What happened?"

"What we expected."

He nodded his iron-grey head. "Ah. Well, they've had their chance. If they won't yield to fair means, we must use foul."

"Good," I said. "Let's be loading her up, then."

Bolitho frowned. "Easy does it, Doctor. We'll take it slow and do a proper job. That's the way to make your profits. Course it's no joke, seeing your friends hungry. But it's no joke getting caught up with the Revenue, neither."

"That won't happen," I said. "Don't you worry."

He tapped with one stubby finger on the table. "Touch wood, Doctor. Touch bloody wood."

All afternoon the gigs went to and from Bolitho's ship, hanging under her peeling gunwales while the bags of potatoes climbed in bunches up to her fore-boom, swung inboard, and descended into the evil-smelling maw of her hold. The captain sat in the Palace with his nose in a bottomless glass of Harry Jack's brandy, and I fretted a good deal during the next couple of days. But he mumbled, "More haste, less speed," stuck his head out of the parlour door from time to time, and drank on. Then, quite suddenly, on the evening of the third day after loading, he said. "All right. Wind's going round to the north-west. We're off."

At that moment, there was the merest zephyr from due south, and I was not sure whether to believe him or not. As I took the mare home, the afternoon sun was sidelighting the ripples of a mackerel sky. By the time I hobbled back over the hill with a carpet bag, the wind was blowing fresh from the north-west, striking short whitecaps from the blue-grey channel.

I met Little John at the quayhead. He said, "You'd better come back."

"I will," I said.

"We'll see." He turned away.

Then I went to say my farewells to Mary, gazing at the schooner straining at her anchor-cable in the reflection of Hangman's Island.

"I wish I was coming," she said.

"So do I." I kissed her on the mouth.

Bolitho's mate was waiting on the quay, impatient. As I clambered onto her deck the hook came off the bottom, a backed jib brought her nose off the wind, and her fore and main filled with a bang. The Palace started to slip by to port. White sand and the fish cellar and the rounded roofs of the gig-sheds went by, then Plumb Island and the green rise of Abbey Hill. The tide was high, the rocks smoothed away by a blue-grey sheet of water. Far behind under the sprawl of the Palace, Mary waved a handkerchief.

We left Nut Rock to port, and twenty minutes later we were under the long stone batteries of Garrison Hill on St. Mary's, and *Jane and Emily*'s barge-like bow was plunging into the first of the hundred miles of long, slow seas that roll between Scilly and Britanny.

Jane and Emily was very slow and decidedly ungainly. Even with the fresh nor'wester punching into her grey canvas from over her starboard quarter, she made a mere

three or four knots. On the morning of the second day I
settled myself by the bowsprit, six feet above the curl and
gurgle of white water. It was cold and misty. The wind
had backed westerly and moderated. Ahead the tedious
billows marched into the morning vapours. There was a
thickening. At first I thought it was a fog-bank. Then a
gust of wind tore the grey curtain aside and I saw a low
green line, grey at its base, with streaks of white where
waves gnawed at the cliff-walls. Inland, there was a suggestion of hills. *Jane and Emily* put down her helm. Three
hours later we were ghosting through a swarm of tan-
sailed French fishing-boats under the neat grey granite
houses of Roscoff.

Bolitho and I went ashore. Bolitho spoke no French,
whereas I had learned a good smattering of the language,
first from Connolly's Abbé and later from Duquesne. We
walked along the quay, which was lined with boats and
covered with a rich mixture of boat's gear, goods and gar-
bage. Bolitho looked straight in front of him, his square
head sunk between his shoulders as if in cement. I kept
up with him as best I could, though seriously distracted
by a shop crammed with pretty women wearing high lace
coifs and clogs and paisley shawls, whose colours made
them gorgeous tropical birds. Bolitho tramped on uphill,
barging his way through throngs of Bretons in a manner
which would have provoked numberless fist-fights in Waterford or Bristol. Here, however, everyone was talking
too hard to notice. He turned abruptly to his left, down
an alley under an archway and shoved open a nail-
studded door at the far end. He had a way of opening
doors as if he intended to walk straight through them,
nails, timber and all.

I followed him into the gloom. There was a smell of
bad drains and spirits. "Cursed Frogs," growled Bolitho,
who had, he claimed, been indefatigable against the Corsican. "Rossoo Drenec!" he roared. "Som Zissy." He
cleared his throat. "Your turn," he said, slightly embarrassed by this display of fluency.

Footsteps were coming up dirty stone stairs, one after
the other, very slow. They drew closer and closer, and
Rossoo Drenec crunched into view. He was very fat, with
a huge black moustache, a nose like a crimson gherkin,
and big eyes like black shoe-buttons.

"Ah! Le Capitaine Boleto," he said. *"Enchanté de vous revoir."*

"And me," said Bolito. "This here is Doctor Nicholls."

"Enchanté," said Drenec, beaming. "But you are a doctor?"

"I am."

"My liver," said Drenec, rolling his eyes up. "Ah! How he pains me. And my bones—" He launched into a lengthy and detailed account of his gastro-intestinal symptoms, the best prescription for which would have been less food and ardent spirits. In view of his trade, however, I did not feel at liberty to suggest this course. So when at last he ran down, I tut-tutted, suggested seawater draughts, and received for my pains a look of the order Lazarus might have bestowed on Our Lord after his raising. *"Un génie,"* he whispered in tones of reverence. *"Un génie extraordinaire.* Come now, you will be hungry."

He took us through into a big, dusty, sun-lit office overlooking the harbour, dragged bottles and pots and cheeses and bread out of a cupboard, and stood over us while we ate. The cheeses stank to high heaven, and in the pots was a paste of offal not unlike brawn. Bolitho went through his like a fox through a hen-run. When we had finished, Monsieur Drenec said, *"C'est bon?"*

"What's he say?" said Bolitho.

"That's all right, is it?"

" 'Course it is," said Bolitho matter-of-factly. "Always behaves like this. Ask him to take us down to the cellar."

As we descended flight after flight of stone stairs, I argued with the back of our host's neck about a price for the potatoes. Finally we arrived at a result which, even after Bolitho's cut, would mean that the growers would receive about twice what Croesus Mumford would have allowed them. It was still little enough to buy corn for the winter; but that was where the second phase of the plan came in. Monsieur Drenec barked instructions at a youth bare of foot and striped of jersey, and signed a docket. The youth ran off to start discharging the *Jane and Emily*'s cargo. From the level of trust displayed by all sides, I concluded that this was not the first time Bolitho and Drenec had had dealings.

The bottom-most cellar was a cave in the granite that stretched away into the gloom as far as I could see. It was divided up into alleyways just broader than my shoulders by rank after rank of piled hogsheads. The smell of brandy was so strong as to be almost inflammable, and I could feel it warming my blood.

Monsieur Drenec stood taking deep breaths, his rosy cheeks glowing like delighted apples in the lanternlight. "Good," he said. with a sigh of contentment. "You will please tell Capitaine Boleeto that I can no longer get myself down the rows, so you and he will have to manage while I give you directions. I became stuck one day," he said by way of explanation. "By the time they found me, I was sleeping peacefully. They had to use a block and tackle." He brightened. "But by the grace of God I was next to the Grande Reserve des Rois Bourbon."

"Come on," said Bolitho. "What's he jabbering about?"

Drenec dug in a cupboard in the wall and found a couple of large glasses. "Monsieur le Capitaine knows what to do," he said. "Tell him that the arrangement is the same as before."

This involved walking down the rows, barrel by barrel, tasting. After four barrels I was glad that, contrary to my normal habits, I had had a large and greasy luncheon. After six barrels I knew I would have to stop soon.

"Next, the beautiful one," cried Drenec from his point of vantage. "Taste."

I tasted. It was excellent, a nose like gaseous velvet, a smoothness that was just not oily, and a poetic slide over the gullet that soothed and strengthened but did not burn. "Astonishing," I said. "Captain."

Bolitho walked across the row, twisted the spigot, sipped, swallowed, and said, "Aaah."

"Something about it," I said. "Cool and like a breath of summer all at once, as it were. Bit smokey, with a—"

"Reminds me of a time down Cadiz way," said Bolitho, pouring himself another stoup and supporting himself on a barrel. "Cape St. Vincent, 'twas. Back in '96. We was chasing on the tail of a damnation westerly when bugger me if we don't see a Friggie froggett—I mean a Froggie frigate—"

"I think Monsieur Drenec is trying to tell us something," I said. It was a little annoying. It would have been far more comfortable to sit down on the nice soft granite floor. But Drenec's voice was bouncing and booming like a wagon-wheel between the rows of barrels. And there was Cadiz and Bolitho's lady-friend to hear about. "He says that if we are to get away on tonight's tide we should make our minds up soon. I think that this is the article. Not so?" I turned round to point at the barrel, to make sure he got my drift, and stumbled.

"Naah," said Bolitho, with scorn. "This stuff? Like mother's milk. They'd drink it by the gallon in Bodmin and not notice what hit 'em. Something with a bit of bite." He drained his glass, took mine, lurched up the aisle to another barrel, and tapped. "Try that."

I tried it. When I had stopped coughing and the buzzing in my ears had subsided enough for me to hear myself speak, I said, "My God!"

"Good, eh?" said Bolitho. "Right we are." And we zigzagged back between the rows to Monsieur Drenec, who was watching us as a proud father might watch two favourite sons.

"Tell him we'll take twenty hogsheads of that stuff," said Bolitho.

I told him. "Ah," he said his moustache drooping. "Is not good. *Feuilles d'automne,* they call it. Very disgusting."

"But cheap. Why Autumn Leaves?"

"Because it makes one change colour and fall to the ground."

This struck me as most humorous. I laughed immoderately, which cheered Drenec. "And for you," he said. "I present you with a keg of the beautiful one. As a tribute to your taste."

"Thank you," I said. "Now. To business."

After we had fixed prices and drunk a final glass to the success of our venture, we took our leave. Monsieur Drenec, beaming and breathing fumes, showed us to the nailed door. *"Au revoir,"* he said. "After dark, the barrels come. I will stay here. I have a wife who does not let me out. She says I am too fat and old. So good luck. Particularly with your Preventives."

As Bolitho and I turned into the street, blinking like owls in the bright afternoon, I felt suddenly sober. When we sailed from Roscoff, I would be taking an irrevocable step. The brandy soured in my stomach at the thought of the black night, where the men in uniform cruised the blockade in swift cutters.

We sailed at midnight, with a fresh sou'westerly breeze. *Jane and Emily*'s new cargo was a good deal lighter than the potatoes, and we slid through the water at a fine rate. The night had turned thick, with a dense layer of cloud hiding the stars. I stood aft by the wheel with Bolitho, huddled in a suit of oilskins.

"Don't you get nervous," said Bolitho, his face shadowed by the dim light of the binnacle. "Won't be nobody out looking for us. Yet."

"No," I said. But I could not stop my eyes flicking port and starboard. And I did not like the sound of that "yet."

The hogsheads lay in the hold tightly packed, stinking of rotten fish. The upper rim of each barrel was extended above the head, to make a tray about six inches deep. Into this the crew had pressed a wad of mackerel half-liquid with age. The stench was tremendous. There was a watertight hatch on the hold, and I was standing upwind. Even so, it made me feel distinctly queasy. Eventually, I went below, to the small dirty saloon, and raised a glass of Drenec's extra special to Scilly and a prosperous winter.

Doctor Duquesne was much given to disappearing. After his promise that my regime would change I tried to discuss the matter further; but either I was at the Anatomy House or working for my clinician's certificate in Sir Patrick Dun's Hospital, or there were patients to see to, or he was simply out. On these last occasions, nobody would tell me where he was. I assumed he was foregathering with potential patients among crystal chandeliers, frivolous talk and beautiful women.

It was a month before I could get him cornered and remind him of his promise. He looked me up and down with his cynical old eyes and said, "Ah, yes. You come to claim your prize." He snapped his fingers for the butler. "You will inform mesdames in the waiting-room that my assistant and I are called away on a case of urgency. Then bring us our coats."

He led me out to the carriage, bade me be seated, asked me if I was quite comfortable. I asked him what was this urgent case.

"You will see." He leaned forward. "May I enquire how you like your new profession?"

"Pretty well," I said. It was not strictly true. Though I felt I had to put a good face on it, the butchery in the Anatomy House and, worse, in Sir Patrick Dun's was not encouraging. It gave me strong intimations of mortality, and at the age of sixteen I found that something of a blow. "I prefer your practice to the hospital."

Duquesne laughed a tinkling laugh. "So many old ladies and pretty things for you to charm," he said. "But still you complain there is too much to do."

I grinned at him sheepishly. "There's little time for . . . myself," I said. Dublin, huge and glittering, was all around me. But the only parts of it I saw were hospital, medical school, consulting rooms. There had been tantalising glimpses. That had been all.

He nodded understandingly. "You must become used to it," he said. "A doctor is everybody's. Always, he must be busy. Or he will never be busy at all. But tonight, you will meet with the new regime."

I looked out of the carriage window. We had left the well-lit streets behind. The coachman was urging on his cattle, nervously, taking us at a rapid clip through mean lanes where the infrequent lamps shone on tall houses with boarded-up windows, people ragged and thin leaning by street-corners. The air was damp. It smelt of bad drains and old rubbish.

The carriage drew up outside a crumbling red-brick building with a lamp over a slime-green marble plaque bearing the words Mercy Hall. Duquesne told me to get out and ordered the coach for nine o'clock. Then he said, "Well?"

I kept my mouth shut. I had expected plush-breeched footmen, double doors, light and magnificence. Instead there were wooden benches, windows curtained with spiderwebs. On the far wall hung a huge and gory Sacred Heart, with a lamp before it. The benches were full of people.

Even on the worst of the country estates I had not seen such people. They were of all ages, from old men and women bent with rheumatism, to skeletal babies too listless to pluck at the shawls hiding their mothers' breasts. But they had one thing in common; they were all agonisingly thin, eyes sunk far back in bony sockets with a dumb misery that was past rebellion. Past anything but death, I thought.

We went to work. Or rather, Duquesne went to work. He raced about the squalid hall, chucking children under the chin, flirting with their mothers, reproving drunken old men, talking hurling with young labourers. And into the crevices of his patter he squeezed a stream of orders. I found myself writing furiously on my tablets. Then before I had finished, we were behind a curtain and he was pulling down a woman's verminous dress from her dirty-grey shoulder, lancing a black-headed carbuncle, leaving me to dress it as best I could while he called for me to write the next prescription.

For three hours it was like that. I worked in a sort of trance. All I could see was misery, dirt, lousy clothes. My nostrils were full of the fecal stink of no hope. I only wanted to go outside and vomit up everything I had seen and smelt and touched.

Duquesne finished his rounds. The coachman brought in two huge baskets, which he gave into the charge of the haggard priest who had been acting as shepherd to this diseased flock. Then he bowed from the doorway, and we left.

In the carriage, we were silent. The scrofulous streets unreeled, and there were more lights, fewer of the quiet people staring at the rain. Finally he said, *"Eh bien,* Mr. Power. You have had your revision of duties. From now on, you will assist me at the Mercy Hall."

I could only nod. Disappointment was raising a lump in my throat.

"You will become used to it," said Duquesne, his voice kind. "I feared that you were gaining the wrong idea. I shall explain. I treat the rich people with those so stupid draughts of eggs. They feel they are ill, and who am I to disabuse them? I need not very much money, so I use what I have left over for the help of these poor ones you saw tonight. I must do it secretly or some other doctors will make trouble and politics. Having lived in the Terror, I detest both." The lamplight beyond the windows was brighter now, and I saw his ironic smile. "I will give you my own maxim now. Doctors know nothing about curing bodies. But the great curer of minds is hope. Rich and poor, all need hope. With the rich, it can be bought. With the poor, it is the only aim of charity. *D'accord?"*

I said, *"D'accord."* My disappointment had gone. Much to my surprise, I found myself liking him enormously.

"Good," he said. "Now you live in the real world."

I awoke next day to a sou'westerly wind and foul clouds dragging their bellies over a grey sea. It was not weather to lift the spirits, but Bolitho, like a block of wood in his cracked oilskins, was cheerful. "Never find us in this," he said. "If she keeps up. Whistle for it." I did not ask him how he thought he would make his landfall at Prussia Cove in the pitch dark in this meteorologic soup. It was not encouraging to entertain such thoughts.

At the meal of French capons and hard biscuit we shared at about five o'clock in the afternoon, there was little talk, except from Bolitho, who delivered himself on the plan of campaign. "If the wind holds we'll make Praa Sands on the last of the ebb," he said. "One o'clock. We show two lights, white, one above the other. Jacko, you look at that." Jacko, a moon-faced youth of about eighteen, nodded solemnly. "Larry and Boz, get them hoggers to the rail when I gives the word. Link 'em with a line, and make sure they're ready to tip. Mister Trevithick." He turned to the mate, who was chewing steadily at a mouthful of biscuit. "You'll work the ship with me."

"And me?" I said. "What can I do?" I was irrationally anxious not to be left out.

"You can keep yer eyes peeled and yer head down," growled Bolitho. Then, relenting, "Useful thing, an extra lookout. Have to be sharp. Right. So as long as the wind holds we proceed as follows. One o'clock, Praa Sands. Up to Prussia Cove on the last of the ebb. Make signal. Drop for gig. Off to New Grimsby. And nobody none the wiser."

After dinner I went to the bows and stood looking out past the bowsprit into the grey rain. Somewhere over the horizon was the Lizard, the rocky peninsula that forms the southern blade of Cornwall's claw. The grip of the claw was Mount's Bay, a thirty-five mile curve of white sand and granite cliff that swept up to the crags of Land's End. And twelve miles up from the Lizard were the wave-lashed flats of Praa Sands, with beyond them the rock notch of Prussia Cove. It was a wild place, and one studiously avoided by most sailors. The prevailing wind blows straight into the bay, and once embayed, there is nothing a ship's master can do but commend himself to his Maker and hope the end comes quick and clean. The inhabitants, fishermen on the coast, tough tin-miners on the barren moors inland, regard wrecks as a gift from God. And there were rumours that they had none of the Scillonian scruple about the taking of life. A man who survived the

rocks and the waves, it was said, as likely as not got a
tinner's shovel across his neck, to save the cost of his
keep. During the past fifty years, the Wesleyans had
made great inroads, and a good proportion of the population had turned its back on the old ways. Even so, the
Preventives were worse hated than the Devil, and seldom
risked themselves near Prussia Cove without a good-sized
escort of the military. Which was why Captain Bolitho felt
himself free to put his goods ashore there without undue
worry. He was an old hand, and I trusted him; still, I
found it difficult to share his confidence.

At about seven o'clock the seas grew steeper and
shorter, and the ship's bow began to plunge hard. I made
my way aft to the wheel, where Bolitho and the mate
still stood. "Getting rough," I said.

"Wind on the tide," said Bolitho. "Lizard's over there."
He pointed into the haze to the north-east. "It's clearing
from the west.

He looked unhappy. Over the port rail, visibility was
improving. Streaks of blue showed between the masses of
cloud, and a wide beam of sun slanted down. The beam
shifted, and a wing of sail shone gold against the sudden
green of the water.

Bolitho had his glass to his eye, bracing himself against
the weather shrouds. He kept it there for a long time. At
last, he folded it with a snap. "Bear off a little," he said
quietly to the helmsman. "Couple of points." The mate
bellowed down the deck to Jacko. Jacko eased sheets, and
Jane and Emily turned her port quarter to the wind. The
bubble of her wake became more urgent. Bolitho snapped
open his glass again and trained it on the white sail.

"Bugger," he said. "You look."

It took me a few seconds to bring the sail into the circle
of waves. When I did, I saw a single mast with a gaff
mainsail, jib, staysail, and flying job. The hull was black
and looked sleek and predatory. There was an ensign at
the gaff-peak and a moustache of white water at the bow.
"What is it?" I said.

"Hornet," said Bolitho. "Revenue cutter."

A black dot climbed to the cutter's crosstrees, broke,
fluttered and stiffened in the wind. "Signal," I said. She
was directly upwind, so I saw the flag end-on.

Bolitho stretched his lips back over his teeth. "Can't

see it," he said Nelsonically. "Get them barrels up on deck."

The west was clearing now, thickening to a hedge of dull orange clouds down on the horizon. The sun was sinking towards them, casting a low golden light over the green and dun Lizard two or three miles to starboard. My throat was dry. "Can they catch us?" I said.

"You'll see," said Bolitho, watching as the two men in the hold rigged a couple of skids to the lee coaming of the hatch and began to reeve a parbuckle through a dead-eye. "Not if we can stay away from 'em till night comes. If the wind holds. If she hasn't got more wind than us."

"That's a lot of ifs," I said.

He grunted and turned away. "We'll be inside the Lizard in half an hour," he said. "Less tide." He looked at the cutter. "She's putting on her topsail. Now you'll see her come on."

During the next twenty minutes the cutter shortened her distance appreciably. When I turned the glass on her I could see the gold letters under her bow and the figures of the men on her decks. The sun went behind the bank of clouds. The light dimmed.

"Any minute now," said Bolitho. "Sooner the better."

A puff of white grew from the cutter's side. A second or so later, the thud of the gun.

"Too early," said Bolitho. "Thinks he's got us."

The wind fell away, and *Jane and Emily* came suddenly on an even keel. Larry, heaving on the parbuckle lines, yelled. There was a rumble and crash and a roar of curses from Bolitho. The smell of brandy wafted aft from the hold.

"Useless buggers," growled Bolitho. "Might as well tip it all overboard, have done with it." I was relieved. If he was so worried about his cargo, he must still expect to deliver it. Catspaws of breeze crept across the water and the sails filled again. "Flukey," muttered Bolitho, looking astern. "Good." The cutter's sails were flapping idly. "We'll get more tide than him," said Bolitho. "Just you exercise yerself by praying the wind don't go altogether."

As the light faded we drifted in an eddy of the ebb, making enough ground to bring us fractionally closer inshore. The distance between us and the cutter stretched, very slightly, until she was about a mile on our port quarter. Ahead the sails of the returning fishing fleet showed

tan against the distant sweep of the hills behind Penzance.
And on we crept, while the sky overhead turned from orange to mauve and faded into deep blue. Venus glittered
in the western sky, and one by one, constellation by constellation, the stars pricked the vault. The barrels were all
up from the hold now, ranged along the lee side beneath
the swinging booms. Their weight tilted us over until the
gunwale came between them and the cutter. When the
wind died, I could hear voices floating across the glassy
water. The air was soft and warm. It seemed utterly incongruous that anyone should be giving chase on a night
like this. Only Bolitho's constant stream of curses at my
side made me believe in it.

"Here we go, and about bloody time," Bolitho said at
last. I looked up. The stars were hazier, and a light breath
of wind fanned my cheek. The sails rumped for a moment, filled. Water gurgled under the counter. "She'll last
till the tide turn, anyway," said Bolitho. "You've got some
luck, Doctor. Five more minutes and they'd have been
alongside in the ship's boat."

Night came down, black and getting blacker. Soon there
was nothing, not a gleam from the water alongside, not
even the glimmer from the binnacle. Only the creak and
rattle of the ship, and the rush of water. Bolitho held the
chart in his mind, tattooed with tide and wind and rock.
He could have swum it, blindfolded. Or so I hoped.

Notwithstanding my confidence in him, I glared into
the darkness aft until I saw phantom cutters coming up
under our stern, heard the gurgle of phantom wakes.

After a long time, Bolitho began hissing quietly between his teeth. I felt an uneasiness coming off him.
"What is it?" I said.

"Half past eleven. We're losing the tide."

I was about to say something when I heard a noise
from behind my back. I was sitting on the rail at the time,
facing inboard. For a second I did not realise what it
meant. Then I tumbled reflexively into the weather scup-
pers and only got my head above the rail in time to see a
tall mass of night slide by the black backdrop. At its rear
end there floated a human mask etched in dim yellow
light. It was so close that I could see the individual hairs
of the beard. I heard the dull running of *Jane and Emily*'s
sheets and steering tackles as we paid off to the north-

ward. Then the shape yawed astern and shrank and vanished.

"Bloody eejit," growled Bolitho. "Keeps his binnacle lamp lit, blind as a bat."

I did not answer. Bolitho's refusal to view the pursuit as anything more than a professional exercise was getting on my nerves.

"Still," said Bolitho. "He's past us now, only he don't know it. And I should say we'm coming up for Praa Sands. Get yer lights ready, Jacko."

The wind on my face felt softer. "It's dropping," I said.

"Would be, with the tide," said Bolitho. "Never you mind."

By the time Jacko's lanterns jerked one above the other into the lee rigging, the wind was hardly more than a stirring. "They'll never think to look behind them," said Bolitho reassuringly. "Would you?"

"No," I said. But then I didn't spend every day of my life pursuing nautical badgers like Bolitho in and out of slots in the coastline.

There was no response to Jacko's signal. A quarter of an hour later, the breeze dropped dead, leaving us drifting. "Again, Jacko," said Bolitho.

"But the cutter," I said. "She'll see us—"

"Never mind that," said Bolitho. "Just keep yer eye out over there." He pointed forward, to where three or four dim points of light swam in the water. Jacko's lights climbed and dipped, leaving me dazzled.

Two hundred yards away, a lantern glowed, occulted, glowed again. It was so close I could hear the clang of the shutter. "There they are," I said, relief bringing the sweat out at my forehead and armpits. "Brilliant, Captain Bolitho. Uncanny."

"Too bloody close." Bolitho sounded apprehensive. "I thought as we was further off. Larry, stand by to cut them kegs loose. Mr. Trevithick, drop the hook, and we'll be on the sand."

There was a bump alongside. I said, "What's that?"

"Larry with the barrels," said Bolitho doubtfully. The anchor ran down with a splash and a roar of cable.

"Please stay exactly where you are," said a harsh voice from the port rail.

There was an instant of dead silence. Then the grate of a lantern-shutter and a dazzle of light. I caught a glimpse of a figure with gold braid at throat and cuffs, with a crowd of others at his back. Then my eyes scurried across to Larry, arm up and frozen, a cutlass glinting in his hand: Bolitho, at the wheel, looking stolidly across the deck, one eyebrow a little raised but otherwise unmoved: Jacko, his moonface white in the lantern's glare, his mouth a black cave of astonishment. There was no movement in it—not until a hatch slammed forward and out of the shadows beyond the firemast came a crouched figure, running with something in his hand that looked like a squat, thick coach-horn.

Suddenly, everything moved at once. Larry's arm came down and I heard the garland of barrels start splashing into the sea as I saw what it was that Trevithick had in his hands and I dropped flat on the deck as the night split in a thunderclap of sound, and the crowd of Preventives wavered and staggered under the tongue of flame that blazed from Trevithick's blunderbuss and the lantern flew into the air, turned over twice, and dropped with a hiss into the water over the side. I heard Larry's cutlass hack again. This time it did not sound like rope. There was a hoarse scream of pain from the night. Then there was a flash and bang, not like the roar of the blunderbuss, but shorter and sharper. Trevithick said, "Gaaah," long and horrible. The Customs voice said, "And the rest of you will swing." I lay where I was, squeezing the sweaty handle of my stick, straining my eyes into the dark. I began to see dim outlines of masts and yards. The cloud was thinning, and a fingernail wisp of moon gleamed through the ice-colours of the sky. There were several dark shapes on the deck. As I watched, one of them turned into a man, smeared itself against the rail and began climbing over. There was a rush of boots on planking and a crunch and short cough. "One," said the harsh voice of the King's man. "Any more?"

I was damned if I was going to be taken. Cringing back in the shadow of the gunwale, I reversed my stick. Footsteps were coming along the deck towards me. "Here's another," said a voice. A pistol exploded forward, and the man turned to look. I heaved myself to my feet, braced myself on the shroud. The cane whirred in the air and I felt the *crunch* as its knob took him in the temple, and saw the half-moons of white as his eyes rolled and he fell straight back on the deck. Bolitho's voice roared, "At 'em!" but I could not see who to get at and I had to stay by the rail, with my short leg, or I would fall over and that would be the end of me.

My heart was hammering in my chest. Moonlight gleamed off blades on the far side of the ship and Bolitho said, *"Urh,"* and someone screamed. Thirty men on the cutter and six of us, one—maybe two—dead. No chance. I jerked my head left and right, straining to see. A dark shape detached itself from the loom of the mainmast and said, "Oh," sounding surprised. Something wide and silvery with moonlight buzzed towards me on the end of its arm and I tried to duck, but I lost my balance and the cutlass-blade caught me just below my crown. I felt flesh tear and the moon swam from between the clouds and into my eyes, swelling in a white glare until I shouted for less light and it shrank into a pinpoint, and the deckplanking smashed into my shoulders and all the lights went out into a big ringing blackness.

VI

I OPENED MY EYES on to a grey fog. Dark as it was, it was too bright, so I tried to close them again. But the lids were like plates of iron, and I found them too heavy. So I lay with them rolled back into my head, listening to the tolling of my skull. The grey mist solidified into a vertical ridge with a depression on either side of it. Faintly, through the tolling, I heard a voice say. "This one's dead." It came from a hole under the vertical ridge. "Get below here," someone said, further away. Hole, ridge and voice receded into the mist. I lay on.

After a while, I found that I could move my fingers. The power spread up my arms to my chest, and down into my legs. The ringing contracted until it was a hard buzzing located at the base of my skull. I could hear

voices in the ship's hold. Above me, the rail cut the night
sky. I clasped my head between my hands to keep it on
my shoulders and sat up. My stick was a pale streak on
the deck at my side. Seeing was more difficult than it
should have been, even in the dark. I could not focus
properly, and when I moved my head the world swung
sickeningly away. With my stick and my good leg and my
free hand I levered myself to my feet until my buttocks
were at the rail. Then I let myself fall backwards. Eight
feet of sea air rushed past my face, and salt water filled
my nose and mouth and eyes. Moving water. I surfaced a
few yards away from the loom of the ship's side, coughing. The top of my head stung like fire.

There were shouts from *Jane and Emily*, and I thought
I saw the blurred shape of heads at her rails as I passed
under her stern, lying diagonally in the water, conscious
only of the pain and the fact that I was being swept away
from the shore.

Soon I could no longer see the ship, only the shine of
pale moonlight on inky water. I was getting very tired,
sinking lower. Goodbye Mary, goodbye Michael, goodbye
everything. Once you got past the chill of it, the sea was
fine stuff. Like silk, or Mary's skin, or Katie's hair, or
Charity's smile. A man could sink into it, float like seaweed, no need to try, no need to think. Sleep, far from
pain.

Water filled my mouth, and I choked, kicking. Something brushed my foot, and again. I straightened my leg
and my head came clear. I was hopping on a hard sand
bottom. Suddenly I was not tired any more. I started to
laugh, until the pain in my head caught me. Then I
started for the shore.

The respite did not last long. Soon the water piled on
my chest grew heavy, and my mind started to wander.
Sometimes I thought that there was a canvas band round
my ribcage and someone was pulling it on a rope, keeping me from the low pale line of the beach ahead. To my
right, lights danced on something black and lumps in the
water. I supposed it was the ship, but I did not care. I
was all alone under the cold sky, shivering so hard that
my gorge rose. At first, I thought it was too far. I would
have to let my knees buckle, sink and drown. My foot
plunged into a gulley. I choked, splashed across, found
dry land again.

The pale line of the beach lifted the horizon. I could hear the splash of wavelets breaking at the water's edge, the suck of pebbles. The water shallowed and I went on hands and knees, my head flopping into the water, dragging painfully up again. And finally the hiss of the waves filled my ears and I could smell the beach-smells, rotten seaweed, bent-grass, sand gritty between the fingers, and I fell forward with my face in it and could move no more.

"Look at the head on him," the voice was saying. It was thick and Cornish and quiet.

"Never you mind that," said another. "Get the coat round him."

Thick cloth passed round my shoulders. It smelt musty, of sweat and tobacco and drink. "Come on," said the voice, as if to an old and exhausted horse. "Walk up now."

"Stick," I said. "My stick."

"Jem's got that," said the voice.

"He's lame," said the other.

"Get an arm, then, and shut yer jaw." The voice was impatient, but not unkind. My arms were dragged over two sets of shoulders and I was hoisted up, dragged on in an attitude of crucifixion away from the hiss and roar of the sea, towards the dark rise of the land. At some point I became unconscious.

I was woken by the sound of singing. I sat up, swilled out my mouth with water from the jug beside me, and put my hand to my head. My fingers touched bandage, not unskilfully applied. I was hungry. The singing went on, loud and clear through the floor which, except for a few boards where I lay was of lath and plaster.

> *"A man who looks on glass*
> *on it may stay his eye*
> *or if he pleases, through it pass*
> *and then the heav'n espy,"*

I looked muzzily around and tried to work out where I was. Not in Heaven; too dark and dusty for that. I doubted very much that they sang hymns in Hell. And His Majesty's jails were constructed of materials more durable than lath, plaster and slate. The words of the hymn turned my attention to the windows, of which there were two, round and set in the triangular ends of the building. I chose the one with the most light, crawled towards it and looked out.

First there was a fenced-off enclosure leading down to a muddy lane. There were long mounds in the enclosure, each with a peg of slate at its head. Beyond the lane there swept up a face of brown moor. On the skyline was a curious building of stone, very tall for its length, with a steeply-pitched roof and a fat chimney blowing whitish-grey smoke. A line of carts moved from the building into a muddy yard with a dirty huddle of sheds. Beyond the moor there were others, brown with outcrops of rock, and a blue chip of sea. It was evening, and the sun sat above the notch and shone straight into my face. There was no glass in the window, and I sat there breathing deep of the clean air that blew off the sea.

The singing finished, and a voice started up in its place. Choosing as its text the lines, *"Wine is a mocker, strong drink is raging; and whosoever is deceived thereby is not wise,"* the voice proceeded to tell the highly-coloured tale of a tinner who, by spending his wages on drink, succeeds in killing his wife by ill-treatment, his children by starvation, and his workmates by his negligence with a fistful of blasting-powder. It was a fine voice, strong and clear, with a hint of broadening about the vowels. Since I had nothing better to do, I settled back to listen, too, and passed a hungry forty-five minutes reflecting bitterly on the ragingness of strong drinks as expressed on its vendors as well as its consumers.

At last the sermon ended in a general Amen, and the band cranked itself up with a tremendous wheezing of serpents and viols into a final, enthusiastic rendering of *Lead us Heav'nly Father Lead us O'er this world's tempestuous sea.* After which there was a scraping of boots on floorboards, and I got back to the window in time to see a flood of hats and bonnets spill out of the chapel door. There were more bonnets than hats, with rusty black skirts below them. The hats were mostly black and round, with a sprinkling of nautical blue caps. There was a brass helmet, too, with a plume. Below it was a pair of broad red shoulders with gold epaulettes. They stood around for a while, and I heard a hum of talk, punctuated with remarks from the voice that had given the sermon. The brass helmet looked ill at ease, reversing through the crowd, nodding and bowing, to get to the black charger that waited in the lane.

When the helmet reached the outer fringes of the crowd, it tilted back. Suddenly I found myself looking straight into a broad, worried face framed in a set of brown whiskers. The eyes focused as I jerked my head away from the window, breathing hard to still the banging of my heart. When I looked again, more cautiously this time, the face was still there. I thought he did not see me, for he turned away, thoughtful, and swung himself into the saddle of his charger. As the sound of hooves died, the crowd by the chapel door strung out towards the gate. Bringing up the rear was a straight-shouldered figure in a black cassock with a leather-bound hymnal under his arm. The sound of voices receded, muffled by the high banks on either side of the lane. Darkness began to spread across the moors.

Footsteps banged on the chapel floor. There was a scraping, and something knocked against a beam by my feet. I looked down. There was a trapdoor, and below it the stamp of boots, growing louder. The hinges of the trapdoor were towards me. The footsteps stopped, and a voice said.

"Doctor?"

I chewed my bottom lip. The silence was so loud it hummed.

"Doctor?" said the voice again. "I'm a friend of Bolitho's."

"Come up," I said quietly. "Very slowly." I reversed the stick in my hand. The trapdoor began to rise. I stood poised to strike, off-balance on my right leg. A head and shoulders came through the opening, indistinct in the half-light. The head was bearded, the shoulders clad in a course woollen jersey.

"Put that thing down," said the head. "Can you walk?"

I dropped the end of the stick and leaned on it, feeling weak. "Yes," I said. "Who are you?"

"Never mind that," said the man. "We must get you out of here."

"Dragoons?"

"If you keep talking you'll find out. Come along of me, my beauty, and make it slippy."

I don't know how I got down that ladder. When I reached the bottom I sat down on the floor and stayed

there, gasping, while the man put the ladder back on its
hooks. Then he said, "You fit to ride?"

"Food," I said.

"Outside."

We left the chapel by a back entrance. Two horses
were tied to the iron railings. Even in the half-darkness,
they looked big and well-fed. My rescuer opened a gate
and boosted me into the saddle. "Quick," he said. He put
something into my hand. "Eat that. Keep close behind."

As we went through the gate, I bit into the half-moon
of pastry. Inside it were vegetables and good lumps of
mutton. Almost immediately I felt better. We skirted a
long slope of bracken. I saw my guide's head turning constantly to the left. "Ride," he said, kicking his horse. I
listened a moment. There was a clatter of hooves and a
jingling of spurs from the direction of the road. The
horse's muscles bunched under me and he leaped forward.
The ground was a blur as we thundered over the brow of
a hill and down onto a track that led northward, into a
cleft of the land roofed with small, wind-flattened trees.
After a while we turned off the track and onto the moors.
My guide reined in his horse to a walk.

"Where are we going?" I said, when I had breath.

"Botallack," said my guide.

"Whose is the horse?"

"Squire's."

"Thank you for this."

"No matter. I seed he had you spotted, after meetin'.
Went back for his squadron. Now, then." He turned his
mount to a steep slope littered with boulders. "Look out.
Old shafts here." The ruins of a pumping-house stood up
gaunt against the sky as we crossed the ridge, empty windows like the eye-sockets of a skull.

We rode for an hour and a half, never slower than a
trot, avoiding the roads and going over moorland paths.
After about ten minutes of it, I ceased to care where we
were going. I drove my knees into the horse's sides,
grabbed handfuls of mane and reins without discrimination, and clung on. The skin of its neck was hot and
sweaty against my beard, and always the great muscles of
the hind legs drove on and on after the crouching figure
of my guide. At one stage we were drumming along a
beach, I know, for I could hear the rush of a small surf.
There were the lights of a fair-sized town ahead. Then we

swung inland and I caught a glimpse of a steep rock crowned with a loom of towers far behind, and we were climbing a small wooded valley where the branches whipped and smacked at my bandaged head. Finally the land sloped down again, a moor criss-crossed with low walls. The moon was up now, and there was no shelter but a few scrubby thorn-trees, tops flattened by gales. And at last a dark row of cottages straggling along a stony lane. My guide said, "Here," and reined up. My horse stopped too, and stood blowing hot wet streams of air from its nostrils. The cottage door opened and yellow light poured out at me. My legs would not move.

"Get off," said the guide. "Hurry."

I kicked my feet out of the stirrups and fell on my face in the road. As I lay flopping like a stranded plaice, my guide shouted, "Giddup!" and he and the two horses clattered back the way we had come. Strong hands took me under the shoulders and carried me into a little room with a fire and shutters painted bright boat blue. They laid me on a bench covered with little cushions worked out of squares of coloured cloth. I let my head roll forward and went to sleep.

I suppose I must still have been suffering from the blow on the head, for I have only very hazy memories of the next few hours. There are a few random moments that stand out. One is of a marmalade cat sitting on a pair of ancient moleskin breeches, and a hand, the nails black and broken and the rough skin seamed with dirt-tattooed scars, moving gently across the ginger fur. There was a voice, too, soft and rough, that went quiet and apprehensive when I asked if there was any news of Bolitho and the others.

After the cat there was the clothing, breeches and a skirt that was coarse and not very well mended, and a pair of enormous boots padded with rags so both my legs looked the same length, though I knew it would make walking impossible and I tried to protest. I remember the feel of scissors and then the sharp edge of a razor scraping at my jaw, and water splashed at me. Someone did something to the bandages on my head and I felt a rim of wool on my neck and brow. Then a woman's voice, hard but not unkindly, saying to me, "And you're pretty enough now," and laughing. There was a face with it, black hair and bright blue eyes and big bones with the flesh gnawed away from the cheeks. It was a good face, but the marmalade cat voice said, "Come on, then, Doctor. Yer name's Arthur Pendean."

"Arthur Pendean," I said. The words tasted of moths, with green grass growing on their wings.

"Right, then," said the cat voice. "Off to bal."

"Where's bal?"

A deep laugh, ending in a cough. A miner's cough, phthisic. "You'll soon enough find out."

Then limping through the night and under the moon with a crowd of other men, the smell of beer and sweat and tobacco, shoving and jostling to the lip of a great hole like hell, with a steam-engine near saying stuff stuff stuff stuff. And the cramp in my right foot jammed into the boot, and the feel of the wind in my smooth face, with a whiff of salt. And then the ladders that dived down and down into the pit, and wet, slippery wood under hands and boots. There were dots of light like fireflies, and when I looked down once I could see a bottomless spiral of them, wheeling. The ladder grew wetter, and my right foot kept cramping and slipping off the rungs. But just as I thought I could go no further there was a ledge, and a candle flickering in a slight draught from a ragged hole in the rock wall.

"Follow," said the marmalade cat voice. Something pressed into my hand. The cane. Wet black rock, with the marks of chisels. The drip of water and the sound of my own breath clattering in my throat. And always the gleam of the candle, held between the first and second knuckles of the fist above the hulking shoulders. The ground grew stonier, with boulders the size of a man's head. The nails in my boots scraped and slid. A corner. Then a dead end.

"Here we be," said the voice. There was an old chair; a bed with a flock mattress evil with fungus; a jug and a bowl; and that was all. "Not what you're used to," he said. "But it'll serve a few days." He shrugged, and his pack hit the floor. "Two dozen candles, so use 'em careful. Bread, cold meat, figgies. Bottle of eye-water agin the cold, and by Jeeze you'm going to need it. Flint, steel, blankets. All well?"

"All well," I said, trying to stop my teeth chattering. "Thank you."

"Good. I hopes you'll have company soon. I'll be off, then." He stuck his candle in a niche in the rock, lit an-

other from the flame. Then he turned, rounded the corner.
The last I knew of him was the crunch of his boots and
his dry cough ringing off into silence.

I tipped the mattress of the bed, rolled myself in four
blankets, and lay down on the criss-cross cording. It was
uncomfortable, but at least it was dry. The silence was not
as complete as I had thought. There was the rush of water
from somewhere close by, and much further away a tiny
clink, like a drop of rain falling on a bell. The candle gut-
tered and went out, but I made no move to light another.
The blackness pressed on my eyeballs; I could hardly tell
whether my eyes were open or shut. Red shadows of
blood glided in the dark.

I suppose I might have slept. Certainly I was tired
enough. Whatever the case, whether it was a dream or a
delusion or a derangement of the mind brought on by the
blow to the head, I sometimes found myself talking aloud.
First Charity was there, Little John standing behind her
with a protective hand on her shoulder. "I'm sorry," I was
saying to her. "Perhaps you wouldn't approve . . . but you
see it was for the best. Hope, you know. We must have
hope." ·

Charity gave me her saint's smile. "That's all right,"
she said. "You tried to help. But my hope is in the Lord."

Little John did not agree. "Lot dead," he said. "All for
no result. Might as well have wrecked 'em."

"It's a new way," I said. "If at first you don't succeed. . . ."

"A good way," said Charity, soothing as a mother.

"Quiet," said Little John. Charity disappeared. "You
failed. You tried to make the Islands soft. It is the Lord
that provides. Not man. You tried to steer us from our
duty. You are cast out."

His face was becoming hazy and flat, more and more
like a cheap chromolithograph of Jehovah. "Into outer
darkness, where there shall be weeping and gnashing of
teeth," said the picture in Little John's voice. "There is no
place for you in Eden." The picture went out.

A slender hand came out of the darkness and brushed a
section of it back, and I realised that what had looked like
empty space was Mary's hair. Her skin was like roses and
ivory. "Come back," she said, turning towards me. "Pay
no heed to John. Try or not try, it makes no difference.
Scilly wants you. *I* want you." She faded, leaving me in

the dark, listening for the jingle of dragoons in the tunnel.

After a while I lit a candle, ate some leather bread and took a swig of the brandy. My head was aching less, but as if in compensation my thoughts were black and miserable. The smuggling expedition had failed; Nicholas Power, Saviour of the off-islands, had lost Bolitho's ship, God knew how many lives, and all his self-respect. Not to mention the woman he loved. And by playing at saviours, I had thrown away any hope the islanders might have had to living through the winter on anything better than sea beef.

The candle went out. I left it for what I thought was an hour, then lit another. I had three left when the man with the voice came next, a crunch of boots and a small, tight cough in the dark. He seemed in a hurry, and I only had time to ask him where I was.

"Botallack," he said.

"Where?"

"Botallack mine. Twenty fathom level."

"I had never heard of the place. "And what's happening?" I said. "Bolitho—"

"No time for that," said the tinner. "You'll find out ere long, God willing."

Now that I was on the map, even if it was a map I had never seen, the waiting was more difficult. My brain, recovering from the blow, was returning to its old habits, and time flapped about me like a vulture, tearing at my nerves. I lay hearing the steady roar of the subterranean waters and the elfin clink of distant picks on stone. And five candles after the tinner had left me, a gnawing like a titan grinding his teeth. That I could not understand.

At the eleventh candle, I heard the distant clatter of many feet in the passage. I quickly nipped the wick, lifted my stick, and shoved myself back into a hollow in the rock just on the blind side of the sharp corner. Light splashed on the weeping stones, and I held my breath. I heard a voice say, 'Hold him steady, there." It was Bolitho's. I lowered my stick and stepped out into the passage.

"Good evening," I said. "I didn't expect to see you so soon."

"The feeling's mutual, and it's morning," said Bolitho. "Give us a hand, here."

There was a body slung over his shoulders. I did not

like to think of him on those slippery ladders above the abyss. The tinner kindled a lantern, and the light improved to such an extent that it made me squint. We laid the body on the bed, and I began my examination. It was Jacko. Bolitho and Box gathered at my side as I tore his neckcloth away. The right-hand side of it was stiff with dry blood. "Where's Trevithick?" I said. "And Larry?"

"Porthleven churchyard," said Bolitho curtly.

It seemed likely that Jacko was headed in the same direction. His shoulder looked as if an ill-intentioned butcher had set about him with a cleaver. The cut went down through the shoulder muscle, clean through the collarbone and had notched the top rib. The whole business was clogged with dried blood, and there was a redness and a heat beginning that boded ill. "Needles. Catgut. Bandages. Opium," I said.

"Joby?" said Bolitho to the tinner.

"Can't get none of that but the needles," said Joby.

"Bring 'em," I said. "And some pack-thread." He nodded, and crunched off into the dark.

"How did he get like that?" I said.

My sense of the probable had been stretched out of shape by my confinement in the dark. Until that moment it had seemed perfectly natural that *Jane and Emily's* crew should arrive in this hole, even if I had last seen them firmly in the grip of His Majesty's Preventive Service.

"All very unfortunate," said Bolitho with great philosophy. "You were still there when pore Trevithick loosed off with his deadly weapon. Not prudent, I fear, seeing as how Larry put the wet goods over the side a second after. Still, what's done is done. Well, they cut Trevithick down. And then they come on us and you went over the side, and me shouting to give up gentle, like, not knowing there was two Preventives stiff and stark and another four picking old nails from Trevithick's hooter out of their hides. So they was rather excited, particular at Jacko and Larry, I don't know why. So they chops 'em down, but they only does half a job on Jacko. Then they buttons us in the cabin and goes over the ships and finds nothing but a few bust staves and a smell, the which," he frowned, "was bloody careless, not to speak ill of the dead. And when the tide takes her off the ground they sails her into Penzance, claps us in a closed coach, rousts out a milingterry escort, and puts us off to Bodmin to wait for the assizes, hempen neckwear guaranteed." He paused, significantly.

"Why aren't you in Bodmin?"

Bolitho raised his left forefinger and his right hand with the black bottle. He wiped his lips, slow and deliberate. Then he proceeded, sighing fumes.

"Well. The Preventives had us, but they didn't have the wet goods, what they was anxious to secure. So they gets out their boats and their lanterns and they starts looking down the tide for it. Which hullaballoo nacherly attracts the attention of a few tinners and Prussia Cove men as happens to be on the same errand. And what with one thing and another, them being sharp lads, the barrels come ashore; they take possession, and someone knocks an end in. Twenty times a hundred and forty," he said, counting on his fingers. "Three thousand gallon, near enough. Allowing for spillage and a barrel or two in the right place, call it two. Well, word got round and they drank the lot. And by the time we was rumblin' up in that carriage, there was the better part of a thousand tinners, fighting drunk, between us and the rest of the Bodmin road. Bugger me, I'm glad I weren't in that milingterry escort." He laughed uproariously, expansive with drink and liberty. "They're a law to themselves, these minery boys. The millingterry took off for the town like scalded cats, and the tinners brung us down here. And a great pleasure it is to see you again, Doctor, all safe and secure." He cocked an ear. "Wild old night out there."

The grating and grinding was louder now, continuous.

"What is that noise?"

"It's the boulders on the sea's bottom," said Bolitho. "'S only twenty feet above our head. Oh, very safe we are here."

"Very," I said.

"So what happened to you?" said Bolitho.

I told him, and at the end he clucked appreciatively. "Good, good, Doctor. Good ride, that. Fifteen mile if it's an inch. You were lucky though. Luck of the devil, you have."

"Well," I said. "Now we've come this far, what next?"

"I was talking to Joby Pembarra, as brought us down here. He was saying as him and another Botallack man was taking passage to America on the *Corinthian,* as was coming down from Bristol any day now."

"America?" I said. "What the hell are you talking about?"

Bolitho shrugged. "No more ship," he said. "Can't stay here, after this. And Joby was saying as they've found gold in Carolina or some such place, and he thought he'd have a dig there. Be better than going to bal every day for no wage. And they're hard men, these Botallack boys. They'll do well."

"Leave for America?" I could not seem to understand.

"It's that or Bodmin gallows or Botany Bay," said Bolitho. "You'd best come."

"But I must get back to Scilly," I said.

"Only thing you'll do is get yourself took," he said. "Best forget about it. Them on Tresco can look after theirselves."

"And so can I," I said, trying to think of my responsibilities but succeeding only in thinking of Mary. "I'll get back. Nobody need know. A disguise."

"Disguise nothing," said Bolitho. "You know the size of that place. Every bugger on the islands'd know who and and where you was in half a month. We need men like you in Carolina."

"I'm going back," I said.

"Then you're a bloody fool," said Bolitho, and pulled the blanket over his grizzled head and began to snore.

When Pembarra returned with more food and candles, I drew him aside. "Can you get me out of here?" I said.

"If you want to leave, we'll not stop thee."

"Can you get me some clothes?"

"Clothes. I can try."

"And a razor?" I passed my hand over the black stubble on my jaw.

He nodded and turned away, coughing.

In the periods of darkness and light that followed I sat thinking, listening to the stones grinding. Uppermost in my mind was the crazy idea that if I got back to Tresco, matters would work themselves out. I could say that I had been ill, in my house. Or with Mary. She would never give me away. There would have been telescopes trained from the Preventive cutter, of course, but that had been when I still had the beard. Without the beard, I would be easily recognised by anyone who had known me in Ireland. But Ireland seemed a lifetime away.

When Joby came back he had a razor and a black bundle. "Compliments of Squire Trengwainton," he said. "He said I was to tell you you was a damned fool." He obviously agreed.

I thanked him, and unwrapped. There was a long black cassock, a shovel hat, a plain silver cross on a chain and a pair of blue-tinted spectacles. Joby, for the first time since I had met him, grinned. "Squire said he hoped as you'd be a better catholic than the first man as wore it," he said. "There'll be a horse for you above. I'll come for thee at crouste."

Crouste, I discovered from a now wakeful Bolitho after he had gone, was the tinners' mid-shift meal. I took advantage of the wait to try on my new garments, much to Boz's delight. He even stopped playing patience to offer advice on the correct behaviour of a bloody Papist taking a packet-ride. The soutane fitted well. The hat was rather too big, the better to cover the bandages. Then I checked Jacko's stitches and strapped up his arm again. The wound's lips were red and inflamed, and there was a discharge of yellowish-green matter. It might be cleaning itself by healthy suppuration; then again, it might not. Only time would tell.

When the boots and the cough sounded again in the passage, I made my farewells to Bolitho and his men, slung the bundle over my shoulders and turned to go.

"You're a fool," said Bolitho. "I'll write, though. Care of Bodmin Jail."

"Tresco, Scilly," I said. "Care of Mary Prideaux."

"Hopes you," he said.

"Quick," growled Pembarra from further down the passage.

It was worse going up the shaft than it had been coming down. High above, there was a tiny circle of starlit sky that grew with dreadful slowness. I had to pause more and more frequently to catch my breath, and when I reached the top I fell down on the ground and lay gasping in my sweat, deaf to Joby's curses.

He pulled me up and led me past the pumping-house to a long shed. It was very dark inside. There was straw on the floor, and a smell of manure and the breathing and shifting of stalled horses. I pulled on the soutane, looped the cross over my head and settled the hat on my bandages. Joby went into the dark and returned, leading a horse. He pointed into the sky. "Keep after Orion's belt.

Stay on the high road. It'll take you straight to Penzance. Packet leaves the quay at nine o'clock. You've got an hour till dawn. If you get lost, follow the daylight."

"I don't know how to thank you," I said.

"That's all right." He boosted me up into the saddle. "Leave the horse at Pearce's Union hotel. They'll know what to do with it. Good luck, now."

I heard his dry cough as he trudged back towards the shaft. I dug my miner's boots into the horse's ribs. The steam-engine panted for a while over the roar of the waves. Then it grew fainter, and I rode on down the high-banked lane towards the lightening eastern sky.

After I had gone up for my examination, which I passed without difficulty or brilliance, I stayed on with Duquesne. It was not yet time for me to set up in practice in my own right, and Duquesne was feeling his age; so we came to an arrangement, whereby I remained with him nominally as his assistant but actually as his partner in all but title. Most young doctors in my position would have gone on the Grand Tour of the hospitals of Europe; I decided against this course for two reasons. First, I was attending Doctor Macartney's Surgery lectures; and second, there was Mercy Hall.

I was walking down Lower Mount Street one day, returning from the hospital, when a stout gentleman in front of me stumbled and fell to the pavement. When I reached him, I saw he was Doctor Murdoch, a Scottish physician whose promptness with a bill and antiquated technique had made him one of Duquesne's *bêtes noires*. His face was dark mauve, and his breathing stertorous. I enlisted the aid of a couple of beggars and had him conveyed the short distance to Duquesne's house in Merrion Square.

Duquesne was away taking the Leixlip waters, by which he swore, and so it was left to me to attend to Doctor Murdoch. I laid him on the consulting-room couch and applied restorative measures appropriate to an apoplectic seizure. After a couple of hours the breathing eased, and the congested appearance of his face and neck improved. I had him carried upstairs to a bedroom, sent a man to the address on his card, and waited for consciousness to return.

When his eyes opened I told him where he was, and said, "You must rest quiet, Doctor Murdoch."

He looked at me, very pale now, and said, "An apoplexy. By heaven you're Duquesne's boy." He struggled up on the pillows, running his hands over his face and neck. "The leeches," he said hoarsely. "Where are the leeches?"

"We did not exhibit the leeches," I said. "A little Cayenne pepper and the clyster of Epsom salts and caster oil, with senna. Also a mustard plaster for the feet. You are proceeding very nicely."

"You took no blood? Blast you, boy—"

"You will please lie quiet," I said. "There is nothing to be gained by struggling, and much to be lost." I wondered if I should exhibit the tartar emetic, as recommended in such cases. "Perhaps I might call on your own practitioner?"

He nodded, with the look of a severely frightened man. I sent out for his doctor, placed the ice-bag on his bald head, and withdrew, realising that I might be in for trouble. So I left Doctor Murdoch to the tender mercies of his own doctor, and in a couple of days he was judged well enough to be removed from the house.

About a week later, I received a furious letter from Murdoch, blackguarding me for criminally masquerading as a qualified physician and failing to administer correct treatment. He would, he said, be taking the matter up with the College of Physicians, and it would not assist me in my pursuit of a licence to practise.

I showed the letter to Duquesne, now returned. He put his finger to his lip and said, "H'm. I see. Perhaps you should have left him to die." He laughed his light laugh. "By now you should have learned that with men like this . . . *charcutier* . . . logic means not much, in life or practice. He has friends at the College, you know. I think I must take myself off. And I think I shall send him a bill, no? Such ingratitude. Most certainly you saved his life." Flapping his hands, he clacked out of the room on his preposterous heels. He must have whispered in the right ears, however, for I heard nothing more about the incident until next time I managed to get away to dine with Michael.

As the port went round, Michael said, "I hear you've been taking some eminent lives in your hands."

"If you mean Murdoch, I'd hardly call him eminent."

"Sure he's a terrible old carpenter. But they're the ones who pull the strings, boy."

"You think I should have let him die?"

"You did the first thing that came into your head again. Deliberation, Nick. That's the word."

"Not if it means a corpse on the streets."

"Ah, you're all heart," said Michael. "But if you don't harden yourself up a bit, you're going to walk into trouble."

I was becoming rather weary of Michael's diatribes on my fervent nature. Ambition was bringing out the worst in him nowadays. Away from the law, he was the same old Michael; but his business was beginning to creep into his private life. So I sighed and drank off my glass and said, "I'll look after myself."

He shook his head. "You don't know the meaning of it." Then he changed the subject.

By the time I arrived on the hills behind Penzance it was full daylight. The town was a grey tangle of roofs below me. Wisps of smoke rose from newly-kindled breakfast fires, and in the harbour fishing boats were crawling seaward under oars, their tan sails furled in the morning calm. The air was cool, with a remnant of the night's dew, and the sun struck a dazzle of light from the sea past St. Michael's Mount. On the outskirts of the town a young man of seedy aspect was leaning against a cottage gatepost.

"How would you like to earn a shilling?" I said. "My son?" I added hastily, remembering my disguise.

He straightened up eagerly, and put out his hand.

"I wish to take joy in God's good morning," I said, hoping I was not overdoing it. "Would you be so good as to take the horse to Pearce's?"

He nodded furiously, making a gargling noise in his throat. Dumb. An excellent omen. I grinned at him in a saintly manner, gave him a shilling from my purse, and watched him lead the horse down the hill into the town. Then, after a discreet interval, I hobbled after him. Walking soon became very painful. But Roman Catholic priests did not normally take their constitutionals on high-mettled hunters. Whatever else Squire Trengwainton might be, there were two things that could be said for him: he looked after his friends well, and he was a fine judge of horse-flesh. I tried to distract myself with gratitude as the houses rose on either side of me, solid buildings of dressed stone with fresh-painted doors and housemaids sweeping steps.

By the Town Hall I caught sight of myself in a window. With my limp and my soutane and the blue spectacles, I was a figure from the murkiest deeps of the Calvinist conscience. The town clock stood at half-past seven, so I went into a respectable-looking inn and was about to order beef and bread when I remembered it was Friday and changed quickly to mackerel. At half past eight I paid my reckoning and hobbled out into the street.

The town was bustling, and in the crowds pushing and jostling in the main street I was well camouflaged. I asked my way of a man who looked at me once, then looked away as though he thought I would have him cursed. There were fewer people on the road to the quays, but more wheeled traffic, and I got a ride on the tail of a cart. We clattered into a cloud of tar and rotten fish and drains lying over a grimy beach covered with boats' bones and refuse and gulls. A detachment of militia rattled up the road; one or two of the blank soldiers' faces passed over me, but they did not register. The grey town swallowed the red coats. My confidence began to grow.

The carter put me off at the inshore end of the quay. The packet was a tubby cutter economically painted with black tar. At her transom gold letters said *Lord Wellington, Scilly*, but for all that she looked like a fat charwoman at a taproom bar. Gulls screamed and fought over the side. I paid a polite, sun-burned sailor for the passage. He looked surprised at my lack of baggage and led me down to the passengers' cabin, an apartment jammed with humanity and an atmosphere compounded of old vomit, older sweat, burnt cabbage and fear. I decided I would sit on deck, which had the added advantage of a commanding view of the shore.

My confidence was running pretty high, but still I swept the coast road with my eye, looking for the blotch of red that would stain the tall, grey houses and spires under the blue morning sky. Nothing. A coach and four rumbled along as the town clock struck nine. A nautical gentleman paced impatiently abaft the ship's wheel, looking first at his watch, then at the coach. *Penzance Mail* was written in a flourish of scrollwork on the door. The coachman was asleep, a bundle of greyish overcoats on the box, but the horses drew up with the precision of long habit. A sailor hoisted the mailbag out of the box, gave the horses a cut with the whip and laughed as he cast off the shorelines, and the coachee woke and bellowed muzzily at his leaders, prancing too close to the edge of the pier. The wind cracked into the headsail and the bow came away from the bollards and began to inch forward towards the blue line beyond the pierhead.

The man who had climbed out of the *Mail* jumped neatly down from the quay. He went to the cabin door, looked inside, wrinkled his nose and came back on deck. He was slim with a very young face, dressed in a square-cut brown coat with brass buttons. He tugged at the skirts of the coat as he strode up the companionway, a curiously military gesture. There was something military in the bow he gave me, too, stiff-backed and formal. Then he turned and walked aft and began talking to a man with a peaked cap, a blue pea-jacket and a gift for unruffled profanity who must, I supposed, be the captain. I kept my eyes straight ahead.

The quays fell away, and Mount's Bay opened up to leeward. My glasses deepened the sea's blue and turned the distant sprawl of the Lizard peninsula dull purple. It was difficult to believe that there I had been half-scalped with a cutlass and washed ashore in the murderous dark. Difficult, that is, until I thought about the man with the military habits; then it came all too easy.

There were ships in the harbour beyond the quay, mostly coasting vessels. We passed a coal barge black with soot, an iron-ship from South Shields red with rust, and a Baltic timber-ship reeking of raw turpentine. The bigger vessels lay on the outside of the pack, fat and serene in the clear morning air. Fishing-boats crawled between them, sails the colour of dried blood in the sun. I watched all this idly, preoccupied with my thoughts. The Land's End peninsula stretched away to starboard, rugged with dark granite. A fishing-boat was ploughing the blue water just off the rocks. As we came near I saw a solid pair of shoulders with an iron-grey head set dead centre. *Lucinda, St. Ives,* said the boat's bow. I did not recognise the man at the tiller, but Boz was there and Jacko, his face the colour of my clerical collar, and the tin-miner and another man. For a moment my eyes met Bolitho's. The grizzled head tilted imperceptibly; then they had passed us. As we went up for the Rundle Stone, I saw the fishing-boat go alongside the fattest and most workmanlike of the merchantment, a brig. Then we passed behind a buttress of cliff.

The *Lord Wellington*'s bow lifted and dived, leaving me momentarily weightless. The military-looking man had been walking forward. He stopped, and I saw that the skin under his eyes was greenish-white. The waves were big and short out here, whipped by the wind against the tide, and they gave the ship an ugly corkscrew motion. The merchantman would be the *Corinthian*. In weather like this, she would not be long sailing.

The shoulders of the brown coat bent over the rail and heaved. After a while, their owner staggered back across the deck and sat down on the cabin roof. "Ooooh," he groaned. Then he saw me and gave a tight smile, embarrassed. "Up all night in that damned coach," he said. There is usually a reason for being seasick that has nothing to do with the sea.

I nodded at him, smiling consolingly. "Indeed," I said. His voice had a hint of Irish in it. Connaught.

"Is this your first visit to Scilly?"

"Yes," I said. He was looking at me as if he thought I could save his soul. The colour of his face certainly gave him the appearance of being not long for this life. I wished I had a breviary; but Squire Trengwainton's disguises box had not run to one.

"And mine," he said. "You don't mind if I talk, do you? It takes one's mind off . . . things."

I spread my hands and smiled again, wishing he would fall overboard.

"I come from Ireland," he said. "The West. Galway. They say Scilly's quite like Galway. I hope not."

"Oh," I said. "Have you been in England long?"

"Five years." I relaxed a little. "Had to come to a civilised country. Thought I'd be in London. And where do I land? Chasing more damned peasants." The *Lord Wellington* rolled steeply, and he lurched to the rail. When he came back, his voice was noticeably weaker. "Think I'm going to die."

"An indisposition," I said.

"S'all right for you," he said. "You don't know what it's like."

"There are always the consolations of religion," I said smugly.

"Yes," he said. "I suppose so."

"But you will be a Protestant," I said.

"I certainly will," he said, becoming aggressive. "The Pope's all right for peasants. But God, how I hate peasants." He was as young as he looked, I realised.

"We are all God's children," I said stiffly.

"Balderdash," he said. "Peasants are animals. Living in their disgusting cabins with their pigs and their potatoes, speaking a barbarous language, breeding like rats in a tannery. Weeping about the hard times one minute and burning ricks the next. They're the same everywhere."

"How interesting," I said. Once, I had thought like that. "I am afraid I cannot agree."

He was not listening. "Chasing them up hill and down dale because they're too damned sly to pay His Majesty's duties." He buried his face in his hands. "It's no kind of life for a soldier."

"You are a soldier?" I said.

He laughed bitterly. "Not even that. I came to England to buy a commission in a decent regiment. But no, they said, no more bankrupt Irish. So I had to join the Customs instead."

"The Customs," I said tightly. "That is useful work."

"Useful? They don't pay any heed. They carry on with their smuggling as if we weren't there. I'd rather be getting myself shot in the back in Galway than trying to get the truth out of this rabble." He groaned, in an ecstasy of self-pity. "It's no kind of life for a gentleman."

"We all have our cross to bear."

"Yes," he said. "And what lightens it now is that I am going to make an arrest. For the first time in six months. An arrest."

"At Scilly?" I said mildly, wondering if he could hear the hammering of my heart under the silver cross on my chest. "Surely they have Preventive officers of their own?"

"But the goods came ashore at Prussia Cove," said the Customs man. "I'm to organise the search."

"I don't understand," I said. "If the contraband is in Cornwall, what good will it do to look for it at Scilly?"

He looked suddenly very young, and laid a finger on the greenish skin beside his nose. "Information," he said. "There's a damned murdering insurrectionist doctor fellow at Scilly who's been stirring up the devil. Smuggling's only part of it. Some peasant with more sense than the rest sent us a little chirrup about it." He grinned smugly. Then his cheeks bulged and he dived for the rail.

I sat rigid, looking out at the wide blue sea. Panic tugged at my throat. Suddenly I wished I had been on that fishing boat with Bolitho and the rest of them, bound for the goldfields.

The Customs man came back and sat limply down. He was silent for some time, eyes glassy and fixed on the planking between his feet. At last he said, "Look here, Father, I told you too much. You won't let it any further? As a fellow-countryman. Seal of the confessional, and so on." He brightened. "I say. You look jolly pale. Feeling a bit low, too?"

"Only a little," I said. "Only a little."

We fell into a silence that lasted a very long time. The thoughts whirred in my head like a mill-wheel. No escape to America. No refuge in the islands. Mainland buzzing with pursuit. There was only one ray of hope, and that dim. Mary. If I could get to her, she might hide me until I could get a ship out.

Late evening was deepening into dusk as the *Lord Wellington* sagged down St. Mary's Sound, went about and began to beat up for the Pool. She came alongside the ramshackle quay to the usual chorus of, "What news from England?" A seaman began selling newspapers even before the warps were on the bollards. Nobody in the crowd noticed me but one small boy, who tugged at my cassock and implored me to stay in his mother's lodging-house, clean, sweet and not a bug in the place. I shook my head and limped into Hugh Town. I followed the coast round past the slipways of Porth Mellon and Porthloo, where half-built ships lay like the rib cages of smashed giants. I came at last to Carn Morval, and sat down on a soft cushion of sea-pinks. Tresco was a dim lump across a mile of water. A gig moved down-channel, bound to put a pilot on a ship to the southward.

Who would have tipped off the Preventives? Little John? But according to him, my place was beside Charity Pender. Perhaps my interference had got the better of his sense of duty. It seemed unlikely. But who else could it have been?

There were a couple of lights showing on Abbey Hill.

For nine months, Tresco had been a haven. Now it was a trap.

Finally, I got up, stripped off hat, cross and cassock, jammed them in a cleft in the rocks. I knew the Scillonian mind well enough to be sure that when the clothes were found they would not be reported; the metal of the cross would see to that. Then, my leg stiff with the dew, I started down for Porthloo in my shirt and breeches. There was a punt riding at anchor just beyond the low water mark. I silently apologized to the owner, hauled in the tripping-line, and began to pull towards Tresco.

When the bow hit the beach I shipped oars and walked up towards Great Rocks, slipping in the soft sand of the dunes. As I came to the lip of the hollow where Mary had her house I paused, leaning heavily on my stick. A dim light glowed in the deep-set windows. Swallowing, I walked into the dell and knocked softly on the door.

She opened it, and stood looking at me for a moment, her face in black shadow. Then she stepped back and said, "Come in." She was wearing a long dark shift with panels of bright stuff. In the middle of the room stood the embroidery frame. As she threw the cover over it, I thought that the figure representing me was smaller than before.

"What is it?" she said as I ate bread and cheese. "There's trouble. Isn't there?"

"Yes," I said, and told her what had happened.

When I had finished she sat very still, the lids low over her eyes. I stared at her, looking for a hint of feeling. Her face was still as marble. At last she said, "I'll hide you."

"Yes," I said, feeling indebted and hating it.

"I hoped it might be . . . different."

I took her hand. It was limp. "It still could be," I said. "If it's dangerous for me, it'll be dangerous for you."

She pulled her hand away. "That's not necessarily true."

"Mary, listen to me. Someone informed on me. Someone on the island is out to get me. And in the process they've made sure that you all starve this winter. There's only one person I know who'd kill the whole island as long as I go with it. The man of principle. Little John."

She shook her head. "You've got it wrong. You like to think of yourself as the last hope. It's not in nature.

There's been hard winters here for ten thousand years, and people have lived through them. Not by putting all their eggs in one basket, though."

"What do you mean?"

"I mean that there are a lot of people who like to see a man happy. And if it makes you happy to think you're the saviour of the off-islands, they'll go a long way to give you that impression. Particularly if there's a chance they'll benefit by the results."

"So they gave me the last of their potatoes to throw away?"

"There's more places to keep potatoes than in a shed. And there's more ways to make money than selling potatoes."

"You'd go back to wrecking?"

"You don't stay alive by making resolutions. Not here."

"You'd stay? Even after the time we spent together?"

"No," she said. Her eyes were uncertain. "I don't think so."

Hope bloomed. "Think carefully. It won't be easy. You'll be stepping outside the law."

"You think that matters?" she said angrily. "I've never been inside it."

"So you'll come."

"Yes." She would not look me in the eye.

"Are you humouring me? Like the rest of them?"

"I don't know," she said. "I just don't know. I can't tell."

"Decide."

Her eyes came up and swamped me. "Oh God," she said. "God but I love you, Nick." There were tears running down her face.

I stood up. "So you'll come?"

She pushed the hair back from her face and drew a long, shuddering breath. "Yes," she said. "Now come to bed, my darling. You've been too long gone."

Someone was banging on the door. "Whazzat?" I said. My mouth tasted horrible, and every joint in me ached.

"Get out," said Mary quietly. "Get to the back of the house while I see who it is."

I forced my legs into my breeches. Memory returned like a bucket of icy water. Mary lit a candle and shuffled over to the door. I waited, half-covered by the curtain. Mary opened up. Then she said, "Oh?" sounding surprised.

There was the rumble of a man's voice. I stepped out from behind the curtain as I recognised it, walked forward into the dull glow of the banked-up fire. Little John Woodcock came in.

He did not look at all surprised to see me. "You're here," he said. "Bolitho said you would be. I've just now come off the *Corinthian*. You know the ship I mean?"

I nodded.

"She's anchored in St. Mary's Roads. Bolitho's man, Jacko, took a turn for the worse. Captain didn't like to get the St. Mary's surgeon to him, and there ain't none on the ship. Said would you go."

"Of course I will," I said. But should I stay, once aboard?

Mary was thinking along the same lines. "What time can we expect the Preventives, John?"

"First thing in the morning. With a fine toothcomb. There's some young rip over from the mainland to put a bit of ginger in 'em. I'd be off the island if I were you, Doctor."

"You would."

"Go now," said Mary. "I'll come out at dawn."

"You will?" I said, not believing my ears. She gave me that enigmatic smile. Then she came over and I kissed her long and hard.

At last she said, "You'd better be off."

I turned back in the doorway. "Until tomorrow," I said. Little John and I walked down to Carn Near, and he rowed me out to where the *Corinthian* lay anchored.

I said, "Judas."

He smiled. "You been very awkward, Doctor."

"You must feel pretty big."

"I have done my duty," he said. "I shall continue so to do."

"Continue to kill innocent folk. Revenuers and Bolitho's men. Dead because of you."

"The mills of God," said John. He pulled away. I went up the Jacob's ladder. A man blocked my way at the top. "Who are you?" he said.

"Doctor."

"Right you are." He stood aside. As I passed I saw that

he carried a musket. There was a pair of pistols stuck in
his belt, and a cutlass at his hip.

Bolitho was below, in what had once been the main
hold. Two new decks had left a mere five feet of headroom between the hatch and the waist. It was lit with
dour lanterns, and by their light I saw that the bulkheads
were lined with bunks. There was a smell of too many
people in too small a space, and the deck was covered
with boxes and bundles. Somewhere a child was crying, a
constant, keening wail.

"Glad to see you hale and hearty," said Bolitho, grinning. "Poor old Jacko's been took bad." He led through
a labyrinth of household goods and sheaves of picks and
shovels, and strange wood and iron contrivances to the
forward bulkhead. It was lined with bunks like all the
others. Boz was sitting at a makeshift table of planks,
playing his inevitable game of patience. He looked up as
we came into the light of the lantern, and said, "Morning,
Doctor," and went back to his cards.

Jacko was lying under a pile of blankets in a bottom
bunk. His moon face was slick and pasty, his forehead
burning. When I took off the bandages they were stiff
with the discharge from his wound. The wound itself was
running still, hot and puffy. When I put my fingers to the
inflamed flesh his eyes flew open and he screamed
hoarsely. He did not recognise me; I do not think he
knew where he was.

As I cleaned away the discharge Bolitho said, "How
are matters with you?"

"Not good," I said. "In fact, damned sticky. I was wondering—"

"You want to come?"

"There's a woman."

Bolitho grinned at me. "There always is," he said.
"And welcome. I took the liberty of discussing it with the
men on the passage. What we concluded was that if you
wanted to be part of the enterprise, we'd write you in for
a share for joining. You'd be useful to us."

"A share in what?" I said.

"New Botallack," said Bolitho.

"What the hell's New Botallack?"

"Don't know," said Bolitho. "But we'll be looking for
gold. We sail at first light."

It was still dark when the boat from Tresco came along-

side, but the sky was greying to the east. I finished doing
what I could for Jacko and came up from the smelly
cabin to find the rigging alive with seamen unfurling the
sails to the light, southerly breeze. The clacking of the
capstan was loud from the bow as we came over the anchor. A sailor ran panting into the waist and said, "You
the doctor?"

I admitted it. He said, "Captain's compliments and will
you step aft?" I cast a look at Mary, coming up through
the entry-port wrapped against the morning chill in a dark
hooded cloak. I wanted to be with her. But there would
be time enough for that.

The captain was sitting in the great cabin, narrow-
shouldered against the stern windows, talking to a fat man
in a pea-jacket whom I supposed was the mate. He did
not look at me until he had finished giving his instructions. When the mate had left, he jerked his head at me
and said, "Doctor. Good. Captain Barlow."

"Nicholas Power, at your service." It felt good to use
my right name again.

"You'll work your passage. Medicine chest in your
cabin." He beetled across the deck, a small stringy figure
exuding energy like a galvanic engine. "Ass of a surgeon
deserted to Bath. Drunk." He handed me a key. "Get to
it, now. Two families on the lower deck got the flux. Can't
have it spread. See to it."

"Aye, aye, sir."

As I went on deck, the *Corinthian* was moving down
the channel under main and fore-courses and topsails.
The southern tip of Samson lay seven or eight cables to
starboard. Little John was standing by the helmsman,
huge and solid. The wind had the smell of freedom. At
that moment, I was almost grateful to the man. In the
waist the breeze caught Mary's cloak, billowing, making
her look bigger than I remembered her.

"Look aft," said Little John's voice from the poop.

Three boats were moving across the water from St.
Mary's, heaving for Tresco. Even at this distance I could
see they were full of men. John said something to the
helmsman and came down the ladder. "Here," he said.
"Take a look."

I raised the glass on the boats. There was a shimmer of
steel from the fixed bayonets bristling up from the
thwarts. In the stern of the foremost boat two men were

standing. One of them was dressed in a faded blue uniform coat. Maltby. Talking to him earnestly, waving his hands, was the youth I had watched heaving yesterday's breakfast into the Atlantic from the rail of the *Lord Wellington*. "Revenue," I said. "I hope you're proud."

"I did the necessary," said John. "You couldn't go back now. Not even if you wanted to."

"Get to it, I said!" roared the captain's voice from the break of the poop.

I went to the cabin and got the medicine-chest and clattered down the companionways into the bowels of the ship to dispense Dover's Powder and comfort; then I went on deck.

Mary was still standing at the rail, the hood pulled down so I could not see her face. The ship was bowling along under the freshening wind, the white water of the Bishop Rock abeam. Ahead, the horizon was a broad blue curve, unbroken. I said, "Mary. I love you." She did not answer. I went to put my arm around her, but drew back. It was a hard parting for her, and she had the right to be alone for it.

Little John came forward to the waist, took out the stopper of the entry-port, and called for his gig's crew. He waited for them to get onto their thwarts and sky their oars. Then he said, "Goodbye, then, Doctor. And goodbye to you, too." He put an arm round the waist of the hooded figure at my side. Then he threw back the hood, slid down the ladder into the gig, and cast off. I watched him go until I became aware that something was whipping the air at my shoulder, something light and insubstantial, the colour of unbleached flax. Hair. I looked round. My heart crashed against my ribs.

It was not Mary at all. Little John had shanghaied Charity Pender.

The wind blew up into a full gale, raising seas that spilled foam down their dirty slopes. Charity locked herself in my cabin, refusing to talk. I could hear her crying, and when I tried to reason with her through the door she refused to come out. So I went to the lower deck and set about my work.

In her prime, *Corinthian* had carried general cargo to the corners of the world. Nowadays the emigrant trade was more profitable and less taxing to her ancient timbers, and to triple her load the hold had been split horizontally into three decks. On a calm day the five-foot headroom and the press of bodies and baggage made them dark and cramped. Now that the ship was lurching and wallowing in the deep troughs, the lower deck was a vomit-slimed hell.

The Carters had taken berths on the lower deck because they were the cheapest on the ship. There were eight of them; Seth and May Carter, Seth's elderly parents, and four children between the ages of one and six. Seth had been a woodman, until the squire had torn out the trees to plant corn; he was a proud man, and with his trade gone he had decided to take his family to America rather than accept parish relief. In the lightless stink of the lower deck, the Carters had gone down with the bloody flux off Lundy. It looked as if old Mr. Carter, Seth's father, would never see the New World.

Seth was sitting on the lowest bunk of the tier of three with his face in his hands. A dim lantern swung from a beam, billowing greasy smoke. He lifted a gaunt face when he saw me and said, "Father's bad." The crying of his children jarred the teeth in my head.

The old man was lying jammed into the narrow bunk. His mouth was open, his breathing fast and shallow. Next to him lay his wife, her ancient eyes fixed in a terrified stare on the planks nine inches above her head. I examined him as best I could. His skin was cold and clammy. He had been sick, often. The flux had started the job; the seasickness would finish him. I tried to look encouraging, laid him on a pallet on the cluttered deck, set his son to chafing his limbs with flannel to restore the vital warmth. May Carter went off to make gruel, moving as if her shoes were made of pig-lead. The old man had lost too much of his body fluid already; whenever I managed to get some water down his throat, the motion brought it up again. Around me the ship groaned and shuddered, flinging baggage across the deck as I looked down at the grey-white face. Astern was Scilly and the blue coats rummaging rock and heather after me, and Mary—eight hours ago I had been with Mary, waking in her bed. And at the time, that awakening had seemed like hell.

When May Carter came back, Charity was with her, stooped under the deckhead, one hand supporting her and the other balancing a pan of gruel against the heave of the ship. The old man's pulse was irregular and thready, his breath a mere flutter in the chest. Charity knelt beside me and put a hand almost apologetically on my arm. Seth stopped his chafing. It was too late for that now. Too late for gruel. I said, "He's going," and left the son with his father. Charity came with me, up the steep companionways through the dark hold and onto the deck. The ship's bow rose and plunged, blowing out a cloud of spray.

"I'm sorry," she said. "I didn't mean to cry."

I lifted my hand, let it fall. "There's enough to cry about." The wind was cold, blustering in my ears and drumming at her blue linen dress.

"I want you to know that it was John made me come. He had a pistol under his jersey. He said he would shoot you if I moved."

I tried to take her hand, but she drew it back. "You should have moved," I said. "The captain would never have taken you . . . I'd rather have taken my chances."

She looked away at the grey horizon. "Do you know, for a moment I thought . . . when you said you loved me . . . but you thought I was Mary."

"Never you mind," I said, trying to stop the tears brewing in her eyes. "We'll put you on a ship. First one we see—"

"No," said Charity with a firm set of her jaw. "I've made up my mind. I'll not go back to Scilly now."

"Very well," I said. She was looking me proudly in the eye, strands of wet hair plastered across her wide forehead. "Then we'll do what we can." I smiled at her to hide the bitter disappointment that she was not Mary. "Come with us to the goldfields. We'll all get rich together."

"No," she said in a small voice.

"Yes. If it hadn't been for me you wouldn't be here."

"If it hadn't been for you—" She put her hand to her face. There was a wetness on her cheeks that was not spray. "Understand this, Doctor. I looked after you because I wanted to. Whatever happened was of my own choosing, or through my own vanity. I won't be making that mistake again."

"I'd like you to be with us."

"I'd like to be with you. But as soon as you can, you'll be sending for Mary Prideaux. I couldn't stand that."

The stubborn mask slipped, and she looked at me as if she was hoping she was wrong. But she was right, and I knew it and she knew it, and more tears brewed. "It's not your fault. But every time I see you together it's like . . . axes. Chopping me up."

There was a silence. Finally I said quietly, "Charity. Will you not take a ship back and make your peace with Little John?"

She made an exasperated sound. "He wants me to have you. And even if he didn't, I wouldn't have him. No, I thank God I shall never see him again. I can nurse. I can sew. I'll make my own way. And I won't ever go back. No-one can make me. No-one." She was crying in earnest now. I put my arm around her shoulders, but she wrenched free and ran to the companionway.

I stood alone by the shrouds, watching the heave of the sea. The guilt was still with me. It made me feel a monster. And the feeling was strengthened by the thought that kept running through my head. "You'll be sending for Mary Prideaux," she had said. That must mean that Little John had kept Mary behind by force. Despite the guilt, there was cheer in that. Hitherto, the day had seemed like an ending. Now I found it possible to see it as a beginning. And in that and only that, there was consolation.

Two weeks after my twenty-first birthday I heard that my father had died. I was qualified now, and Duquesne's partner; I took the chaise and arrived in Carthystown in the cold, grey morning. There were not many people in the Palladian church. As his only surviving relation I sat alone in the front pew. We had never been close, so I was rather surprised at the regret I felt as the clods hammered on the lid of the coffin. It was not grief: more the regret that one might feel at the passing of the father of an old friend—an old friend whom one no longer saw.

As I walked, more thoughtful than sad, under the lychgate, a groom took me over to a closed carriage which had stood in the road throughout. The Drumcarty arms gleamed in the black lacquer of the door. The groom opened it, and I climbed in. The blinds were drawn. It was hot, with a smell of camphor.

"My commiserations," said a voice that I had last heard in Drumcarty library. "He will be sorely missed."

I was in a peculiar mood. "Will he, My Lord?"

He laughed, a sound like sandpaper on pig's bristle. "An honest man," he said. I did not know if he was referring to me or my father. "Will you dine with me?"

After I had taken a glass with Mrs. Fitzpatrick—her husband, Michael's father, had died amid general rejoicing the previous year—the chaise took me up to the castle.

We dined tête-à-tête in a cavernous room where the draughts sent the candle-flames skittering at their wicks. It was a sombre meal. Drumcarty talked like a man not used to company, with long pauses, asking me about the details of my life in Dublin. He seemed in some obscure way gratified by my progress, for he lowered the long lids over his eyes and gave that tiny inclination of the head, saying, "Good. Good."

The Earl was very tall and thin, with a pale, ascetic face and copper-red hair receding from a lofty forehead. He had changed since last I had seen him. He had never been a man of fast movements, but now there was a painful slowness to his gestures, so that he seemed to be moving in a glass jar of some viscous fluid. He had a wasted look, as if in his languor he could not find the energy to eat. I thought his skin had the luminosity one sometimes sees in consumptives. But it was not my place to tell him so.

With the port, he began to talk about my father. "He was a useful man," he said. "In the good days. He served me long and well. But I think he was too bitter. One does not look for . . . kindness in a steward, but he was perhaps lacking in fire. Do you think?" The long, white fingers with the domed nails played with the stem of his glass.

"I find it difficult to pass judgement on my father in those terms," I said, slightly irritated.

"My dear Power . . . I am sorry. I am alone too much to be tactful. Really these are difficult times. Sometimes I think there is no gratitude left. The tenants. . . ." His voice trailed away. "But your father. I am grateful for his life. Are you?"

"I am," I said. "He was a good father in his way."

"In his way," said Drumcarty, sighing. "If you knew, Power. The straits to which one is reduced. The lawsuits. . . . Matters were easier once. Now it is all Emancipation again, and if one cannot be sure of having one's candidate returned at the Elections, how can one run an estate? It puzzled your father sorely, I know. And now there is the Catholic Rent to finance lawsuits against land-owners. . . . I see only chaos, Power." He drank. "But to chaos all things must return."

I remained silent. Emancipation seemed no bad idea to me. In fact, I had joined O'Connell's Catholic Association and contributed to the Rent. My father would have thrown me out of the house if he had known. But I was my own man now.

Drumcarty brought himself back from his abstraction. "I shall not be employing a new steward. I shall run the estate myself, with my attorneys. So for your life you may consider the Steward's House your own."

"Thank you, My Lord," I said. "That is most generous of you."

"It would only fall down otherwise," he said, with a return of his old tactlessness. "And if you ever wish to use the Library, of course. . . ."

I bowed.

"There is one other thing," he said. "Katie—Lady Katherine—will be returning from London soon. I am sure she will want to be in Dublin. She is a clever girl, but sometimes a little wilful. I wonder if you would be so good as to give her the benefit of your protection?"

"I should be honoured," I said.

Once, such a request would have overwhelmed me with joy. But memories of love fade faster than memories of pain, so I felt a vague trepidation. And why me? Dublin was full of the Earl's acquaintances. Any one of them would be better qualified.

He seemed to sense the question in my mind. "I feel I know you, Power. In a manner of speaking, I watched you grow to man's estate. . . . You have your wild times, but I think you are over them now."

"I am flattered by your confidence."

He rose. "Kelly will show you a room, no doubt. Time enough tomorrow for your melancholy duties in the Stew-ard's House."

After he had bidden me goodnight, I sat over my port watching the candle-flames flicker across the long faces of past Drumcartys on the walls.

Freed of my infatuation, I saw clearly that a new and unpredictable epoch was opening before me. If Katie was still the Katie I had known before I went to Dublin, I would be not so much a protector as a lion-tamer. Before I went to my bed I resolved to make sure that my father's duelling-pistols accompanied me back to Dublin in the chaise. I very much hoped I should not have to use them.

But with Katie, you could never be sure.

Book Two

VII

Book Two

Ship Corinthian,
Charleston Harbour,
November, 1829.

My dearest Mary,

I do not know whether this letter should be one of reproach or commiseration, so I shall resort to neither. It is
enough to say that whatever your feelings in the matter, a
light has gone out of my life—a light of such power that
even the Charleston sun looks pale and dim. Not a moment passes but that I wish you were at my side. Yet here
we are about to cast up on an unknown shore, with no
prospects but strong backs and stout shovels. So I cannot
say, "come now," for I know not where I shall be. My
only address will be with Charity Pender, care of Mistress
Elizabeth Stump, Stump's Academy, Charleston. You can
tell Little John Woodcock if you like. It may give him
some satisfaction. You can also tell him that Charity is
going to Mistress Stump's of her own free will, to be a
lady's maid, on the captain's recommendation. She says
that she wishes to make her own way in the world, without benefit of his advice or mine or anyone else's. I have
tried to reason with her, but she will have no part of me,
declaring that her mind is made up. There is no place for
her in the goldfields, her new situation is exactly what she
has always desired. And furthermore, Little John's ca-
price is nothing but the manifestation of the Divine Will.
Personally, I consider there is more of the diabolic in it,
than the divine.

I am called to see to a Scots child sick below, for whose
benefit I have remained on board this week past. A doctor aboard an emigrant ship eats seldom and sleeps never,

178

*even after journey's end. Write, please; I think of you
constantly.*

Your loving Nick.

Tresco,
March, 1830

Dear Nick,

*How it did Delight me to hear that you are Alive and
Well, on the Sea! And by now, I suppose, on land. I am
sending this in the care of Charity Pender, in the hope
that her Saintliness will see fit to forward it. Oh, Nick!
What delight there is in talking to you again What grief
in separation!*

*First, though, I must disabuse you of the idea that you
should either Reproach or Commiserate. The Facts of
that last horrid night were as follows: I was all ready
packed up for the Boat when Lit. John came back in a
touring Passion, hit me by the temple, tied me with my
back to the Chimney and told me that he would get Charity and take her aboard in my place. I tried to point out
to him that this was ill luck for Charity and indeed your
sweet Self, but he would have none of it. So by the time
you were Gone I was still bound Fast, spitting no Little I
can tell you. And after that I had no Idea where you had
gone. So what joy when I got your letter! Since then all
my dreams are with you, I am quite cut off from Life.
My feet walk on old Tresco, but my soul walks with you
among Wild Indians on Strange Shores. O that I could be
with you, my heart, my soul!*

*The Preventive man has been through the house three
times since you left, very thorough. He ast many a question about you, and got sorry riddles in return. He is a
young chap with a face like a slab of cheese. Last time
there was a bit of flop from the south-west and he Pewked
between St. Mary's and Carn Near! The Island is full of
questions without answers, about Little John, and why he
told of you and Bolitho and the wet goods. He said it was
for Charity's sake, God bless his sweet consideration; but
I know it was because you and I spoilt his wrecking of
the Montezuma. Little John has other answers, but he is
becoming quite a Merry-Andrew to all but himself.*

There have been no wrecks, or at least none reported,

though the winter has been bad, with gales and much rain. We shall need one soon, but the heart has gone out of me since you left. Scilly will pull through, though, as it always has. I am feeling a Little Indisposed, so I shall finish now. I have had Wid. Webber read the cards for you, and it seems that Good Luck attendeth, which would be all the better were it influenced by the wishes of,

Your loving Mary

Charlotte,
North Carolina.
August, 1830

Dearest Mary,

I did not realise it was possible to be on tenterhooks for nine months, but getting your letter was like rain after a long drought. I received it in my lodgings here, Charity having sent it up from Charleston. As you will see, the mail is very slow, coming up the Catawba River by steamboat as far as the cataracts—fast enough, one would think, but the floods bring down an enormity of snags, and the steamer is always in dry dock—and on by waggon, drawn by oxen so slow it would take a week to fry a steak off one of their rumps.

You may judge for yourself my relief in hearing that you were detained, the day I sailed for America; I wish I had Little John Woodcock under my care, so I could reason with him. Still, I shall probably not see him again, in this life. What is important now is that I become established—I should say we become established—so I can send for you from Scilly. The privations here are considerable. I write from a so-called inn, which is no more than a shed of clapboard on the outskirts of Charlotte, once, no doubt, a pretty enough village, but now besieged with gold-seekers. I have today sewed up a gentleman who attempted to settle a commercial argument with bowie-knives, picked in the hip of another for a bullet, and applied vinegar and brown paper to three broken heads. All these made payment in gold dust, which made me wonder whether mining lead in flesh might not be more profitable than mining metal from the ground. Bolitho, however, assures me otherwise, and our partners are with him in this opinion.

We have already made one sortie with our gold-pans,

which proved fruitless; now we have been working to build up our supplies, and depart tomorrow for the back country, on the foothills of some western mountains called the Blue Ridge. An Indian whose arm I set after it was smashed in a brawl, has offered to show me some pits where he says his forebears once dug gold; he is a pleasant fellow, rejoicing in the name of Jabez Twochild. He calls me Mountain Walker, because of the shortness of my right pin, which he says qualifies me admirably for walking clockwise round his native peaks. Bolitho and the rest of them do not put much faith in him; but times are hard, and good claims rare; so we live in hope.

I often think of you in the round house under Great Rocks. The hardest of times at Scilly can only be a paradise compared with this beastly Gehenna; even Little John sometimes appears a saint compared with the canaille who stab and shoot and brawl in the saloons. But whatever its disadvantages, it would indeed be Paradise itself if only you were here. So, my darling, wish luck to,
your ever loving Nick.

Tresco
December, 1830

Dear Nick,

I have just received your Letter, how curious to think of it under your Hand in that little town of Wild Men and Savages across the water! There was a stain on the Packet that looked like blood, I hope not yours. By now you will be up in your Mountains, and perhaps you will have had success? I do most devoutly hope so. Success is what you deserve and it is none of your Fault that it eluded you at Scilly and in the time before, of which you never spoke.

News from the Island: there has been only one wreck this year, brig Hope *on Plumb Island north of Tean Sound, from which friends brought me a little bag of Gold and a Book, but it was only a Novel by Walter Scott and not at all interesting. The harvest was much better, so tho' Little John has as usual been roaring about the Place trying to get the lanternmen out onto the Northern Rocks he has found no support. I think that since you the heart has gone out of them. The Parson has left, because of the loneliness it is said, but I think because he spent too much time talking with a certain dark-haired Siren whose repu-*

tation is no better than it should be. I am fully occupied myself, as I have started to catalogue the little chips of Creation under rocks etc., which you Undertook, it is a good Task and a happy Memory of You. Great Turmoil about the Leases, old Johns has disappeared from view, so no man knows where he stands. Prophesy and augury are rampant, some saying that there will be a new Lord Proprietor who will come in a boat like a swan in a rain of gold.

There is a ship in the Roads for Charleston, windbound now, but the Weather is changing and it will be blowing black from the E. by Morning, so I will take this to the captain now and only say that I am Forever,

your Mary.

We had travelled through a land of low, forested hills. It was early spring, and as we pressed on we saw the mountains still capped with snow far between the green-hazed branches of oak and maple. The nights were icy cold, the days hot and getting hotter. Myriads of a kind of black midge with which I was not familiar descended on us, digging holes in the skin until the blood ran down in streams. The river was fast and shallow, fed by creeks which ran down from their valleys like the little bones into a herring's spine. Occasionally there would be a farm, a log house and a few fields perilously tilted on the hillside, fenced in against bear and deer. As we penetrated further, the homesteads became fewer, engulfed in the tree-furred flanks of hill after hill, the ripple and thunder of the river reflecting the blue sky, the mocking-birds like a lash on a wet back. And on the fourth day, we turned into the mouth of Lose Sky Creek.

"Here," said Jabez Twochild. "Further up, the pits."

That night there was hard talk of gold. Later I lay in my blankets under the cold moon, and watched pale night-hawks whirring after bugs while the sleepers shifted and muttered. We had supplies for a month. After that, we would have to return to civilisation and work up a new grubstake, and another year would slip away.

In the morning we descended on the creek with pans and pry-bars. Joby Pembarra and Jamesy Paxton, the miners, worked slow and looked as if they would believe in the gold when they saw it and not before. Jacko Samms and Boz Boswarva, Bolitho's former crew, started out skylarking, full of confidence, and were disheartened by noon. Bolitho ploughed the fast water with his shins, furious at his own clumsiness. When we took a break at midday he was quiet and sullen. Jabez Twochild said, "More work, captain. Must work harder."

Bolitho swivelled his head threateningly and said, "You'd better be right."

We panned until sunset, and we found colours. But it took the seven of us all day to get enough gold to dirty a well-bitten fingernail. Jacko and Boz chattered like monkeys round the fire until Bolitho snapped at them as if they were still his hired hands rather than his partners. That evening we were quiet. Solid Pembarra sat tailor fashion and scribbled one of his endless letters to his wife. Jamesy Paxton sawed tunes from his fiddle, surprising the pines and maples and carrying me back to the Jenkins kelping and Mary dancing on the hot beach. Bolitho threw twigs petulantly at the red embers. I slept deep and early, the bones of my lame leg aching from the chill of the day's wading. Next day we worked on up the river, and the glittering specks of yellow in the black sand at the pan's bottom were still there, but very few.

So it went for two weeks. Then it rained.

The clouds cut off the hills at their shoulders and spewed water, and the creek became a raging brown beast that chewed at its banks and gulped whole trees into its muddy belly and chased us into the dripping forest, to sit miserable and sodden, eating up our dwindling stores and waiting for the flood to pass.

By the time the creek was workable again, the food supplies were low and Bolitho's spirits were even lower. I could understand that. He was a man of considerable dignity and used to being his own master. He had, after all, been captain of the *Jane and Emily*. To earn the money to buy his share of our supplies he had had to work as a common labourer, and in the raw boomtown of Charlotte there was little dignity in that. He worked off his hostility on Jabez Twochild, until it was only the loyalty that Jabez had conceived for me when I had set his arm that kept him with us. Part of it was that Jabez, whom Bolitho had typecast as an ignorant savage, was now the most useful member of our party. It was he who had brought us to the Cherokee goldpits that pocked the overgrown slopes above the creek; it was not his fault that they were all worked out. It was he who guided me into the hills to hunt deer to supplement our meagre stocks; it was not his fault that deer were scarce this year.

As for the rest of the party, Pembarra and Paxton worked patiently on, while Jacko and Boz passed from disappointment into homesickness and from homesickness into sulky apathy. It was a dour and unhappy party that assembled round the fire on the eve of the thirty-fifth day.

When he had scraped the last of his ration of beans and deer-fat from his tin-plate, Bolitho said, "We're finished."

Nobody spoke. Finally I said, "There's always tomorrow."

"Tomorrow I show you very good place," said Jabez, encouraged. "Up the creek, where there is old farm."

"Oh is there?" said Bolitho, slamming his plate into the dirt. "And what do we eat when we've found nothing in your very good place, again? Grass?" He rounded on Jabez with a heavy swing of the shoulders. "White man's bellies need food, not hay."

Jabez rose slowly to his feet, tall and dignified, his black eyes reflecting the firelight without expression. "I have held my peace. Now I speak. Perhaps it is best you go back," he said. "Perhaps this is not the place for you."

"Perhaps you're bloody well right," said Bolitho. "Perhaps it's not the place for anyone who's looking for gold. Perhaps those pits are latrines."

"Yes," said Jabez. "You go back." He turned away to the dark woods.

I went after him. "You must not listen," I said. "His heart is sick, for he is far from home."

"That is true," said Jabez. His copper skin reddened with the distant firelight as he looked down. "You healed my arm," he said. "With you I will go hunting, to get meat for the journey. But I will not go back to the fire."

Next morning Jabez and I rose in the misty dawn and started upstream. The day became hot, a steamy heat that brought the sweat pouring off me. The rifle on my shoulder grew heavier and heavier, and my feet were like lead. My thoughts were as ponderous as my feet. The treadmill. Raising grubstakes, prospecting, exhausted stores. Panning empty streams, losing heart as the valleys filled with other prospectors. No Mary, no freedom, no new life. Only the drudgery and the search, the constant search.

Ten miles up the bank of the creek, we stalked and

killed a deer. It was a good stalk, high in the ridge, in and
out of gullies and hemlock-groves; at another time I might
have enjoyed it. But the shot, the fall of the beast, the
gralloch were only more steps on the treadmill. It was a
big buck—too big to carry; so we dragged it down to the
creek and Jabez began building a raft while I lay on a
beach of fine white sand and tried to get my breath back.

"This is the place," said Jabez.

Across the water, the sun lit on a tangle of cat-briers
and rank weeds. A mat of vines crawled over something
that might once have been a cabin. Ours were not the only
blasted hopes in the valley.

I lay back against a boulder, letting the sun soak in.
Many of the settlers had moved west when the rains had
leached the goodness out of the steep valleys and flushed
it down the creeks. There must have been others here who
had looked over the creek and the worn-out fields on their
last day, waggons loaded for the mountain passes and the
new lands beyond. It would have been a sad place to
leave, I thought. Lower down, the valley sides were as
steep as cliffs, which was why we had panned there. They
would fall in easily as the water undercut them, and the
heavy gold would sink to the bottom while the lighter debris trundled off downstream. Here, the slopes of the hills
were almost gentle, with a soft roundness that reminded
me of Ireland. It had not impressed our expert prospectors, though.

Jabez said, "It is ready."

I got up, reluctantly. The deer's carcase was strapped to
a bed of logs grounded on the beach. "Well," I said, with
a final look round. "Let's be off."

Jabez nodded, but made no move, as if he wanted to
say something but was not sure of his ground. Suddenly, I
wished I could stay here by the bright water in the rapid's
roar. Of course, it was impossible. But the journey back to
civilisation was singularly unappealing.

Jabez stretched his closed hand out towards me. "We
have a custom in my clan," he said. "When we have made
a kill, we take something from the place." The fist turned
over, palm up. "Now you take this."

On the brown palm there lay a stone. It was of the
same white quartz that covered the bed of the stream. We
had levered stones like it with pry-bars, rattled them in

our pans until our legs ached and our backs were sore. They were pretty pebbles, smooth and bland. We had grown to hate their smoothness and blandness.

Jabez moved his hand a little. The stone rolled, catching the sun on its plane base, a glint of mirror-silver and red-yellow. Red-yellow. The flash of it dazzled my eyes and I put out my fingers very slowly and took it, while the first rumours spread along the optic nerves to my brain. Under my eye, the landscape of it was a sere waste of jagged crystal, split with faults. Beneath the scarps of the faults there ran broad rivers yellow as butter in the high sun. It was the landscape that had filled my dreams, and those of my partners, these eight months past.

Gold.

I do not know how long it was before I looked up at Jabez. His eyes were still on me, black as deep water above the long, flat cheeks. He nodded, once. He knew what he had given me.

"It is yours now," he said. "This place is yours."

"You knew," I said. "All this time?"

"It was with you I had the debt," he said. "Not those others."

"But they are my partners."

He shook his head. "They are not meant for it."

I weighed the nugget in my hand. It was heavy with a good weight, warm as the sun. I could hold my peace, return alone, stake the claim. The others would not know until it was too late.

"Would they have told you? Any one of them?" he said.

I did not answer. Probably not. But it was through Bolitho and his men that I had escaped with my neck. The tinners had sheltered me from the hunt. "Them, too, I owe a debt," I said. "But it is yours. You found it. You sell it. You could be rich."

"I do not care for dead metal," he said. "I have seen my brothers who fill their pockets with it. It weighs them down and they sink."

"I owe you a debt," I said. "You must at least be a partner."

"All debts are paid. If I cared for gold, I might work with you. But not with Bolitho. I value my life above gold. Search your own heart, Doctor."

"We have agreed."

"So be it," he said, turning away to the raft. "May you never regret it."

We lived on that buck for a week. As soon as we arrived at the camp, Jabez vanished; but nobody noticed he was gone. Next day we moved up the creek and started work. It was hard and our bellies were empty; but nobody was noticing the hunger. The colours were thick on the bottom of the pool below the rapids; but halfway up the fast water they vanished.

The hillside was a tangle of cat-briers and dogwood, but by the end of the day it was as barren as the desert, and soon there was a good shaft heading down for bedrock in a gulley twenty feet above the creek, with the dirt panning out at a pinch of dust the rinse. So up we went another twenty feet and another, with a sluice by the river trapping black sand and those little yellow flecks in the burlap covering its bottom, the whoosh of the flume sounding like gusts of a big wind over the rapids' song. It was three weeks of deer meat and green shoots and eight more shafts before we found the vein of rotten quartz that ran into the hillside twelve feet below soil level. And by that time, the lumber gang had a pile of green logs stacked on pegs driven into the steeps, and there was a hydraulic ram to bring water to the flume. When I went down to Charlotte to register and get the supplies, I took fourteen ounces of dust and nuggets and the two Botallack men with guns, because Charlotte was no kind of place for a lame man with a full poke and peaceable disposition.

> *New Botallack,*
> *Lose Sky Creek.*
> *May, 1831.*

Dear Mary,
I received your letter two months back, but have waited till now to answer so I could send you what I hope will be the best news you have ever had. I enclose a note for £100. Take ship for Charleston at once. I shall make all arrangements. In haste and expectation—
Your happy Nick.

New Botallack,
Lose Sky Creek.

Dear Mary,
  *Since it is possible that my last letter to you may have
gone astray, I repeat: come at once! We have our own
village, our own mine, wealth inexhaustible, a new life, a
new Eden!*
  I enclose a further note for £100.
                    your loving Nick.

There were only two correspondents who addressed me
personally; Charity and Mary. When Jabez came up from
the creek on the 10th September, I could hardly breathe.
There was a small white packet in his hand. I had received a letter from Charity only the week before. She
was well and happy and Mrs. Stump had set her to in-
structing the young ladies in needlework. A young gentleman of the town was paying her marked attention. It
had to be Mary.
  The handwriting was small, the vertical strokes broken
by little tremors. Not Mary's scrawl. I was so disappointed
I nearly flung it into the mud. But Jabez, who liked to be
appreciated, was watching, so I tore it open.

Stump's Academy,
Charleston,
August, 1831.

Dear Doctor,
  *I write to apprise you of sad News concerning yr friend
Charity Pender, who was with me here, a good Companion and valued Servant. The Yellow Fever hath been very
Bad this year and poor Mistress Pender being badly afflicted by the Miasms fell sick and departed this Life yesterday in the Hospital. Her last thoughts as they were relay'd to me were of your person and welfare. If there be
aught I can do to soften this most Grevious blow, please
accept my Assurance Dear Dr that I shall do it, if it be in
my Power; and meanwhile dear Dr count as yr most humble and obedt servt*
                    Elizabeth Stump.

I walked slowly down the hill and across the ford. Bolitho was working the twenty-foot sluice, stripped to the waist, his gnarled shoulders knotting with muscle as he shovelled. When he saw me coming, he straightened up and wiped the sweat from his forehead with the back of his hand. I said, "Charity's dead. I'm going to Charleston."

"Sorry to hear it," he said. " 'eed I am." He stopped, filled his shovel, crashed the dirt into the trough. "You might do the bank run on yer way."

"The bank run?" I said.

"Drop in the take at the store, man. Make yourself useful."

It took time to register. "She's dead." I said stupidly.

"Bad business," said Bolitho. "Devilish bad. Make sure you get a receipt now." He went back to his shovelling. I stood watching him, wondering whether I would batter his head in with a pick and kick his corpse into the creek. But it was only his way. Dogged old blunt Bolitho. I pulled out the poke from under its flat rock in the riverbed, took down my rifle and set off.

On the evening of the second day I pulled up in Charlotte. I deposited the gold in the little clapboard store, choked down a dinner of jerked beef and rye whiskey and started south.

A week later, the riverboat's warps pulled her onto the quay. I picked up my carpetbag and walked into the town to do my duty to my conscience.

Mrs. Stump's academy was an imposing edifice of white wood, with a mansard roof and a piazza. I rang the doorbell, and was ushered by a black woman in a crisp blue-and-white uniform through cool rooms to a little parlour, in which sat Mrs. Stump herself. The misgivings I had entertained about her were quickly dispelled by her appearance and manner. She was a small, sharp lady of about fifty-five years, with a ramrod back and a mouth whose lips had long since retreated nun-like from the world. I introduced myself. She looked me quickly up and down with eyes that made me acutely aware that I had not shaved or cut my hair for three months, and that my clothes left a good deal to be desired in point of cut and cleanliness. Her conclusions did not seem entirely unfavourable, though, for she called for lemonade and said, "Ah, yes.

Poor Miss Pender. I declare we did get along so famously.
'Twas a great sorrow to us. A great sorrow."

"Yes," I said. "I am sorry I was not here sooner."

She nodded, like a bird. "She asked for you, In her . . .
illness."

I looked at my feet. "I was thinking. . . . Perhaps you
would tell me where she lies buried?"

"I'll take you there myself." She rose to her feet. She
wore a high-waisted dress at least thirty years out of fashion. Hung from her shrivelled wrist was a fan, which she
plied with a style that was as much a relic of the last century as her spelling and syntax. As we walked through the
house, a door opened a crack. I saw three pairs of eyes
and heard giggling. Mrs. Stump jerked her bonnet. The
giggling stopped.

The place where Charity was buried was on a hill overlooking the harbour. It was a clear day, very hot. The sea
was blue, and it was just possible to imagine I was at New
Grimsby in July. There were flowers on the long mound
of earth. They were new, but already they were wilting.
The church was white and small, with a stubby spire.

"The young ladies keep the flowers fresh," said Mrs.
Stump. "They were much attached to Miss Pender. I'll
leave you to yourself for a moment.

Poor Charity, I thought. Poor, good Charity. Charity
who had nursed me back into the world with her love.
And I had been three hundred miles away when she was
sick. Only three hundred miles.

After a while I went to look for Mrs. Stump. She was
standing by a white marble urn, watering a red geranium.
"Mr. Stump," she said. "Poor dear Ezra, he did love flowers so much. Best music-master in all Charleston."

We started back through the hot afternoon. The people
in the narrow, shady streets moved with the languor of
carp in a ditch. "I'd like to put up a stone," I said.

Mrs. Stump nodded.

I hesitated. There was a question I hardly liked to ask.
"Did she go . . . easily?"

She folded her hands in her lap. "You're a doctor. You
know yellow fever."

"I've read it up. But—well, we don't get much of it in
Ireland."

"How stupid of me. Yes, she went easily enough. It
didn't last long. The day after they took her to the hospi-

tal. Doctor Degas advised her removal. The contagion, you know." She nodded her bird's nod. "It surely does seem hard. Poor Charity. To die among strangers. Perhaps you'd like to meet the doctor? He's well thought of in the city. He is medical adviser to the Academy."

"No," I said. "I'm sure he's done his best." I wondered why I had come to Charleston. There seemed to be no reason, now I was here. Nothing I could do would make any difference. "If you could ask the mason for a simple cross? White marble?" I wrote on a piece of paper "Charity Pender 1810–1831. Safe in the arms of Jesus."

"I surely will," she said. "And, Doctor. Don't feel too bad about her. It wasn't your fault."

"I fear it was," I said.

"No. Charity and I became good friends while she was here. She told me about you. She was a strong girl with strong convictions. One of those convictions was that she had her own way to make. She told me once that she thought you were braver to let her go than to keep her with you."

"I wish I believed that," I said.

"I do," said Mrs. Stump.

I forced a smile. "That's very encouraging," I said, and meant it. I got up. "Thank you for your consideration. I must be off now."

She gave me her dry claw hand, and I bowed deep and kissed it. "Any time you think an old lady could be of assistance, you only have to ask," she said.

Suddenly, through the bagged skin and the wrinkles, I saw the beauty that must have turned Ezra Stump away from the pianoforte and into the nuptial bed. "Thank you," I said. Then I left.

I rode into New Botallack a week later in heavy rain. Bolitho and Pembarra were at the sluices, shovelling. At their feet the creek roared, the colour of melted chocolate. I went up the opposite slope to my cabin. The roof-shingles were glazed with a running film of water, and streams of the stuff drummed and splattered into the mud under the eaves. I saw to my horse, shouldered the saddlebags, and limped through the door. The place smelt of damp and mice, as usual. There was a plank bed, a table, a chair and a fireplace. On the walls were a few books. I saw that the mice had been at my *Cooper's Surgical Dictionary* again; they seemed to find its binding irresistible.

I picked up some of the gnawed-off fragments and went to start the fire. The letter was on the table.

Tresco
August, 1831.

Dear Nick,
I am writing this on a day so hot I can barely keep the Ink liquid between Pot and Paper. It has been most Glorious weather, the winds having been westerly and Light, which has occasioned great Distress because the pilots have been without employment. Croesus Mumford on St. Marys—you will remember him, I think!—has begun a shipyard, and is now diskusting prosperous on the proceeds. It is giving employment to St. Marys, though on Tresco and the other Off-islands Life continues much as usual, save for the rumours about the new Lord Proprietor. Actually I have discovered that there is to be no Lord Proprietor, the Duchy of Cornwall not being able to find anyone stupid enough to pay for the privilege of being bankrupted.

I looked at my Almanac the other day and found that Soon it will be two years since you left! It seems like a minute. I can still see you if I shut my eyes. It is almost as if you are still here. Some of your books that you left. And your Journals. I am afraid that my cataloguing has been a poor business. I never seemed to have the time.

Nick, I cant come to America. I just cant. I cant leave here. It's my home. If I left I should die. I know I should. You're the kind of man who can live with no past, only a Future. I cant conceive of the future, but the past keeps me tied down. I love you, Nick. I do really. I'll wait for you till hell freezes. But I wont—cant—come to America. I cant explain. But I cant.
Forgive me, your Mary.

The two hundred-pound notes were pinned to the back of the sheets. I smoothed them carefully on the table, folded them in half, and put them in my wallet. Then I re-read the letter and threw it on the fire. There was a bottle of whisky on the shelf by the books. I drank it and went to bed. Next morning I got up early and started work. And from then on, for a long time, there was nothing but work. Not doctoring; I had had enough of flesh and blood and will and reason. Digging was the work I did, tearing at the ground to rip out soft yellow metal, to make a wall to stop the world getting in at me.

I learned to love the *chunk* of pick in face, to see the tiny glitter of quartz in the matrix, to drool over the tender weight of a crumbling lump of crystal shot with wires and crumbs of pulpy gold. The shafts ran deep after the vein and then we began the first level, following the thin crooked line towards the heart of the hill. Winter froze us solid, but the picks still swung and the nails in my boots squeaked on the iron-hard ice of the tunnel floor. The creek dwindled and froze, but we kept at the face until the ore-piles spilled down from the shaft mouth and we dug the level back to daylight, so it was a hole bored straight into the side of the hill, and then we faced the arch of the tunnel with stone. It looked across the valley at my cabin like an empty black eye, that arch, with the ore and the deads splashed down the white snow like mineral tears. At the river the gang worked on the mill-dam, racing the thaw, hacking the frozen ground into a pile ten feet high and sixty yards long, while the shrunken remnants of the river trickled down the narrow slot of the leat.

Spring melt came. The white hillsides turned to foul mud, and every path, every tiny longitudinal notch in the ground took water rushing down the fall-line towards the cheek. The rivulets banded together and made streams, and the streams hurled themselves at the topsoil and prised at the masonry lining the level mouth. Thin trickles of water flowed down into the dark of the level. The floor was wet underfoot, tinkling with the drips from the roof. By March, the barrowmen were moving bouse up to their knees in cold water, and Joby Pembarra was talking about drainage. But the rest of us were talking about gold.

The sun came out and the wet steamed up from new greenery and sat in lakes of fog along the valley bottoms. The flies hatched. There was no escape but at the face, where the air was now so bad that the flies would not follow. Joby still talked about drainage, but the groundwater seeped away and the barrowmen's wet-sores began to heal. And pretty soon it was beginning to be summer, and there were other things to think about.

With the clear days and the hot sun, the timber we had felled over the winter was rolled down to the south-facing

slope, and the little cabins which had served last year began to sprout wings and porches and new storeys. The
work of building was hard, but we were ready for it. The
Cornishmen moved slowly, but they never wasted an
ounce of energy. They trudged through the piles of logs
and the half-built walls in their scarred boots and their
buckskin breeches, and I worked with them. Winter in
the main level had put muscle on my shoulders and arms,
toughened my legs, until I no longer needed my stick.
None of my clothes would fit me any more, but they
had been no use for this kind of work anyway, so I wore
nailed boots and buckskins and rough flannel like the rest
of them. There were only six of us; but as I sat on the
steps of my cabin with Joby Pembarra and looked over
the results of our work, I thought that twenty ordinary
men could have done no better. On the far side of the
river, running up to the foundations of the mill, the new
waggon road was a scar of red dust against the green. The
water sparkled silver in the sun. Normally it was foul with
the washings of the ore; but today the flumes lay idle. It
was a special kind of day, for everyone but me.

Joby said, "There they be," and heaved himself to his
feet.

I listened. Over the ripple of the creek and the bird-
song from the woods came a regular creaking and a high,
shrill laugh. A woman's laugh. I drank from the bottle in
my right hand. My second bottle that day. Pop Schmelk,
who farmed ten miles down the branch, brought it over
the hills once a fortnight. The Botallack men drank hard,
but I was easily his best customer. "Drink, Joby?" I said.

"Thankee no," said Joby. "The old lady'd kill me." He
grinned his gap-toothed grin, and the blue patch of
blasting-powder on his right cheek moved up toward his
eye. "Reckon I'll be off to meet 'er."

He began walking down the hill. His feet quickened
over the grass until he broke into a run, into the creek
leaping and hopping, six feet tall and two hundred
pounds of him scattering rainbow fans of water into the
sun, a middle-aged giant capering like a spring lamb and
yelling, "Welcome home to thee, Tamzin!" until the birds
shut their beaks, and all that was left was the creak of the
axles on the waggon pulling up by the mill. Miners,
women and a chattering swarm of children spilled out of
the waggon and I heard that shrill laugh again. Joby

came up the hill towards the new-sawn logs of his house, with the new-dug patch out front, inside a new pale fence against the deer and the bears. He had his huge arm round the shoulders of the woman I had met at Botallack pithead, she of the blue eyes and the black hair, and the flesh bitten from under her cheekbones. She smiled at me as they came up the hill, and for a second she looked like an older Mary. One of her children looked at me and hid his face in her skirts. And on they went into the new house, and I heard her say, "Oh but Jobe it's lovely! Oh Jobe!"

And then I went into my filthy cabin and locked the door. I got out another bottle of whisky and threw the cork out of the window.

Later, Bolitho came up. I gave him the bottle. He drank and wiped his lips and looked around him, deliberately, with that heavy swing of shoulders. Then he said, "I haven't seen you for a while. Not to talk to."

I said, "There's been nothing to talk about."

He shrugged massively. "Maybe not." There was a silence. A woman was singing somewhere on the hillside, clear and happy. "You ought to go into the town, sometime."

"Why?"

"No sense in making yourself a bloody hermit."

"I'm quite happy."

"If that's how you want it," said Bolitho. Another silence. Then he said: "Do you know how much we're worth?"

"A good deal, I suppose." The bottle was empty again. I threw it into the fireplace.

"Quarter of a million dollars. Your share, a round forty thousand. We'll double it by this time next year. More than double it."

"Good," I said. I supposed it was what he wanted me to say.

"So what the hell are you going to do with it?"

The question had not occurred to me. It seemed quite unimportant. "What does it matter?"

"It may not matter to you. It matters to me. There's a lot of things I want."

"What I want can't be bought," I said.

"You might as well sling yourself in the creek."

"That's my business." There was another bottle on the

shelf. I went to fetch it, my boots crunching on broken glass.

"All right," said Bolitho. "I know you've had some bad luck. We all have. Just take it that I want to get rich. Stinking bloody rich. Deep sunk in blunt. Quicker the better. That means you, too. You don't mind how I go about it?"

"Fire away," I said. "Just don't come up here preaching."

"I won't."

"Have a drink."

He shook his head. "No more."

"You've changed."

"It's one thing hauling round Scilly in a rotbucket like the old *Jane and Emily*. You can see further here. I like what I see. I want to get that mill up fast. Then dig another shaft. We haven't got the men. I'm going to get a slave-driver up from South Carolina."

"Dig on."

"You're sure about that?" said Bolitho. "No damned Radical stuff about Liberty and Equality?"

I hardly heard him. The bottle slipped from my hand and broke.

Next thing I knew it was morning, and I had a head like a manure keg. I started for the creek, for my morning bath. At my usual bathing place, there was a woman washing clothes. She had brown hair and a comfortable bottom, and when she heard me behind her she straightened up, wiping her hands on her apron. I said, "Good morning," rather miffed. It was my custom to bathe naked.

"And good day to you, Sir," she said. "You'll be the doctor, will you? James told us about you, in his letters." She blushed. "You'd know, of course, having wrote them."

"You must be Mrs. Paxton," I said. Jamesy Paxton was a small tinner with fiery red hair who played the fiddle like an angel, but had never learnt to write. "Did you have a good journey?"

"I don't know as you'd call it good," said Mrs. Paxton. "Still, all's well as ends well. I wonder would you come and have a look at young Billy? He took sick at Charleston, and he's poorly yet. If it wouldn't be too much trouble?"

"With the greatest of pleasure," I said.

Nobody was working that day. Bolitho had left for Charlotte early in the morning. So I limped back to the cabin with a bucket of water, splashed my face and went to the shelf where I kept the bottles. My hand reached out. Then I took it back. "Not yet," I said. I had fallen into the habit of talking to myself in the winter, and it had stuck. I lit the fire, heated water. While it was heating I stropped my razor and polished the bottom of a pan with sand until I could see my face in it. Then, slowly and carefully because of the shaking of my hand, I began to shave. It was the first time I had seen myself for nearly a year. My eyes looked like two tomatoes, and I was shocked to see a couple of streaks of grey in my hair. Under the beard the skin was white, but there was a toughness to the face that I didn't remember. The resemblance to a debauched Napoleon was still there, but now it was a Napoleon hardened by air and exercise. "Not bad," I said. "Handsome devil." I put on the cleanest shirt I could find, climbed into my breeches and went across to the Paxton's cabin.

The last time I had seen the inside, it had been in much the same state as mine. Now the floor was swept and sanded, the household gods ranged neatly on shelves. Jamesy was sitting in a chair, looking slightly stunned. When I came in, his mouth opened and stayed open. "Morning, James," I said. "I've come to see to the little one."

"Bugger me," he said. "Well bugger . . . I . . . me. It's old Nicholas. Looking like a Methody preacher."

I grinned at him. The shock was perfectly reasonable.

"Would you stop that language," said Mrs. Paxton from the next room. "What will the doctor think?"

I could see James about to tell her that she could go to the Devil, and that the doctor had said worse in his day. But he clamped his mouth shut, and his wife took me into the bedroom, apologising all the while for the mess. I looked at Billy, who seemed to have a touch of the intermittent fever. Then I reassured Mrs. Paxton and went home.

New Botallack possessed a medicine-chest, but I had not opened it except in search of catgut and opium. I pushed a pile of dirty plates off it, washed out a bottle—there was no shortage of bottles—and prepared an infu-

sion of the Peruvian Bark, which I took back to the Paxton's. Mrs. Paxton took it with gratitude, introduced me
to Mrs. Samms, who turned out to be Jacko's wife, and
Mrs. Pembarra, whom I already knew. The old Mary
pain came back when I saw Mrs. Pembarra. I was given
tea and asked a variety of questions about the healthful-
ness, climate and prospects of New Botallack, which I
answered as encouragingly as I could; at which the ladies
seemed much relieved. And with the slackening of the
strain on their faces, I began not to think about Mary. Instead I began to think about New Botallack, and the way
it was going to change, and whether I was going to
change with it.

But in the next few days the celebrations became more
and more private, and finally the women and children
were taken for granted, and life continued much as before. There was one difference; much to Pop Schmelk's
disgust, I stopped drinking. During the days I worked
down the pit or at the sluices; in the evenings I held con-
sultations in my cabin, and afterwards I read and stayed
sober. With women on the place, our social life broad-
ened. Before, New Botallack had kept itself pretty much
to itself. Now, our neighbours began to come in, on foot,
on horseback, in waggons, buckboards, and other con-
veyances with no known name. At first they came out of
curiosity; then they came to my surgery; and finally, they
came out of friendship.

And so I became a miner by day and a back-country
croaker by night, and pretty soon I had so much to do in
the here and now that I had no time to think about the
past. I began, with work, to feel better. New Botallack
had other explanations. I heard Jamesy Paxton talking to
Joby Pembarra about me one night. They were leaning on
the snake fence at the top of the hill, smoking their pipes.
Joby said, "Th'old doctor seems to've cheered up."

"Ar," said James. "I reckon he had woman trouble, and
now he sees the way they do carry on he conceive it
weren't no trouble after all."

Four weeks after the arrival of the women, a cavalcade
of a different kind came down the creek road. At its head
rode a long, thin specimen in a straw hat. Below the hat
was a white moustache, a cigar and a face composed
mainly of bags and pouches. He wore a dirty white riding-
suit and black Blucher boots. His horse was a fine chest-

nut, glossy with sweat. At its heels trotted a pair of bloodhounds. Behind the dogs there trudged about forty black men and one woman. Behind them were a couple of flatbed buggies drawn by mules and piloted by a couple more black men. Bolitho went to meet them. I had just come out of the level, and I went after him.

"Oh," said Bolitho when he realised I was in his midst. "Colonel Tuke. Doctor Power. Colonel Tuke's gang has come up to build us the mill."

"They have," I said. "Well, that's a great thing." I had seldom seen such a run-down bunch of human beings as the slaves. Lids hung heavy over eyes, ribs stuck out over scrawny bellies, and elbows and knees were great knobs of bone. "They don't look as if they could build a card-house."

"Deceptive, 'pearances," said Tuke. He turned round and snapped orders.

The men sat down in the dust and the waterboy went round. After a few minutes Tuke said, "Right. Where's yer timber and where d'ye want the mill?"

Within half an hour of their arrival, the human skeletons were hewing logs, rolling boulders and digging trenches. Above the track, the women put up tarpaulin tents and lit cook-fires. When it got dark, the slaves stopped work and trooped silently back to the drab tent village. Tuke went to Bolitho's cabin. I followed.

They had the mill plans laid out on the table. Bolitho was talking about the foundations, Tuke puffing huge clouds of smoke from his moustache. I said, "I'm sorry to butt in, gentlemen, but I'm curious about how much we're paying Colonel Tuke."

"Fifty cents a head a day," said Bolitho.

"Cheap," I said. "Fifty cents don't go far on food."

"What the hell—" said the Colonel.

"I'm concerned that your men don't die on the job. I don't like people dying."

"They won't starve. They're only animals," said Tuke illogically.

"The Colonel's animals," said Bolitho.

I saw Tuke the next morning, watching operations from the top of a boulder. The bloodhounds lay at his feet, panting in the early sun. Like his horse, they looked glossy and well-fed. A gang was digging a sawpit up the hill from the river. I had seen slave-gangs at work—in

South Carolina; up here in the back country, a slave was a rare animal—and I had often stopped to listen to their work-chants. These men were working in silence, picking listlessly with spades and mattocks. Bolitho was on his way to the sluices, and I said to him, "I'm not surprised you got that gang cheap."

He watched them for a moment. Then he said, "See what you mean," and went over to the Colonel. I did not hear what he said, but Tuke slid down from the boulder and went over to the sawpit, slapping his riding-quirt into the palm of his hand. I went on up to the level mouth. As I lit my candle and went into the dark, I heard the *whack* of leather on flesh.

At about noon I went out to eat bread and cheese on the hill by the level. I met Jamesy Paxton, red hair flaming in the sun, coming up with Jacko Samms. Jamesy said, "Good day."

"How's Billy?"

"Comin' along well. Don't take to his physic. What d'ye think of that all?" He jerked a thumb at the square of mortared boulders and the deepening scar of the sawpit, overrun with thin black figures like slow ants.

"It'll be a good mill. Good plans."

"The mill's all right. What about them darkies, though?"

"What about them?"

"They've just took two of'em away back to their tents. Clean out, they was."

"You'd better ask Bolitho."

Jamesy shook his head. "We agreed on usin' 'em. I tell you now though, I don't like it. I din't know it'd be like that."

"Like beasts," said Jacko. "Wuss nor beasts."

"Are you going to do anything about it?"

"It's Bolitho," said Jamesy. "I don't. . . ."

"He ain't a man to tell he's wrong," said Jacko. His moon face was badly worried. "He'd tear the guts out of you."

"You're a partner," I said. "He's not your captain any more. Why don't you tell him?"

Jacko looked at his feet, and Jamesy hissed between his teeth and spat. Neither of them spoke. Finally, Jacko said, "We voted."

"So did I. I don't like it any more than you do. I'll tell

him." I could feel the relief in their watching eyes as I walked down the hill.

Bolitho was at the sluices, as usual. I said, "What's this about the help dropping like flies?"

"Malingering bastards," he said, without breaking rhythm.

"I'm going to have a look at them."

Bolitho stopped and aimed his eyes at me. "Now don't let's have none of your milk of human kindness. You promised me."

"I was drunk," I said. "I don't mind what I promised. I'm not going to let those men work themselves to death."

"None of our business," said Bolitho. "This is a mine, not a girl's school. We paid the ganger for the job. He does it his own way."

"Not this way," I said. I walked over to the slave-camp. The fires were lit, the cauldrons bubbling. I said to the mammy, "What are you cooking?" She was thin and nervous-looking.

"Corn pone, massa."

"Looks like there's more water than corn."

"Oh, he ticken up," she said without much conviction.

"Any meat?"

She looked at me as if I was crazy. "No, massa."

"Where are the sick men?"

She led me under a tarpaulin a little back from the fire. The men were lying on the bare ground. Their eyes were crescents of white under the lids. Exhaustion. Not enough food. One of them had a bright red weal running from shoulder to groin, corrugated by the protruding ribs. Ants crept busily over him. "How old's this man?" I said.

She shrugged. "I don' know. Forty, fifty mebbe?"

He looked seventy. "Why don't you feed 'em better?" I said. "Corn's cheap. So's pork."

"Mastah say, small corn enough for lazy men."

"I see." I scratched my chin. "Fetch water. Put it on to boil. Make a big fire."

Boz was wheeling a load of bouse down the walkway to the sluices. When he had tipped it onto the pile, I said, "Let's have that barrow." I wheeled it over to the store-shed, pulled out a hundred weight sack of cornmeal, and dumped it in. There was a side of bacon hanging in the rafters. That went in, too. I wheeled my load back to the slave-camp and said, "Boil it all up." The hillside was lined with watching miners. The slaves had stopped work. Bolitho was advancing down the waggon-road, shovel in hand. He said, "What the hell are you doing?"

I said, "I don't like watching men starve. I told you. They'll get a good meal and then they'll get away from here. We'll hire our labour at an honest price or do it ourselves."

"Who the hell do you think you are?" he said. "I made a contract with Colonel Tuke, and you agreed to it."

"The Colonel can go to the Devil with his contract." The blood was hammering in my temples. "There's not a man on the place wants this kind of thing."

"They voted for it."

"So they voted for it. Unless I am gravely mistaken, we came over from England because we wanted a chance to make an honest living. In the Land of the Free. This isn't what I understand by freedom. Or honesty."

"Who's going to pay for the meal? The bacon?" Bolitho looked as if he had been sandbagged. All the partners were standing in a knot, now.

"I will, if necessary."

The other partners looked at him steadily. Jamesy said, "And we will."

Bolitho's head pivoted slowly on his shoulders. "A bloody girl's school," he said. But he went over to Tuke, and shortly after that the slaves went back to their encampment.

That evening I was called over into the next valley, to sew up a farmer who had put an axe through his calf-muscle. It was a five-mile ride, and after the operation was finished I stayed and talked to the patient and his wife. I told him of our troubles with the mill, and he laughed. "What ye doin' callin' in the negras?" he said. "I'll put the word around and you kin have all the help you need. Y'all put two men on the sawing now, and in a week'r so we'll get the folks over. Be done before harvest!"

I found my way back over the ridge by the light of a heavy half-moon. The frogs and crickets were singing partsongs, and the woods were haunted with owls. The lights of the cabins twinkled like rubies, with a bigger, hotter jewel in the slave camp. As I rode down towards the stable, I saw a lantern moving.

I recognised Boz, who looked after the horses because

he liked them. "G'night," I said, preparing to slip out of the saddle."

"G'night," he said. "Couple of them black fellers cut and run." He slung his forkful onto the manure heap.

"Good luck to 'em," I said. It had been a long day. I was tired.

"They'll need it," said Boz, a gloomy soul. "That Colonel went after 'em with his dogs."

"Which way'd they go?"

"Back down the waggon-road. You can hear."

The noises of the night seemed very loud. But at the back of them was the *yoop, yoop* of hunting bloodhounds. I dug my heels into the horse's ribs and went down the hill, splashing through the shallows of the creek and on past the slave-camp. I caught a glimpse of fire gleaming red on a half-circle of black faces. This afternoon, they had been slack and weary. Now they were tense and serious. I put in my heels again and the gelding sprang forward. Pop Schmelk's horses were as good as his whisky.

The moonlight splashed livid stripes through the tree trunks. Over the pounding hooves I could hear the bloodhounds, closer now. They would be running a hot scent, but they were no match for a galloping horse. I did not want to think about the slaves. I had been hunted once too often myself.

Ahead, the road curved to the left, following the bank of the creek. There was a slide round the corner, and the moon lit it grey and naked. The horse at the far end slipped into shadow like a rabbit into the burrow. Low and in front of it, I saw the gleam of a wet jowl. There was a crash of brush and the yelling of the hounds grew more urgent, frantic now. I plunged into the shadow of the trees.

On the left, a tiny stream trickled from a spring higher up the hill. New Botallack hated it like hell because whenever there was a spate it washed out the road; but the runaways must have seen it as a stairway to heaven. Water meant no scent, and no scent meant—well, whatever it meant to be free in the bush forty miles from the nearest village.

They had reckoned without the ferns on the runnel's steep sides. The fronds must have brushed their bodies as they scrambled up the rocky bottom, scraping off sweat and oily secretions. To the bloodhounds, it was better than a pillar of fire.

I pulled the gelding's head into the ravine. He flattened his ears, then plunged up the hill, spraying my breeches with cold water. The rump of Tuke's chestnut scuttled around a zigzag thirty yards ahead. Tuke was yelling, "Attaboy! Good dogs! Get them black bastards!" His voice cracked, and he laughed, as I had once laughed with the hounds across the river from Drumcarty, plunging off a bank and seeing the tan-and-white pack streaking after the low-bellied russet fox. I began to feel the rage building under my breast-bone.

Above the spring there was a little patch of open ground where rock came too close to the surface to support anything but a few blades of grass. I came up out of the stream with a yell. The hounds were shrieking now, racing after the two gleaming black figures. I saw Tuke rein in, nodding to himself like a wine-taster as the bloodhounds nosed their way at the canter after the stumbling runaways. A moment of silence, in which I heard the breath sobbing from their lungs. I shouted, "Stop that!" Tuke laughed again. His horse went back on its hind legs, came down with a snort and arrowed for the hinder of the two slaves, Tuke waving his quirt like a dragoon's sabre. He went straight over the hounds. I heard the click of hoof on bone, and half the howling turned to a shrill yelp of pain. I jammed in my spurs.

The black man stopped and turned, spread his hands and said, "Mastah! I sorry—" Tuke's horse swerved a little and went straight into him, full gallop. There was a scream, a crunch, then nothing. Tuke looked down and laughed. I saw his heels go out.

The other man did not stop. He was going like a hare for the wall of trees. Tuke moved across to intercept him. Over pricked ears I saw the pouched face, silver and black in the hard light. His head turned and he saw me and realised what I was going to do, and the mouth opened. Then the gelding's shoulder took his horse in the withers and the moon and the trees turned upside-down, slow and floating. I saw the black back sliding into the thicket, and then I put my arms around my ears and the ground smacked me hard in the belly. The breath whoofed out of my body and I entirely lost interest in the proceedings.

After a long minute I rolled over, sucking wind. The gelding was grazing quietly in the moonlight. I could hear the sound of his teeth on the thin grass. The body of the runaway was quite still. The head was twisted under the shoulder, and I did not have to dissect the cervical vertebrae to know what that meant. Behind me, the chestnut flailed its legs and wriggled onto its feet. Loyal to the last, the bloodhounds were snuffling at a white-suited body prone by the edge of the trees. I went and took the pulse. It was slow and full. I was almost sorry.

On the way back to the houses, Tuke groaned and began to wake up. I left him where he was, lashed like a blood pudding over the chestnut's saddle. Bolitho and Pembarra met me by the slide. I told them what had happened. Bolitho shook his head and said, "Well, hell. He did it on purpose?"

"He did." I still felt sick at the memory.

We rode on in silence. Eventually Bolitho said, "Look, Nick, I think I owe you an apology. You were right, I was wrong. We'll hire men to do the work. I never did realise—"

"That's all right," I said. "The men'll come. It's already fixed."

"Good man," said Bolitho heartily.

The trouble was, I didn't believe a word of it.

Colonel Tuke came to see me before he left. When he kicked open the cabin door his nose was smashed over his face, his white coat covered with blood and green grass-stains. He wasted no time on pleasantries. "I came to tell you I'll see you swing, you bog Irish pretty boy," he said. "Abetting a runaway's a hanging matter."

"So's murder," I said.

"That was no murder." His teeth curled away from his lips and I saw him again, laughing, last night. "Feeding my niggers meat! What in Christ's name d'you expect! I got friends in this county. Good friends—"

"Listen," I said quietly. "I am a rich man. A very rich man. People respect me." The taste of the words was unfamiliar, but not unpleasant. "I do not believe that the word of a penny-ante slave jobber will hold much weight against mine. So I should let the matter rest here, if I were you."

He looked at me with his bruised eyes. What he saw seemed to make him uneasy.

"Shall we set that nose?" I said, advancing, finger and thumb out.

He turned and stumbled out into the sun. I watched him curse up his bloodhounds, scramble onto his horse and trot away down the waggon-road after his stock-in-trade. The sun was warm; and so was the sensation in my belly.

It was nearly a year after my father's death that I received the news that Lady Katherine would be arriving at the Pigeon House on the fifteenth of September, and I had almost forgotten about the charge laid on me by her father. But I asked Duquesne to mind the store and took the coach and four down to meet her.

As usual, the quay was thronged with ragged men bombarding recently-landed passengers with offers to carry their luggage. I could see Katie sitting in the packet's longboat, laughing with one of the men at the oars, attracting scandalised glances from an elderly lady who, I presumed, was her chaperone. The boat came alongside and Katie was helped up the slippery steps with great ceremony. When she saw me she looked hard, and said, "It cannot be Nick Power, surely!"

I bowed. "Your Ladyship," I said. "I trust your journey has not been too fatiguing."

It was four years since I had seen her. She was wearing a green bonnet that brought out the colour of her eyes, and a rakish travelling-gown of heavy silk to match. The years had fined the patrician elegance of her face to a proud symmetry that might have been cold, were it not for the smile. The smile had not changed, and for a moment my pulse quickened.

"His Lordship asked me to convey you to Alban House," I said.

"How kind of him," said Katie. "And how kind of you to come. You have become quite handsome, Nick. And you look most respectable."

"I was thinking the same of Your Ladyship."

She laughed. A tendril of auburn hair had escaped her bonnet. At least it looked auburn; it was only when, as now, the sun caught it that you saw the red lights in it.

"Shall we proceed to the carriage?" I said. "The baggage can come on later."

Katie's eyes strayed over the crowd of beggars and would-be porters. "Oh, there's Captain D'Arcy." An officer in a red tunic was making his way through the press, waving. "Nicholas, it was so kind of you to come, but I think I shall go with the captain." She paused, reflecting. "But perhaps you would be so good as to take Lady Nellie. You have met Lady Nellie Henderson?"

I said that I had not, and was duly introduced to the elderly lady in black. I bowed with as good a grace as I could muster. Lady Nellie said, "Do you think it is right for you to drive with the captain? Should I not—"

"Oh, stuff, Nellie! Really, all will be quite suitable. The captain drives a curricle and I am sure that my virtue will be quite safe, up in the seat for all to see!"

"Very well, dear," said Lady Nellie, with the air of one for whom life had been a long series of similar defeats. "If Doctor Power thinks so."

"Of course he thinks so," said Nellie. "Don't you, Nick?"

I knew there was no sense in disagreeing. But I had learned subtlety. "Very well," I said. "But we shall follow close behind. Do you not think?"

"Who is this fella?" said a drawling voice. It was D'Arcy, a willowy Hussar with the face of a Canova angel. "Are you ready, Lady Kate?"

Katie gave him the full force of her smile, tucked her mauve kid hand under his elbow, and said, *"Au revoir."*

I quickly gave orders for the baggage to be brought to the house later and led Lady Nellie across the quay to the waiting coach. We followed the curricle through a press of waggons and jingles, the dilapidated one-horse carriages that ply for hire in the streets of Dublin. It soon became evident that the captain was trying to shake us. I knocked on the roof and told Healy, the coachman, not to spare the horses; and off we flew.

We thundered round Killiney Bay and through the dung-heaps and cabins of Ringsend, keeping the curricle well in sight. There was considerable traffic, but I was not unduly concerned about losing them. Although D'Arcy had a reputation as a good whip, Healy had been driving in Dublin since he was six, and his speed to a sickbed was legendary. So I was able to concentrate on Lady Nellie, who was sitting jammed into a corner with her eyes tight shut, less worried by the threat to her charge's honour than by our breakneck progress.

By the time we drew up before Alban House, a splendid edifice on the north side of St. Stephen's Green, Lady Nellie had recovered sufficiently to inveigh weakly against her charge's lack of consideration. I sprang out, helped her down, and told Healy I would walk home. Katie was descending from the curricle on D'Arcy's arm. The captain's face wore a sulky look, and I heard Katie say, "Dear me, I do think you should talk to Doctor Power about selling you some horses."

"Deuced fine cattle, mine," said the captain. "Can't be beat. 'Twas the traffic."

"Well, I think the doctor has the victory," said Katie, turning her smile on me. A few years ago, it would have reduced me to a quivering pulp. Not, I was surprised to find, now. "Perhaps he would care for a dish of tea?"

"I fear I have an engagement," I said. "Perhaps I might call another afternoon?"

"By all means," said Katie, faintly startled. "I am sure the captain has an engagement, too."

D'Arcy turned pink and said, "Well, actually no—"

"But I am sure you have," said Katie. "You are only being modest. Most becoming. Good-bye, captain. Really you have been most obliging."

"Actually . . . I do have an engagement. I had quite forgot," said the captain, making a last-ditch attempt to save his face.

"I do hope your poor old horses survive long enough to get you there," said Katie. "Come, Lady Nellie." Again she turned her smile on me. "We shall see you very soon, I hope, Doctor." The double doors of Alban House closed behind her.

I laughed. Katie had not changed. But I had, and I was thankful for it. D'Arcy paused with his foot on the step. "You find something amusing, sir?" he asked.

"I do," I said.

"May I enquire what?"

"You may not."

For a moment, I thought he was going to manufacture a quarrel. Instead, he said, "You will have learned better manners next time we meet."

I said, "You too, I trust," and began to walk home.

I heard D'Arcy's lash on his cattle's rumps. He and his friends occupied their extensive leisure time in drinks, cards and duels. As I heard his wheels rumble off over the paving-stones, there was a faint smell of powder-smoke in my nostrils. Oh, yes. She was the same old Katie.

The New Botallack mill-raising became a back-country legend almost before it was finished. When Tuke was well over the horizon we levelled out the foundations, squared off the socket-holes for the beams and wondered when the labour was going to arrive. It took six days of waiting; just after dawn on the seventh, the neighbours came over the hill. There must have been a hundred men, with God knows how many women and children. Bolitho said, "What is all this? Do they think they're coming to live here?" His eyes went towards the mill-dam and the stone safe where the poke lay.

Pop Schmelk, listing slightly to starboard, pulled his buckboard up with a volley of Pennsylvania Dutch oaths and slid into the dust beside us. "Big crowd," he said. "Hope you got a good supper, lots visky."

"They want to eat us out of house and home as well as get paid?" said Bolitho.

"Paid?" Pop's forehead creased with astonishment. "Nobody wants pay. Raise up mill, lotta food, visky, music. All haf a goot time." He cast a judicious eye over the foundation. "Fifty-gallon mill, looks like."

"Fifty gallons?" said Bolitho. "Of what?"

"Visky."

I took Pop Schmelk by the arm. "Look," I said. "You'd better get right back on your buggy and bring over everything you've got."

"You ain't got no visky?"

"Maybe five gallons on the place. We're not used to . . . mill-raisings."

He nodded. "Chust kilt a hog. Better bring him too."

Before Pop's dust cloud had properly died, the pins were out of the logpiles above the level and the men were in their gangs. The frame, white oak morticed and pegged, was up by afternoon; then the rolling gangs shot the logs up the skids to the axemen and the sun glittered off the razorsharp blades, and the shavings flew fine as paper, and the walls grew out of the ground like mushrooms.

Pop Schmelk arrived back a couple of hours before sundown and gave of his plenty. There were log fires burning by the creek, and over them the women worked like furies, sweat running down from under their bonnets, and hissing into the ashes, one hand on the pans and another batting the children away from the flames. When it was too dark to work, the food went on the tables and there was a long interval of silent eating. After the eating, the ones who lived close went home, with a quick, "See y'all in the morning." The ones who lived a long way off slept in the cabins, packed like pilchards in the barrel. A few bold bachelors, much to Bolitho's fury, took themselves up to the level mouth and passed the night in song.

I bade goodnight to Pop Schmelk, and observed that it seemed rather tame. There had been very little talked or drunk.

"Gott Almighty doktor de mill ain't raised yet," he said. "Tomorrow now. You vait." He towed a blanket under a tarpaulin on his buggy. As I turned to go inside I heard his first snore.

There was a little knot of men standing by the leat, under the black shadow of the half-built wall. As I walked towards them I saw it was Boz, Jacko and Pembarra. Pembarra put out a hand and tentatively patted a new-hewn dovetail.

"Fine, isn't it?" I said. "The goodness of people."

Pembarra grunted, head thrown back to see the black roof-frames gridding the stars.

Bolitho's voice came from behind me. "I don't like it."

"Don't like what?"

"This good-neighbour stuff. It's not business-like."

"Nor's looking a gift horse in the mouth," said Pembarra, and walked away.

Next day the walls went up and the roof crawled over the rafters. Just before sunset a lanky, red-haired youth nailed down the last shingle, flung his hammer in the air and slid down the ladder without touching a rung. Someone put an axe through the head of a barrel of Pop Schmelk's finest, and the festivities commenced. There were long tables set up in what was to be the stamping-floor, under the roof. We ate in a roar of talk in the smell of wood-shavings and pine resin. After supper the tables were cleared and someone got out a fiddle, and the dancing began and didn't stop until the dawn showed pink in the eastern sky. The mountain ladies loaded the mountain gentlemen into the buggies and waggons, said their farewells, and went away, but not before they had swept the place clean as a whistle. I threw a blanket over Pop Schmelk, overcome by his own merchandise. Bolitho said, "Did you hire?" I had no desire even to think about hiring anybody, at that moment; I was tired as hell. But I said, "Two wheel-wrights, for the wheel and the heavy gears. Ten face-hands. Few horse-boys. Satisfied?"

"As long as the money's right," said Bolitho.

"It is."

I went up the hill and opened the cabin door. When I looked back, the mill was shining big and squat in the sun. It looked as solid as the ground itself. If you ignored the newness of the timber shingles, it could have been there forever. A monument to friendship. I hoped it would still look that way in a year.

VIII

It was a hard winter. By November the hills above New Botallack were white with snow, the creek frozen blue and green. The children played in and out of the drifts under the level mouth. The mill-wheel was built, soaking under the ice on the pond, waiting for the spring. We broke the ore on the stamping-floor and came out in the evening with our ears singing from the hammers' concussion. When there was a partial thaw we used the flumes; but the thaws came seldom. There was gold enough to pay our hired hands—forty of them, now—and we used them on a new project.

Late the year before, Joby Pembarra had discovered a branch in the vein at the end of the main level. The top branch continued with a two-degree upward slope, while the lower plunged away at an angle of eighty degrees into the bowels of the hill. Joby burrowed after it, and after six weeks' digging delivered his verdict: the lower vein would be a big producer. Joby's instinct for metal in rock was as keen as the noses of Tuke's bloodhounds, so we gave the matter serious thought. The result was a fifteen-fathom shaft where the vein had been cored out, and a big fat face where it levelled off at the bottom.

We had now seriously to consider how to dispose of the metal once we had got it out of the ground. In February I rode over to Pop Schmelk, to see how his whisky-pickled constitution was lasting out the hard weather. I found him hale and hearty, and stopped over a couple of nights, trying to find a way of improving his still, which was currently a threat to the county's eyesight. When I had finished explaining to him the importance of tempera-ture control in fractional distillation, we got to talking about New Botallack. He told me that he had heard of a couple of Germans who had set up in Rutherford County, minting coin and making jewellery and ornaments. I took the news back to New Botallack, suggesting that it might be a way round the chanciness of the Charlotte market; so Bolitho and I and two heavily-armed guards set off with a pack-train mid-March.

The thaw had come, setting the creek roaring in the mill-leat and changing the waggon-road's white drifts to hock-deep muck. We left on a day of raw cold, riding un-der dripping pines past the little shacks which had sprung up downstream of New Botallack, each with its sluice and pile of deads. The gold-hunters had spread far into the back-country in the past two years; such was the speed of claim and boom and bust that New Botallack was re-garded as old-established and copper-bottomed. Not everyone had Jabez Twochild to lead them to the lodes; half the men labouring at the shaft had come in out of the cold with hardly a shirt to their backs. They had been employed against Bolitho's will, some of them. Success was doing nothing to increase his faith in human nature.

It was a tense journey to the Bechtlers' mint, with bet-ter than a hundred thousand dollars of species in the packs. We slept in the wet woods, as far away from hab-itation as possible, taking watch in the stealthy night-noises around the fire. But there were few travellers

braving the abominable roads, and we reached the mint
and concluded our business without incident. The guards
returned to New Botallack, but Bolitho and I went on to
Charlotte. Bolitho had friends in Charlotte now, and he
particularly wanted me to meet them. Besides, there was
business to attend to in the town.

We put up in the Catawba Hotel, a tall wooden establishment in a street off Constitution Square. A black servant brought a tin bath and hot water, and I sluiced off
my thick layer of road-silt, listening with a profound sense
of unreality to the rumble of waggons and the sound of
voices from the street outside. Then I arrayed myself in
the stiff black serge coat and trousers Mrs. Pembarra had
made me, grasped my stick and went down to the bar. It
was full of men, smoke and loud talk. A voice said, "Doctor Power! I want you to meet my good friend Abe
Cawthrop." It was Bolitho's voice, but I could not see
Bolitho. I walked on into the room in a sudden hush.
There were a lot of people looking my way. I brushed
shoulders with a square-set individual in a grey frock-coat
and high white gills, and apologised. The man laughed.
It was Bolitho's laugh. He said, "Didn't recognise me,
eh?"

"No," I said. "I didn't." The boots were shining, the
trousers well-cut. Across the white waistcoat there
swooped a watch-chain of thumbnail-sized New Botallack
nuggets.

Bolitho was saying, "Doctor Power—General Cawthrop." I remembered my manners and bowed. The General raised his hat, and said, "This sure is a pleasure.
We're honoured at Doctor Power's visit to our little town."

I looked at him narrowly. He was perfectly serious.
Suddenly I remembered that I was a rich man, from the
old-established New Botallack mine. "The honour is all
mine," I said.

Bolitho called for drinks and the General and I discussed the appalling state of the weather and the roads,
the excellence of the Bechtler mint, and the money the
boom was bringing into Charlotte. The General had a
long, bony face and a drooping grey moustache, carefully
combed. He spoke with his right thumb hooked into his
waistcoat pocket, frowning down at his red-veined nostrils
in a manner calculated to give every word its maximum
weight. With the forefinger of his left hand he made jab-

bing gestures at the smoke-browned ceiling. I got the impression that he was used to addressing large numbers of people, and that he was only talking to me because of my immense wealth and importance.

"And how do you like our city?" he was saying, as Bolitho turned back from the bar.

"A fine city," I said, perhaps more from courtesy than conviction. "I spent some little time here before we moved to New Botallack, you know."

"Ah, yes," said the General, screwing up his forehead as if gazing into the murky deeps of prehistory. "Before New Botallack. A long time ago. Our city is changing. Bigger, more bustling. The commercial spirit, Doctor. The very air of freedom."

"The General has more interests than a goat's got whiskers," said Bolitho with a note of proprietary pride. "Land, politics, mining. . . ."

"And my family," said the General with a sentimental grin into his glass. "My little brood of chicklings. You as a man of religion will appreciate the close ties that knit a family under God—"

"I'm a doctor of medicine," I said.

The General finished his drink, scything the air with his left hand as if bracketing the liberal professions into one splendid pantheon. "And now," he said when he had carefully wiped his moustache with a white silk handkerchief. "Shall we repair to the domestic pleasures of my humble hearth?"

The hearth, as it transpired, was by no means humble. Outside the hotel there waited a coach with four fine bays, two black grooms and a black coachman. In this conveyance we forged out of the town through the warm drizzle and, after a few miles, turned between lamplit white pillars onto a long carriage-drive. When the coach drew up, there were black footmen with flambeaux to hand us out onto the steps, under a huge pillared pediment and up to a front door the size of the end wall of my cabin at New Botallack.

We were ushered through a circular hall decorated with white plaster impressions from the antique, into a drawing-room with a log fire, dark portraits on the walls, and high wine-red velvet curtains. "Mrs. Cawthrop," said the General. "We are honoured with company."

Mrs. Cawthrop was tall and worried-looking, wearing a

dress of blue silk embroidered with marigolds which must once have matched her hair. She smiled nervously and said, "Oh, wonderful, honey," her thin hand straying to the bell-rope.

"My daughter, Bella Cawthrop," said the General.

Bella smiled, too. She had auburn hair and brown eyes and a face long like her father's, but considerably prettier. Her smile showed rather pointed teeth, and I got the impression that there was something sharp about her whole person. But she said, "Charmed, I'm sure," and her long hands were delicate against the sky-blue shot-silk of her dress, and I was charmed, too. It was a long time since I had seen faces or manners prettier than the wholesome but rough graces of New Botallack.

After more polite chit-chat about the state of the roads and the weather, a liveried butler announced dinner, and we proceeded to the dining room. Silver gleamed in the light of the cut-glass chandeliers, and impassive black footmen brought clear soup, which was despatched in silence, the hour being late and the company hungry. After the fish and more small talk, the entrée made its appearance, flanked by a roast of beef to which General Cawthrop addressed himself. The business of carving apparently turning his mind to business, he said, "And how goes it in the goldfields?"

"Well," I said guardedly. "We are hoping for a useful year come spring."

"Driving a new level," said Bolitho. "We should about double last year."

"Good, good," said the General. "A little of the outside for you, Doctor? I like to see a man take his meat, though the ladies will have their made dishes. I am sure we wish you every prosperity in the coming year, and after that. Not so, my dears?"

Mrs. Cawthrop nodded distractedly, and Bella applied her napkin to her mouth, blushing.

Bolitho cleared his throat. "And how are your projects, General?"

"Good," said the General. "Very good. We'll be putting a thousand acres to cotton. Sowing any day now. When we were at the Charleston races I profited by the opportunity of seeing to the stock."

"Got some good ones?" said Bolitho.

"Prime. Just prime. Powerful dear, of course——" The

General's knife paused in the bloody interior of the sir-
loin, and he smiled archly—"but we can't all be miners. I
envy you, Doctor. Dig a hole, make money. Simple as
that."

"It's not all downhill," I said.

"Hell of a gamble," said Bolitho. "Paid off, though."
He looked across the table at Bella, who blushed again
and said, "And while Daddy was with his men of affairs,
we were at the spring balls."

"You find Charleston an amusing city?" I said. There
was something afoot between Bolitho and the General,
and Bella and her blushes might have something to do
with it.

"Oh, the spring balls!" cried Bella, clasping her hands
Everybody was there. The Izards, Rutledges, the Pinck-
neys, the Alstons!"

"And young Mr. Alston paid Bella the most marked at-
tentions," said Mrs. Cawthrop, with pride, then put her
hand to her mouth. Cawthrop said something that
sounded like, "Puppy," and champed beef.

"We see very little of that kind of thing at New Botallack," I said, to break the silence.

"That might change," said Bolitho. "Will change. Eh,
Bella?"

Bella dropped her eyes. On the third finger of her left
hand there was a heavy gold ring, set with a diamond the
size of a lima bean. I looked across at Bolitho, whose
weatherbeaten face wore an expression of supreme smug-
ness. "Do I detect . . . an understanding?" I said.

The General laughed a hearty laugh and said, "Sharp,
Doctor. Very sharp."

"Miss Cawthrop has done me the honour of consenting
to become my wife," said Bolitho solemnly.

I stared at him, at the grizzled brush of hair, the shrewd
blue eyes, the hard jaw working on the beef among the
improbable frills of his shirt-front. He was a good thirty
years older than Bella. The General was watching me
closely. I said, "Well, well. You are the dark horse. My
congratulations to both of you." Then I ran out of steam.
Bolitho married? I would have been less surprised if I had
heard that Joby and Mrs. Pembarra had been seen dancing at the Jockey Ball.

The General said, "A bumper! To Captain Bolitho of
New Botallack, and the future Mrs. Bolitho!" We all

drank, I reflecting on Bolitho's rank. If the General had known that he had earned it running brandy to half-savage tinners, he might not have been so free with his claret. Then again, the General struck me as a man who weighed his advantages on a pretty sensitive scale. He was losing a daughter. So what was he gaining?

Bella turned to me with a sentimental tear in her sharp, brown eyes. "Is it not wonderful?" she said. "Are you a married man, Doctor?"

"No," I said shortly.

"You look quite downcast," said Bella. "We must try to find you a wife. I am sure there is some charming young lady who would suit you nicely."

I laughed, sweeping away the remembrance of Mary's soft voice, the night-blue eyes. "Oh, I can look after myself."

"I am sure you can," she said, laughing too. "I am sure that Horace and I shall approve of your choice."

"Horace?"

"Captain Bolitho, of course."

"Shall we leave the gentlemen to their wine?" said Mrs. Cawthrop nervously.

The ladies withdrew, leaving the General to address us on the iniquities of the North Carolina Legislature's discrimination against the State's Western counties. Bolitho nodded and grunted and made useful suggestions. I sipped at my wine and gave myself over to delightful speculations as to Jamesy Paxton's reaction to the news of Bolitho's Christian name.

But later, when I retired to my comfortable tent bed on the first floor of the Cawthrop palazzo, I felt less frivolous. The General had sent for our bags from the hotel, swearing that no future son-in-law or friend of said son-in-law would rent a room while he still had a roof over his head. I sat for a while in an armchair by the fire, trying to read a newspaper that had come back from Charleston with the Cawthrop party. It was full of invective against Federal import tariffs. I could not keep my mind on it. If the General was planning to plant cotton, he would need slaves to work it for him. If he was buying a lot of slaves, he would need money. And if he needed more money than he already had, what better way of coming by it than a rich son-in-law? But the General seemed to be a rich man. And presumably Bolitho knew what he was doing. It was his life, his money. It was not my place to ask awkward questions, particularly since Bella did not seem averse to the idea. Nonetheless, my feelings as I blew out the candle were not those that might have been expected of the old acquaintance of a happy bridegroom-to-be.

Next morning I was early into Charlotte, and spent the day ordering up supplies for the mine. There was a lot to be done, with the new shaft sunk and spring coming in; by four o'clock in the afternoon I had bespoken ten waggon-loads of iron, cordage, and chemicals. When I had finished that, I went to do some private errands for the ladies of New Botallack in the way of haberdashery. The clerk at the notions counter was small and garrulous and when I told him to send the goods out to the Cawthrop house he said, "Red Hill? You'll be Miss Bella's intended? A lucky man, Sir, a lucky man."

I disabused him, at which he fell into a flutter of apologies. "Oh dear me, how tactless. Forgive me do, only we're real pleased that Miss Bella's got a man who—well, a man of *substance*. Got a couple of bucks to rub together."

"I should have thought she'd have all the substance she needs," I said.

"Real old family, Cawthrops," said the clerk. "Rumour around town was that they were stretched pretty thin. Yes sir. But you know what rumours are! Will there be any other article?"

"That's it," I said. "Thank you."

"Good day," said the clerk. I left him parcelling up Mrs. Pembarra's puce ribbons, wondering again whether Bolitho knew what he was doing.

My next visit was more consoling. Late in the fall of the previous year, we had appointed Cadwallader Jones Attorney to New Botallack Mines, and one of the purposes of our expedition was to pick up the company papers, among which were the share certificates, six thousand of them, representing one thousand shares per partner. Mr. Jones was a wiry, sanguine gentleman, unsoured by watching the failure of most of the mining companies to which he had been midwife. He greeted me effusively, gave me a cup of coffee, and congratulated New Botallack Mines on its profits and the alliance of one of its partners with a Cawthrop. I said to him, "You regard it as a useful alliance?"

"Well, God yes," he said. "Why not? New money, old family. Cotton's the coming thing now, lotta good sand-hill land. Fine prospects, Doctor. Fine prospects."

"I had heard talk. . . ."

"They'll always make it sound worse than it is. Folks 'round these parts is used to small farming. Scotchmen. Soon as a man starts improvements they start looking for bailiffs in the bushes."

"That's a consolation," I said, finishing my coffee.

"Just as well to be sure," said Jones. I liked him, but he was still a lawyer. I noticed that he had not committed himself one way or the other. "Will you join me at the saloon?" He said.

"Thank you no. I wonder if I might beg the use of paper and pens?"

"By all means." He led me into a little side office, where I wrote two letters. One was to Michael Fitzpatrick and the other to Mary. I gave them both the baldest possible account of the winter's doings. Into Michael's packet I folded one hundred of the New Botallack share certificates. Then I sealed it up. Mary's I left open, while I scratched my beard and wondered whether I should add another paragraph, telling her once again to come. I wrote a couple of lines, crossed them out, gnawed my pen. In the end I merely added, "If ever you change your mind, you know where I am; I shall be waiting." Then I folded in a hundred and fifty certificates and consigned both packets to Jones' care, with particular instructions for a safe courier and a fast ship. After which, I rode back out to Red Hill.

Bolitho and his fiancée were in the drawing room, chaperoned by Mrs. Cawthrop, who was knitting in a high-backed chair. Behind her, Bella was explaining to Bolitho the provenance of the water-colours in an album. Bolitho's hand rested on her shoulder, and he was not even trying to look interested in painting. When they saw me the lovers separated, Bella getting to her feet and saying, "Well, I declare, I didn't know it was so late!" She tripped from the room. Her mother, usefulness ended, followed. I said, "I'm sorry. I didn't mean to play gooseberry."

"All the time in the world," said Bolitho, rather smugly.

"Beautiful woman. I couldn't wish you better."

"She is," said Bolitho. "And by God I've seen some women in my time. Plenty of blunt, too. Funny thing, you know, I had an idea I'd end up with some widow, comfortable fortune. I never did imagine I'd get anywhere near . . . all this." He waved a stubby hand at moulded ceiling, Italian marble mantlepiece, long-dead Cawthrops gazing gloomily down at him from their portraits.

"When's the wedding to be?" I had never thought of Bolitho as a man with aspirations to gentility.

"Saturday."

"But—Good God, man, it's Wednesday already. What about the people up at the mine? Why so quick? You haven't. . . ."

Bolitho laughed a jolly bridegroom's laugh. "Almost wish I had," he said. "But they're damned strict. Never have seen her alone. As for the people up at the mine, what do they want with weddings?"

"They'll kill you if you get married without 'em. Can you conceive of Mrs. Pembarra being left out? Or Jamesy? Let alone the rest of them."

Bolitho frowned. "See what you mean. But we've got to do it quick. All arranged with the General. Question of dowries, guarantees. . . . We'll have a grand old hell-raising when we come back to New Botallack, never you fear. That'll satisfy 'em."

"I hope so," I said. It was on the tip of my tongue to ask him what dowries and what guarantees, but I left it unasked. He was his own man. It was none of my business.

"Glass of wine," said Bolitho, and sent the footman off for claret with a powerful air of custom. As we drank, his chest looked larger, his watch-chain brighter, his iron-grey hair fiercer. It was quite evident that whatever reservations there might be about Cawthrop's style or substance, Bolitho did not share them. "And you," he said, smacking his lips, "will be my best man."

"It will be an honour," I said. "Long life to you both."

The night before the wedding, Bolitho became exceedingly drunk. Red Hill was in a turmoil of preparation, so we had taken the coach into Charlotte, to the bar of the Catawba Hotel and later to a succession of less desirable waterholes. I contrived to stay sober; since my drink-sodden winter, I had decided that even the most leaden sobriety was preferrable to the after-effects of home-made whisky. Bolitho passed through three stages of drunkeness. At first, he was the young bridegroom, nervous and callow. Next, he roared and slammed glasses about and sang songs he had learned in port with the *Jane and Emily*. And finally, he became sly and confidential.

The final stage occurred in a saloon floored with slimy sawdust and patronised by four morose Indians. He put his elbows on the table, sank his head into his shoulders, and said, "I'm a damned lucky man."

"Lovely woman," I said.

"Not only that. Y'know what we've arranged for the dowry? The estate."

"What estate?"

"Red Hill. Lock, stock, and barrel. Took some doing, I can tell you."

"Will you be moving down from New Botallack?"

"Not in the General's life. He has it for his life, y'see. See? But when he dies, poof! Old Bolitho's got it. It and lovely Bella and a coach and four and cotton and Charleston and—"

"And until the General dies?"

"New Botallack. Needs an old hand at the helm. Old Boz and Jacko and all of them. And you. You're a clever lad, Nick, I'll grant you that. But you haven't got the firm hand of the helmsman. First thing you know you'd be feeding Red Indians or harbouring runaways, or giving gold away in the street."

"That's an interesting point of view," I said.

"Very sly," he said. "Very, very sly. That's me."

All this was less of a revelation than Bolitho had intended. I had suspected for some time that he considered himself the guiding hand at New Botallack, and I had thought it might cause trouble. For tonight, however, the trouble could keep. Bolitho's head was approaching the table. I got him out and into the coach, and we drove back to Red Hill with the window-glass rattling to his snores.

It took a few stiff jolts to get him going the next day, and when we saw the rows of carriages drawn up outside the white clapboard church I thought for a moment that he was going to cut and run. But he set his jaw grimly and charged the doors at his old pace and sat down to await the bride as casually as if he was waiting for the tide out of New Grimsby harbour.

The church was packed with the *ton* of the surrounding area, and there was much whispering. I heard a woman's voice behind me say, "O Lord but he's handsome," and another say, "That's the best man," and a muted storm of giggles. Then a pianoforte started banging chords and the General slow-marched up the aisle with Bella a tent of virginal muslin on his arm, and next thing any of us knew the happy pair were hopping into the big black carriage, covered today with green branches and white ribbons, and rumbling through the drying puddles towards Red Hill, and Bolitho, self-styled helmsman of New Botallack, was a married man.

"Like a bloody hearse it looks, doesn't it," said a cheery voice at my elbow. It was Cadwallader Jones, all wild hair and rolling eyes in black swallowtail and breeches. "Come up the house on the buggy." It was a fine spring day, with only a haze of high cloud between us and the sun. There was a newness in the air that tugged at my worry about last night's revelations and tore it away. So off we jounced behind the scraggy rump of Jones' mare while he, with a remarkable lack of discretion, told me dirt about every local worthy within sight in a subdued mumble, as if he were rebriefing counsel in open court.

Then there was luncheon for sixty and whisky for the men and champagne for the ladies, and I flirted with the bridesmaids. The General made a speech about the merging of old blood with new vigour, which worried me rather on Bolitho's behalf. But it all went over his head, sitting next to the undeniably radiant Bella. Then I made a speech about hospitality and the joys of young love in spring, which went down well enough. And after it all, bride and groom left in a hail of rice and a forest of waving handkerchiefs, with Mrs. Cawthrop sobbing from the shelter of the General's protective arm on the portico. And a very pretty bridesmaid caught Bella's flung bouquet and batted her eyelashes at me, while her mother smiled indulgently on. And Cadwallader Jones, behind me, said "You next, Doctor. They'll all be after you now." And the guests straggled home, leaving me with a curious sensation. The sensation that the ceremonies of the day had been not so much a wedding as a glorified cattle market. I said my farewells, slung packs on Bolitho's horse, and set off for New Botallack.

As I rode north-west, the clouds came lower, trailing veils of mist among the dark slopes of pine. It was a heavy mist, wet on my face and distilling in little globes over my harness and the lead horse's pack-saddle. The veils thickened until the trees were jagged black-green spikes projecting from a pearly sea. The ford over the Catawba River, normally a fetlock-deep splash, was a belly-deep brown torrent. After I had crossed it, the rain began, soft at first like a Drumcarty morning, then gathering weight. I made miserable camp in a pine-grove, and trailed into New Botallack late the next day. The rain had not abated. The spring had washed out the waggon-road again, and the wheel-ruts were baby rivers. New Botallack looked dour and mossy, the smoke from its chimneys smeared down over the hill towards the day-labourers' shacks at the flooded creekside.

Jacko and Boz took the news of Bolitho's wedding with a quiet resignation learned after years under his command at sea. I had long realised that neither of them could get used to the idea of being equal partners with their captain; at our periodic conferences, they always waited for Bolitho to vote, and voted the same way. Mrs. Samms looked a thought put out, but softened when I told her that Bolitho had promised a major festival on his return from his honeymoon three weeks hence.

Joby Pembarra only nodded when I told him, and went to the window and stared out at the rain half-hiding the far hill and pocking the soil of his vegetable patch. There were tiny valleys eroded in the soil, with fans of mud at the bottom of the terracing. "Wish him joy," he said. "Wet for it." Mrs. Pembarra was off at chapel over the ridge, and Joby seemed disinclined for company, so I went on to the Paxtons. Jamesy was practising his fiddle, his wife having taken the children with Mrs. Pembarra. He was the only one who reacted as I expected. "Bloody pompous old hog," he said. "Too good for us, is he? We'll see about that." He then offered me a drink, took one himself, and commenced sawing away at the *Devil among the Tailors*. The head of steam Jamesy worked up of a Sunday was legendary. I hoped for Bella's sake that Bolitho arrived back on a weekday.

The rain did not stop. All that week it came down, and

the next, and the week after that. Five new hands arrived up the flooded waggon-road, saying that they had been sluicing down-stream in a small way and that the creek had risen so far that it had swept away cabins and sluices and wiped them out. We took them on the strength. There was going to be a lot of work to do when the rain stopped. If it ever stopped. Jamesy was slamming nails into the new wing of Bolitho's house, and wondering aloud whether it wouldn't be a good idea to put a hull on it and call it an Ark. Behind the mill-dam the hammer-pond stretched back up the valley and out of sight. The sluices were wide open, but the water lapped within inches of the top. And still the rain came down.

Spring came to New Botallack four hours ahead of the new Mrs. Bolitho. The newlyweds came out of the bush on foot, their carriage having bogged at the slide. Bella was seen to be rather pale, leaning on her husband's arm in a suitable apprehension. The husband's jaw was set and his eyes forbidding. I sent five men to see to the road, bowed deep, and said, "Mrs. Bolitho, welcome to New Botallack."

Bella gave me a smile more wan than sharp, and went on to be introduced to the ladies of New Botallack, resplendent in the ribbons I had purchased in Charlotte. That night we supped on the stamping-floor, and the ladies with their excellent Cornish manners tried to put Mrs. Bolitho at her ease. But Bella had turned unexpectedly shy, and it was almost a relief when after supper the gentlemen adjourned for a conference.

Bolitho had insisted on this conference. When all six of us were seated at the democratically round table we used on these occasions, I said, "We should decide on the spring offensive. How to use the men. Any views?"

"Aye," said Joby Pembarra. "There's a hell of a lot of water. The new vein levels off a bit at fifteen fathom, but she's still a down-sloper. I don't like it."

"And what would you propose to do about it?"

"Run an adit into the hammerpond."

"From where?" said Bolitho. "From the bottom of the shaft?"

"One from there. One from further down the vein."

Bolitho frowned. "Hell of a job," he said. "You'd have to take half the men off the face and the stampers. Can't be done."

"Got to be done," said Pembarra in his slow, deliberate voice with the little cough in it. "You'll lose the lot if you don't."

"How do you know?" said Bolitho sharply.

"There's a lot of water in that hill. 'Sgoing somewhere, and it ain't all in the creek. Else the hammerpond'd be over the dam by now. She's sitting up there in the hill."

Bolitho chewed at a fingernail. "How d'you know?" he said. "You've no proof. There's no profit in building adits. None."

Pembarra folded his massive arms and leaned back in his chair. "There's no profit in drowning fifteen fathoms down, neither."

"If I might make a suggestion," I said. "Only a certain number of men can work on the adit. Why couldn't the rest dig the upper level face? There's less water up there, and even if you did hit a pocket it'd run down the shaft."

Pembarra laughed a hollow laugh. "Ever seen a pocket go? Never mind it running down the shaft. Blow you away and take the level with it."

"There's no guarantee there's a pocket," said Bolitho.

"Possibility's enough for me," said Pembarra.

After which, they sat glaring at each other. Finally, Bolitho said, "Vote. Do we carry on with the shaft and dig the adit up towards, or do we put all the men on the adit. Adit first."

I raised my finger. So did Paxton and Pembarra.

"And then there's three of us vote the other way," said Bolitho, without even looking at Jacko and Boz. "Month's chairman has the casting vote." He consulted the minutes. "Chairman's Jacko. Jacko?"

Jacko's round face screwed up uncomfortably. He gave me an apologetic grin and said, "I votes with you, cap'n."

"Stupid bugger," said Pembarra. "Doc should have left you to rot."

"Now come on, Job, there ain't no call to talk like that," whined Jacko. But Pembarra kicked back his chair and stumped out of the room. . .

I got up. "I think you're crazy not to listen to him," I said.

"Pusillanimosity," said Bolitho. It was by no means warm, but there was a shine of sweat on his forehead. "Now let's get the men down that hole and dig some gold."

After the pursuit from the packet-landing, I found myself regularly invited to Alban House. Duquesne was
much pleased; his age was interfering seriously with his
practice, and he was more and more relying on me to
bring in the influential patients whose guineas supported
Mercy Hall. At first I was somewhat nervous of accepting
these invitations, fearing for my dignity at Katie's hands.
But she found my fellow-guests better butts than me, and
I soon became as close to her as anybody, I think. Dublin was rather frightened of her. Her reputation was by
no means good—I had even heard that she had left England to avoid imprisonment for debt; but her glitter
brought a certain element flocking to her salon, in much
the same spirit as McGinchy visited the Mauritius Rooms.
You could always be sure of fireworks at Alban House.

One evening I was surprised to see Michael Fitzpatrick
come into the drawingroom, sleek and grinning avari-
ciously beside an exquisite young gentleman I knew was
heir to ten thousand acres in County Cork. I say surprised
because Katie made no secret of her dislike for Michael; I
think she knew that he was a match for her, but she always thought that, unlike me, he could not be moulded
into a trustworthy ally. I did not care; I found their society equally amusing, though naturally Michael lacked
Katie's physical attractions.

When he had made his salutations, Michael came over
to me and said, "I have your rents for you."

"My rents?" I said.

"I didn't know you were a landlord," said Katie, aban-
doning Michael's exquisite heir. She had an astonishing
gift for picking out a potentially scandalous remark from
the general hum of talk.

"Sure and didn't he tell you about the hundred acres
he won off McGinchy at a badger-baiting?"

"To tell the truth I had quite forgotten about that," I
said.

"At a badger-baiting," said Katie, losing interest.
"Oh."

"Will you double up this year?" said Michael. Katie
brightened, sensing trouble.

"The rents, you mean?" I thought of the dispossessed
wrecks, grey and sick and verminous, on the benches at
Mercy Hall. Katie was watching me closely. I pulled my
chin. "No. I don't think I will."

"And why not?" said Michael. " 'Tis grand country. We could squeeze 'em easy."

"No," I said again. "We'll let 'em have it."

Michael looked puzzled.

"Give it to them. You might have the papers drawn up. Each tenant to have his land. Freehold."

"You're crazy," said Michael. I had never seen him so shocked.

"What do I want with land?"

Katie's clear laugh rang icy among the chandeliers. "Oh, good, Nick," she said, clapping her hands. "You get better and better." As always, I found great satisfaction in having that laugh on my side.

"But reflect, man," said Michael. "Giving away land— they're Catholics, for God's sake."

"They're farmers," I said. "That's good enough."

Michael shrugged. "If you want it like that." Since the Act of Union, more and more landowners found it convenient to run their estates by proxy. Michael had profited considerably from this arrangement. Now I was striking at the very roots of his prosperity. It was not an unpleasant sensation.

Katie said, "But I think that's wonderful." Michael went back to his heir, with whom he would undoubtedly have business to discuss. Katie remained at my side. "Will you stay and take some supper?" she said, putting her hand on my arm. The green eyes were soft and tempting.

Katie's suppers were as famous as her afternoons, but for different reasons. They were usually tête-a-tête, and old women tended to whisper that carriages were called for at disgracefully late hours.

"I fear that I am engaged," I said.

"Then cancel it."

I was due at Mercy Hall at six. "I am afraid that is impossible." She lifted her pointed chin. The softness left her, and she fixed me with the haughty stare that made all Dublin quail. But I was long past quailing. "Perhaps you would care to join me?" I said.

"What is it?"

"You will see. But perhaps it would not amuse you . . . ?"

She bit. "Of course it would."

"Then we should be going."

She told Lady Nellie to look after her guests, and five

minutes later we were rolling down the narrow, squalid streets of the Liberties.

"Where are we going?" she said. "This had better not be a joke."

"Not a joke," I said.

The carriage came to a halt in the greenish light over the dingy plaque. "This is where we get out," I said.

She wrapped her cloak around her, a marvellous thing of flame-coloured silk that matched the red lights in her hair. And she followed me into Mercy Hall.

She paused on the threshold, swaying a little. Father Allen came up and shook me by the hand. I introduced him to Katie and he fixed her with his gentle eyes and said, "So glad you came. I wonder would you care to assist?"

"Assist?" said Katie. I had never heard that voice before. It was low and it trembled. The emerald eyes travelled the rows of ragged misery on the benches. "How—what—what could I do?"

"Perhaps you could bear a hand with the soup?"

"The soup," said Katie, as if the word was a floating plank and she drowning. "Of course."

I went about my business, writing up the prescriptions and working like fury in the smelly alcove behind the curtain. As always happened, I became lost in my work. But soon I heard laughter from the long table with the pans and the loaves of bread, and when I looked, there was Katie in an apron, laughing her head off with a street-girl.

When it was over, Father Allen took Katie by the hand and said, "God bless you for coming to us, my child."

Katie blushed. She actually blushed. I heard the clink of coin as she put something into his hand. Then she mumbled some indistinguishable words and we went out into the drizzle.

For perhaps a mile she did not say anything, only huddled in the cushions with her cloak pulled over her face. Finally, she said, "So that's where you go. Why did you take me?"

"I don't know," I said. Perhaps it had been merely a matter of putting her out of countenance. Perhaps it was to show her that loneliness was not the worst thing that could happen. For I knew, now, that she was a very lonely woman.

"I'm glad you did," she said. "It was only that . . . it seemed such a little thing to do. To give charity. Food. Money. It would so soon go."

"Not only charity," I said, echoing Duquesne's remarks on my first visit. "Hope."

"Is that enough?"

"What do you think?"

Again silence. Then she said, "Nick. Do you think you could give me hope, too?"

The weather held, the sun burning down day after day, sucking up the winter wet until the grass was dry and the leaves stood out new green on the whiteoaks and maples on the ridge. There was green on the red soil of the gardens and fields, too, as the seed planted after the melt shoved its first tentative leaves towards the light. So hot did the sun shine that it should have been too dry; but it was not. The springs in the hills spouted water in double their usual quantities; it looked to be a prodigious year for the gardeners. For the mine, too. With two faces under simultaneous attack, the quartz poured down to the mill. Long plumes of deads muddied the river, and the thud of the stampers was an iron heartbeat that measured the valley's day.

The new Mrs. Bolitho did not show herself much. Bolitho's cabin by the side of the hammerpond was now a splendid edifice by New Botallack standards. Its large central part had two storeys and a pillared portico looking over the pool. There were two wings, one with bedrooms, the other with a kitchen and quarters for the black lady's maid Mrs. Bolitho had brought with her. Bolitho had installed a fleet of white ducks on the hammerpond, and had plans for swans. Myself, I found it too close to the din of the stamping-engine, but Mrs. Bolitho did not seem to mind. I saw her from time to time watching the ducks, dressed in brilliant colours that caught the sun like jewels. Once or twice I went and passed the time of day with her, but her talk was mostly about Charleston and the wonderful time she had passed with dear Horace on their honeymoon, and I found I had little to say to her. She, for her part, had had no time to develop an interest in New Botallack. It would come, I had no doubt; Mrs. Pembarra was making it her task to draw her out, and once Mrs. Pembarra had drawn you out you stayed drawn.

Now that the hired hands were doing most of the dirty work, I had a good deal of time for my rounds. I went off for days at a time to visit the families living on the fringes of the Blue Ridge to the west. They were a poverty-stricken, rugged, independent lot, and I liked their company. They reminded me, in their tough self-sufficiency and their cheerful disregard for the law, of Scilly folk. There was a lot of consumption and it had been aggravated by the soaking misery of the early spring; but as the sun showed itself the mountain air turned to tonic wine, and there was a general improvement.

On my return from a sixty-mile round, I met Joby Pembarra at the back of his house. His face was grim and pale, the patch of blasting-powder standing out deep indigo. "Come with me," he said. "I want you to see something."

I gave my horse to one of the stable-hands—we employed four now, under Boz's supervision—and followed Joby's worn flannel shirt across the mill-dam and up to the level mouth. It was a warm spring evening, but the chill of the dark tunnel struck through my clothes and made me shiver. Joby took a lantern from the rack and we stood aside to let a bouse-barrow past. After the rumble of the barrow there was a moment of silence, broken only by the drip of water. "Wet," I said.

"That's not the half of it," said Joby.

The level mouth became a speck of light behind, went out. Barrows passed, one every two minutes. The lantern-light threw our shadows huge and grotesque on the gleaming vault of the roof. I could hear the smack and clink of picks on rock far below. The level bent slightly to the right, and widened. There were men with barrows and a windlass bringing bouse up from the shaft that yawned black in the floor before us. To the right of the hole a walkway skirted the gulf, and Pembarra strode across it, ignoring the barrowmen. They looked worried. On the far side of the shaft was a clay dam a foot high. The dam continued round the lip of the walkway. The walkway was two inches deep in running water.

"Where's that coming from?" I said. Last time I had been down here, a couple of weeks ago, there had been no dam, no stream of water.

"You'll see," said Pembarra.

The upward slope of the tunnel floor steepened into the jagged curves where the diggers had followed the vein's meanderings. I could hear men's voices up ahead, and a tinkle of falling water. We rounded the last curve, and came into a bright little chamber of lamplight, the roof of raw stone. On the ground there were lumps of quartz, shining white. White as the skin of the face-crew who stood leaning on their picks, watching the wall where the tunnel ended. The face of the quartz here was a foot wide and thirty inches high, and it glittered. I could not understand why it was glittering, shimmering. The lantern-flames were still. Then Joby Pembarra pointed up, and said, "Look."

Where the face joined the roof, the rock changed colour. There were traces of quartz up there, squeezed in by the upheavals that had raised the hills. Across the join in the strata there ran a crack, as if they had once been glued together and now the glue had fallen out. From that crack there poured a stream of water, running down the face and onto the floor and out, following gravity to the shaft and the walkway and the daylight.

"Is that one of your pockets?" I said to Joby.

He shook his head. "Couldn't say. Wouldn't like to put it to the test."

Was it my imagination, or was the stream of water running harder?

"Better get out of here," I said. Suddenly I realised that I was two hundred yards into the side of a high hill, in a place that might at any moment become a roaring drain of rock and water and smashed bodies. The narrow tunnel began to close in on our little glow-worm of light. I licked my lips. They were salty. Despite the chill, I was sweating. Pembarra said, "Steady, the croaker." I tried to grin at him, but I could not seem to get my breath. The air tasted as if it had been breathed hundreds of times. I said, "Let's go."

Pembarra nodded. As we walked past the shaft, a whistle blew. Two minutes later we were in daylight, gulping clean air, and the shaft-hands were spilling out after us.

"What now?" I said to Pembarra.

"Hard to say. She might be just a trickle, a little sink-hole. It's not coming out under much pressure, so even if it's a pocket we'll be right at the top of her. Or it might be seepage through previous rock. Out of ·a great big bloody bubble of 'er."

"In which case?"

"In which case we'd better start learning to be farmers."

"We'd better close down, wait and see if the water stops."

Pembarra laughed. "Close 'er? Jesus no, man. I'll take the boys down and we'll make a burrow round to the side, see what we finds." He looked at the men sitting on the platform outside the level-mouth, smoking and talking. "I'll take Jamesy and Jacko and Boz," he said. "They know what they's·doing. And them two." He pointed at a couple of squat gentlemen in filthy buckskins. I knew them only as the Barstow brothers. They had turned up in the middle of the winter, all taciturnity and Yorkshire. They occasionally spoke with familiarity of the Peru lead-pits on Grassington Moor, and I had heard rumours of a dead foreman and a precipitate flight.

"What the. hell's all this?" said a voice from down the hill. It was Bolitho, ploughing up the pile of fill, red-faced. "What are these men doing out here?"

Pembarra left me to answer. Already, he was organising the gear for the return to the face. "The world's sprung a leak," I said.

"I don't see any water. Get these men back inside. Wasting bloody time."

I found myself getting angry. "I suggest you calm down," I said. "We're doing what we can."

"Well, get a bloody move on," said Bolitho.

"If you want to be a ship's captain again, go and buy yourself a ship," I said. "In the meantime, you remember you're only a partner, like the rest of us."

Veins in his neck swelled, and his face took on an apoplectic tinge. But after that, he held his peace.

Pembarra had his party organised now. There were the Cornishmen, the Barstows, and a gang with logs and beams for shoring, in case the tunnel ran into soft stuff. I said, "Do you want me to come?"

"If we need you, we'll send for you," said Pembarra. "If we have time." He turned with a gallows laugh, and blackness swallowed him.

When it got dark I went down the makeshift saloon in

the shanty-town by the creek. There was an old Ukrainian face-hand who liked a game of chess, and I often
played with him. I half-expected gloom and despond-
ency; but the conversations I overheard were mostly
bitching at the loss of half a day's pay. Pembarra was
universally respected, and the general feeling seemed to
be that as long as he was in charge, nothing could go too
far wrong.

I was giving the Ukrainian a hard time. Two moves
away from a certain checkmate, the door slammed open
and Jackō came in. He was panting, his big face frightened and daubed with red clay. He said "Doctor! Come
quick! Robin Barstow. . . ."

I said, "Get my bag from my house," got up and ran for
the level-mouth. It was raining hard, and by the time I got
there I was soaked. The lanterns were on the rack, two lit,
as usual. I grabbed one and ran in with my awkward lamp
run, my footsteps syncopating echoes in the lonely narrow
vault, the lantern swinging crazy in my hand. Far ahead,
I could hear a high, chilling sound, a keening as at a
wake. As I skirted the gaping shaft-mouth, I could distinguish the words, "Jesus O Gentle Jesus." The voice was
crying, "God Jesus don't let it come back on me." A rumble of normal speech. Joby Pembarra's dry cough. A
shout. Then a grunt and a dreadful scream and a hideous
caricature of Robin Barstow's voice howled. "AAAAAAH!
MY LEGS. NO, DON'T LET HER COME BACK. AAAAAAH."
Then silence. I came round the final bend.

There was a slot of tunnel among mounds of broken
rock to the left of the face. In its mouth stood Boz and
Jamesy Paxton. They were looking into the tunnel, but
when they heard me their heads turned. They were
smeared with red clay, too, their eyeballs rolling white.
"Doctor," said Boz. "Thank Christ you come." His voice
was high and he was swallowing too much.

"What is it?" I said.

He stepped back, and said, "Take a look."

The new tunnel was tall and narrow. The walls were of
dry red clay, shored with timber. Behind me, the trickle of
water was a clock measuring off the seconds of my life.
Twenty feet in, there were two backs. One of them was
Joby's; the other, stocky and squat, belonged to Fulk Barstow. I could not see Robin.

"He's waking oop," said Fulk's voice, dull Yorkshire.

"Tha's all right, lad. We'll have 'ee out on't." He heard me coming and stepped back, his shirt brushing crumbs of clay from the wall. I stopped dead.

Robin Barstow was lying face down on the floor. His hands gripped the clay in a white-knuckled grip of agony. Across his upper thighs there lay one of the ten-inch pine beams the gang had brought into the level to shore up the new digging. And on top of the beam there was a pile of rock and clay that might stretch up as far as the air three hundred feet above.

"Christ," I said.

Under the right-hand end of the beam, Pembarra had a lever. The lever kept the beam perhaps four inches above the level of the floor. Its end was propped on a rock.

Robin's head lifted, the eyes opening. A small keening began again in the back of his throat. "We'll have to have him out of there," I said. "Get men and a barrow." The howling rose and became words and died again, and behind me the smashed man's brother said, "O bugger it, can we not do summat for 'im?"

There were voices in the level. Jacko and six men, all talking hard. Pembarra said, "Would you close your bloody jaws," looking at the tunnel ceiling between the beams. There were drips of water starting out of the clay, falling on the injured man's hands in red drops darker than blood.

"All right," I said. "As many on the lever as we can fit. Fulk, take his other hand. Lift as high as you can and we'll draw him out." I bent down to Robin's head. "This is going to hurt," I said. "Do you want a drink?" He showed his teeth in a rictus of agony, shaking his head. "Right," I said. "Ready. Steady. Lift!"

There was a collective grunt from the men on the level. The beam lifted two inches. Robin screamed and began to slide forwards. Then he stuck, screaming, until he fainted.

"Can't hold her," said Pembarra. "Pull, God damn you."

"Stuck on his knee-joints," I said. "Up another inch."

"Aaaah," said the men. I heard a crack of sinew. The beam lifted and Robin slid out. His feet flopped sideways, boneless. "Oh Christ," said Fulk. I heard him being sick.

"Timber's giving," said Pembarra. "Down she comes." Wood creaked. Earth groaned, shifted, settled. Again the dripping.

We loaded the unconscious man onto a door laid on a barrow. Pembarra said, "All out."

"You coming?" I said.

"We'll stay and see if we can't fill 'er back," he said. "Could save us some trouble later."

"What about the water?"

"It's only a drop here and there. No harm in it." There was the sound of something huge and heavy settling alongside us, away in the hill. Pembarra said, "Can't fall no further now."

"No," I said. "Good luck with it." And I started back down the passages with the barrow. Under my shirt I was soaking with sweat. The lifting-gang were very quiet. They were walking faster than usual, I thought. When we got out into the rain, they all started talking at once, loud. I said, "Bring him in the shed, and bring me a lot of lanterns."

I laid Barstow on the plank table and cut his breeches away. The left thigh bent in the middle at a nasty angle. The right, which had been closer to the wall, was worse. It was blue and flattened, and I only had to look at it once, quickly. Fulk Barstow said, "Are they broke?"

"They're broke all right," I said. "We'll set the left. The right'll have to come off."

"Come off?"

I took off my coat, rolled up my sleeves. "I'll amputate. Sooner the better. Where's my bag?"

I laid out my instruments on a crate. Knives. Forceps. Thread for ligatures. The saw. Fulk's broad face was greenish-white. "D'you want to assist?" I said. He hesitated. "Quick, man." He nodded. "Good lad. Get another man. A friend. Two slats the length of your thigh."

Robin's pulse was fast but full, his face bluish-white, his breathing shallow. I cleaned up the legs with a rag dipped in water. Superficial abrasions only. Fulk returned with another man. I got him to brace down on the pelvis while I set the left leg, thanking the Lord that the man's muscles were relaxed by unconsciousness. We put the splints on him. I said, "Tie him down."

"What?"

"Tie him to the table. So he won't thrash about." I realised I was being too harsh. "Don't you worry," I said. "We've caught him early. Sooner the better, quicker the better." Fulk nodded miserably, poor devil. I continued with my preparations. When I had finished, I said, "Good. Now what you have to do is stop your brother bleeding to death. You needn't look at what I'm doing, but I want you to keep your fingers clamped in there." I showed him the beat of the inguinal artery in his brother's groin. "Understood?"

"Aye."

"Then let us commence. You," I said to the other man. "Wash your hands well. Then whenever I ask you for an instrument, I want it straight away. Understood?"

"Understood."

I lifted the right thigh. It was quite relaxed.

"Knife."

It was a good knife, of Sheffield steel, and very sharp. I reached my right arm under the thigh, judged the line. The point bit skin and fascia and I brought the blade round in a clean circular sweep. Drops of blood oozed from the red line round the white flesh. I said, "Come here, you," and showed the man how to put tension on the skin so it would retract and I could make the incision to the point where I would use the saw. I cut the loose, superficial muscle with another sweep of the knife, then pointed the blade upward into the leg and sheared the tough, deeper tissues.

Robin woke and began screaming. The muscles jerked under the knife. There was blood, but only from small vessels. "Hold him," I said. "Sponge."

When I had sponged away the blood I began to dissect away the tissue next to the bone. When I had finished I said, "The napkin."

Before the operation I had torn the napkin halfway down its middle. The bone showed bloody white in the centre of the circular incision. I passed one half of the napkin underneath, so the bone rested in the bottom of the tear. Then I said to my assistant, "Pull upwards on that. It'll keep the muscles out of the saw." The man nodded and swallowed. The napkin reddened with blood. Robin had stopped screaming. The sweat was pouring off his face and he was saying, "Aaah. Aaah. Aaah," and Fulk was telling him, "nearly over . . . all but finished . . . doing well."

I took the saw, breathed deep. There was a raw, sweetish smell in the shed. Outside, men were shouting. It was as if they were in another world. Here in the yellow lanternlight there was only the Method and the sounds of agony from Robin Barstow's throat. I drew the saw over the exposed bone. The sound of it was very loud. Robin screamed again and his brother made a sound like a sob. "Hold him," I snapped. Then I began to saw, in the groove, without pressure, letting the weight of the instrument do the work. The thigh went limp. The shouting outside was louder now, but all I heard with my conscious mind was the steady grate of the blade in the wound.

The leg came away clean.

I pushed the amputated part onto the floor and said, "Silk. Forceps."

The door burst open and a man roared "Doctor! The mine—"

I said, "Get out." I caught a glimpse of a white face, an open mouth and eyes with the white showing all the way round the irises. "Get out," I said again. The door slammed. I began tying off the arteries, first the femoral, pulling it out with the forceps, looping, pushing away the branches of the anterior crural nerve. Then I tied the rest of them and cut away the loose ends. "Take the pressure off. Slowly," I said. There was very little bleeding.

I cleaned the stump with a napkin. It was a good one; the empty cone was smooth and perfect. Not too shallow, not too steep. I compressed the base of the cone, stuck it up with plasters, bandaged. Then I said, "You can take him away now. You'd better get him up to my cabin."

I went to the door, heedless of the blood on my hands, looked out. The shouting had stopped. Then I heard Bolitho's voice roaring, "What the hell is all this?" and another voice, unsteady with fright, saying, " 'Tis the upper level, sir. It's gone."

"Gone?"

"Flood, sir. Roof's gone. Shaft filled."

Somewhere a woman's voice began screaming.

"Where are the men?" I said. There were a lot of lanterns, and I skimmed my eyes over the heads of the crowd, looking for Pembarra's great height and bulk.

"Inside," said the man.

I did not believe it. I could not believe it. I stood watching the dull eddy of the crowd at the shaft-mouth. Then I recollected myself and said, "All right. Stand back. Digging parties, stretcher parties. Form up."

"There's a couple in there, digging," said the man.

The level floor was soaking wet, covered in a slippery layer of silt. Where the shaft-mouth had yawned was a round pool of water, black and dirty in the lanterns' glow. Twenty yards up from the shaft, there was a new end to the level, a wall of clay and boulders stretching from floor to ceiling. There were two men, picking at it. They were making very little progress.

"Stop that," I said. "Dig it out near the top. That way if it's full of water it won't come down all at once.

The stretcher-man beside me said, "Holy Christ."

"What is it?"

He pointed at the base of the dam. "Hurry up," I said, ignoring him. "There may be men alive in there. Any sounds?"

"No sounds, Doctor."

"But, Doctor. . . ." The stretcher-man went down on his knees, and began scrabbling at the pile.

"The top, damn you," I said, grunting as my pick sank into clay. "Dig at the—oh my God."

Where the rubble dam joined the floor, there was something white, the size of an octavo book, curled up at the end. It was smeared with red clay, but I had no difficulty in recognising it for what it was. Jamesy Paxton's left hand. I could see the callouses at the bases of the fingers. The marks of the fiddlestrings above the nails.

I bent down, dug away the clay and tried for a pulse. There was none. The hand was quite cold.

This was not a rescue party. It was an exhumation.

It took us eight hours to get them out. Jamesy had got as far as the dam. Jacko and Boz we found lying together halfway to the face, red as Indians with clayey water. Joby Pembarra was up by the cave-in. When we went to carry him away, we could not loose his hands from the shaft of his pick. So we put him on the stretcher like a crusader in stone, still holding the ash helve which had come with him from Cornwall. Beyond, water dripped hollowly in the pocket in the clay. For what it was worth, Joby had been right. It had been only a small pocket. But big enough.

Outside the shaft the women were waiting for their menfolk, shawled against the black drizzle. They were quiet now. Only young Mrs. Samms made a sound and Mrs. Pembarra puts an arm round her as she walked away behind the covered stretchers. I watched them go, wanting to follow, to give comfort. But I knew there was no comfort to give.

Footsteps whacked out of the level-mouth and Bolitho's voice said, "God damn it all to bloody hell."

"I know," I said.

"How the hell are we going to get that shaft open?"

I could not believe my ears, "What do you mean?" I said.

"I want that shaft open. Soon. Get the place producing."

"Your sympathy is really quite overwhelming," I said.

"Sympathy's no good."

"Listen," I said. "Unless you shut your bloody mouth I'll tear your head off. It was your idea to keep at the faces. You voted against digging the adit. And look where it's got you. And your friends."

"You don't understand," said Bolitho. "I needed the money. For the Cawthrops. . . ."

"What have the Cawthrops got to do with it?"

"I'm financing the General into cotton."

"I see. So you can live in a big house and be Captain Bolitho the Nabob, you're prepared to murder your friends. Quite reasonable—" I did not see Bolitho's fist coming at me out of the dark. It smacked into the side of my face and sent me rolling in the dirt. I said, "You shouldn't have done that." Then I got up and went for him.

I was always a good boxer. Now I forgot the rules. I felt his fist slide off the wet and grease my forehead, but it might as well have been a fly landing. I hit him with a left to the solar plexus and a right further down, and as he folded up I gave him another right in the chin and followed it with a chop to the back of the neck that had all my weight behind it. Then I went down after him and got my forearm to his larynx and heaved back with all my strength until he was making rattling sounds and the fingers plucking at my sleeve began to lose their power. Someone dropped a lantern with a crash and I felt hard miner's hands dragging me off, and then I was pinned back against the level-mouth and an American voice was saying, "Now don't you murder that man, Doc. He's had enough." And I struggled like hell while the red fog swirled behind my eyes and Bolitho raised himself on his elbows and fell forwards, coughing, into the mud. The

American voice said, "Is that his blood? There's blood all
over." Memory came back. The mists condensed into the
hard thump of my heartbeat. "No," I said. "It's Robin
Barstow's. I'd better go and see to him."

As I walked through the black rain to the lighted cabins opposite, I did not look back.

We buried them two days later, in coffins of white-oak
boards from the hill above the cabins. Then we raised a
cairn of stones over the graves. The women and children
stood white-faced in the sun. There was no weeping. It
was too hard a blow for weeping. There was only a deep,
numb shock. The eye of the level-mouth looked impas-
sively out over the crowd by the cairn. Nobody looked at
it, except Bolitho, who stood a little apart, his grey head
sunk in the bandages on his neck. His wife, beside him,
had the stains of tears on her face. There were black rings
under her eyes.

When the last stone was on the cairn, Mrs. Pembarra
came across to me, leading her eldest son by the hand.
She said, "I just wanted to thank you, Doctor."

"I'm afraid I haven't done anything."

"You were a good friend to Joby. And all of us."

"And always shall be. If there's anything, ever—"

"There is," said Mrs. Pembarra. "I was talking to the
other women. We're going away." She gestured across the
valley. "I couldn't . . . I mean every time I look at that
tunnel I see . . . Joby and the rest of them, and I can't
believe it. I know it's there all right, but . . . well, I just
can't believe it. That's all. And I don't want to be reminded of it."

"Perhaps in time," I said.

She shook her head. "Never. You wouldn't understand. But to us mining folk the pit's like a person. And
when that person's turned bad. . . ."

"Where will you go?"

"Back to England. Somewhere where there aren't
mines. Just the land. Somewhere green. Away from this
damned gold. I hate it now, Doctor. Because it killed my
Joby." She bowed her head, and began to cry.

Her son, pale and set-faced, said, "Come on, Ma. Cup
of tea. And Doctor Nick, what Ma wanted to say was if
you could fix it with the captain there. . . ."

"Of course I will," I said. I watched them, the black-
shawled woman and the small, upright boy. Then I went

down to Bolitho's clapboard palace by the hammerpond.

Mrs. Bolitho let me in. When she saw me she smiled, looking relieved. Bolitho's voice, hoarse and cracked, said, "Who's there?" Her smiled disappeared. She said, "Doctor Power, darling. Shall I get Effie to make tea?"

"Don't bother," said Bolitho, coming into the hall. "Doctor won't be here long."

"I just thought—"

"Don't think."

The expression on Bella's face reminded me of her mother's. Defeat, exhaustion. And something close to panic in her eyes. "No, darling. Very well, darling." She half-ran into the kitchen.

"What d'you want?" said Bolitho.

"The women are leaving," I said.

"What's that to me? They'll get their money all right."

"I'm taking them as far as Charleston."

"There's work to be done."

"Then pay the men to do it. Joby had the plans for the adit all drawn up. You can sink another shaft, blast back—"

"Don't you be giving me orders," said Bolitho. "I'll do as I please."

"Suit yourself," I said. "Just remember I'm still your partner."

"How could I forget?"

The door slammed behind me. White ducks cruised the sky-blue waters of the hammerpond. The mill was silent, and mocking-birds called high on the valley slopes. The constitution of the partnership provided generous insurance for the families of deceased partners: shares in the company remained with the original partners, unless specifically allotted. The dead men had made no such allotments. Their families were well provided for, and I was a very rich man. But I would have given every cent of it to see Joby, Jamesy, Jacko and Boz come trudging out of the evil, black semi-circle above the mill.

IX

Two weeks later, I committed the ladies and their children to the care of Captain Childers of the packet *Sure*, Bristol-bound. The longboat brought me back ashore and I stood in the bustle of the waterfront, watching her paddles churn the sea to dirty foam. Then the steam-whistle blew, the sound tossed from horn to horn of the harbour, and she dwindled beneath the ostrich-plume of her smoke in the heat-hazed sky. And I, mounting my horse, rode back into exile. An exile made sharper by the letter from Mary I had intercepted on the road from New Botallack. It must have crossed my last to her.

> *Tresco,*
> *February, 1834*

Dearest Nick,
A line, no more, which will reach you after Valentine's Day but which is Valentinian in intention. It is quite Extraordinary, I feel I should miss you more each Day but I have the feeling you never left! I wonder how this can be. So here, anyway, I rest contented, a very Nun to the Memory of you.

Great alarums in the islands. There is still no Lord Proprietor, thus no landlord, thus no leases, tho' of course St. Marys collects the rents as usual. Place overrun with little beaky men from the Duchy of Cornwall throwing up their hands and saying O dear all must Improve. It never will, thank God; not while rich men still have too much sense to saddle themselves with a place that would be a Vampire to their Fortunes. I hear that they are looking for a Proprietor, but that all of good sense are refusing. So for the moment, we are free.

Little J. Woodcock has disappeared! There was several wrecks this winter, and if the bad gales persist there will be more. He left straight after the last one, because the captain would have it that the anchors did not drag but were cut, and St. Marys is becoming very sharp in such matters, being full of new brooms resolved to sweep clean. Nobody knows where he has gone; it is most peaceful without him.

Keep well, my Nicholas: I think of you daily, and nightly too—

your loving Mary.

I read it again and again. Now the women and children were gone, the links stretching across the Atlantic seemed far stronger than those which bound me to the valley. While I was in Charleston I went to put flowers on Charity's grave. From the churchyard on the hillside I could see the stain of the steamer's funnel on the horizon. The headstone was in good order, and the inscription was well enough done. I did not stay there long. Already the mound of earth had sunk in on itself. But for the headstone, there was no sign of her passing.

I rode straight back to Charlotte, in no very optimistic frame of mind. New Botallack had turned sour. Scilly was out of the question. Ireland—well, it was time I forgot about Ireland. Forever. Besides, there was work to do at New Botallack. We would have to take on extra men until we had the shaft drained. With the upper level face out of order, there were new shafts to be sunk in the hillside. The waggon-loads of equipment I had ordered at the time of Bolitho's wedding were standing idle, unassembled. There was enough sickness in the hills around New Botallack to keep a doctor occupied for the next two hundred years. Keep useful, Power, I said to myself. Don't mope.

In Charlotte I went to see Cadwallader Jones, who was his usual genial self. Most of my other acquaintances were somewhat dumbfounded by my accidentally-acquired wealth; not so Jones. I dined with him at the *table d'hote* at the Catawba Hotel while he poured the gossip of the town into my ear. Afterwards we had coffee and revolting black segars, and he said, "How are Captain Bolitho and the beauteous Bella?"

"Fair to middling," I said.

He nodded. "Always did wonder what it was about. General's cutting up rough, shouldn't wonder."

"Oh?"

"He's playing a lot of cards, and he don't play well. You know he's a Judge now?"

"I didn't."

"Gone to his head, my 'pinion. Sits over at the Rose Magnolia all night, poker mostly. Big money. Don't know where he's getting it from."

"Bolitho. He told me."

"That would explain it. Still, New Botallack can afford it."

Suspicions which had been on my mind a long time took solid form. "I think Bolitho's taking it out on Bella."

"Surely not," said Jones, frowning. "He ain't that kind of man."

"That's what I thought," I said. "But I don't know any more. The money's got to him. He doesn't seem to care about much else."

"Happens," said Jones, gazing morosely at the oily surface of his coffee. "All too often. Me, I like to do a little choral singing. Puts things in perspective." He threw his head back and carolled in a penetrating baritone, *"Ar hyd y nos."*

"What?" I said, laughing at him.

"All through the night." He gulped his coffee. "Which reminds me you haven't been to the Rose Magnolia."

"I don't gamble much, any more," I said.

"Gamble? God bless you, it's not just a gambling-den. It's a club. Private. Come and see for yourself, man!" He sprang to his feet, slammed a couple of silver dollars on the table, and said "Quick, quick. No time to lose."

It was a warm, pleasant evening. We strolled out of the town, talking, bowing to the people who greeted us. A lot of them seemed to know my name, and they were very deferential. We passed through the shanty-town on the outskirts and into open countryside. It was almost dark now, but Jones seemed to know his way. After a walk of perhaps a mile, we turned through a gate towards a big, new-looking clapboard house. There was no sign except a weedy magnolia tree, new-planted and moribund under a yellow lantern. The windows of the house were dark, but not lightless. The blackness of them hinted at drawn curtains, secret conviviality. The sound of piano music came

muffled across the dry lawn. We crunched up the drive
and hammered at the door. It opened suddenly, holding
us pinned in a shaft of light. "Good evenin', gemmen,"
said a black butler in white gills and red brocade. "Boy
take you' hosses?"

"No horses," said Jones. We went in. The carpet was
deep as blown sand, spread on parquet that shone like
ice. There was a big double staircase lined with bad, dark
paintings after Rubens, lit by a gigantic chandelier with
the hard bluish shine of cheap plate. There was a smell of
spirits, cigar-smoke and scent. The effect was of magnificence achieved at the minimum possible cost. It was quite
at variance with the house's dour exterior. A door closed
upstairs, cutting off a cascade of brittle female laughter.

"Come along in," said Jones. "Meet the company."

The footman opened the door of the piano room, un-
stopping a billow of noise and smoke.

The piano player was black and drunk and he wore a
straw hat. He was thumping away at the overture to the
Magic Flute like a blacksmith in a hurry. Nobody seemed
to be paying any attention. To the left of the door were
the card tables, each with its group of players in a nimbus
of smoke. On the green baize I glimpsed the buttery shine
of heavy gold coin.

Cadwallader Jones waved to a man sitting at the far
end of the room from the card-players and said, "I want
you to meet somebody."

"Fine," I said abstractedly. I was looking at the women.
There were perhaps fifteen of them, sitting demurely chatting with the gentlemen. The room was warm. Had it not
been, the women would have been distinctly cold. I began
to understand why the Rose Magnolia was a private club.
Charlotte's morals were high and severe. The morals of
this bright flock looked to be quite the reverse.

Jones piloted me across the carpet, greeting left and
right. A black-haired girl, decolletée to the navel, caught
him by the arm and said, "Hi, sweetie. Comin' to see me
tonight?" He patted her indulgently on her round bottom
and said, "Later, Clarice. Maybe."

She pouted her red lips at him and said, "Try, honey."

"You bet your life," he said, steering me on. A couple
of gentlemen I recognised from Bolitho's wedding said,
"Howdy, Doctor. Mr. Jones."

In the corner there was a bar, staffed by a black man

with a white apron and a smile to match. Leaning on one end of the bar was a small individual in impeccable dove-grey pink of face and baby-blue of eye, stomach exactly filling a convex waistcoat of red shot silk. "Allow me to present Mr. Trianon Woods," said Jones. "Doctor Nicholas Power of New Botallack."

"Of course I know Doctor Power," said Mr. Woods.

"Then I fear you have the advantage of me," I said.

"I saw you at the Cawthrop wedding." The voice was high and light, with the suspicion of a giggle. "We have seen your partner Captain Bolitho at the Magnolia already."

"Not since the wedding, I hope," said Jones genially.

"You might be surprised," said Woods. "You just might. All Charlotte comes to the Magnolia, for one reason or another." The blue eyes looked past me. They were as light and giggly as the voice, but I noticed they had a way of becoming calculating. "Judge Cawthrop seems to find reasons. I see he is taking a rest from the tables." I looked round. The Judge was walking out of the room with a girl on his arm. She appeared to be chewing his ear. Her negligée was red and semi-transparent, and under it she was naked. The Judge looked as if he was enjoying himself.

"I sometimes wonder if Captain Bolitho knew what he was letting himself in for," said Woods.

"I should have thought that was his business," I said, irritated by the freedom the inhabitants of Charlotte allowed themselves in commenting on private matters. Cadwallader Jones frowned at me. Woods gave a little tinkling laugh.

"So sorry," he said. "We are awful gossips, aren't we? A glass of wine?"

"Thank you," I said. "I think I should be going."

"Oh, just one," said Woods. "Simeon!"

The black bartender poured champagne for Woods and me, whisky for Jones. Woods' eyes roved the room constantly. "Excuse me a moment," he said. "Simeon. Give these gentlemen what they want."

When we were alone Jones said, "Take it easy. It's only his way."

"Is he the brothel-keeper?" I said.

"Among other things," said Jones. "Thought you ought to meet him, that's all. He's a big man."

"Oh," I said. "Really."

"Look," said Jones. "You don't have to like him. But sooner or later you're going to want to do things with all that money you've got. Woods might be your man."

"I don't think I'm interested in buying shares in a brothel," I said.

"Nor in cotton? Banking? Railroads? He'll be in all of them soon. He's a comer." Jones was full of honest indignation. "Look, Doctor. I'm your attorney, and I know what goes on round this town. There's too much money and too little done with it. There's talk of a branch of the U.S. Mint opening here. I'd like to see you in on that. And a lot of other things."

"And what's in it for you?"

He grinned at me. "I'm your attorney. A good old blood-sucking lawyer. What's good for you is good for me."

"Cadwallader," I said. "You have the principles of a fifty-cent whore."

"They're not all bad, fifty-cent whores," he said. "Your very good health."

"And yours," I said. Twisty as an eel, and quite ruthless, Lawyer Jones. But you couldn't help liking the man.

Wood returned, and we talked a little longer. Then I said, "I really must be off. I ride to New Botallack tomorrow."

"Come again," said Woods. "When you've more time. Always glad to see you."

"Maybe I will," I said. "Thank you for an interesting evening."

"If you ever need anything," said Woods. "A woman, a game of cards. Advice, assistance. You only have to ask." Behind his plump, dove-grey back, Jones rolled his eyes and winked. I shook hands—Jones' dry and wiry, Woods' plump and hot—and made for the door.

A woman with white skin, red hair and narrow green eyes caught me as I passed, and said, "Don't I know you?"

"I think not."

"We could change that." She ran a pointed tongue round her mouth and laid a hand caressingly on her hip.

"Perhaps some other time," I said, smiling at her.

"Well, Christ, if it ain't the Good Doctor," said a voice behind me.

I turned and said, "Colonel Tuke."

Tuke blew his dirty yellow moustache out at me. "Bin helpin' any more runaways?" he said. "Or do you on'y do that when yer welshing on contracts?" His consonants were thick, and there were clouds of whisky on his breath.

"I was on my way home," I said. He stood blocking me, his little black eyes shifting under his battered hat. "Would you kindly step aside?"

"Ye'll have teh go through me, boy," he said. Under the rumpled white suit, his limbs were like sticks. "Well? You feared of ol' Tuke?"

"I don't want to hurt you," I said.

Woods was by my side. "I think you'd better leave, Colonel."

"You know what this niggah-lovah did to me?" said Tuke.

"I'm not interested," said Woods, smiling a baby-pink smile. "Simeon!"

A white coat brushed my sleeve. Simeon said, "Sorry, Doctah, sah." His fist moved a foot, very fast, into the third button of Tuke's grubby waistcoat. Tuke folded up with a whoof of whisky fumes and lay rooping.

"Put him outside," said Woods.

Slave-driver or no slave-driver, the man was too old for that kind of handling. "Was that necessary?" I said. "I am perfectly able to look after myself."

The baby-pink smile did not quiver. "I run a neat house, Doctor. Can't have important customers insulted, can we now?"

I went down on my knees by Tuke. He would live. I caught the eye of a gentleman with a distinguished white beard. He smiled and shook his head. "On'y way," he said. "Teach him what's what."

"So sorry you were troubled," said Woods. "Let me see you out."

We left to a chorus of reverent goodnights. Tuke followed us, feet-first, his white coat sliding along the parquet. As we reached the front door, he got enough breath back to curse.

"Goodnight," said Woods. "So glad to have made your acquaintance."

"Yes," I said, looking past his fat, pink ear. Tuke was on his hands and knees, weaving. "Goodnight."

The night was a black vault jewelled with stars. The

air outside the house smelt green and good. I took big, deep breaths of it, trying to blow the smell of the Rose Magnolia out of my lungs. But it clung. I thought of Tuke's pouched face, his bantam-cock stance, and tried not to feel sorry for him. My tangle with him at New Botallack had been in hot blood. Despite his pinkness, Mr. Woods was cold as a hake; and if that was the deference due power and money, I wasn't sure I wanted any of it.

My practice began to flourish, and so did my prestige. The consulting-rooms at Merrion Square were always full. Duquesne had slipped further and further into the background, and it was me the patients now came to see.

I dined often at Daly's Club, and frequently attended the meetings of the Dublin Society in Leinster House. All in all, I felt entitled to consider myself a coming man. This impression was reinforced by a ballad, ill-printed on spongy paper, that one of the more dissolute of my patients one day brought me.

DOCTOR POWER
(air: Nancy Dawson)

Don't talk to me of Paris quacks
or London men with all the facts
who'll keep your groaning on your backs;
they lie—and you lie lower.
I'll sing of a boy I know
who'll set you on your feet just so
no lungs the breath of life can blow
like those of DOCTOR POWER.

He'll lance your boil, he'll cut your stone
he'll probe your bullet, set your bone
he'll quiet down your gouty groan
and light your darkest hour.
He'll make a lame man dance all night
illuminate a blind man's sight
no man alive will set you right
as quick as DOCTOR POWER.

When Paddy Celsius scratched his head
above bold Brady, flat in bed
—for Brady he had six pints bled—
and Brady thus did cower.

He straighthway called on DOCTOR NICK
who very promptly did the trick.
O there's no harm in being sick
in sight of DOCTOR POWER.

So ladies, never shed a tear
who bold Nick whispers in your ear
he whispers it in Merrion Square
and in no leafy bower.
A gentleman may trust his life
and just as easy send his wife—
there never was a surgeon's knife
as gay a blade as POWER.

I showed it to Duquesne, who laughed. "It will not
make the College love you," he said. "But it will do no
harm. Provided always that you do not think yourself an
improvement on"—his eyebrows arched on his white
forehead—"Paddy Celsius."

"No," I said. "Not while there's Mercy Hall."

Next day, I returned to New Botallack.
The valley was full of noise and rush. The millwheel
groaned, the stampers crashed, the gang-bosses hollered
and the women screamed at each other by the shanties,
and a pack of curs snapped at my horses's heels as I
trotted down the dried-out waggon-road and splashed
across the ford. But there were no childrens' voices from
the cabins high on the north slope, and later, as I sat in
my cabin reading, I found myself listening for Jamesy's
fiddle and Mrs. Pembarra's shrill laugh.

Much later, I walked down to the cairn. The stones of
it gleamed white in the moonlight, and I thought of the
loneliness of it, those men lying cold and still in the
ground they had dug with the hot gold-lust driving in
their arteries. Then I realised that it was me who was
lonely. Joby and Jamesy and Jacko and Boz were beyond
all that. Their wives and families would soon be back with
their people. Me, I had no people. Only Bolitho, a
changed Bolitho with a sore neck and a sorer head,
brooding on money. And Mary, who said she loved me
but kept herself in a place where I could never reach her.
I wanted to go back to her, at that moment, away from
the muck and greed of the mill and the shanties and the

cold, white house by the hammerpond. But there was nowhere to go.

Once, I might have turned to the bottle. But I had a
better drug than that, now. Work. And I dived into it like
a hungry wolf at a carcase.

My practice grew and grew. People were coming in
from thirty miles away to get physic, and I doled it out
from what had once been Jamesy Paxton's cabin. And
on the four days each week that I was not doctoring I
was down at the mine, with the gangs, hacking at the
adit-face, hammering up the clapboard sheds by the mill,
digging new try-shafts further up the valley, drawing
plans for the ore-conveyors Joby had sketched over the
winter. We found two new veins, one while we were driving the adit, and another a little upstream, and pretty
soon we were working them too, and the gold-dust went
pouring down to the Bechtlers' mint. We had men who
were paid to do nothing but carry guns and watch the
pack-trains and waggons that went up and down the
waggon-road, now drained and culverted. There was no
trust in the place any more. I watched Bolitho and
Bolitho watched me, and neither of us liked what we saw
but neither of us did anything about it, because there was
something bigger than both of us, and that was the pile of
gold and deeds and share certificates, fat and heavy, in
the vaults. New Botallack had become a machine for
turning dirt into money, and there was no joy in it.

It was a feeling that spread like a sore, the joylessness.
Though we paid well, hands tended not to stay long.
There was pilfering, and more watchmen, and once
Bolitho tried to prosecute a man who had stolen an ounce
of gold to send to his wife, who was waiting in a New
York slum for him to come back a millionaire. That
meant a two-hour shouting-match, with Bella locked in
her room away from her husband's snarls. By late summer we were seriously undermanned and the prospecting
season, on whose failure we relied for casual labour, was
coming to an end. I told Bolitho I would go to Charlotte,
to recruit new men and to restock the medicine chest; and
Bolitho agreed.

I was sitting in my cabin the night before I was due to
leave, writing up my journal. One or two of the longer
serving hands were developing unpleasant coughs and
rattles, and I was working on the links and differences be-

tween the miner's phthisis and the consumption endemic
in the mountain cabins. I heard the latch lift. When I
looked up the door was open a crack. It went no further.
I said, "Come in." The crack widened. It was Mrs.
Bolitho. She was very pale, and there were pink edges to
her eyes. "Oh," she said. "I'm sorry . . . I didn't mean to
disturb you . . . I'd better go." She put her hand to the
latch. She was shaking so badly that her fingers would
not grip.

"No," I said. "Here. Have some brandy."

She said, "Oh. Yes." I poured. The glass clattered
against her teeth.

"Won't you sit down."

"No. Really. I won't stay." She took a long breath,
shuddered.

"I'll take you home."

"No!" It was a shriek.

"Then perhaps you'd better tell me why you came."

She took a gulp of brandy. It seemed to steady her.
Something of the old sharpness came back. "I want you
to take me to Charlotte with you tomorrow," she said.
"To my parents."

"To your parents?" I said. I knew she might not be
happy, but that was between her and Bolitho. In Dublin
I had seen some surprising accommodations at the foundations of some of the serenest households.

"I have come to the end," she said, as if to herself.
"Not one more day. Not one. Not with him."

"Have you told him?"

She laughed. It was not a pleasant sound.

"He's your husband," I said.

"Do you know what he'd do if I told him?" She let the
shawl slip from her shoulders. There was a raw, blistered
abrasion, red and yellow on the white skin.

"Let me look," I said. She had been hit with something
heavy and hot. "He did that?"

"With a log out of the fire. I found him with Hannah.
My maid." I covered the wound with raw cotton, began to
bandage. "You have very gentle hands, Doctor."

I grunted, halved the end and tied it.

"You're my only hope," she said. "He'll kill me. I know
he will."

"And what will your father say? Your husband told me
the terms of your settlement."

"Daddy wouldn't watch me be killed. Not if it ruined him."

"You're sure you couldn't go back to your husband?" The first time I had met Bella, she had been full of whims. I had to be sure whether or not this was a whim.

"Very well," she said quietly. "I'll tell you from the beginning. I was a damned fool ever to marry him. But I thought—well, I couldn't conceive of anything different. I didn't know you could be rich and still live in a place like this. And then on our honeymoon, in Charleston, I began to realise. He'd leave me at the hotel and come back drunk, and I'd smell other women on him. Cheap women." She laughed. "I suppose if they'd been women . . . like me . . . I wouldn't have minded so much. Lord help me, I was a little fool, then. Was that only four months ago? Could I have some more brandy?" I gave her some. Her cheeks were a better colour. The shock of the burn was leaving her, and she was getting a little drunk. Not a bad thing, in the circumstances. "Then we came back," she said. "I hoped he might . . . settle down. I wanted to meet the other women. You. The men. The poor men. But I tried a few times and I could never find anything to say. As if we spoke different languages. I suppose we did. And then the cave-in . . . after that he never said a word to me, except to curse me. I remember the first time he hit me. A fox got one of the ducks. I liked the ducks. He told me to stop snivelling, and that made it worse, and then he knocked me down. And after that he seemed to get the taste for it." She shook her head. "I'm not going back. Take me back to my father, Doctor. Please."

I took her, there and then, over the moonlit roads in the buckboard. I was not worried about being followed. She told me she had put laudanum in his whisky. I hoped she had not killed him, but she said she did not care. It was evening when I put her down in the gravel sweep in front of the big white house. A field-gang was singing a sad chant in the cotton-field beyond the park fence. As I clattered back towards the gate, I thought that she looked very small under the heavy portico. I hoped she would be allowed to have another try. But nowadays life was being pretty tight with its second chances.

I spent the night at the Catawba Hotel. Next morning I took a ground-floor room, hung a sign in the street and promised a couple of ragged, tobacco-chewing children a dollar each to carry placards round the shanty town, bearing the legend NEW BOTALLACK MINES A GOLDEN FUTURE —ABLE BODIED HANDS REQUIRED—GOOD PAY. Then I put my feet on the desk and waited. There was a great calm hanging over me, like a pregnant thundercloud. I was able to consider in a manner quite detached, Bolitho's probable reactions. I thought that they would be the cause of the storm; but as it turned out, I was wrong.

At about nine Cadwallader Jones came in, shaved and scrubbed under his mop of wild, black hair. He shook me by the hand, poured himself a cup of coffee, and sat down. "What's all this I hear?" he said.

"About what?"

"Don't play dumb. Judge was down at the Magnolia last night, drunk as a skunk and losing Bechtler golden eagles. And he was roaring about his daughter."

"That's between her, her husband and her father," I said. "Nothing to do with me."

"Watch out," said Jones. "Judge weren't pleased to get his daughter back."

"He'll be all right," I said. "Cotton-picking time soon. Then he'll be in the money again."

"He's got used to the extra," said Jones. "Mind if I stay around for the day?"

"A pleasure," I said. "You can earn your keep writing up the contracts."

The men began to trickle in. I examined them rather as I might have examined horses—teeth, legs, hands, shoulders. Most of them were Mexicans. As the morning drew on, the trickle became a river. A lot of later arrivals already smelt of booze, and I turned them away. There were already a couple of saloons at New Botallack, and soaks meant fighting. There was enough fighting already. I had a fast luncheon with Jones at his club, and then we returned to the fray. By six o'clock we had forty men signed up, which was enough; and Jones said, "Dinner. Then some Rose Magnolia. Fine new girls since you was there last."

"Dinner anyway," I said.

"You should talk more to Trianon Woods," said Jones. "You made quite an impression. He's going a long way, that man."

"Not with me," I said.

"I told you, you don't have to like him. Just do business with him."

"You're a lawyer," I said. "I'm not—what's that?"

There was shouting in the hotel lobby, and the crash of breaking glass. Then running footsteps.

"He's coming here," said Jones, fumbling in his coat pocket. "Bolitho. You got a gun on you—"

The door crashed open, splinters spraying from the latch.

"There you are," roared a voice. "Whoremonger!"

"You're not Bolitho," said Jones in a high, fast voice.

"Who's Bolitho?" said the visitor. "I want that doctor." His shoulders filled the doorway. The lintel was seven feet high, but his grey-streaked mane of hair brushed its paint. The vast arms hung loose by the thighs, fingers curled like crane-hooks. He wore a stained shirt and foul brown breeches. His feet were bare. I sat transfixed in my chair. Last time I had seen him he had been standing at the tiller of the *Emperor,* looking like Jehovah after the destruction of the Cities of the Plain. I shut my eyes and opened them again. It was no phantom. My head spun with the questions. But by the look of him, I was going to have no time to answer them. "Oh you flatterer," he said, low and conversational, Cornwall blurring the last syllables. "Oh you palterer with falsehood, scourge of the innocent. Say your prayers, if you know any."

Jones got up quickly, tipping his chair to the foor. "Be very careful," he said. "Who the hell are you to burst in on my client at a business meeting?"

"He's Little John Woodcock," I said, quiet and precise to still the whirlwind. "He used to make a habit of it."

Little John moved forward. He was breathing hard enough to stir the coarse pelt of his beard. "I'm going to kill you now," he said. "As I should have years ago."

He seemed to fill the room. Jones was behind me, edging away. I could not blame him. "What is it, John?" I tried to keep the shake out of my voice. I watched his hands. They came up, slowly.

"You know," he said. "You sold her into captivity. You thought I wouldn't reach you here. Well, I have. And now I'll do for you. I promised myself."

"Sold who?" I said, fighting for a handle to grasp.

"Charity Pender." The name was halfway between a hiss and a bellow. Then he lunged.

I was quicker than he would have remembered, since I had been working in the mine. I got out from between those two flailing hooks, but in the process I took a glancing blow on the shoulder that sent me spinning into the wall with a crash that shook the hotel. He rounded at me and came on slowly, eyes glinting above the mat of beard. "I never sold Charity Pender," I said. "You've got it wrong." He snorted. His left came up from behind his knee and I twisted aside and it tore air, but then his right caught me behind my left cheekbone with a noise like a cannonshot, and the room took a quick quarterturn to the left and I tasted dust and blood in my mouth. I said, "She's dead, you fool. Listen to me, will you?" but it came out a feeble whisper. I heard Jones shouting, "Get out of the corner!" like a second at a prize fight, and I began to crawl foggily along the wall. John's foot slammed into my ribs and I felt something give in my chest. Through dark fog I saw the hands come slowly down at my neck, and again I tried to tell him it was all a mistake but I had no breath and anyway it was no use.

Jones' voice said, "Don't move. This is a gun."

The hands stopped. The fog began to lift. I saw John straighten up. There was a frown on his face, as if this was a local rule nobody had told him about. I began to drag myself away from the wall, towards the door. "Don't shoot," I said. "I want to talk to him." There was a sharp pain in my chest when I breathed. I spat. There was no blood. Lungs intact.

"What are you doing here?" I said. "Why—"

He shook his head. "You know. In your heart you know. Your deeds have found you out."

"Believe me, John. In God's name what do you want?"

His eyes blazed and he started at me again. I yelled, "Don't shoot," and saw Cadwallader Jones go for the big wardrobe by the wall and then Little John had me by the shirt, and I screamed with the rip of white-hot agony in my chest. Then there was a crash of splintered wood and I fell to the floor, Little John on top of me, loose-jointed. I pulled myself out from under him, groaning with the pain of it.

"You all right?" said Jones.

"Rib broken, I think," I said.

I stood breathing as hard as I dared while Jones chased away the interested bystanders from the wrecked door and shouted for whisky. Only John's legs showed from under the wardrobe. "Hope you didn't break his neck," I said. "No idea you were so fast."

" 'Mazing what you learn at will-readings," said Jones. "I'm only sorry I didn't shoot the bastard earlier."

"I'm not," I said. The whisky arrived at the same time as the manager, who was inclined to bluster. Jones told him to go away and said, "Drink?"

I shook my head, trying to believe my eyes.

"You know the man," said Jones drily.

"I do," I said. Why had he come? What was this about Charity Pender? I leaned against the wall, breathing shallow against the pain in my chest.

The bottle clattered against Jones' teeth. He was very pale.

"Thanks," I said. "Glad you were here."

"Don't mention it," he said. "All part of the service."

"One more thing," I said. "Lend me your pistol."

It took six men to get John Woodcock up the stairs to my room. I told them to put him on the bed, sent out for a doctor and got my ribs strapped up. Jones left for dinner and, as he put it, so on, looking worried. I checked the priming on the pistol, ordered up a roast chicken and a pot of coffee, and settled down to wait. Little John owed me some explanations. The wardrobe had hit him a hell of a whack, but there was nothing broken. Whether he would be in his right mind when he came back to his senses was another matter.

At about eleven by the clock in the lobby, he stirred and began to mutter unintelligible words. I went over and took his pulse. Instead of the intermitting beat I had expected, it was slow and full. The pulse of a sleeper, not of a man suffering from a concussion of the brain. The pupil was slow to react, but not as finely contracted as I would have expected. I went and sat down in my chair. There were pronounced streaks of grey in John's hair, and the flesh was wasted from the facial bones, giving him a gaunt, hungry look. I trimmed the wicks of the lamps, poured myself a last cup of coffee, and picked up my pistol. Then I made sure there was no missiles within reach and applied the sal volatile bottle to his nostrils.

He choked, snorted. The eyes opened, closed again. I waited a moment, reapplied the bottle. The eyes opened and stayed open. He groaned.

"You are among friends, Little John," I said.

He groaned again. "You—" he said. The pain got him and his face turned fish-white and his head fell back on the pillow.

"Listen to me," I said. "I am pointing a pistol at you. It is loaded. I don't want to use it, but if I have to I shall. I should like to know what you are doing here and why you see fit to try to kill me. If you feel moved to attack me again, I shall put a ball in your right bicep, where it will incapacitate without damaging too severely. You follow me?"

He made no answer, but he did not move either. I pushed a glass of water over to him with my foot. After a while he drank it. After a little longer, he said, "I was looking for Charity."

"She's dead," I said.

He stared at me with concussion-vague eyes. "Don't you play your games with me."

"I'm not playing games. I wish I were. I have seen her grave."

"So you say."

I felt in my coat for my notecase. I had kept the letter there, flimsy and worn at the folds. "Read that," I said.

He held it in big trembling hands, screwing up his eyes to focus. When he had read it he said, "That don't prove nothing."

"You heard from Charity?"

"She wrote."

"What did she say in her letter?"

"That she was getting on all right. Moving up in the world. That you'd ditched her."

"She left of her own free will."

"Same thing. Your duty was plain."

"You must allow me to decide where my duty lies."

He was silent a moment. Then he lifted the letter and said, "So you tell me what's wrote in this is the truth. Then explain this. How come I seen her in Charleston and followed her up here?"

I stared at him. "You're mad," I said. "Crazy. She's dead. I saw her grave. I even put up a headstone."

"I told you," he said. "She wrote to me, and after I left Scilly I took ship to Charleston to see after her. When I came to Charleston I went to look for her at that Academy. But I got lost in the town and then I seen her up on the balcony with a screen to it with a lot of ladies and gentlemen. All laughing they was, but her. And in wine. Wine the mocker. So I went up to the door and ask to see her, and they threw me out. So I went back in again, angry I was, and they took me off to gaol. Sixty days I was there. And when I came out I went straight back, after dark, and got hold of the one that threw me out and I . . . made him tell me she were coming up to this Charlotte place. And I remembered hearing Mary Prideaux the scoffer tell that you was round these parts. And I seen that boy with the placard, and I thought I'd come and seek you out. You weren't hard to find. They know you well in this town."

I said nothing. My mind was spinning with it all. Charity alive? In Charlotte? Why had she not sought me out? Either it was not Charity at all, or it was Charity but she did not want me to know her whereabouts. But to let me think she was dead? It was quite unlike her. Even if she had a reason, she was not capable of that kind of subterfuge. "You must be mistaken," I said at last. "It's not plausible."

"I got good eyes," said John. "It was her all right." He swung his feet to the floor. "I'll take you to her."

"Very well," I said. "But I still don't believe you."

"You can put that gun away," said John. "I won't hurt you. Not just now."

"You think I'm telling the truth?"

"Time will tell," he said with chilling economy. He swept the room with his eyes. "Any food up here?"

I gave him the remains of the chicken and a loaf of bread, and despite my shock I marvelled at the thickness of his skull. Any normal man would have been teetering on the brink of death. But John tore into the food until not a crumb remained. Then he wiped his hands on his ragged brown breeches and said, "Off we go."

"After you," I said. When his back was turned I slipped the pistol into my coat pocket. The tortuous logic of John's mind had caught me on the hop too often.

We walked down into the street, through an alley between the houses and across fields. I fingered the pistol. We were getting well away from the town. Above, clouds rolled under a gangrenous moon. But John kept on at a steady clip, and he seemed to know where he was going.

After half a mile or so I said, "And what if we find her?"

"We'll find her. And you'll do the right thing by her."

"You have mentioned that before. What do you mean by it?"

"You took her away from me. She was promised to me. I'll see her an honest woman, one way or another."

"It was not me that took her from you. You drove her away because of your own fantasies. Did she never tell you that?"

"Of course she did, but I knew she was lying."

"What led you to think that?"

He stopped. " 'Twasn't hard to see. The way she looked at you."

"Did I ever give you cause to think that I returned her affection?"

There was a silence. "You betrayed her with Mary Prideaux," he said at last.

"There was nothing to betray. John, was it that you were hurt in the pride?"

"I did my duty," he said sullenly.

"Did you? You made her home a misery to her. You used her shamefully. It was you that sent her away. Not me. Was that doing your duty? No. Let me make a suggestion. You loved Charity. You love her still. But because of your jealousy and your absurd notions of duty, you cut off your nose to spite your face. Is that true?"

We walked on. Finally, he said, "It might be."

Ahead there was a picket fence and a long, low clump of big bushes whose leaves shone black in the moonlight. "Here," said John.

I looked for a gate.

"We go through."

"Like burglars?"

"Like burglars." The pale light brought out the hollows of his skull, threw eye-sockets and cheekbones into deep shadow. "They wouldn't like it if we knocked."

"They wouldn't?"

He gave me a long look. Then he climbed over the fence.

I followed him. The bushes were laurels, and the dust got in my eyes and the branches whacked at my strapped-up chest. I followed John's crashing, wishing that he could examine his soul before he used his fists, not after.

Beyond the bushes rose the pale gable of a fair-sized

house. A big cloud covered the moon and an edge of shadow swept across the pale lawn. We went out of the bushes crouching low. To the left was the dark loom of buildings, stables or slave-quarters. The place was big and prosperous. It was the kind of place in which I would have liked Charity to be staying, if it was indeed her. But why the burglarious entry?

We were right under the high loom of the gable. There was a hiss and a clatter of iron that made me jump half out of my boots. "Cat," said John. We stood stock-still among the remains of three wash-tubs and a couple of buckets. A door opened, and a cheese-coloured wedge of light fell over the yard.

"Someone dere?" said a voice. It was a Negro, dressed in shirt and breeches. He was a big man, young and muscular-looking. I was sure he would hear the crash of my heart.

"Puss, puss," said the Negro. "Dat dam' cat. Puss, puss." He came out into the yard, hands close to the ground, making inviting hissing sounds between his teeth. "Done spill all de washin' stuff. Dam if I touch it. Leave he for de garden boys," he said to himself, groping in the iron debris three feet away. "Dark like coal—what dat?"

My eyes being used to the dark, I saw that his hand had closed on Little John's ankle, and that Little John was taking measures. There was a sound like a rock dropped in a boneyard, and the black man fell on his back in the yellow light, twitched, and was still. His breeches were of red brocade.

"Move," said John, and slid through the door.

We came into a little hall with coats and turned right up stairs of scrubbed wood. There was a smell of strong soap and sweat and boiled cabbage, a servants' quarters smell, with behind it a hint of perfume. Green baize doors gave off the stairway; we passed them unopened. At the top, three storeys up, there was a narrow passage of bare boards with doors opening on either side. John crept along like a silent bear, his vast shoulders hulking black against the window at the far end. I heard him grunt with satisfaction. He opened a door, and I followed him. Inside the room it was warm, and the smell of perfume was stronger. John lit a candle. There was a narrow iron bed, a pair of black stockings crumpled on the floor, an ewer and basin. By the window was a cheap dressing table with a looking-glass and powder-puffs, little brushes with shadowy colours of paint still clinging to the fibres and complicated bottles labelled *Balm of Cytheria* and *The Constantinople Essence.*

John felt the dressing-table chair. "Not long gone," he said. "Quick now."

"Wait a minute," I said. "This isn't Charity's room. She wouldn't use all that stuff—"

"Wouldn't she?" said John, with a strange look. Then he was out of the door, clumping down the stairs.

At the second landing I saw the red glow of a smouldering candle-wick on the shelf by the door, and smelt the wax-smoke. I could hear laughter, the tinkle of a piano. "What—" I said. "We can't just walk in on them. It's not—"

Little John twisted the brass handle with his left hand, and pushed me in the centre of the back with his right. My feet ran over carpet, and I put my hands out to save myself from the mahogany balustrade ahead. I hit it with a rib-jarring crunch, and hung for a moment blinking the tears of pain out of my eyes.

A blur of metal and flame. The big chandelier with the bluish sheen of cheap plate. The light from the candles glowing on varnished nymphs and satyrs. The balustrade like a gallery above a thickly carpeted hall. And below, a woman, broad-hipped, full-breasted. Ash-blonde hair in a chignon at the nape of her powdered neck. A gown of black satin cut low at the back, tight as skin over the smooth swell of buttocks, moulding the long thighs. The sway of the hips as she turned through the door. Charleston harbour. That same woman, hands clasped in the lap of a dress of practical blue linen with a little white collar, nervous but expectant as the porter carried her bag to the Academy carriage. I remembered the feeling then, the worry that she was going to a strange place, into service when all she had known was Scilly and its freedoms and its simple poverty. And now, the practiced roll of the hips, a glimpse of lips scarlet with paint, eyes shaded with black. No. Not possible. Not Charity. Charity was dead. Or I found myself hoping she was dead. But in a moment of sick horror, I knew.

"That's her," said John.

There were other people in the hall below. Men, well-dressed. I remembered the smell. Cigar-smoke, liquor, cheap perfume. The smell of Mr. Trianon Woods' Rose Magnolia. "It can't be," I said automatically. But it was. There was no doubt about that. A couple of men raised their hats to me and said, "Evening, Doctor." I went down the stairs, fast, strode across the hall and into the drawing room. There was a brief lull in the conversation—a hush which lengthened when they saw Little John.

Mr. Woods' voice cut across the silence. "Well, Doctor, this is a pleasure," he said. "Good to see you again. And may we," he said, running his eyes quickly from John's bare feet to his mane of dirty hair, "may we be introduced to your *friend?*"

I ignored him. The woman with the blonde hair was turning, slowly, with a languid twist of her broad hips. She let her eyes rest on me a moment. Then they travelled on. Little John's hand tightened convulsively on my arm. I brushed past Woods and said, "Charity. Oh my God, Charity, I thought you were dead."

The high-boned face with long dark eyebrows, plucked now. The paint on cheeks and eyelids could not hide the quality of the skin, the resoluteness of the chin.

"Her name's Freya," said Woods. "Isn't it, dear?"

The woman's lips moved. They were full and red, without firmness. She said, "Freya," and smiled at me. "Good evening to you, sir." It was Charity's voice, with a husky purr to it. But the eyes were not sad any more. They were empty, the blank blue of shallow water with sky on it.

"Charity. What have they done to you?" I took her hand. "We're taking you away. You mustn't worry about anything. Come, now."

"Why don't we sit down and be cosy?" she said.

"She's very talented," said Woods. "I can't tell you." He gave a bright little laugh.

"Shut your bloody mouth, pimp," I said. Shock was giving way to rage. Who had turned her into this painted shell?

The suspicion of a frown creased her smooth forehead, and the white swell of her breasts quickened to her breathing. "Do sit down," she said. "You're very pretty."

"Rather strong," said Woods. "Do please control yourself."

Little John made a sound deep in his throat. When I looked at him he had his eyes fixed on Woods, glittering and famished. There came to me the knowledge that this would need to be handled delicately. "All right, John," I said. "We'll fix this." He looked at me. To my relief, what he saw seemed to reassure him.

I took Woods by the arm and drew him aside. Little John stood with his hands dangling, glaring round at the women and their customers. The talk started up again, and the card-players turned back to their games. I said, "I'm sorry. Carried away. But . . . I knew that women, before she came to this. I want her out of here. Name your price."

Woods said, "Oh, how very gallant. But I couldn't possibly. Such a prize. Quite stupid, you know. Only does one thing, but she does it awfully well."

"I'll give you fifty thousand dollars for her."

His eyebrows arched on his glowing pink forehead. "My, my. You are keen. But I'm afraid she's not for sale."

"I'll double it."

He pursed his lips. "Very tempting. But I am afraid your insight has failed you. Honestly, she is beyond price." His eyes flicked to John. "Tell your friend not to get violent. It won't help."

"Easy, John," I said. "There's too many of them."

He nodded slowly, watching Charity.

"I'll have her," I said. "For the night."

Woods smiled. "I am so glad you understand. To you, one thousand dollars."

"My credit is good, I suppose?"

"I am nothing if not accommodating, Doctor. Simeon, the key to Number One." He smiled. "We call it the Bridal Suite. I *do* hope you have a pleasurable reunion." Charity leaned against me with a confidential press of belly and thigh. "I shall leave you two young things together," he said. "And if you could do something about your friend? He is a little *rougher* than our usual people, as I am sure you will see."

I gave him a big smile. "We'll just have a little drink. Then he'll leave."

"Wonderful."

I watched him bob jauntily through the crowd. Little John looked into Charity's face. She gave no sign of recognition, only the coquettish smile.

"Charity love, do you not remember me?" said John gently.

"Oh yes," said Charity brightly. "Sure I do." Her eyes were bright and blank, and she stroked his arm with her white fingers. The nails were long and varnished, now.

"What is it?" said John. There was agony in his eyes. "How— Why is she like this?"

"Later," I said. "Now we have to decide how to take her out of here."

"You did think she was dead. I see that now. I'll take her."

"And get killed. Those black boys are all prizefighters."

"Not worth trying," said a voice at my elbow. It was Cadwallader Jones. "I heard how much you offered for the lady. You must want her pretty bad."

I explained to him just why I wanted Charity, while she smiled emptily at her reflection in the mirrors behind the bar.

"My God," he said at the end. "Not very nice. I think . . . that is I heard stories about this. Seems that there are some surgeons in the fever hospitals—"

"Never mind that," I said. "How do we get her out?"

"Oh, that," said Jones. "Can't see any way. There'll be adoption papers, I suspect. Unless—of course, you could marry her."

There was a commotion by the door. I saw the long, hollow face and grey moustache of Judge Cawthrop across the heads of the crowd. He was lurching, as if very drunk. "Marry her," I said.

"Marry her," said John. He was looking at me. "Do your duty."

"You know what I think about you and your duty," I said. "It was you put Charity in this position. She did not want to be shanghaied to Charleston. But you decided you were the Angel of Justice. I owe her a debt of gratitude, because she brought me back to life. You love her. You told me as much. Damn it, man, will I have to put it into your head with an axe? If I did marry her, it would be against her will and mine. Because in my soul I am married to Mary Prideaux."

John stared at me as if he did not recognise me. Finally he shook his head and said quietly, "I hated you for living after the wreck. I was jealous. Even until tonight. But nothing's certain no more, off Scilly. And my eyes are open. I see my duty plain."

Jones cleared his throat. "You'd better get your friend out."

"Yes," said John, ignoring him. "I'll marry her."

He moved past me, beside her, put a ragged arm round her white shoulders and said, "Charity, love." Jones began making frantic hand signals. She smiled up at him. For a moment, they could have been a pair of lovers.

"Christ if it ain't the doctor." Judge, late General, Cawthrop was wobbling hard as he tried to get his eyes to focus. "The doctor that brought li'l Bella back. What have you got to say for yourself, Doctor?"

"That I did the right thing."

He screwed up his face, his moustache pointing out at right angles. "Maybe you did, maybe you din't. What you got to say to that? Simeon, gimme a drink."

"That if you love your daughter, I did you a favour."

He applied glass to lips. "Love's one thing. Money's 'nother."

I found myself not liking the Judge. But likes and dislikes were irrelevant, for the moment. "What's money to a man like you?" I said.

"Nothing. Long as I got a lot of it."

"I hear you're a gambler. Pretty high roller."

He hooked his thumb in his waistcoat pocket. "You heard right."

"Wanna bet?"

"Name it," he said. "Stocks, horses, cards, dice. Jus' name it."

"I'll bet you five thousand dollars you won't marry these young folks here," I said, indicating John and Charity. "Now. This minute."

"Well, you start countin' your money, boy." He turned to the happy couple, shaggy John in his filthy rags towering over painted Charity in her clinging, black satin. "You sure 'bout this, now? Throwin' away your money."

"Best dollar I ever spent," I said. "The man's new gang boss at the mine. Taken a big fancy to the young lady."

The Judge started to recite the marriage ceremony, from memory. Charity looked puzzled and then clapped her hands and said, "Oh! It's a wedding!" John looked down at her with a gentleness of which I had not suspected him capable. The Judge glanced out over the crowd that had gathered, saw Woods forging through with two black footmen, and accelerated his gabble. He said, "Ah now pronounce you man and wife. You may kiss the bride. Awright, Doctor, let's see your dough."

"What's all this?" said Woods, elbowing his way through. "What are you doing."

"A little wedding," I said. "Great year for weddings."

"A pretty charade," said Woods. "But the girl is my adopted daughter. She can't be married without my permission. And I most definitely withhold my permission."

"Well, I'm afraid what we have here is a little elopement," I said. "My condolences. But remember; you may be losing a daughter, but you're gaining a gang-boss at New Botallack."

"Very amusing," said Woods, the pink glow of his face deepening from rosé to Côtes de Rhône. "But time to stop. There is no licence. Please behave yourselves, all of you."

"There is a licence," said Jones. "Lodged at my office, signed by the Judge hisself. Not so, Judge?"

"Sure, sure," said the Judge, appalled by the prospect of losing his five thousand.

"Come on, boys," said Woods, his urbanity slipping, "I done you all favours. You going to let this big brute walk off with little Freya? Game's over." He took Charity by the waist. "Up to your little room, sweetie."

"Take your hands off," said John quietly.

"Mind how you speak to your betters," said Woods.

I saw John's great fingers open, spread over Wood's dove-grey shoulders, and lift. He held him for a second above his head, the little arms and legs going like windmills. Then he threw him. The mirrors and bottles behind the bar folded over the plump body like glittering blankets, and for a breathless moment he seemed to hang suspended. Then Woods, bottles, glasses and mirror collapsed to the floor with a crash like a herd of buffalo in the Galerie des Glaces.

"Perhaps we should be going," I said, looking round. Until now, the crowd had been friendly. A bet was a sure way to their hearts, and any game Little John played became instantly as good as performing bears. The sight of Woods groaning on the floor, saturated with mixed liquors and bleeding profusely under his covering of looking-glass, was different. He had distributed his patronage cleverly. There was not a man in the room who was not

beholden to him. The laughter stopped, and in its place
came uglier noises. Even the Judge twitched his moustache and looked a little nervous. I heard someone say,
"Common assault." Someone else went and asked Woods
if he was all right.

Jones murmured, "Quick now."

My hand went to the gun in my pocket.

"Not that," said Jones. "There's some wild ones."

We started towards the door, Little John leading Charity by the hand, she frowning now, as if puzzled by an
ugly ending to an amusing game. I heard Woods' voice,
high and sharp, shout, "Simeon!" And Simeon came over
the bar. In his big hands there was a wooden club, and he
looked as if he knew how to use it.

Simeon said, "Please leave de lady, massa."

John said, "Never."

Inspiration came. I said to John, "Could you fight that
man? Feel up to it?"

John growled in a manner that made me glad I was not
Simeon.

"Look out," said Jones in his county-court murmur.
"He's been training that boy six months now. Well-
fancied fighter."

"That's all right," said John.

Simeon took a step forward. His eyes narrowed and he
said in a voice deceptively quiet, "Please, sah." The
crowd was hushed now, except for Judge Cawthrop offering six to five on the black boy, in thousands. Woods
started to say something, but a hard voice with a lot of
Scots in it said, "Shut your mouth."

Someone took the Judge's bet. A circle widened round
the two big men. I caught a glimpse of Jones slipping
through the door. Simeon took another step forward.
Voices shouted, "Drop the bat! Fair fight!" His thick lips
spread in a confident grin. He opened his hands. Little
John stood watching him, hunched over, his fists low. As
the bat fell to the floor, he hit the black man slap in the
middle of the grin. A groan went up. I expected to see
Simeon's head leave its moorings and whizz like a cannon-
ball across the room. But the smile did not budge. He
merely shook his head from side to side, once. Then he
went up on his toes and said, "You goin' to be sorry for
dat." His left fist flicked out twice, tap, tap, on John's
chest. And I saw by the look in John's eyes that this fight

was going to be no walkover. I began to edge Charity closer to the door.

John's left went out, but Simeon came inside once more and again there was that tap, tap, and on the second tap John said, *"Oof"* and tried to gather Simeon into his arms. But Simeon went out like an eel and on the way John caught him with a left to the neck that shook him. Judge Cawthrop said, "Look out, nigra." But John could not beat his own inertia. It was amazing he was upright at all, after the hammering he had taken earlier that evening. Simeon got out and came in again with those two fast punches, and when John broke back there was a scarlet river on his upper lip, and his head was going down. But there was still that famished look in his eye. Simeon was a moving ebony statue. Big muscles rolled under his shirt, and he kept smiling that same smile. He threw a feint with his left. John caught it with his guard, and his left hand went out for the black man's throat. I shouted, "The right!"

It came up from Simeon's knees, that right. It collided with Little John's jaw with the sound of a nine-pound hammer on a drill. I heard the click of the vertebrae as his head snapped back, another solid whack as Simeon put the left into his stomach. Someone behind me said, "Good Christ." John took one step back, tottered, and Simeon went after him, dancing, the grin carnivorous now. I saw his left foot touch down on the club. The club rolled, and he hesitated, caught his balance. John's eyes were almost shut. But as the black man stumbled, John's arms flew out in front of him, round the sweat-soaked white shirt. The huge right hand locked on the left wrist. I saw the biceps swell under the filthy flannel. Simeon's fists hammered at the side of his head. He swayed. Sweat poured into his beard, carrying blood with it. The veins in his neck stood out like thick stalks of ivy. Simeon said, "Oh. Oh my God no," and quickened the beat of his fists. He was hitting with the inside of his hands, panicking. And Little John began to bend forward from the waist. For a moment they might have been two lovers embracing. Then Little John laughed deep from his belly. And after that, the sound came.

As a physician and a surgeon, I have heard some very unpleasant sounds; the final cough of the consumptive, the grate of saw on bone. But I have never heard a sound that sickened me like the hard, sharp *crunch* produced by the parting of Simeon's ribs from his sternum.

After that sound, silence, while I tried to beat the horrible nausea that crawled over my belly. Then the thump of a falling body, and John and Charity and I hurrying through the hall and out into Jones' buggy, away from the shouting in the drawingroom, like the hard yelping of hungry dogs. And after that, dark driving over rutted country roads, and at four o'clock the next day, New Botallack and Bolitho.

I had had no sleep. My ribs hurt badly. I sent Little John and Charity up the hill to my cabin and walked along the margin of the hammerpond to the pretentious white house. My mind was a tightly-stretched drum, and the pounding of the stamping-engine boomed a time for the thoughts.

My guilt. If I had not been cast up at Gun Hole she would never have been my nurse, and if she had never been my nurse she would have married Little John, lived out her life at Scilly and none of this would have happened. . . .

Bolitho was in the room he used as his study, behind a desk covered in papers. One of the gang-bosses was with him. His name was Mathew Cross. Bolitho had hired him. If it had been me, I would have let him go. He took one look at me and said, "I'll be off, then," and left, hitching up his breeches.

Bolitho did not look as if he had been doing much sleeping either. The skin of his face was grey and sagged over the deep lines running to the corners of his mouth. His head was sunk between his shoulders. He looked at me for a moment. I could not read his eyes, but they did not look as hostile as I expected. Only bloodshot. I sat down, without waiting to be asked. He poured himself a drink, pushed aside a pile of papers, squared it carefully with his blunt seaman's hands, taking his time. I decided that he could talk first.

"Well?" he said. "What news?"

"Your wife asked me to return her to her parents. In view of her injuries, I thought it best to do as she asked."

To my astonishment, Bolitho laughed. He said, "I knew I could trust you to do right by her, Nick. I wish 'em joy of her. Don't look so bloody amazed, man! Did you get some good hands?"

"Damn the hands. What about your wife?"

"Too expensive," said Bolitho. "Couldn't be doing with the General pissing away all the money I sent him in that knocking shop."

"There might have been a kinder way."

"Do it quick and do it sure, that's my motto," said Bolitho. "Besides, I couldn't stand the whey-faced bitch whining at me."

"So why did you marry her?"

"That's my business," said Bolitho. "How many hands did you get?"

In view of his drunken confession the night before his wedding, I decided that I didn't believe his casualness. Faced with the loss of his in-law's big house and broad acres, he was feeling less smug than he liked to pretend.

"Forty," I said. "And a new ganger."

"They'd better be workers," said Bolitho. "No cripples, I hope. Didn't find yourself feeling sorry for any blind men or old women?"

I got up. "You can decide for yourself," I said.

"Siddown, siddown. Can't take a joke. Tell me a bit about the great city."

I told him about John and Charity. He would have to know, and now was as good a time as any. He was laughing as I described my fight with John, but when I told him of our entry into the Rose Magnolia his mouth opened. He had his glass halfway to his lips, but he put it down without drinking. "Woods?" he said when I had finished. "You stole that woman from Trianon Woods?"

"We didn't steal any woman."

He made a short chopping movement with his hand. "You bloody fool," he said. He spoke in a rattlesnake whisper, lips stretched tight over his small yellow teeth. "You damned pious cretin. Do you know what you have done? You have got yourself across a man who could have made you a millionaire as many times over as you liked. And all for the sake of a pox-rotten Charleston whore."

"That is one way of putting it," I said, cold fury jumping in my belly. "What would you have done in my place?"

"Left her there," shouted Bolitho. "Rented her for the night. If you itch, scratch. Then have done." His voice rose to a quarterdeck bawl. "Don't you understand? You've ruined us, you herring-gutted pig's arse!"

"Go and sleep it off," I said, very weary.

"Why didn't I kill you long ago?" screamed Bolitho. "Why?"

"Perhaps you felt you had enough on your conscience already." Then I left.

Merrion Square became the resort of more and more of the fashionably ill. My well patients I found more tiring than the sick ones; sometimes I felt so weary that I was ready to give it all up and retire to the Steward's House. It was on the evening of a particularly meaningless day of vapours, nebulous aches and seedy livers, that Michael Fitzpatrick walked into the consulting-rooms. I was glad to see him. "Let's go and get some dinner," I said. "I need two bottles tonight. Three."

Michael grinned. "Business before pleasure," he said. "I've a client I want you to see."

I groaned. "What is it now?"

"Come with me," said Michael. "You'll find out."

I picked up my bag and got into his carriage. As we rolled through the streets, Michael briefed me. "Funny case," he said. "You remember Clarissa Bulstrode?"

I did. She was the daughter of the agent on an estate in County Tipperary. I had spent considerable time in adolescent flirtation with her before I had come to Dublin. "Didn't she marry George Fakenham?"

"She did, bad luck to him," said Michael. "He died a week ago. Delirious tremendous."

I nodded. The least of Fakenham's eccentricities had been keeping two packs of foxhounds in the drawingroom of Cloone House, his family home. "She could be well rid of that one," I said.

"You'd think so," said Michael. " 'Tis an odd business, though. Dirty dealings. Her father's asked me to represent her. He's in the Marshalsea, for debt."

"Is she ill?"

"That's what I want to know."

The carriage set us down half an hour later at a seedy house near the decayed spa of Finglas. An elderly butler let us in, and a governessy woman took us over worn hall carpets into a small sitting-room and said, "The doctor to see you, Clarissa, dear."

There was no answer. By the fire in a wing-chair there sat a woman of about twenty-five. It was only with difficulty that I recognised her. The Miss Bulstrode I had known had been a plump, high-coloured young woman of the type you might meet hunting with any of Ireland's better packs. Now, she was fatter, with a pasty complexion and curranty eyes that looked down at the pudgy hands in her lap. I cleared my throat, fixed a confident smile to my face and said, "Well, well. Clarissa."

She looked up and said, "George! Oh George, is it really you? Now I have made my penance and now I will be good. Oh, how good I will be."

"It is Nicholas Power," said the governessy woman. "You remember Nicholas Power?"

"Oh, yes," she said brightly. "One of George's friends." She laughed, a brittle titter, quite false. "How lovely to see . . . George will be back soon, I am sure." Her hands picked at the arm of her chair. "Only he is out just now. Out."

"I came to see you, not George," I said gently.

"Oh. Oh, I see. Well, then." She stood up, and to my astonishment, began fumbling at the back of her dress. "Bother these laces, they do try the fingers so," she said, struggling with her bodice. "You would like me to undress? Only some of the gentlemen like to do it with the clothes on." She came across and patted my arm. "I am sure we will get a son. You look very strong. Handsome, too."

I said, "There's no need to undress. Shall we just talk a while?"

A look of intense fear covered her face, and she began to tear at the ties of her skirt. "Oh, no. We mustn't talk. George said . . . Oh, no, you must *service* me. Indeed you must. Or George will put me in the cupboard. Please."

"George is dead," I said. "Nobody will put you in the cupboard."

"He's dead?" She sat down suddenly. "I don't understand. How could they be his sons if he was dead? I don't understand. I must give him a son, you see. But I can't." Her face went down and her knees came up, and she rocked back and forth, the knotted strings of her clothes swinging with the motion. Michael raised an eyebrow at me. I shook my head, went over to her and put my hand on her forehead. It was cold and clammy.

"She'll be like that for days," said the governessy woman. "We've tried everything."

"Perhaps you'd better tell me about it," I said to Michael. We left Clarissa with her companion and went into the drawingroom.

"Bad business," said Michael. "Her father called me in after old George died. Seems that George was up to his ears in debt, looking at the bottom of too many empty glasses. When they went into the house after he died, they found Clarissa shut up in a cupboard in the attic. Servants told us the rest. George's father's will said he could only inherit when his wife had produced a grandson. Matters went swimmingly, baby delivered, boy; born dead. Clarissa down with childbed fever, only just pulls through. Duns behind every bush. George then finds he can't—well, he's impotent. So he asks his cronies to rally round, holds Clarissa down while they try their best to do what he can't. Only I suppose the fever's done for her innards, and the long and the short of it is, she's no better than George. More duns in the bushes. Hounds everywhere. So George goes for the brandy like a mad thing. Opium too. And he keeps trying. Every time Clarissa fails to . . . give satisfaction, he shuts her up in the cupboard. Forgets about her. Days on end. And after a couple of years of that—well, you saw."

"Has she any friends?"

"Only that governess. What do you think?"

"I think someone should have done for George Fakenham a long time ago."

Michael waved me aside impatiently. "What's the prognosis, man?"

"Change of scene. Sedatives. Kindness. Could you send the governess and a physician with her to Switzerland or Italy?"

"That costs money."

"Your department, Michael."

"I don't know if I can properly ask—"

"If you don't, she'll be in the Bedford Asylum. And nobody gets out of that."

Micheal was silent. He had known Clarissa in earlier days, too. At length he said, "I'd be exceeding my brief."

"Then exceed it."

He grinned at me. "If you say so, Saint Nicholas. I'll do my best."

I hoped he would, but I should have known better. Six months later, Clarissa was in the asylum. I visited her there often, until she died.

When John and Charity were settled in Pembarra's old house, I gave him my views on his wife's case. I had never liked the orthodox procedures; constant purges and the frequent exhibition of mercury certainly cured, but more often than not they killed. Charity had her change of scene. She had her physician in constant attendance. And she had John, who cared for her with a single-mindedness of which only he was capable. And her condition did begin to show signs of change.

Memories stirred faintly, like fish deep-buried in mud scenting coming rain. They were not happy memories, it seemed; she grew fretful and wild-eyed, puzzled by her new surroundings. But any alteration, I told John, was an improvement.

John she liked, and she showed it in the only way she knew, then. She made up to him as if he were one of her favourite customers, patting the muscles of his massive arms and cooing endearments to him. These endearments were often of shattering physical frankness, and I think they hurt John badly. But his ponderous mind, having once assumed a new course, rolled on immutable. He treated her with astonishing gentleness, exactly as if she were the Charity Pender he had known on Tresco; and she responded, at first. The fretfulness died away to a timid placidity, returning only at night. I tried to soothe her with valerian. But it was not enough. One night, John came across to my cabin and said, "She's bad, Doctor." As he walked back, I heard the smash of breaking glass.

She was standing in the middle of the floor with a hammer. The panes of the windows were all shattered, and the shards of Mrs. Pembarra's looking-glass lay glinting on the floor.

John went over and took the hammer away, saying, "There, there. All right, my beautiful. Don't you worry yourself." She pulled away from him, weeping. The fair hair hung in strands about her face, stuck to the skin with tears.

"That surgeon!" she was moaning. "Oh that surgeon with the big ring on his finger came and got me away, and what will I tell Mistress Stump? Here in the house all alone. All alone." She looked wildly about her. The shallowness was gone from her eyes. In its place was a crazy, lost vacuum much more sinister.

"Now then," said John. "You aren't alone. I'll look after you, God willing."

She paused, looking at him very sly, her hand poised in the act of brushing the hair from her forehead. "You will?" she said. "All night? All night long?"

"All night," said John. "The doctor'll give you your draught."

"You're the doctor?" she said, snapping her head at me. "Oh yes you're the doctor. The square hard man with the short leg." She skipped across to me, put her lips to my ear and whispered, "But I know you, Doctor."

"You do? Good, Charity." I poured the sleeping-draught into a measuring-glass.

"Yes. You're the Devil, aren't you?" She put her hand caressingly on my thigh. "Don't take me away. I know how to be very nice to you, Devil. Just don't take me away out of the hospital. I know about doctors, you see, Devil."

"Nobody'll take you away," I said. "Drink that, now. It'll help you sleep."

She made a violent movement with her hand. The measuring-glass smashed into the fireplace. "Oh no," she said. "You'll make me look at glass and you'll steal me away and only leave a reflection. They buried my old reflection. The Surgeon told me. You can't get me that way." She laughed. "Never. Not in a million years. Think you're clever!" The laugh got her by the shoulders, went up the scale until it was a jagged shriek that hurt the ears.

John came over and put his arm round her. The laughing went on and on, higher and higher, until it cracked and she fell on the floor, drumming her heels. Then the sobs came, shaking her with great hiccups, and faded gradually away. We picked her up. I poured the draught between her lips and put her into her bed. The last I saw of John he was sitting at the bedside in the candlelight, watching with fierce eyes as she slacked away into sleep.

When the next mail came, Bolitho was furious. He had ordered a lot of equipment up from Charlotte, and it had failed to arrive. Then he had demanded explanations, and they had not arrived either. I found it worrying, too. Our suppliers had never failed us before. We needed the gear to develop the new shafts and levels planned for the winter.

It was late September already, and within a month the roads would make it next to impossible to freight in the heavy equipment. But when I saw the mail, I forgot about the errant stores. There were two letters, one addressed in Michael Fitzpatrick's bold, legal copperplate, the other in Mary's curious scrawl. I read Michael's first. It was short and to the point.

> *Moyle, Bevan and Fitzpatrick,*
> *Stephen's Green.*
> *June, 1834.*

Dear Nick,

I am writing to tell you that I shall soon have occasion to visit the United States of America in pursuance of a charge laid upon me by Drumcarty, the old vulture. I am to find immigration agents for some of the less desirable of his tenants, of whom he wishes to purge his land. This will bring me at least as far as New York, from whence I propose to go south, on errands of my own. I hope I shall be able to visit you in your golden lair. I leave by the packet in a fortnight and shall much look forward to renewing our friendship and thanking you in person for your munificent allotment of company stock. I can hardly express my delight at hearing of you firmly settled in a new land, and becoming rich as Croesus into the bargain. I have the honour, my dear Nicholas, to remain
your friend,

> *M. Fitzpatrick.*

I looked again at the letterhead. The elevation to a full partnership would more than account for the new pomposity of his epistolary style. I hoped that to one of such importance New Botallack would not be a disappointment. It would be interesting to see him again. I opened Mary's letter.

> *Tresco.*
> *May, 1834.*

Dearest Nick,

Now it is the end of a long and dreadful Winter, and the sun at last shines through the beastly wrack brought

*by the East Wind, which has blown these ninety days, to
the great Detriment of all of us. There have been no ships
in, so no place for the selling of early Vegetables; the Pilots are much in Hardship, and I think some might have
gone back to the old Ways, if there had been a ship come
close enough. But Temptation stayed far off, and as a result there is again much hunger and sadness. Many is the
limpet eaten this Winter past.*

*I have heard from a little shrimp of a surveyor sent by
the Duchy to inquire into the state of things, that the reason for the delays in our getting a new Landlord has been
a squabble between the Duchy of Cornwall and the
Crown. Mr. Driver (the surveyor) tells me that the Duchy
looks like winning. I was thinking that if you are really a
rich man now, you might even consider becoming Landlord at Scilly? I know how you feel about Landlords, I
think, but I am quite sure you would be better than any
others, having now witnessed both Sides of the question.
As to the matter of your being recognised: most of the
Preventives have changed; Maltby as I told you, drowned
while trying to land on Melledgan: and St. Mary's is now
so prosperous that they are quite bound up in themselves,
and would hardly trouble to look for Proofs against you
even if there were any, which I am sure there are Not. J.
Johns is dead now, his son W. T. Johns will I suppose at-
tach himself to the new Proprietor, if the Proprietor be not
you. So you have nothing to fear from the Law, and I am
sure you are Rich enough. The idea is so Exciting I can
hardly bear to think about it! To have you back and the
islands too! Be quick: I shall hope to see you Soon and am
as always,*

your loving Mary

I told the man who had brought the mail to wait. Then
I ran to my cabin and wrote a letter to the Secretary of
the Duchy of Cornwall, offering to meet any reasonable
terms for the Lord Proprietorship of the Isles of Scilly. I
hesitated before the signature: then I wrote, "Nicholas
Nicholls, M.D.," and away went the letter, down the road
by the river.

X

THE LEAVES began to turn and the maples glowed like flame, and the mornings were grey and misty with the smell of dead leaves and coming frost. The waggons did not arrive. Bolitho became impatient, then furious: finally he took his courage in both hands and rode down to Charlotte to demand explanations.

Since her hysterical fit, Charity would not see me. The idea that I was the Devil had taken firm hold. I had hoped that my professional detachment would see me through, but I found it very distressing. I had to content myself with discussing her case with John. I proposed that he should try to delve back through her captivity in the brothel to the days at Scilly, in the hope that some memory might serve as a liferaft to bring her back to the real world. He agreed with the idea, though I think he was not very diligent in its execution; he was afraid of reviving memories more horrifying than she could bear. And perhaps he was afraid of reviving memories of her old affection for me, too, and souring the trust she now placed in him. For in their own strange way, I think they lived a life as mutually satisfying as that of many of the married couples I had known.

I was working in the mill office when Bolitho returned from his errand. It had been raining. His boots and breeches were splattered with mud, and he looked tired. He flung his whip into the corner, thrust his hands into his pockets, and planted himself in front of the desk. "I want a word with you," he said.

I finished the sentence I was writing. "What is it?" His face was slack and dour. "Give you a rough ride, did they?"

"What would you know about that?"

"I shouldn't have thought that you and Judge Cawthrop would exactly be bosom pals."

"I've made my arrangements with the Judge," he said. "That's all right. It's Woods."

"What about Woods?"

"I told you not to mess with that man," he snarled, conveniently forgetting that he had done no such thing. "He's done us."

"What do you mean?"

"He won't sell us any more stores. Nobody in town'll deal with us. We're lepers."

"How are our stocks?"

"They'll last the winter."

"Then in the spring we can go to market again. And if they won't have our money in Charlotte, they'll take it in Salisbury."

"But there's no road to Salisbury."

"Then we'll have to build one. We can sell gold to the Bechtlers easy enough. They'll pay no heed to Woods. So what are you worried about?"

"Christ, but you're simple-minded," he said. He retrieved his whip and left, slamming the door behind him. I could hear the iron heels of his boots crashing on the boards, even over the pound of the stamping-engine. I sat for a moment wondering whether all business partnerships had the simple sweetness and harmony of ours. Then I went back to work.

After Charity's arrival I had written to Mrs. Stump at the Academy, outlining the circumstances. I could not believe that she had anything to do with the false burial, and the horror she expressed in her reply confirmed me in my belief. Charity had been placed in a thoroughly reputable establishment, she said; but Charleston was so difficult now, a crossroads for the world, and some of the types were . . . well, frankly undesirable. She had given me the address of the fever hospital, together with the name of the chief physician there, a Doctor Kennard. Now I was writing to Doctor Kennard with a request that he furnish an explanation. I did not hold out much hope.

When I had finished the letter I sealed it and put it with the rest of the mail, among which was a letter to my bankers asking for statement of my net worth. I had made my own calculations, in preparation for my offer for Scilly, and had been not unfavourably surprised.

Thanks to the fatness of the New Botallack veins and the vigilance of Cadwallader Jones, I reckoned that I was now worth some half a million dollars, of which perhaps a third was redeemable within a couple of months. As far as I was concerned, New Botallack's days were numbered.

A couple of weeks later, Michael came down the waggon-road. One of the children from the shanty-town, a half-Indian boy whose father was at the face, brought me the news, so I was expecting him ten minutes before the buggy rattled out of the trees; even so, I could hardly believe my eyes.

"Michael," I said. "Well, hell. Welcome to New Botallack."

"Jesus but it's good to see you," he said. "Now help me off this damned thing would you? Me legs is froze under me."

I handed him down. His palm was soft, a little sweaty. "Looking prosperous," I said. He had always been big and broad, and high living had thickened him out. He took off his wide-awake hat to scratch his head, taking in town, mill, mine and valley in one shrewd glance. His hair was black and oily as ever, but now a patch of white skin gleamed at his crown. His face was red and shining between the thick hedges of whisker.

"And you," he said. "You look like a Mohawk who's made a million."

"Half a million," I said, as the crafty eyes sized up my worn buckskins, the hollows in my face. "Come up to the house. You'll be needing a drink."

"We will," said Michael, smoothing the hair carefully over his bald patch with his big, soft hand. It was a new trick, that one. The boy heaved his carpet-bag down from the buggy. "Careful, Hawkeye, there's bottles in there. Damn fool of a porter in New York got the oil of macassar into a dozen good shirts," he said, by way of explanation.

I said, "I'll take it," and flipped the boy a half-dollar. We splashed across the ford and started up the hill.

"Bit of a change from when I saw you last," he said. "You're getting on." Same old patronising old Michael.

"Well enough. We're lucky. We've got a good lode."

"You've had trouble, though."

"We did." I did not want to talk about it with Michael. Other people's troubles made him uncomfortable, unless he stood to gain by them. "But there's always trouble."

"They don't seem to like you in Charlotte. Took me a long time to rent a buggy." There was more to it than that, from the way he looked at me out of the corner of his eye.

"How about you?" I said, to get away from the carefully buried memories stirring under the grass of the hillside.

"Oh, famous," he said heartily. "Grand. Partner now. Big practice, lot of absentees. Lovely stuff. Skin the tenants one end, sting His Lordship the other. Like your old man. You should know."

"I know. Been anywhere near Drumcarty?"

"Time to time. Time to time. Himself isn't an easy man to see." A big forefinger tapped at an oily temple. "Hasn't been quite right up here since . . . well, you know. Spends most of his time locked in the solar. Runnin' the place down like a bloody train. Lawsuits, more lawsuits. Good as a pension for me. And still spittin' black fury about a certain person." He nudged me with his elbow. "You're well out of that one, Nick Power."

Bolitho was coming towards us. He threw a suspicious glance at me, bowed to Michael. "Good day to you, sir," he said. "Don't think we've had the pleasure?" Normally he never came this far up the hill. He was seldom curious unless he was suspicious, nowadays.

"Michael Fitzpatrick," said Michael gravely. "You'll be Captain Bolitho. Heard a great deal about you, sir. A great deal."

"Shouldn't wonder," said Bolitho, warily. "What brings you to these parts?"

"Burnin' desire to see my old friend Nick Power." He winked at me.

Bolitho seemed to find encouragement in his tone. "Perhaps you'll put some sense into his head."

"Oh, I doubt it," said Michael, with a shrewd narrowing of the eyes that did not quite fit the big laugh. "Quite beyond reason, long as I can remember."

"So we all find," said Bolitho. "Come up for a crack some time. I'll be in my house."

"I will," said Michael. When he had gone he said, "So that's Bolitho."

"In the flesh. You will have heard of him in Charlotte."

"There was talk."

We went into the house. Michael looked at plank walls, crude shelves, mountain furniture, and said, "Better than the last place."

"I suppose it is."

Michael laughed, and went to have his bath.

He came into dinner in a brown shooting jacket and tweed trousers, looking like a successful farmer; I knew the effect was carefully calculated. It was part of the great charade that had made him the confidant of Ireland's richest and added his name to the much-polished brass plate in Stephen's Green.

We talked about the past; I let him steer me round the sensitive areas, and after we had eaten we sat by the fire drinking whisky-punch. The conversation turned to New Botallack.

"What kind of a man is Bolitho?" he said. "I thought I smelt something between the two of you."

"You did. The money's got to him. He threatened to kill me the other day." I explained the circumstances.

Michael looked shocked. "That's bad," he said. "Why would he say a thing like that?"

"I was wondering. You'd think he was pressed for cash. But God knows he's rich enough."

"Ah," said Michael, with the air of one to whom all things have been revealed. "I think I might be able to help you there. Something I heard in Charlotte."

"Oh?"

"I was talking to a man. Seems that Bolitho mortgaged himself to a fella called Woods. Wanted to raise money to get married, was it?"

"That would be about right."

"Well, I heard that Woods was squeezing him. Sounded like a damned silly contract to me, but your man's in it up to his neck."

"That would explain it," I said. "Thanks for the hint. But he won't be worrying me long."

"Why so?"

"I've had enough of it here. I was thinking I'd clear out, sell up while the selling's good."

Michael's glass was halfway to his lips. He set it back on the table without drinking. "Where would you go?"

"Back to Scilly, I thought."

"In God's name you're crazy," he said. "If you've a brain in your skull you'll keep as far away from Ireland —Europe—as ever you can. They'd hang you soon as look at you."

"I've changed," I said. "I'll be there with a new name. And you know Nick Power's in the Parish Register, dead and buried."

He gave me a long, level look. "You never did grow up, did you? Will you not see reason, this once?"

As often happened with Michael, I found myself growing stubborn. "I'm grateful for your advice, but I'll do as I damned well please."

He sighed. "I know. But Christ, Nick. You ought to be stopped. You're riding for a fall." His red face was jolly as ever, but the eyes were harder than I had ever seen them. "For the last time. Settle your differences with Bolitho. Do whatever you have to do. But don't go back across the Atlantic."

Next morning I offered to take Michael round the mill, but he said he was tired after his journey, so we sat on the stoop in the Indian summer sun and talked about old times. Anyone who knew Michael less well than me would have seen a man of affairs, boots on the rail and glass in hand, taking his ease after an arduous round of business. But knowing him as I did, I had the distinct sensation that beneath the oily black ringlets the cold brain was ticking, mincing some problem fine. What the problem was, I had no idea; but from his polished boots to his greasy crown, Michael was a monument to his own single-mindedness in the acquisition of money.

In the afternoon I took him over to meet Little John and Charity. He was not impressed. He had always been ill at ease with the sick, and Charity, rocking in her chair, sensed it. So when he bowed and murmured an insincere courtesy over her hand she cringed away, knees coming up to her chin, and Michael stepped back abashed. Perhaps his manners reminded her of the Rose Magnolia.

As for Little John, he ran an eye over the smooth-shaven chin and flash country clothes and shut up. Not one word could Michael get out of him. So I cut our visit short, to spare Michael the mortification, forgetting that he was a hard man to mortify. As we left, he said, "Still harbouring cripples, eh?"

I tried to change the subject, out of politeness; he persisted, with a lack of sensitivity that was new even for him. "Travel light and travel far, I always say. The more people you have hanging on your coat-tails, the slower you move."

"And friendship?" I said.

He looked at me sharply, then recollected himself and laughed. "That orang-outang?" he said. "Come on, Nick. The girl now. I can just about see her. Pity about her mind, but she's deuced pretty. Take it where you find it, eh, Nick?" He screwed up one hard black eye in a wink.

It took me a moment to realise what he was suggesting, and then I got angry. But I remembered it was Michael I was talking to, and said, "You're wrong, and you're in damned bad taste."

He saw he had gone too far and began to talk about the gold market. He did not mention Charity again, so we passed a pleasant enough evening. Finally he got up and said, "I think I shall call on Mr. Bolitho. Will you join me?"

I shook my head.

"I was thinking. . . ." He looked almost embarrassed. "I've had some experience as a . . . mediator. I know you think your partnership's past repair, but how would you feel if I did my best to effect a reconciliation?"

So that was it. He thought he could reunite Bolitho and me, get Woods off Bolitho's back, and claim a reward for his trouble. It would not be like Michael to let a chance of profit slid by. "Try away," I said. "But remember this: Charity stays put."

"Charity?" he said. "What's she got to do with it?"

"You'll find out."

I was asleep by the time he got back. He must have talked long and hard, for there were grey pouches under his eyes in the morning. When I asked him if it had gone well he shook his head with an uncharacteristic lack of enthusiasm and said, "Well enough. Well enough. But he's devilish angry."

"That makes two of us."

"Yes." He tugged at his chin. "But have you thought how he must feel about it?"

"If he's in a hole he dug it himself," I said. That was the kind of logic that appealed to Michael.

"Try to look at it another way. He made a business

deal with you and a business deal with Woods. And you can say what you like about him, he makes a straight deal. So it seems to me that it's only natural he should get upset when you cross the man he owes money to." He shook his head. "It ain't business-like, Nick. It really ain't. You can't be going around stealing other men's property like that."

"I'm afraid I've no sympathy for that argument," I said, trying to keep the anger out of my voice. "If you're referring to Charity Pender, that is."

"God damn it, Nick, don't be such a baby," he said. "A deal's a deal. Property is property. And if you're too sentimental to see it that way, you shouldn't be in business."

I said, "You've changed."

"Of course I've changed. So have you. You get older, you get tougher. That's life. Now listen to me. What would happen if everybody let their emotions get in the way of their business? How would you run an estate if you listened to every damned croppie's tale of woe? How—"

I slammed my glass down on the table and shouted, "That's enough!" I was shaking with fury. "That may be how you behave in Dublin. But you won't get away with it here. You can keep your damned nose out of my business from now on. Understood?"

He looked at me, his eyes round under the busy brows, his mouth hanging open. He looked so astonished that my rage abated. His absurd pomposity had not changed. His mouth closed, and for a moment he had the expression in his eyes that at Carthystown school had meant revenge at any cost. But he mustered up a frank grin and said, "Ah, hell. It was worth a try. Now give us another drink, would you?"

After that, we talked of hunting. Mose Potter, an old man who lived in a cabin in the hills behind the ridge, had been complaining about bears raiding his beehives. I suggested we go over next day and see what we could do about it.

We retired early and rose when it was still dark. Already the day's clamour was beginning in the huddle of shanties down by the creek. As we rode past the old Pembarra house, I thought I saw a curtain lift and fall back. The dawn came up shell-pink as we crossed the ridge, and by the time we turned the horses out in Mose's split-rail paddock it was full daylight, a bold blue day with a yellow sun blazing across the fiery maples on the slopes behind the log house.

I told Michael to load his gun, and we started up the narrow trail towards the spring. It was a stiff, steep walk, and when we came out in the little clearing I could hear him breathing fast and hard, and the sweat was shining on his red cheeks. The mud by the pool was full of deer-slots; over the slots marched the deep paw-prints of the bear.

"Look at the claws on him," said Michael, awed.

"Not so big as some," I said. We followed the scuff-marks up the slope for a mile and a half, to the mouth of a dry valley. I had hunted here before; at the blind top of the valley the berries grew thick. Mose said the bears went up there after a feed of honey to get the sweetness out of their teeth. "You keep up the right-hand lip," I said. "I'll go up the left and see if I can't push him over to-wards you."

We parted. I went on up, the cool flow of air from the ridge bathing my face. To my right, the valley sank away into the flame-red and sun-yellow of the treetops. After about a mile, I stopped and listened. There was only the rustle of the wind in the leaves. On the far side of the valley, I thought I heard a twig pop, too far back for Michael. I shrugged my shoulders and walked on between the sunlit trunks.

A couple of miles later, the trees petered out into a scrubby patch of briers and vines. Three hundred yards away, the valley ended in a twenty-foot wall of grey rock. I sat down to watch.

The bear came up out of a hollow, his pelt glowing rich chestnut, sharp head waving like a snake. He stuck out a paw and began to strip berries from a bush, pausing from time to time to sniff the air, chewing. Blue juice ran down into his thick neck-fur. He was fat and sleek, full of fall fruits in preparation for his long sleep.

I crept back over the lip of the ridge into dead ground and worked my way up. When I looked down again, the heavy shoulders were seventy-five yards down and away. I could hear the snuffle and crunch of his eating. I checked the priming in the pan, muffled the lock with my coat, and cocked. Then I put the foresight on the hog-killing place behind his left shoulder and waited. Michael had never shot a bear before, so he could have first blaze, if he could get it.

Bruin stripped another bush and rolled onto the next with a slightly nautical gait that made me think of Bolitho. A Carolina wren looked at me from under its white eyebrow and whirred off into the underbrush. No sign of Michael.

I lay and thought about him. It took Michael to get me as angry as I had been yesterday. He had always had a blind spot where other people's feelings were concerned, particularly if there was money to be made trampling them. There sometimes seemed to be two different men in his skull. One of them was my friend, the hunter and boozer and the good companion, the man who had got me out of Ireland and kept the hounds off my back. The other had always been hard and cold and calculating, and I had never liked it. It seemed to be growing, that part of him. I had slapped him down, and the calculator in him would not forget it.

The bear sat up on its hind legs, ears pricked. Then it dropped its forefeet and began to lumber up the slope towards me at the canter. I pressed my cheek into the rifle's stock, drew a deep breath and held it. From the other side of the valley there was a bang. Something whizzed over my head and whacked into a tree-trunk. The bear turned, exposing his flank. I swung with him, squeezing the trigger. The rifle jumped at my shoulder, and when the smoke cleared the big brown carcase was rolling down the slope, limp and dead. Men's voices were shouting on the far side. I found I was shaking.

I looked behind me, at the tree. There was a raw hole in the trunk. When I poked in the first two joints of my right forefinger I could feel the soft metal of the bullet, still hot. Putting my elbows back in the marks they had left in the dirt, I craned my neck round. If I had had my head up, that bullet would have hit me in the left eye. I got up and began to walk down into the valley. The men were still shouting, hip-deep in briers. There was Michael, red-faced between the heavy black whiskers. The other was huge, stooping, bearded. Little John.

As I drew closer, Michael caught sight of me and said, "Will you take this ape off my back?"

My heart was still beating too fast. I said, "Jesus, man,

you should look where you're shooting. You nearly had the head off me."

"He was looking all right," said John. "He had you dead to rights. I seen him."

"You're crazy," said Michael. "I'm sorry if I shot wild, but your man jumped on me just when I was lining up the beast, there."

"He was trying to kill you," said John stubbornly. Michael the calculator, I thought. But kill me? Surely not.

"By God you should be locked up, and if you wasn't a lunatic I'd be bringing an action for slander and assault," said Michael. "Me shoot Nick Power, indeed. Sure and isn't he the oldest friend I have?" His face was flushed with anger and he was breathing hard, his black eyes darting between the two of us.

I said, "All right, John. Get along with you. I'll talk to you later." He turned heavily away, shaking his head, and began crashing towards the bear. "Sorry about this, Michael," I said. "I suppose he didn't take to you and he's— well, he's a strange customer."

"Strange!" said Michael with a bark of a laugh. "I should think he is. And I'd be obliged if you'd keep him well away from me."

"I will," I said. "I'm sorry about it."

When we arrived back at New Botallack I sent Michael to his bath and went over to John's house. He had the bear-carcase flat in his yard under the last of the sun. His arms were red to the elbows.

I said to him, "Tell me why you followed Mr. Fitzpatrick up the hill today."

He worked his knife between hide and membrane. "Because I knowed he had evil in his heart."

"How?" Through long practice, I had come to realise that the only way to get what you wanted out of John was to prod him gradually into monologue.

"Because I saw it in his eye when you brought him over yester eve," said John, sawing his way round the big muscles by the spine. "He is a speaker of falsehoods and a schemer."

"John," I said patiently. "The man's my oldest friend."

"I looked at the tree," he said. "That bear was thirty feet below you. He missed you by six inches. That's too close to be friendly. And I'd say he's a good shot."

"Yes."

"Ay, ay. A smooth tongue he has. But no friend he. I saw it with these eyes. The gun was on you, not the bear. Full a minute I waited before I took him, and I waited so long to be sure that nearly was I too late."

"John," I said, summoning my patience. "Why would he want to kill me?"

He drove the knife into the base of the foreleg, slit the skin to the hairy wrist. "I followed him down to the pool last night, the serpent. Did you know he was talking with Bolitho?"

"Of course I did. He was making a misguided attempt to patch up our quarrel."

John laughed, hacking at the bones of the paw. "Is that what he told you?" He worked for a long time in silence. At last he said, "Didn't sound like that to me."

"What didn't?"

"I went and listened at the window. I heard Bolitho saying that if you were to die your share would pass to him. He said that he often wished as how someone would kill you. He would make it worth their while. Then he laughed. They both laughed."

"It was a joke," I said. But my stomach was cold, and once again I heard the whizz and whack of that quick bullet.

John grunted as he tore the bloody pelt from the beast's skull. "Maybe it was, maybe it wasn't. I only say that if Fitzpatrick's your friend, you've no need of enemies."

"I see," I said.

"I'll be staying close while he's here," said John. "You may walk in blindness if you like, but I am resolved I will do my duty in the Lord."

After that, I went back to the cabin. Michael was full of jokes and charm, and pretty soon I was convinced that Little John was wrong. Having drunk to my narrow escape and Michael's abominable marksmanship, we retired. But the whisky brought the thoughts tumbling through my head too fast for sleep, so I got up and lit the lamp and opened my case-book.

My studies of pulmonary disease in the foothills of the Blue Ridge had progressed so far that I was now working on the elements of a *Materia Medica*. The isolation of the mountain communities was such that remedies were either herbal or arrived at through common sense; both of these ideas in their simplicity would have had little appeal to the fashionable practitioners of Europe, half awash in mercury and corrosives and the simplistic theories of the Brunonian school. But they seemed to me to possess considerable value, and I hoped I might persuade others to see it the same way.

After a couple of hours I put my pen down, closed my book and got up. I blew out the lamp, drew the curtain and looked out of the window across the valley, at the sprawl of the mill and the new oreways. The shadows of a three-quarter moon lay across the frost-grey grass. There was only one light, a yellow rectangle in the east wing of the house by the hammerpond. Bolitho's study. He had acquired the habit of working late when Mrs. Bolitho still lived with him, and it had taken. The light was the only sign of life in the valley. The reflection of it tinged the memorial cairn faint gold. From Bolitho's house across the grass led a black trail of shadow. Someone had walked that way, recently. I followed it up the hill with my eyes, idly. Then I stopped breathing.

There was a man standing under the cypress-tree down from my house. He stood very still; I had to look twice before I could be sure he was there. A long moment he was motionless; then he stepped forward and started for the house. He walked quickly for his bulk, and warily. His face was in dark shadow, but I got the feeling that his eyes were moving, constantly moving. As he came closer the light fell on his face. It was set hard and tight. Normally, Michael Fitzpatrick was affable and cheery and bluff. There was none of that now. It was the true face of the calculator, tense and purposeful. Why would he be visiting Bolitho at this time of night? A cold breath of suspicion froze my spine. At the front of the house Michael hesitated a moment, then turned to his left and walked through the garden and disappeared. I could hear him puffing after his climb.

The floorboards were fixed with pegs, not nails. The autumn damp made them swell. Just inside the kitchen door there was a loose board. I knew it well and I avoided it. Thirty seconds later I heard it creak. I walked quickly into the hallway, making plenty of noise.

When I went into the kitchen, Michael was standing by the water-bucket. His hair was in disarray, his face red and cheery as ever. His coat and boots were off, his shirt outside his trousers.

"Evening," I said.

He screwed up his eyes at the candle. "Oh, it's you. Care for a noggin?" He waved the dipper at me. I shook my head. "Terrible dry mouth," he said, taking a draught by way of explanation. "Couldn't sleep."

"No," I said. "Nor could I." His shrewd eyes looked at my clothes. "Well. Take what you need. Good night. Hope you sleep now."

"And the same to you," he said. "Shall we look at the mine tomorrow?"

"By all means," I said. "Good night."

I slept hardly at all, and left my bed before dawn. As the sun crept red-eyed into the frosty sky, I walked over to Little John's cabin. Across the valley above the smoke of the breakfast fires, the tiny figures of the miners crawled reluctantly from the shanties to the shaft. John was sitting with Charity, talking to her, soft-voiced, as she fed herself little sips of tea. She preferred coffee, but I was of the opinion that it overstimulated her. John nodded at me without pausing, and I sat down. Charity was not so bad in the mornings. The only attention she paid me was a suspicious sidelong glance, and went on listening to John. When they had finished their breakfast, John said, "Now you go too, Charity. Go talk to Abby."

"Yes, John," she said. "I'll go talk to Abby." She left the room, keeping her head twisted so as not to see me.

"She's improving," I said. "You're doing well with her."

"She's good in the mornings," said John. "Getting better at nights, too. Less frantic. Not that she's anywhere near her old self."

"She seems happy."

"Ah," said John, smiling a smile quite unlike his old famished grin. "She is. And that's a mercy." Across the valley, the pounding of the stampers started up.

"It is," I said. "Now listen here, John. I've been thinking about what you were saying about Mr. Fitzpatrick."

The smile disappeared. "You have," he said. I got the impression that he would have said more, if he had not of late become rather sensitive to my feelings. I sometimes suspected that he felt that in marrying Charity he had done me some mysterious wrong, for which he must atone.

"I'll be showing him the workings today. I'd be grate-

ful if you could keep fairly close behind in case of ...
difficulties."

"Ah," said John. "I see."

"While Mr. Fitzpatrick is an old friend of mine, I fear time may have changed him. You know how it can happen."

"I know. I'll be down when I've brought up the water."

Since our first visit to Mercy Hall, Katie and I had been spending a good deal of time together, there and at Alban House and in the country. There were even rumours current among those who disapproved of her tête-a-tête suppers, that she was lowering herself by encouraging the advances of the steward's son. Which was rubbish. We enjoyed each other's company, and that was all. And one of Katie's delights was gossip—not the tedious recital of little bits of news about little bits of people, but real gossip, careful dissections of motive and result and personality that seemed to me as useful to the understanding of human nature as any learned discourse on the mind. I did, however, feel that she was usually wrong when she was dissecting Michael Fitzpatrick. She did not like Michael. She could find nothing good or even amusing in him; he merely irritated her.

"So," she said after I had bent over her hand in her private drawingroom that evening. "Did you hear the bad one about His Loyal Slyness?"

"I did not," I said. She had on the sharp smile she reserved for particularly succulent items.

"He's branching out from worming round the little rich chaps. He found someone easier to sell, and he sold her. His own mother."

"No," I said. "That's a bit trite." But I knew about Michael's feelings towards his mother. If he could work up the nerve, he would have done for her somehow, or so he always said. Personally, I did not believe he ever would.

"Oh, yes. Don't look so stuffy, Nick. Shall I tell you?"

I smiled at her. "If you must. But you'll please remember he's a friend of mine."

"And what am I?"

I bowed. "Your Ladyship is too kind."

She looked suddenly hurt and turned away, tapping her

knee pettishly with her fan. "Why do you say things like that?"

"I'm sorry," I said. Since Mercy Hall, I had come to know new, vulnerable parts of Katie. "Tell me."

She brightened and gave me a wide, soft-eyed smile. "Considine wrote to me from Carthystown. Mrs. Fitzpatrick has packed up and left the house. It is to be reserved for the sly man's rustications, complete with servants."

"Is that all?" I said. "Perhaps she wanted to go."

"No it is not all, and she didn't," said Katie. "She wrote to Considine from Bath, where she is residing as paid companion to a Mrs. Buffett. Apparently she has no money and no prospect of getting any. So in Bath she will stay until she or Mrs. Buffett dies." She swivelled the green eyes at me. "What do you think of that?"

"Preposterous," I said. "Old Larry Fitzpatrick must have left the best part of twenty thousand. She couldn't have gone through that."

She had hooked me. Now she struck, sharply. "Considine said that before she left she told him that Michael stole the lot from her."

I shook my head. "If she said it, that wouldn't mean it was true." To anyone who knew Mrs. Fitzpatrick as I did, the idea of anyone getting a farthing out of her was absurd. Larry Fitzpatrick had been a hard man with a deal, but even he had acknowledged when alive that his wife was the tough one of the pair. I said as much to Katie.

"Ah, but he got her with her greed. He'd have known it was the only way. Considine said it was copper mines in Connemara. He took her into partnership and put down money of his own to match hers; and a bit later, lo and behold, no copper. All the money's gone but a couple of thousand, and you can't live on that at four per cent. So good old Michael, dutiful boy, swallows his own losses, takes the house off the ma's hands and finds her a fat old widow in England. And Considine said that good old Michael made certain that all that money they were supposed to have spent digging big holes in Connemara landed in his own pocket." She raised a beautifully plucked arch of eyebrow. "Well?"

"I'd say they were unlucky," I said. "Have you or Considine got proof?"

"Only a long acquaintance with Michael's winning lit-

tle ways," she said. "You're a good friend to have, Nick.
You're so loyal." She meant it with a return of her irony,
but I had the curious feeling that she meant it in a way I
could not fathom. "What do you think? Really?"

"I think anyone who'd believe Mrs. Fitzpatrick about
Michael needs head surgery," I said.

"No you don't," said Katie, laughing at me.

And loyalty apart, she was right.

Michael was wiping the remains of cold venison and
eggs from his whiskers on the stoop of my house. "Fine
morning," he said.

"It is. I hope you slept well?"

"Like a top," said Michael, bluff and breezy as ever.
Had I really seen him grim-faced in the moonlight?
"There goes the old captain." He pointed down at Bolitho
walking up the steps by the oreway towards the level
mouth, a blocky figure in breeches and gaiters. "Better go
and tell him no deal, eh?"

"We'll run into him," I said, suddenly quite relaxed.
If Michael wished to pretend he had not met Bolitho last
night, there was something afoot. The certainty of it was
almost a relief. "Shall we go?"

We walked down the hill to the dam.

The belts were on, and even from the far side the
ground trembled to the march of the stampers. The great
undershot wheel rolled ponderously on its axle above the
leat. "Across," I said. "Lead the way."

Past the sluices at the far end I overtook him. Behind
him the buckets of the wheel sailed up and past. I opened
a door set in the thick stone foundation wall. "Stamping
engine," I shouted over the din from inside. He made
elaborate faces to show he understood. We went in.

Under our new, improved system, the broken quartz
arrived from the shaft in trucks that rolled down the hill,
hit stops, tipped to spill their loads, and went back empty
to the shaft, hooked on the endless loop of chain driven
by the wheel. The big lumps of quartz came rolling down
a chute through a door in the wall opposite the one by
which we stood. The chute ran down onto an area of
ground, perhaps twenty feet square, paved with what
looked like flagstones. But flagstones they were not. Each
two-by-two section of granite was merely the cross-section
of a long pillar extending ten feet to the bedrock below.

It had taken nigh on three months for the original Botal-lackers to dress those dolmens. But none of the nailed boots that had rung on the flags the night of the mill-raising—not even Joby Pembarra's—had been a patch on the dance for which it had been designed.

Above us, under the joists of the next storey, great fly-wheels and belts hummed in the air. At the end of the belts were long live-oak camshafts, cams pinned to the butt-ends of vertical beams that passed down through a white-oak frame which steadied them as the arrow is steadied on the heel of the archer's thumb.

A sort of hiss in my ear above the racket of the place told me that Michael was trying to say something. I pre-tended not to hear. As always, I was watching the stamping-floor.

The grid that steadied the beams was perhaps ten feet above the floor. Below it, they were polished smooth by the perpetual friction against their slots. Their feet were shod with huge iron sandals, each one weighing five hun-dredweight. There were twelve beams on three camshafts, and they marked their time like three iron-shod ele-phants. The movement was slow, but for the last five feet of their drop, when a ratchet and pawl on the cams let them fall free. It was that free fall that had made it nec-essary to take the floor down to bedrock. Even so, it shook the ground so hard that the soles of my feet were numb in my shoes. But it did not worry the Mexicans who moved calmly down the line of hurtling iron; shovel-ling the crushed quartz out onto a water-covered chute that disappeared through an embrasure in the down-stream wall of the mill. The place was thick with dust, cut by shafts of sunlight that streamed through little windows set high in the walls. The brown skin of the shovellers had a grey, caked look, quartz dust and sweat mixed to a thick paste and dried. Michael and I stood watching the gush of glittering white rock, the steady march of the ma-chinery, the stoop and lift of the shovellers like egrets in a crocodile's mouth. Finally, he tapped my shoulder and jerked his head towards the door.

Outside, we both coughed and spat. I could feel the grit of the place between my teeth. It seemed very quiet.

"Fantastic," said Michael. "Marvellous machine. Who designed it?"

"Joby Pembarra," I said, and proceeded to explain

who Joby had been. Then we passed on, down through the washing-houses, to the shed with the lye-vats where the crushed ore soaked while it loosened its hold on the metal. And after that to the quicksilver house and the crucibles, where mercury boiled away, and white-hot metal poured into the moulds and took the New Botallack stamp and rumbled down the river to the outside world.

The vault struck Michael dumb. It often had that effect. Mulligan, whose charge it was, had a good deal of the showman in him. He had the bars, two or three hundred of them, piled high in the centre of the room like turves, before he began packing them in their shipping boxes. They looked almost edible. Michael looked at them for a long time with greedy eyes. "Can I touch one?" he said. He was jovial as ever, but I knew he would be thinking, *just one. Well, maybe two. It's not as if anyone would notice. It's not fair. Why him? Why Power? Why not me?* His eyes were on mine, expressionless. "Luck of the draw," I said, grinning. I could not resist it.

That startled him. He tossed the ingot back onto the pile, opened his mouth to say something, then changed his mind. "We'll go and see where it comes from," I said. "If you like."

"Of course I like," he said. "Of course." We walked back to the chain of trucks. There were rough steps cut beside the rails, and up these we trudged, towards the arch of masonry framing the entrance of the main level.

"How many of them bars in a day?" Michael asked, suddenly.

I paused to let a loaded truck roar by, rocking and shedding chips of quartz. "Five. Six," I said. Far below, Little John was strolling up from the mill, shovel over his shoulder.

"Three a day. All for you."

"Not quite," I said. "We have to pay the men."

Michael nodded absently, watching the rush and roar of the next truck. His tongue ran around his lips, and the cheery frankness had slipped. Something was going on. Little John looked up and nodded to me. I was very glad he was there.

Another truck thundered down. They held five hundredweight of ore, those trucks. At four ounces of gold to the ton, that meant an ounce a truck. Looking back, you could see the white beds of crushed quartz stretching down the bank of the river below the herring-bone of sluices.

There were three men at the top of the shaft. We waited while they unhitched a truck from the traces of a pony that stood blinking in the daylight by the level mouth and shoved it over the points onto the steepening incline. An empty truck rattled up. They clipped it to the pony's traces. "We'll get in," I said.

One of the men touched his forelock and held the reins. He was sturdy, thickset. He coughed badly. It had taken me a week's heavy arguing with Bolitho to get him taken off the face, where he would have died in a year. Here, he would still die, but at least he would die in daylight.

The pony took the strain and heaved. Above us, stout ropes squeaked through pulleys concreted into the living rock, bringing power from the waterwheel in the valley to the lifting-gear that serviced the shaft.

Behind us the glimmer of the entrance faded to a speck, then a pinpoint. We passed the entrances to new levels, dug that summer. The level curved to the right, following the vein.

Another truck rumbled past us. Somewhere, a very long way away, a whistle shrilled. I counted to ten. There was the distant *clang* of a shot-blast, and pressure dented the air. The pony did not break stride. A couple of minutes later we came round a corner into a pool of yellow light. The shaft was a yawning hole in the tunnel floor. Now it had a rope hoist with tipper buckets. The first full bucket came up as the pony pulled the truck onto the turntable. "Out," I said, scrambling. "Quick." Michael went over the side like a rabbit out of a sack of ferrets, and half a hundred weight of quartz chunks crashed into the truck. There was a man there, and he went to the pony's head. When the truck was full, he would shovel up the spilt lumps and wait for the next cart. His was not an interesting life, but he was saving for a grubstake, as I had once done. I tried not to let my eyes stray past him into the damp blackness where Pembarra and the others had drowned in the dark. The level was closed, now; the men would not have worked it even if there had been anything to work. I swung my legs over the edge and found the first stemple, a beam set like a rung across the corner of the shaft. "It's not far," I said. Michael's face was green-ish in the yellow light. "You still want to see?"

"Of course," he said, and for a second it was Nick and Michael again, at the bottom of a bloody great tree and neither of us wanted to climb it but each of us would rather have died than admit it. But there was more to it than that, now. I started down. The shaft was fifteen fathoms deep, and black as Hades. The buckets of bouse scraped past very loud. Halfway down, Michael said, "How much further?" in a voice with a bit of panic in it.

"Not far," I said. "Look there below." A very long way under our feet was a square of topaz light, dim, but bright enough to glitter on the quartz piled below and the man shovelling it into the empty tip-buckets.

At the bottom I talked to the shoveller until Michael caught me up. As I turned back to him, he was putting his watch away. "Stuffy," he said.

"At least it's dry," I said. In point of fact the air was very good, thanks to the adit. Michael must be close to panic. "It flooded after the accident. Lucky we had the men out. We had to dig the adit up and blast through the last ten feet. Bad business. Dangerous."

"Yes," said Michael, looking down at the floor. There was a continuous drip of water from the shaft sides, running away into a hole two feet by three at the base of the wall. "That's the adit drain," I said. "There's another, lower down. Do you want to go on?"

"Of course," he said.

I took a candle from the box on the wall, lit it. The level sloped downwards. It was much narrower than the upper level, wet underfoot, the shape of a coffin in section, with just enough room for a man with a barrow. Every ten feet there were passing places. Ten times we had to step aside, crushed in with the empty barrows returning to the faces.

Waterpower and ponies came only as far as the shaft. Down here at the fifteen-fathom level, it was all muscle and bone and sweat locked into a tight dance that did not waste a second.

After a hundred and fifty feet the level widened into a hemispheric cavern about twenty feet in diameter. From it led three more coffin-section passages. The cavern served as a junction-point for the barrow men, and as a collecting point for the streams of groundwater that glazed the levels. From a depression at its bottom a little black brook flowed into a drain-hole in the wall. Two men were

standing by the drainhole, talking earnestly. One of them
was Mathew Cross, the level foreman. The other was
Bolitho.

As we came out of the passage he looked up, first at
Michael and then at me, with that movement of the head
of his that made it look as if he was resting it on his clav-
icle the better to take aim. "Looking round, is it?"

"And most impressive," said Michael. "Deuced impressive." The eye furthest away from me twitched a little. A
wink?

"Takes a lot to get the doctor down nowadays," said
Bolitho. Cross wiped his nose on his sleeve and disappeared up the left-hand tunnel. "Like what you see, do
you? Good, good."

A whistle shrilled up the tunnel. Cross came back out,
followed by five or six men carrying shovels and picks.
"Hold it," he said to the barrowmen. "Firing." He consulted a fat watch. "Cover your ears and clear the
mouth." Michael stepped hastily away from the tunnel
entrance. The rest of us knew already. The *wham* of the
shot made my ears ring, even through the palms of my
hands. Dust and small stones flew out into the round
chamber, and the lamps danced and flickered until the
place was a tiny hell populated by half-naked demons. As
soon as the rumble of falling rock died, they piled back
into the billowing dust. They were in a hurry because
Bolitho paid them piece-work. The dust ate their lungs,
but Bolitho did not care, and nor did a lot of them. I insisted that they worked a week below, a week above
ground. It was a sticky compromise. One of many.

"You want to see the face?" I said. Michael looked over
at Bolitho, who said, "Just a minute. I want to talk to
you." His face was hard in the dim light, the eyes hot and
angry.

"Can't it wait?" A full barrow came out of the tunnel.
The waiting empty barrow went in. I looked across at
Michael. His face was blank, judicious. But he was sweat-
ing. *This is it,* I thought.

"No," said Bolitho. "One last time. You're going to give
that woman back to Trianon Woods."

"I am not." *Where was Little John?*

"Then I will," said Bolitho.

"Over my dead body." *Why, Michael?* I tried to catch
his eye but he was looking at his feet.

Bolitho smiled. "Yes. Now you listen to me. I owe Woods a lot of money. He lent it to me to pay off Cawthrop when I married his bitch of a daughter. If he doesn't get that woman back, he'll foreclose. I'll be out. Just like that. You wouldn't want that to happen, would you? Woods as a partner?"

"I'm selling up. Leaving. You can settle your problems your own way."

"So Mr. Fitzpatrick said last night." The smile stayed fixed. "You are making our lives very awkward."

"Really, Nick. You should give her back," said Michael, smoothly. "For your own good. You've a great future here. Why ruin it for a lunatic whore?"

"How much did he offer you?" I said. "You'd be a fool to trust him."

"Mr. Fitzpatrick knows a practical man when he sees one," said Bolitho. "One more time. Will you give the woman back?"

"Over my dead body," I said again.

"Sorry you see it like that," said Bolitho. His hand went to his pocket. "Then there's no other way out." His hand came out of his pocket with a pistol.

"My holdings pass to you on my death," I said. "Is that where the blood-money comes from?" The barrows had stopped coming. "Richer and richer, Michael?" I clenched my fist to stop my hand shaking.

"Richer and richer." *Where was Little John?* "Goodbye, Nick. Sorry about this." He turned and went back up the shaft, quickly.

The black muzzle of the gun steadied on my chest. Michael's footsteps receded into silence. But now there were other feet, nailed boots, crunching on wet rock. Bolitho said, "Who——"

I dived aside. The sound of the boots echoed in the cavern. The gun spat and boomed. As the echo died there was a grunt of pain, and I saw a huge figure standing over Bolitho, blood spreading on the left shoulder of his shirt.

A head appeared in the tunnel mouth where they had blasted, white with dust that glittered. Then another and another, and Bolitho screamed, "Take him! Take him!" The facemen poured out of the tunnel, Matty Cross, Joe Bolt, Jimenez, Garcia. The bad ones. The ones who thought I was an interfering idiot to stop them working themselves to death. They had their picks and shovels, and they came at me and John shoulder to shoulder, narrow-eyed. They were big men. So this was it. I was dead. I picked myself up, waiting for the smash of shovel, the drive of a pick in my ribs. But it was Little John who got up and turned round and went for me. His face was the colour of melting wax, running down the beard in shining drips. His hand pulled me off balance and the other one caught my good leg under the thigh. "God be with you," he croaked. "Strait is the gate. . . . I'll deal with these." I felt myself swing back in the air under the twinkling faces of the miners. Then I began to roar like a frightened baby. For after the swing back came the swing forward. And it took me down, head first, towards the black drain-mouth of the adit. I tried to get my arms out, but he held me fast. My shoulder grounded hard in the pool of water. The last thing I saw was Little John's hand, a huge yellow-white spider, running up the wall to the red chest with the black skull and crossbones and stencilled letters that said SHOT CARTRIDGES.

Then cold, wet tunnel-stone breathed in my face. My shoulders hit a mat of beastly black lightless slime, and slid. The drain sloped fast away. I scrabbled and roared and broke my fingernails. But the slope was too steep. Somewhere behind me there was a huge bellow of noise, too loud for a gun. My guts churned. From below there came the rush of water.

On the plans, the adit was a beautifully simple piece of engineering. Effectively, it was a long tunnel three feet square, sloping down at an angle of twenty degrees to the horizontal, its highest point more or less at the twenty-fathom level. Into it ran three vertical drains, three feet by two—one from the bottom of the shaft; another from the round chamber in the fifteen-fathom level; and another up far into the hill to drain the vessel that had burst and killed the Botallack partners. The volume of water it carried can be judged by the fact that since its construction, the spring that washed out the waggon-road in wet weather had virtually dried up. There was enough water running down that yard-square pipe to drive the mill by itself.

For a moment, I was falling free in a black tube of rock. Then I hit water so cold it knocked the breath out of me, and I was in the six-hundred-foot drainpipe of the adit. I knew there would have to be air in here. But the current of the rough pipe jostled and battered at me until I could no longer tell whether my face was wet or dry. I ground my face into what I thought must be the top wall, opened my mouth, got water. And again, the panic building. On the third try I caught a bubble, which gave me leisure to think. Length of pipe, five hundred and eighty-two feet precisely. Speed of flow, between six and eight miles per hour. Closer to eight. Provided I did not panic, I could make it. Oh, the comfort of mathematics. But there was a curious osmotic process at work, not at all mathematical. My senses kept leaking into my intellect and telling me to scream and thrash about, because I was going to die. Bubbles of panic rushed round my system. But my body fluttered down in the turbulent eddies, still as Ophelia.

Air was getting short. My chest was making breathing movements, but my lips and nose stayed closed. To keep my mind away from the water, I began to say goodbye. Goodbye to Charity, John, Mary. Goodbye to the ghosts of the men under the cairn in the valley. Goodbye to greedy Bolitho, sly Fitzpatrick. Goodbye to New Botallack, the place I now found I hated. The need to breathe swelled like a balloon, pushing away all the other thoughts. Goodbye to Nicholas Power. There was a great roaring in my ears. My mouth opened itself. Flashes of red light danced in my eye-balls, brightening, dazzling. I took a sob of water—

A sob of air.

I shot out of the hillside like a human champagne cork, turned twice in space, and landed smash on my face in the hammerpond.

I turned over. Above me a single white puff of cloud floated in the blue. The trees on the steep hillsides rose in tender walls of flame. A mourning-dove skimmed the water, clapped its wings, and glided out of sight. I could feel the stamping-engine like the pulse of a great heart. Up by the level entrance little men were running. For a while I watched them, quite detached. The subject of a miracle is a man apart. The normal preoccupations of life do not concern him. Still to be alive is enough.

The current was taking me gently down towards the dam. As the mill grew in the corner of my eye, it began to come back. My hands bit water and I swam.

When I pulled myself ashore I ran for the mill. My knees were beginning to shake with the reaction, and twice I fell. I found a fence-pale in the torn grass and hobbled to the first of the pylons bearing the empty trucks up the hill. A truck rumbled towards me. I made a lunge for it and clambered aboard. The towrope caught with a jerk and we started up the track.

Halfway up, the rails crossed a slight shoulder in the ground, and the mouth of the main level came into view. Men were still milling on the flat area in front of it. The points were closed. I saw the truck two in front of me turn unheeded, start to roll down, rocking. More men came pouring out of the mine. There was a suggestion of more inside, and lot of shouting. My truck started up the last steep pitch. I heard swearing and the smash of a pick and a yell of pain. A man reeled out with blood running into his eyes and fell across the tracks. I shouted, "Move him!" Someone looked round and dragged him away from my wheels. I jumped onto the front, unhitched, and hopped to the ground. The truck rolled on round the points, towards the start of the downhill gradient.

Little John came out of the mine. He was white as bone. His shoulders seemed to fill the whole arch. He was dragging something in his right hand, something that kicked and struggled, something black and scorched-looking that wore the remains of a frock-coat. Bolitho.

"John!" I roared.

He looked up. There was a bluish tinge at his lips and temples. He said, "I'm taking him down," his voice hard and distant. The next empty truck rolled round. With one hand he unhitched the coupling, and dropped Bolitho in. A man came up behind him and swung a pick at his back. He caught it almost absent-mindedly by the shaft, and drove it into the man's stomach. Then he gave the truck a shove with his shoulders and climbed in. The spokes of the wheels became a blur. Mathew Cross raised his shovel at me. Someone hit him from behind and he went down. Silence fell.

The down tracks ran through a carefully graded cutting. I watched the plummeting truck as if through a rifle sight, shrinking away towards its vanishing-point in the black door in the mill's wall. John was standing up, braced against the sway of the truck. The big red stain on the back of his shirt shone wet in the sun. A puff of smoke whipped back, and the flat bang of a pistol. John's arms flew out at right angles to his body and he jerked backwards. I could almost feel the slam as he hit the dirt between the rails. He had landed badly. Bolitho stood up precariously, looking back.

I shouted "Behind—"

The truck which had gone down before Bolitho had started badly. It had gone down empty, too light to be stable, so it had finished worse. The walls of the cutting funnelled up the screech of its wheel-flanges on the rails, the rumble of Bolitho's chariot, and, as he turned, his shout of surprise. As if scared by the noise, the empty truck jumped, turned sideways in the air, and landed with a splintering crash athwart the track at the end of the downhill section, twenty yards from the black hole in the side of the mill. There was a gentle uphill gradient here, to slow the trucks before they arrived at the sharp tipping-curve. Bolitho was travelling at perhaps fifty miles an hour when he hit the wreck. His truck stopped dead. He went straight on, end over end. I saw his mouth open and screaming in a face white against the darkness of the doorway. Then he was gone into the mill, and the screaming rose and stopped, abruptly. After that there was only the crash and pound of the stampers on the granite floor. And after thirty seconds someone had the presence of mind to take the belts off and that stopped, too.

Silence swelled up the valley floor and filled my ears. I walked down the tracks, haltingly, to where Little John lay sprawled. His eyes were closed, his face white and pinched. There was a dark-rimmed hole in the left shoulder of his coat, and a scarlet weal at his timple. That was not the trouble, though. As I touched him a tremor went through his neck and arms. His legs stayed slack and lifeless. Down in the mill someone shouted in a voice on the edge of panic.

"Get a hurdle," I said. "Take him across to the house. And be careful. His back's broken."

Then I went on, to the stamping-house. The wheel creaked and spun free, unbelted. One of the floor-hands was leaning against the doorpost, vomiting into a tip-truck. When I went in, I saw why.

The shoe of the stamper post had caught Bolitho in the middle of the back. From the knees down and the sternum up, he was the same old Bolitho, Between these two points, he was one-eighth of an inch thick, at most. The floor around him was shiny red. Strawberry jam, said a voice from my childhood in my mind. It's quite true. It looks exactly like strawberry jam.

He was lying on his face, his coat and shirt torn and singed so the skin showed through, surprisingly white. I hopped onto the stamping-floor and went across to him. The skin was waxy. There was no pulse, and already he was cooling. The face was not so much shocked as gently surprised. It struck me as curious that Bolitho, who in life had seldom resorted to half-measures in his moods, should feel so mild an emotion at his decease.

As I walked out of the mill I met the half-Indian boy who had taken Michael's bags off the buggy. "Where's Mr. Fitzpatrick?" I said. "Did you see him?"

"He went. Half hour ago. On one of your horses. He didn't take his luggage," said the child, aggrieved at the loss of his tip. "He was riding fast."

"More than likely," I said. Then I went up the hill.

There was a crowd of men standing round the door of John's house. I pushed my way through and went to his room. He was conscious, just, his huge frame strangely shrunken under the bright patchwork quilt. His reflexes worked above the waist. But there was no feeling or muscular control in his legs. Carefully, I palpated the spinal spicules. There was no sign of fracture; but with vertebrae, there seldom is. All I could do was strap him up, and wait. Through the wall I could hear the sniff and whimper of Charity's crying. Even in her tight-shut world, the circle of grim faces outside the window had a story to tell.

When I had finished with John I changed into dry clothes and went outside again. Evening was coming on and it was getting cold. But none of the men wanted to go home. There were still people round the level-mouth, among them Robin Barstow, leaning on his crutches, watching. "Lo, Doctor," he said. "How be John Woodcock?"

"Worse then you ever were," I said. Robin had mended well, and he could get about pretty spry, as long as he didn't enter any foot-races.

"And Bolitho's gone, I hear."

"Yes."

Robin spat. "Good riddance, not to speak ill of the dead." He shook his head. "Strong boy, that John."

"He was."

Bit by bit, I found out what had happened. After John had slung me down the adit, there had been a general scrimmage. Bolitho must have picked the face-crew with a view to murder; John had fought five men, and big men. But he had, it seemed, had one advantage up his sleeve beside his size. Being a seaman and not a miner, he had none of the miner's respect for explosives. As far as I could make out, he had beaten a retreat covered with explosions of blasting-powder that had brought the roof down in three places, though not seriously. This had not unnaturally made the face-gang cautious. John also had Bolitho over his shoulder, and the gangers did not want to hurt their paymaster. By the time he had reached the shaft-bottom, John had run out of blasting-powder, but he had picked up a small army of barrowmen who had no love for Bolitho. There had been a running battle in the shaft and the main level. I went down to minister to a man who had fallen forty feet into an ore-barrow, and left with the feeling that it was quite possible that I had been better off in that nightmare adit than in the workings. After that I went to see John again, and thanked him. He did no yet understand what had happened to him. His mind was hazy, half-asleep. I was feeling very tired. I went back to my cabin, kicked the door open, flopped down in a chair.

Michael Fitzpatrick. My oldest friend.

The first thing I did after the proving of Bolitho's will was to settle his debt with Trianon Woods. The second was to arrange the floating of a public company in the name of New Botallack Mines; and the third was to contact the Bessels, miners bigger even than New Botallack, and offer to sell my holdings. News of my offer sent the shares soaring. It was well-timed; the talk of establishing a branch of the U.S. Mint at Charlotte had precipitated action, and it was to start operations in six months. Bessels balked at the price, took a deep breath, and bought. I told Cadwallader Jones to transfer the money to Hoare's Bank in London in the name of Tar Heel Holdings, a company he concocted for me on the spot. And two days later I received a letter

from the Duchy of Cornwall. I was already packing up
my gear, prior to moving out of my house.

London,
July, 1834

Sir,

*We note your favour of May of this year. I would con-
firm that the lease of Scilly has not as yet been taken up.
The Secretary of the Duchy has asked me to secure from
you a proposal on which we may base a serious consideration of your bid. In expectation of a speedy reply I am
Sir*

your Obedt. Servt.

George Harrison, Kt.

I groaned and threw the letter into the fire. Six months,
more or less, from London. I had intended to move to a
house in the lowlands, finish some work, and make sure
John and Charity were well cared for. But they would be
better off at Scilly; and from Scilly itself I should be in a
better position to make my proposals to the Duchy.

At the same time, I received a letter of frantic apology
from Dr. Kennard of the Charleston fever hospital in
which Charity was supposed to have died. There had been
on the staff, he told me, a surgeon of apparently impecca-
able qualifications by the name of Brangwyn. Since
Brangwyn had the power of certifying death, he had been
able, with the help of accomplices, to remove from the
wards several patients, notably young and attractive
women. These he conveyed to a house where, having
staged a mock funeral—there being no shortage of corpses
in the yellow fever season—he would set about breaking
their wills and training them in certain arts which ren-
dered them easily marketable to the proprietors of houses
of ill fame. Kennard told me that I would be pleased to
hear that Surgeon Brangwyn had been lynched by an in-
furiated mob in a small town while attempting flight to
Savannah after his exposure. There was no fear of a recur-
rence of the outrage, the systems of registration and certi-
fication having changed. He could only express his horror
and his sympathy for the poor young creatures sold into
the worst kind of slavery, and so on and so on. He begged
the honour of my acquaintance and would naturally do
everything in his power to right these appalling wrongs.

None of which would unlock the prison in Charity's

mind. I threw the letter in the fire, and got on with my packing.

Two days later, I left New Botallack for the last time. I did not look back. In a sprung bed in the carriage, Little John rolled his eyes at the shanty town, the bare, dripping trees. Charity sat huddled in the corner, looking every way but at me. The rain drummed on the carriage roof, and the roads were very bad. In Charlotte we rested two nights, and I made my farewells to Cadwallader Jones and a couple of other friends. Cadwallader told me I was crazy to be leaving, look at the size of the place; and indeed, Charlotte was growing like a mushroom. Then we went over my holdings. They amounted to a million and a quarter dollars. I was stinking rich. Cadwallader could not understand why I was going back to barbarism, away from the burgeoning New World. But I knew. My mind was full of the green and silver islands set in a sea of clearest turquoise, where the soft winds blew from the south-west and the roaring gales were the breath of God. Where the people were part of the land, not swarmers over its surface or burrowers in its deeps. Where I would find Mary Prideau.

The company in the after cabin of the brig *Macclesfield* were not exactly select. Besides Mrs. Rankin, a pious old biddy in rusty black with a wet sniff that must have driven her late husband mad, there was Major Slipton and the captain. God had given the major a face like a ferret and thirst like the Gobi, and had then persuaded him to justify the latter affliction in an unusually inventive hypochondria. So while Mrs. Rankin glared at me and huffed in indignation at my transporting unchaperoned so beautiful a lunatic as Charity, Major Slipton spent much of his time sidling up to me and implying that his sore head and aching liver were in some way caught from Little John. Captain Poe watched the proceedings with a sardonic eye which I at first thought masked a lively intelligence, but subsequently discovered hid a dense and invincible stupidity.

With such undesirable company, it was hardly surprising that I spent most of my time either reading in my cabin or with my charges. We had fair weather for the first ten days out of Charleston, which, in view of the

Macclesfield's condition, was a mercy. In the evenings it was even warm enough to haul Little John up on deck, well wrapped as to the lower back and legs. We set him on the quarter-deck and there he sat until night fell, apparently quite content, tended by Charity. John's helplessness had touched something in her which I had feared cauterised forever. She nursed him devotedly. And it did him good—not that he benefited much from the beef tea and gruel she made him; but that she could do even this much represented to him a glimmer of hope. He was living almost entirely for her, now. He knew it; and I knew it too. There were certain indications to his condition that I did not like. There was a long swelling and some tenderness beside the spiculae of the vertebrae. I did what I could, short of operating; but that was very little. What worried me more than the physical symptoms was John's state of mind. He was taking, I felt, a morbid interest in sunsets. The only things that would bear him through were patience, hope and luck. Patience he had; but his hope centred now on matters beyond the fiery ruin of the sunsets. And luck—well, he had never believed in luck. What was written was written, and John was convinced that part of what was written was a speedy departure for the next world. At his present rate of progress, I could not find it in me to quarrel with this prognosis.

On our twelfth night out, he called me over. I stopped pacing the deck and went to lean on the rail in front of him.

"I wanted to ask you something."

"Yes?" The dying sun cast a false glow of health over his face. The flesh was sunk away above the great tawny beard, the cheekbones stretching the skin like knives. There were blue circles under his eyes, and since that day down the mine he had never got his colour back.

"When I'm gone you will look to Charity? Will you not?" He had asked me the same question every night for the past two weeks. Every night I had given him the same answer.

"You're not going anywhere. But of course I will."

"What is written is written," said John, looking at me hard, the red glare of the sun in his eyes. "You're not the lightminded brat you was when you come ashore by the Gun Hole. You'll do what's right now, for Charity or

Scilly, choose which. And that's a satisfaction. To come through Hell Bay and be cleansed." His eyes closed and the now frail fingers laced together. It was hard to credit that one of those hands had once knocked my horse unconscious. He appeared to be praying, so I left him. When I returned Charity was beside him, her grey cloak blowing in the breeze, watching him with big soft china eyes.

That night, the swelling on John's back was big and angry. His pulse was frequent and thready, his skin dry and hot to the touch. He lay in his cot without a word, but I could see he was in great pain. All that night the fever raged, and the next day. By noon I knew there was nothing that could be done. He became delirious, raving at people I did not know or half-remembered from my time at Scilly. Once he was back in the brig under Zantman's, yelling orders to his oarsmen. Another time he was somewhere else, on a less merciful errand. "Joshua!" he roared, starting up onto his elbows, eyes staring wildly at the deckhead. "Get thy lantern on the pole and let her come! Can't you hear? Can you not see? The slatting of her sails and the roar of the waves at her timbers and she's coming! She's coming, Joshua!"

"Now, now," I said. "You must compose yourself."

He tore himself away from my grip with a return of his old strength. "Hold me not back, Josh! Follow on! Follow on! She'll have silk and tobacco, boy. So never mind getting yer feet wet!" He paused, his face convulsing. "But it's cold," he said. "My God in heaven, but it's cold." His teeth began to chatter. "And Josh. Where be you, Josh? OH MY GOD!" he roared. His voice died to a whisper. "Face down in the foam, missing an arm. And others like you. Women too. God be merciful unto me a sinner. And it's cold. Cold as death. Too cold." His head fell onto the pillow.

After a while he said, "Doctor?" In the feeble light that stole through the salt-crusted porthole I could see that his eyes had lost their mad glitter. "I was dreaming," he said. "About the worst thing I ever done. I brought a ship ashore on White Island, one time, with a lantern on a pole, God forgive me. They was all killed, women and children too. And my brother Joshua, as repented at the final moment and went to save them. But I hardened my heart and they all died. And since that day . . . since that

day I have tried to be strong in the Lord. Since I failed
once in my duty, I resolved never again to fail, no, nor
suffer another to fail. But now I see that each man's duty
is his own. For each man a Hell Bay of his own."

Those were the last words he ever said. That night, as
the sun sank like a red-hot bullet into sullen banks of red
vapour, his soul left his body.

We buried him the next morning, under a grey sky in a
short sea lashed by a raw northwest wind. Captain Poe
read the service over the long sailcloth bundle, and a couple of seamen slid it off the soaped plank and into the
cold water. Bubbles rose for a couple of seconds. Then
the ship left him astern and the sea was the same as ever,
the great pouring surge of it, ruffled by the wind. Charity
was whimpering beside me. I put my arm round her shoulders and led her below. She kept asking for John. I told
her that he was gone, but she did not understand. Twice
I found her sitting his cabin, by his cot, fiddling with his
sheets. When I tried to persuade her to come away she
smiled at me politely, averted her eyes and told me she
would wait until John came back.

After John's death, the sight of my fellow-passengers
became intolerable. Charity was sad and confused, but
she had lost much of her fear of me, and even at times
seemed glad of my company. Occasionally, in order to
show willing, I went up to dinner in the saloon. It was on
one of those nights, when we were perhaps two weeks
from home, that Major Slipton cornered me. Mrs. Rankin
was sitting under a lamp, half-moon spectacles perched on
her nose, knitting a horrid garment for some unlucky
heathen at her favourite mission. The captain had excused
himself and was drinking in his own cabin. I was heading
for the door, seeking peace in which I could talk to Charity and attempt to digest the sloppy pork and biscuit on
which we had dined, when the major stepped between
me and my escape route.

"Yes?" I said. He had been drinking whisky punch by
the pint, and his little pink eyes were vague and disor-
ganised.

"Thing was . . . wondered if you could have a look . . .
feeling seedy. Dashed seedy. Wonderin' . . . well, wonderin' what it was all about. Like your advice as medical
man."

"Tomorrow morning," I said. "Come and see me then."

"Oh," he said, crestfallen. "Not now, eh?" And for some reason he stuck out his tongue. I suppose he was trying to arouse my professional interest. It was a fairly ordinary tongue, warmly covered in green and white fur. Asking him to put it away, I left the room.

Next morning, the steward knocked on my door and told me the major was confined to his bed and asking for me. I went to see him. The cabin was airtight and smelt very unpleasant. The major complained of pains in his kidneys and groin, and said he had had a low fever last night and had been sick twice this morning. His mouth, he said, was full of saliva.

I told him to take off his shirt, which he did. He was white and flabby. His upper chest was covered in a red rash.

"How long's that been there?"

He looked down, surprised. "Hadn't noticed it," he said. "Had a bit of shavin' rash this morning. Seems to have spread."

"Hum," I said. "You'd better keep to your bed."

"What is it?" he said, looking more like a terrified rabbit than a ferret.

"Too early to say," said I. "Probably just a touch of fever. Don't fret. I'll send you up a powder."

"Thank you, Doctor," he said, as if he was already cured. "Most grateful. Truly am."

I left the cabin, mixed him up a powder of calomel, jalap and rhubarb which would have opened the bowels of a concrete elephant, and sat down to wait out the next twenty-four hours. It could easily, I told myself, be a fever brought on by bad food and excessive drinking. But there again, the symptoms bore a startling resemblance to something more specific—something I did not even want to think about.

When I went to see him the next day, the rash was still there, and it had spread to cover his face and his whole body. He had been vomiting steadily, and he complained of terrible pain in the pit of his stomach. I removed a decanter of whisky from his bedside, and examined him. The rash was dotted now with little red points. One or two were crowned with tiny blisters full of a clear liquid. I took a deep breath. The major was watching me from between swollen eyelids. "What is it?" he said.

"You've got smallpox," I said. "And if it's any consolation, you won't be the only one." Then I went and told the captain.

In a week there were five more cases. I had been vaccinated, and so had two or three of the crew. The captain had not, nor had Mrs. Rankin, and both of them got the disease—Poe mildly, but Mrs. Rankin seriously. Coincidentally, she and the major died on the same day. I took little interest in these events, however, for on the fourth day after the major took to his bed, Charity became ill.

I did what I could, but the only effective remedies were the ones that should have been applied years before. The tide of pustules spread up from her breast to cover her face, so close together that they ran into each other. I tried to keep her strength up, but she could not take the only food the ship could offer; day by day she weakened. As is often the case, after the first onslaught the fever abated. But still she was in pain, her whole body an eruptive mass. Often I found myself thinking of the attic on Palace Row, of the glow of lamplight on her skin, the clink of spoon on bowl as she fed me. She would have liked to know that now I was nursing her. But it was doubtful that she ever would.

On the eighth morning of her illness I went as usual to sit with her. Normally she lay with her eyes closed, her hands bandaged to the sides of the cot to stop her scratching. Today, however, her eyes were open. And much to my surprise, as I prepared her morning dose, she watched me, with intelligence. I drew nearer, and put the bowl to her lips, stroking her hair as she drank. Afterwards, she whispered something I could not catch. I bent my ear down to her mouth.

"What are you doing here?" she said. "Why?"

"Can you not remember?" I said.

"Remember what? Mrs. Stump? The Academy. . . ." Her voice trailed off into silence. Finally, she said, "I am going to die."

"So are we all," I said. "Don't distress yourself."

"It is not distressing," she said. "Send my love to Scilly, would you."

"More than that," I said. "You're doing very well."

"How?" She shuddered. "I have been dreaming . . . I

had a dreadful dream. But I was . . . In the dream I was John's wife."

I could not tell how much she remembered. "That was true," I said. "No dream."

"Was I a good wife?" she said.

"You made him very happy."

She smiled at me. Her face was dark and swollen, and it must have been agonisingly painful. "He would have been a very devoted husband, I am sure."

"He was," I said.

She smiled again. Then she went to sleep.

All the next day and the day after she slept, muttering sometimes in the surly delirium of her fever. It was increasing again, the fever. The marks on her face took on a flatter, browner look. Her pulse was rapid, faint and hard. The eleventh day after the appearence of the pustules is the most dangerous. She was starting it badly. I did all I could with cooling cloths and sedatives; but still the fever mounted. At dawn, I saw that there was a blackish foam at her lips. She was rolling her head restlessly on the pillow. The heat of her body was so fierce that it seemed to fill the cabin.

At nine o'clock in the morning, I heard the thump of bare feet on deck and an unintelligible hail. I went to the porthole and looked out. Poised on the deep blue rollers was a small boat with two foresails and a gaff mainsail over a deep hull with an axe bow. She was a boat I knew. Under her transom, the gold letters said *Gugh. Scilly*. I thought of Little John, and a mist of tears blurred the horizon. Then I turned back to Charity.

Outside, the westerly breeze blew us through the clean Atlantic, after one of *Gugh*'s gigs. No pilot, seeing the plague flag flying at the crosstrees, would come aboard; but they would cheerfully lead us. At eleven o'clock I went on deck for air. Annet and Agnus were a low blue lump, fine on the starboard bow, and the long swell was creaming in the Western Rocks. I found a broad grin on my face. A gannet folded its wings and dived. I turned and went below.

Charity's eyes were open. I said, "You can see the islands." She did not answer. I bent over her, my heart beating hard. There was a little smile on her face. I hoped that she had managed to struggle to the porthole before

she died. One thing was certain. She would never see the
islands again.

Because of the quarantine, she could not be buried in
the Tresco Churchyard. So we buried her close to Gunners, in twenty fathoms. At at three o'clock that afternoon we dropped anchor in St. Helen's pool and the boats
took the sick across to the Pest House.

Book Three

XI

THE PEST HOUSE STANDS on the southern shore of St. Helen's. It is built of dressed granite and it has a tall chimney like a mill's, but in the Pest House nothing is ground except teeth. I was sick of the sight of the place. Above it, St. Helen's Down reared round shoulders of russet bracken below its green cap. The Pest House was empty now; quarantine up, *Macclesfield* had received her pratique, and even now her black spars and dirty sails were shrinking over the horizon beyond Deep Ledges. To the south, St. Helen's Pool was a brilliant rink of aquamarine, and beyond its rocks, Blockhouse and the green fields of Borough rose in a tender swell from a fringe of white sand and rock soft with lichen.

It had been a bad six weeks. At first the boats had come flocking from Tresco and St. Martins, bringing fresh vegetables and cargoes of curious islanders. The vegetables had come aboard, but the plague flag fluttering from *Macclesfield*'s signal halliards had done its work, and after the first curiosity had died down, only the hardiest had ventured close to the quarantine harbour. I had been penned up with the sick, looking out over the spring-green islands but unable to communicate; a letter might carry the contagion. My only encouragement had been a note from Mary. She had spied me through her glass; she would come and take me off when the quarantine was done; and that was all. So now I walked restlessly on the strip of turf above the jumbled rocks by the pesthouse quay, waiting. I could hardly believe I was here. The anticipation was like a shell that stopped me seeing and smelling and hearing. The anticipation was not only for Mary. It was the anticipation of possessing this mass of water and rock and sand and soil, of changing it so the people who lived on it need not fear that one bad harvest would mean misery and starvation. Of changing it so the men on St. Mary's and the mainland, who saw no further than their own comfort and enrichment, would find that they could no longer regard the off-islands as a burden, to be plundered when convenient and ignored when not.

In the late afternoon I moved my boxes and bags down to the quay. The wind dropped, and the low sun cast a great green light out of the west, blazing over the hummocks of rock and turning the water to liquid jade. I heard the creak and thump of oars in the tholepins as the punt glided out of the lee of Northwethel. We watched each other while the ripples from the punt's wake lapped against the quay. To norrard there was the dull murmur of swell on the Golden Ball bar. Herons made their long yarring croaks on Hedge Rock, and a pair of immaculate oystercatchers piped each other down towards Blockhouse. She held water with her left oar, shipped the other. The punt came alongside with a little thump. I took her hand.

Her black hair was caught in a chignon at her nape, and her face was small and pointed, lit with the flare of those night-blue eyes. She had not changed. But when she smiled, there was none of the inwardness there once had been, the feeling that she was only half with me, that the other half was reserved for something private to her. The smile still had mockery in it, but now I felt included, as if with that smile and the slim, cool hand in mine she had reached across the years and drawn me home. She said, "Welcome back." And the shell about me cracked, and I smelt again the clean salt smell of the sea, the faint perfume of her mixed with the aromatic essences of heather and wild herbs. I stepped out of bitter memories of New Botallack and Ireland and poor Charity and Little John, out of my landlord's schemes, out of money and position. I felt the hard Scilly granite under my boots and the power in arms and shoulders and legs, and it was all real again. The joy of it built up in my throat until I opened my jaws and let loose a whoop that echoed in the rocky cairns and sent a crowd of gulls clamouring from their nesting-places in the crags. I pulled her out of the punt and folded her narrow, wiry, soft body against me, she yielding and finding my mouth with hers, and the curve of her lashes against her brown cheeks slid me away.

After a while I felt her laughing. "The boat," she said.

"Devil take the boat." I kissed her again and she kept her eyes open until they misted and the lashes swooped down again.

I do not know how long we stood like that. All I remember is seeing the punt drifting fifty yards away, heading for the edge of the tide swirling through Beef Neck. I tore off my clothes and dived off the quay and swam after it, laughing like a fool, and when I caught it and began pulling back, I saw her over my bare, cold shoulder laughing too. She dried me with my shirt and asked me questions too fast for me to answer them. Then I dragged on my clothes and threw my gear into the punt, and we pulled back to Old Grimsby Harbour.

We left my boxes at the Ship Inn, to come on later in Israel Jenkins' cart. Then we set off over the Green, past the low grey church and up Dolphin Hill between the green hedges. The sky above the brow was scattered with red rags of cloud. We passed three people, all of whom greeted Mary and looked at me with inquisitive eyes. The only one who recognised me was John Sinclair, motheaten as ever, and he, old villain, was not going to give anything away. He only winked and asked politely if I would be staying long, to which I replied that I hoped I should. But Mary said, "Of course he is," smiled at John and dragged me on to the top of the hill. There we paused a moment, looking out over the kindling lights of New Grimsby and Bryher and the Webber hovels on Samson, and beyond to the far horizon where the sun carefully lowered its disc towards the sea.

Everyone has a moment in his life which alone justifies what has gone before and what is to come. For me that moment was standing with Mary in the warm twilight on that road, hearing the evening sounds of the island declining into night about me, feeling the light touch of her hand in the crook of my arm. The feeling of homecoming was so intense that I do not think I would have cared if I had died on the spot. We started down the hill again, into the lake of shadow over the harbour and around the houses; and after the top of that hill, nothing was ever quite the same again.

Halfway down the hill there was a new house. On that site before had stood a tumbledown hut of turf, tenanted by Lawrence Bond, two lodgers, three children and pigs without number. The new house was of straight-sided stone, whitewashed, with windows. I said, "Lawrence is coming up in the world."

Mary said, "Oh, Lawrence doesn't live there any more. He went Away."

"Why?" Lawrence had been fifty-five years old. I could imagine him moving Away—Scillonian for the mainland —less easily than I could imagine an oak-tree going for a morning stroll.

"Never mind Lawrence," said Mary. We were passing the cottage porch where I had first seen her, flitting like a wraith over the silver ribbon of the moonlit road. There was the sulphurous smell of rotting seaweed. "We're nearly there."

"Nearly where?"

She held tighter to my arm, but she did not answer. The road ran a hundred yards along the low cliff of the shore, with houses on the left. She turned into a gate and said, "Here."

It was the last house. Beyond it, the road ran on past fields and the end of the Pool up under the beginning of Abbey Hill into the dusk. "My new house," said Mary.

Instead of the old, round walls, there were sharp angles. No lichen on the granite blocks; only the late gleam of the sky's reflection on grey stone. No towering cone of golden thatch; only slates, ranked flat and crisp as a regiment of Engineers. Instead of the old hollow in the dunes where the wind hissed and roared in Great Rocks, a prospect busy with ships and boats and little houses. I stood appalled.

"Isn't it fine?" said Mary. "I did hope you'd like it."

"Different," I said.

We went in. A fire was burning in the grate, casting red lights over the salt-bleached Turkey carpets, the gold-blocked calf of her books. There seemed to be more books now. An old woman was sitting bent by the fire, the click of her knitting-needles homely and muted. She looked up, startled, and I saw it was Susan Odger, for whom I had fought off the sheriffs. She bundled up her needles, curtseyed and said, "I'll be off then."

I said, "Well, well. And how are the hands?"

"Terrible poor," she said, holding up a withered claw. "I do have the rheumatics in 'em summat dreadful." She screwed up her old eyes at me. "Do I know 'ee, sir?"

"The doctor," I said.

"Oh, ah," said Susan. She did not look convinced. "Well, I'll be getting along." She scurried out of the door, wrapping her shawl round her old shoulders.

"You've changed," said Mary. "It's no wonder she didn't recognise you."

"Perhaps it's just as well."

She laughed. "No need to worry about that. You know Scilly. Gossip like fiends, but if it's something important they'll clam up tight."

"Good," I said. For a moment my belly was cold. But I was with Mary now, so the coldness went away.

"You'll be hungry."

I was. We sat in the kitchen, which smelt of new wood and paint, talking with our mouths full, trying to cram the loose ends of the separate years into minutes so we could start living together again. At last she came to the part I had been dreading. "And what of Charity Pender?" she said.

Charity and John and New Botallack were ages away. I did not want to think about them. It was enough to be in the warm room with Mary, the scent of her verbena, watching her watching me. But as usual, the eyes dragged it out of me. When I had finished, she said, "So what now?"

"Bed."

She put her hand on my cheek for a moment. Then I followed her to the stairs. In the little dark hall at the bottom I stumbled on something I thought was a broomstick. I bent and picked it up. It was a child's hobby-horse, a three-foot pole with a painted horse's head nailed to its top. Mary said, "Come *on*, Nick," low and urgent. I leaned the hobby-horse against the wall. At the top of the stairs were two doors. Into one of them Mary led me, and there was a bed, and for the moment that was all we wanted.

I was woken by a hand on my face. It was a small hand. It ran over the stubble of my jaw and poked a finger up my nostril. There was a sound of giggling. I opened my eyes.

"Good mornin'," said a high voice, still with the remains of the giggle. The voice belonged to a wide face with a domed forehead topped with black hair, two large dark-blue eyes like Mary's, a short nose and an absurdly curly mouth above a chin which was easily the most determined I had ever seen on a five year-old child. "What you doin' in my mamma's bed?"

"Trying to sleep," I said. Then it hit me, and I sat up, fast. "Your mamma's bed?"

"Yes it is. Not yours. What you doin' sleepin' in it? It's hers," said the small boy, driving his point home.

I stared at him. He looked very like Mary. But he reminded me of somebody else, too. Mary's footsteps sounded on the stairs. "Nick," she called. "Nick, are you there?"

"Yes," said I and the boy, together. Then we looked at each other again until the child had had enough and ran for Mary, who was leaning against the doorpost, a finger nervously to her lip.

"I see you have already met," she said. "Nick, may I present you to your son? And Nick, this is your father. He's come to live with us."

"Does he have to sleep in your bed?"

"Yes," said Mary. "He does. Now you go and shake hands with him."

"Shan't," said Nick. He twisted free of his mother's hand and clattered down the stairs. I heard the door slam.

I swung out of bed, pulled on shirt and breeches, and went after him. He was sitting on a rock at the tip of Plumb Island, chin resting on his thin brown knees, staring across at Bryher.

"Nick," I said. Then I could not think of anything else. He did not turn. "What do you want?"

His profile was angry, brows drawn down over his small nose. I struggled for words. "I'm . . . glad I came back," I said. "You must try not to mind."

"I will." He picked up a stone, threw it into the waving fronds of weed. "Why did you have to come?"

"I wanted to see your mother. I was in America."

"She said." He looked at me sideways. I saw the quickening of interest in his eyes before he composed his face to blankness. "I don't see why you had to come."

"It was a bit complicated," I said. "There was an explosion in a gold mine."

"Go away."

"I brought a nugget. The first one I found, actually. I was exploring in the black country with an Indian—"

"A red Indian?" -

"His name was Jabez. I helped him once, when he had a broken arm—"

"And he became your faithful friend?" He had turned, the big eyes boring bright and excited into mine. "Did he have feathers?"

"All down his back. Moccasins, too. I brought some. I suppose they might fit you."

He wriggled his bare brown toes, looking down.

"They're in my box," I said. "Do you want to try them on?"

His face turned bright red. "Oh, yes! When? Now? Can we do it now?" He got up and began bounding from rock to rock. I panted in his wake, caught up with him at the house. He tried on the moccasins. They were too big, but that did not matter. Mary came down and he said, "Look! Look what the man gave me!"

She looked down then at me, smiled. "That's not a man," she said. "That's our Doctor."

The boy looked at me with a return of the old suspicion. I knew that bribes were not the answer. Still, I was overwhelmed with relief. "Say 'thank you'," said Mary.

"Thank you," said the boy. Then he ran away and I coud hear him yelling and whooping in the road. It was the most comforting sound I had ever heard.

"I'm afraid he's terribly spoilt," said Mary.

"Spoilt," I said, feeling the grin start in my stomach and work itself up to cover my face and open my arms and take her in. "No." After that, we did not speak for some time. Finally we drew apart. "Now," I said. "Why don't you tell me what's been going on?"

"There's not much to tell," said Mary. "I knew he was coming before you left. I didn't know what you'd think of it, and I didn't want to be pregnant half across the world."

"That's why you wouldn't come?"

"Partly. But only partly. The rest of it was wanting to stay at Scilly." For the first time since I had known her, she looked nervous. "You're not angry?"

"Oh my God," I said. "All that time—" I jumped out of bed and grabbed her. "You never told me? I would have come back on the next boat. Why didn't you tell me?"

"Because you had your own way to make. Scilly was

just a port of call. I didn't think you'd be happy here. And they were looking for you."

"But later. When they had stopped looking. . . ."

She shrugged. "I don't know. I thought . . . well, I thought I'd lost you to America. I knew you were made for big things. I didn't want you to come back for the boy's sake and regret it."

"But my letters—you must have believed me."

"You asked me to join you. You never suggested that you might come back."

I did not say anything. I was crossing the time I had waited in the valley at New Botallack, with the hammer of the stamping-engine ringing through my lonely cabin and Mary's face glowing in the ashes of the fire, her voice in my ears when I woke in my hard, narrow bed. "Why didn't Little John tell me anything?" I said. "He must have known."

"He did. But you know John. He would not admit that the child even existed. He was so wrapped up in you and poor Charity that he couldn't allow himself to believe in young Nick."

"Yes," I said. I began to see things more clearly. One thing in particular; Little John's realisation in Charlotte that under no circumstances would I marry Charity.

"You're not angry?"

"Angry? To have a son? Your son? And be back at Scilly with you?" I took her hands. "This is the best morning of my life, Mary. I only wish it could have been five years ago."

She smiled, but there was still something nervous about it. "Don't speak too soon," she said. "There's something else." She dug in a small chest on the table. "This came for you. In the winter."

It was a letter, addressed to Doctor Nicholas Nicholls, in a clean, fluent copperplate. It bore a London postmark, dated December 1834. I broke the wafer.

Dear Sir,

I have yours of August last to hand, and note your intentions regarding the lease of the Isles of Scilly. I much regret to inform you, however, that a lease has been satisfactorily concluded this year with Augustus Smith Esquire of Berkhamsted, and that we are thus unable to entertain

*further offers. I am Sir your most humble and obedient
Servant,*

*George Harrison,
Kt. Secretary to the Duchy of Cornwall.*

I crumpled the letter and tossed it aside. Then I looked
up at Mary.

"I knew what was in it," she said. "I thought it would
be better if you read it."

"Yes. I suppose it was."

"We had last night," she said. "That was good, anyway."

I got up and went to the window. The wind was raising
spiky little waves in the channel, blue-green like Cherokee
turquoise. One of Amor Odger's boys was driving a couple of black cattle along the road, whistling. Missed by an
inch. But for the slowness of the mails, all those islands
and rocks might have been mine, to have and to hold.
"Who is this Smith?" I said.

"A banker's son, from somewhere near London. Full
of notions and improvements."

"A banker's son." Some Cockney princeling with the
Cornhill soot still black behind his ears, thinking he would
have himself a pretty toy. Scilly a rich man's yacht, anchored forever in the Gulf Stream for Mister Smith to
strut on and give himself airs and think himself a little
king. A place to paint watercolours and play bezique and
to rhapsodise over the prettiness of it all. "What does he
know about Scilly?" I could not keep the bitterness out of
my voice.

"Not much," said Mary, laughing. "But he'll find out.
He's that kind of man." She dropped her eyes. "He'll
make changes. Will you . . . will you stay?"

"Of course I will. Why do you ask?"

"He won't like you on the island. You're too rich and
strong for him."

"I see. Do you want me to stay?"

"Of course I do," she said.

"Then I shall," I said. "That's all there is to it."

"And you're sure you'll be content? With all your
money, living in a cottage?"

"I'd rather live with you in a cottage than with anyone
else in a palace."

"You're sure?"

"Sure."

She was silent a moment. Then she said. "Oh, Nick. I am glad. But I'll keep you to it." And there, for the moment, it ended.

Later, I set off to see Jimmy Pender and Aunt Woodcock. Jimmy was badly lame now, and the rheumatism had got into his hands, but he was still working at his carpentering. I made out that Charity had died in Charleston, that she was buried there under the headstone I had ordered. I had written to him about it at the time I had first heard and believed the news. Now he sat down and looked over the green rows of early potatoes in his garden, and nodded an old man's nod over the handle of his walking-stick. Charity's death was a part of history for him now. I told him of Mrs. Stump's high esteem for her, and her progress from maid to instructor. And that seemed to please him, in a theoretical sort of way, though his shyness prevented him from expressing it. "As long as she done a good job, Doctor," he said, blowing out his long yellow moustache. "Just as long as. 'Tis hard how time do pass, and children with it. But you do see a lot of it when you do be my age."

Aunt Woodcock had grown enormously fat, but she was as hale and talkative as ever. I found her in her garden, hoeing, and got her to sit down while I told her the news. She took it surprisingly calmly. "Oh dear, poor dear Johnny," she said, brushing tears from her great red cheeks with the hem of her white apron. I made no mention of Charity. I only told her how John had saved my life and lost his own in the process. When I had finished, she looked hard at the ground, while the fat tears ran down and splashed on the linen covering her enormous bosom. Finally, she heaved a gusty sigh and said, "I s'pose I'm glad he died, I mean you can't imagine our Johnny cripped up in bed forever, can you now? And I'm glad he did right by you because I always did say as he was powerful hard on you, Doctor." As before, Aunt Woodcock's house teemed with children, some of the older ones hers, and she waved a big red arm at them. "Least there's the rest of 'em for consolation. I been a lucky woman other than John and Joshua and poor dear Mr. Woodcock as drowned, God knows I have and I'm thankful for it. And I must say I give John up for dead when he left the island. Poor little Johnny. He were always that stubborn."

"If I can ever be of assistance—"

"Bless you, Doctor, you'll be moving on soon enough."

"I shall be staying."

"Well that is a wonder and a good thing too," she said. "Powerful glad to hear that. And so will Aunt Ellis be." She beamed at me maternally. "Well I declare that makes up for all our sorrow." As I left, she was shouting for one of the children to fetch Aunt Ellis to share the glad news.

The way back to Mary's new house took me over Middle Downs and along the ridge by the Abbey Pool. The south-facing slope was cut into tiny fields, and in them men were lifting potatoes. I recognised one of them, a smallish man with bushy side-whiskers and a red nose. "Harry Jack!" I said, astonished.

He looked up, with the myopic squint that was the legacy of years in the ill-lit Palace taproom. His clothes were still those of a man accustomed to an indoor life, but they were worn and stained with hard labour. "By the Christ," he said. "If it ain't the doctor." He wiped his streaming forehead with a red handkerchief. I jumped over the wall—in remarkably good repair, the wall—and shook him by the hand. "By God it's good to see you back," he said.

"And good to see you," I said. "But. . . . Well, it's not like you to be digging. God, man, you should be indoors looking after your customers."

He looked at me hard. "Not too many of them, nowadays."

"And pigs have wings."

He leaned on his spade. "You haven't been long back, have you."

"Since yesterday."

There was something bitter in the squint of his bright brown eyes. "And it looks like you been doing good for yourself while you was away." He clucked his tongue in his teeth, seeming to search my face. "Hardly recognised you. Well, it's good to know the world's treating somebody right."

"Bad times?"

"Oh no," said Harry with elaborate sarcasm. "Only a bloody St. Mary's pimp of a landlord agent says no more Palace because there's too much eyewater and not

enough dooty paid. Only a bastard of a gentleman landlord says I works six days a bloody year building granite
'edges for him. Only that same landlord says he wants a
tenth of all the bloody fish I catch. And says Missis Harry
Jack can't fire the ovens with turf no more. You haven't
been back long, you say. Well, you bloody look out when
you goes to the jakes because Hemperor bloody Smith is
counting 'ow many times you goes and if your tally don't
jibe with his he'll make you pay. Like living in a bugger-
ing goldfish bowl," said Harry Jack, eyeing his spade with
disgust.

"Fierce, is he?" So it was Smith who was responsible
for Harry Jack's reduced circumstances.

"He is. There's some as likes it, mind. But I don't and
there's more like me. A lot more. Only nobody says nothing because if they do they're off Away before their
hands can clap." He picked up his spade again and
jammed it in with his boot as if the spud-row were Smith's
neck. "How's that Bolitho?"

"Dead. In America."

"Sorry to hear it," he said. "Didn't know he was killa-
ble. Always did say that when God made granite he decided it weren't hard enough and knocked up the
captain."

I waited until he had his barrow filled, and walked
back with him to the shed. "So what are you going to do
now the Palace is gone?"

"Dig bloody spuds, i s'pose. That and fish. I'd go
Away, only I don't fancy it somehow." He spat. "If ever
you wants a good bottle of eyewater as hasn't got the
Curse of the Customs on it, you'll find me up there." He
pointed across to the sprawl of the Palace. Half of the
roof was torn off. I made some remark about it. "Hemperor Smith done that," he said. "One of his favorite
tricks. That or saw your boat in half." Bidding me a fond
farewell, he went on his way.

When I went back to Mary's house, Nick had returned.
The first excitement of the moccasins had worn off, and
he was quiet, almost sullen. Mary had obviously been
speaking to him about me, but I could see that he was by
no means keen on the idea of a father who might supplant
him in her affections.

He vanished on sight of me. Mary, seeing me downcast

at his mistrust, said, "He loves the moccasins. I read him *Last of the Mohicans* at bedtime this year."

"I don't think he likes me much."

"He'll get used to the idea of you."

"And what about the island?"

"What about it?"

"It's important that he gets encouragement from other people. Not just us."

She looked puzzled. "What do you mean?"

I found it difficult to say. "That he should have a mother and a father with the same name. . . ."

She said, "Are you telling me that we should get married?"

"Yes," I said, knowing I was lost from her tone of voice. "I suppose I am."

Her laugh was like a window opened in a smoky room. "Ach, Nick!" she said. "Marry you? I told you before, I'll never marry anyone. If I did, it would be you. But I won't. You're the lodger and the father of my child. That's not enough for you?"

"The child," I said. "He needs a father."

"He's got one. And if anyone on the island says different, they'll have me to deal with."

This was the Mary I had seen on the night of the wreck at Old Grimsby. That part of her nothing would ever change. But understanding her reasons did not make her refusal any less painful.

That afternoon I went walking. Where the fish cellar had once stood, there was work in progress. A gang of men was carting and laying stone for a building that, to judge by its chimney, was designed for a mill. Big machines stood shrouded in tarpaulins against the wind and spray. Beyond in New Grimsby harbour, there were six or seven boats. I tried to pretend that this was only normal for the time of year; but I knew it was not. The paint looked spruce, and several of them were obviously new. Before, it had been a rich, rare and meticulous Scillonian who applied brush to planking oftener than once every five years. In the deep water beyond the quay, masts rose against the rocky spine of Bryher. Three cutters, a schooner, and a small brigantine. Here for the potatoes; and to judge by the size of the fleet, the crop must be very good this year. There was even a flagpost at the inshore end of the quay, with the Union Jack fluttering bravely in

the breeze. If you liked that sort of thing. At this precise
moment, I did not. I turned away and walked up the road
that led under the crest of Abbey Hill. The road was better than I remembered it.

At its southeasternmost point Abbey Hill slopes steeply
down to a neck of land separating the two Pools. It is a
commanding point of vantage, the islands spread around
and below to the east, south and west. Once, the crest of
this promontory of hill had been a splash of heather and
wild daffodils, split by rocks mossy with orange and lovat
lichen. The path to the Abbey itself had curled up and
across like a sunbathing snake. You could get a horse
across without too much trouble, but it was a difficult
place with a cart.

Now, you could have taken a waggon and six across
it without noticing it was there. The ridge had a notch
hacked out of it, a thirty-foot cliff of blasted granite whose
foot plunged into a flat desert of ram and rock. Across
the southerly part of it ran a maze of low walls, five feet
high at its highest. A couple of sheerlegs projected above
the walls. I watched a man raise a lump of granite from
a barrow, swing it across into a bed of mortar. There were
ten or twelve other men there, working. I picked my way
over the trenches and into the maze.

I was wearing a short dark coat, with a collar and a
cravat. My trousers were of good cloth, my boots polished. The masons and labourers worked hard and earnestly as I crunched through the foundations, pausing only
to tug forelocks. I only recognised one of them—David
Ellis, a small, dark man with a wise satyr's face and a
reputation as a terror for drink and women, which had
stood him in poor stead in his attempts to deny paternity
of Ursula Jenkins' child. I wished him a good afternoon,
and he remembered me aloud. At this the pace of work
slackened visibly. A pack of cards came out from under a
rock, and a gentleman I dimly remembered as a master
mason returned to a seat in a sunny patch, drawing a
black bottle from his overalls. David and I chatted about
times past, he with a confiding air, as one recalcitrant father to another. Then he took it upon himself to show me
round the house, assuming for the purpose the character
and speech of Augustus Smith, Esquire, of Berkhamstead.
If David was anything to go by, Smith had the manners of
a Nero combined with the language of a Satanist bargee.

He conducted me first through the servants' quarters and kitchens, and thence to a hall and a long drawing-room with the sills of Gothic windows looking out over a terrace. The windows looked due south, across Great Rocks to St. Mary's, and the distant grey houses of Hugh Town. "And here," said David, his face growing long and pompous under the black mop "Here I shall sit and count my rents and watch my subjects work like niggers in my fields for my benefit. And I will watch bloody great ships come in and unload carriages and 'orses full of lords and ladies, and I will feed them my potatoes and we will all get wet as shags in a thunderstorm, inside and out. On this 'ere table I will cheat their britches off at cards, when my carpenters 'ave made me the table. There will also be dancing girls brought over from Injer, expense irregard-less. And after tea we will promenade in the gardens, as you see below." He indicated the terraces of shattered granite running away to the left. "In 'ere you will find my bedroom—"

A granite block fell off a sheerlegs with a crunch. There was loud cursing. David looked round, whipped a trowel from his belt and began scraping half-dried mortar off the top course of masonry. In his own voice, he said, "It's bloody Johns." The site began fairly to hum with ac-tivity. Round the corner came a weedy individual in a wide straw hat. He had a worried face and a nose that darted about him like a bird's beak. "Smith's agent," said David, out of the corner of his mouth. The master mason had replaced bottle in pocket and was squinting in an in-tellectual manner at the pointing of the external wall. I had half a mind to slip away. But Johns had already seen me, and was forging towards me like a heron with some-thing on its mind. His face had that same closed, wary cast I remembered on my father's, as if he constantly ex-pected the world to be lying in ambush behind the hedge-rows. He said, "Good afternoon," pleasantly enough, but with the hint of a question in it. I knew I would have to be careful with this man.

I returned his greeting, but I did not introduce myself. Despite Mary's assurances, I had no desire to put the memories of St. Mary's to the test, at least this early. In-stead, I said, "A very fine house."

"Finest in the islands," said Johns, with perhaps a hint of sourness. This man's father had ruled Scilly for a long time. I could sympathise with his feelings at having the kingship snatched from under his nose.

"Indeed. I hope I am not taking a liberty in looking round?" I made my accent just a touch American.

"By no means. By no means. Keeps the men up to it. Sorry lot."

"Glad to be of service," I said. "It's not by any chance your house?"

He laughed. "No. Belongs to the new Lord Proprietor." Again the hint of sourness. "Have you been on the islands long?"

"Indeed no," I said. "Since only yesterday, in fact." Whatever I told this man would be all over St. Mary's by tomorrow night. "I was landed on St. Helen's for quarantine. I'm a bit of a natural philosopher—made some successful speculations on the New York market—thought I'd tour the great Universities of Europe. But do you know—" I borrowed a gesture from Judge Cawthrop and hooked my thumb in my waistcoat pocket—"I kind of took to this place. And I thought why would I not stay here a time and see if I could find any support for a little hypothesis of mine. Gulf Stream vagrants. Yes sir. I opine that up the broad moving highway of water that connects these Islands with the gulf of Mexico, there travels a host of creatures. Take *chrysaora hysoscella,* for instance. You may know him better as the Compass Jellyfish." "I began lecturing. I had no idea if *hysoscella* ever swam the Gulf, but that was not the point at issue.

Johns' eyes were glazing over, his nose jerking as he tried to agree himself out of the conversation as fast as he could. I could almost see the thoughts forming in his mind. Talk the hind leg off a donkey. Lot of money by the sound of him, but—well, Tresco was welcome to him. Man's a lunatic. "Yes, Sir," I said. "I look forward to a long and fruitful study. I have taken lodging with a Mistress Prideaux, and I am pleased to say I find it most comfortable. Most."

"Ah," said Johns. "Well, good. Very good. I am sure you will find much to interest you. If you would care for a hand at cards some evening. . . . ?"

"I never play cards, Sir. Quite apart from my ethical objections to games of chance, I find such diversions impinge on the process of scientific inquiry." He looked relieved. I treated him to a further five minutes on the need for rigorous discipline in the seeker after truth, then took my leave and set off for Appletree beach. When I looked back, he was quarreling with the master mason, paying me not the slightest attention. I thanked God that the current Nicholas Power, clean-shaven, solidly built, with only the trace of a limp remaining, bore no resemblance to Nicholas Power gaunt and bearded, dragging his useless leg round the island five years ago. And I had told no lies to Johns. When I was recognised—and I was quite confident that it would happen, sooner or later—that would be important. I only needed to claim that I wanted to live without harassment. Even if they put me on trial, they could not find me guilty on their evidence.

In the meantime, I was home, and the summer lay ahead. And there was Mary and the child.

Although I was now one of the five most fashionable doctors in Dublin, I had my worries. My youth made me less than popular with a sizeable number of my competitors. Mercy Hall was taking more and more of my time and money, and if I had spent as many hours there as I wanted, I should never have been able to earn enough at my Merrion Square practice to keep the place going. And Michael Fitzpatrick, who had weathered the gossip surrounding his mother's removal to Bath, never failed to point out to me that I was associating with too many people of, at best, doubtful reputation. I still spent a good deal of time with Michael. Gossip or no gossip, I had known him since a child; and his work had brought him excellent sporting connections. There was nothing like a day riding to hounds in the Wicklow Hills to blow away the stink of Mercy Hall and the twitter of Merrion Square.

Katie and I continued good friends, and if Michael was to be believed, the talk about us became louder and more acrimonious. He had no more affection for her than she for him, though he was a better dissembler; and he was appalled at our involvement with various Catholic causes, which he construed as a threat to his livelihood and accordingly loathed.

As it drew on towards Christmas, it rained. The streets were foul and wet, and the taverns smelt of wet wool and boredom. I felt stale and tired and Katie began to look white and thin. I think she was also drinking too much; although she seemed to make a special effort to hide it from me, I sometimes smelt brandy on her too early in the day. One day I was taking tea with her. I noticed that her hand shook as she poured, and she topped up her cup from a little flask when she thought I was not looking. I said to her, "I really think you could be doing with a change of air."

She laughed. "Why so? I'm feeling quite marvellous. Or is it that you want me out of the way? Sissy Ormonde, is it?"

Sissy Ormonde was a young lady of undoubted attractions whose mother thought highly of the earning-power of young, handsome physicians. "Jealous?" I said.

"Of course not," said Katie. "What would I have to be jealous of?" But she gave me a surprisingly tentative smile, to show it was not a set-down. "Very well, then. We'll go to Drumcarty for Christmas, you and I and Nellie. That suit?"

It would. It was three years since I had been out of Dublin. So two days later, we set off in my coach, Lady Nellie less than overjoyed at leaving the comfort of Alban House for the howling passages and drawingrooms of the Castle.

His Lordship was not in evidence when we arrived. Kelly the butler informed us that he was working in the solar and would probably—he sounded unconvinced—be down for dinner. He did not appear. We ate a bad dinner in great discomfort, and afterwards Katie disappeared to see her father. I, having received no summons, sat for a while over my wine and then adjourned to the library, where the books at least prevented the heat from the three huge fires escaping into the damp walls.

Next day, we rode. The stables were the only part of the great house that prospered, since Pat Considine, Katie's correspondent, was making a good thing for himself out of stud-fees. We toured the home farm, which was in a terrible state. The grass had gone to mud and weeds and what beasts there were in the raths were emaciated and small from bad breeding and worse hay. My father would never have permitted it. I said as much to Katie, who laughed and said, "What's the use? Papa's too busy with his lawsuits. He'd never find a man to work for him who wouldn't steal him blind, now. He's past it."

I said, "But it'll be yours. Aren't you interested?"

She looked at me as if I were mad. "In farming? Why should I be? Come on, now. I'll race you to the lodge."

Next morning—Christmas Eve—I received the summons from the solar. It was a cold grey day. Draughts whipped in the round hall on the bottom floor of the keep and rustled the papers in their neat stacks in the muniment room. But the solar itself was hot, with the smell of camphor. Drumcarty was sitting on the sofa in front of the fire. Round him were heaped piles of paper. He made me think of a rat in its nest; but there was nothing ratlike in the long, pale face, the sensitive hands in the old-fashioned lace cuffs.

"Ah, Power, dear boy," he said with surprising warmth. "So glad you could come," as if the journey from the Jacobean part of the house to the Norman keep was an affair of bad roads and many days. "Looking very fit," he said, with a little cough. "I hear you're doing well. I am pleased."

"Thank you, My Lord. I am most gratified."

He raised his long hand, let it fall. "And I think you are a good influence on Lady Katherine. Sit down." He shovelled papers aside.

We sat on the soft sofa before the fire in a long, uncomfortable silence. He was even thinner than I had last seen him. At last he said, "I should like a picture of you."

"A picture?" I said, taken by surprise.

Drumcarty produces little enough of merit," he said. "You have looked the place over, no doubt. The tenants . . . the lawsuits. . . ." He picked up a handful of papers, let them drift down like huge snowflakes. "Lady Katherine, now. She has merit. Do you think?" He looked at me sharply.

"Indeed," I said, embarrassed.

"She is all I have. Mine is a proud name. She is the last of my line . . . Yes. She bears it well." I wondered how her creditors would react to this statement. "She has the pride. That is what matters."

"Yes," I said.

"And you yourself have merit. You have cared for her. Fought for her. I should like a portrait of you, Nicholas. Your name is one bound to ours. Give the commission to whomever you think suitable."

He picked up the sheaf of papers he had been reading when I came in. "Goodbye," he said. "I have much to do

. . . too much, really. A labyrinth of law . . . I am most pleased with you in your care of Lady Katherine. You have turned out well."

The Earl did not appear on Christmas Day, but we spent it merrily enough; even Lady Nellie became quite cheerful. In the evening we dined out, and Katie, cool and beautiful in French tulle over a white silk petticoat embroidered with roses and ears of wheat, was witty and pleasant, and the gentlemen sat over their wine for an unusually short time in order to get back to her.

On St. Stephen's Day, hounds met at Glasheen Cross. Katie had threatened and cajoled Considine into giving of his plenty, and we were both well mounted, Katie on a perfect Arab with a tight-bowed neck, I on a big chestnut stallion. The Glasheen meet was a great festival, and there was a huge and ragged crowd of foot-people—more ragged then I remember them; that would have much to do with high rents and low prices. They made me think of Mercy Hall, and I was selfishly glad when the hounds found and we left the foot-people far behind in a straight six-mile run across neglected grassland with big, exhilarating banks.

It was dark when we hacked down Drumcarty Drive. Katie stopped before the bridge, looking at the overgrown mass of the Steward's House. "Funny to think of you there," she said. "All those years we never met. Did you know I was jealous of you?"

"Why?" I said.

"Oh, you had a father who talked to you. Who had loved your mother. Papa hated my mother, and he never said anything that wasn't about Pride and the Name. I always thought of you as the love-child."

"My father never let it trouble him," I said. We rode on in silence, over the puddles where I had floundered while she watched from the carriage. "I was in love with you. Did you know that?"

She said, "Oh! No. How wonderful, Nick!" There was warmth and laughter in her voice.

"Yes. It took me four years to get over you."

I felt her freeze. Then she jammed her spurs into the Arab's flanks and shot forward over the bridge, sparks whizzing from the horse's hooves. I did not see her again that evening.

It was a curious summer. Part of it was an idyll. In the
terraces below the slow-growing walls of Smith's new
house, there were fleshy-leaved mesembryanthemums,
their flowers aniline eyes that stared up at the raw stone
and the lazy masons with an indifference I found quite
appropriate. St. Mary's was always there, but I never
went to it and it never came to me. I worked on my cata-
logues, carefully preserved by Mary, did some doctoring
in the other off-islands, and talked to young Nick. It took
a long time, and there were occasions when I thought I
might as well move out of the house and be done with
him; but little by little he began to accept me.

He was a strange child, Nick, with a most decided will
of his own. I feared at first that his lack of a father would
make him too dependent on Mary. But she treated him
as an adult and a friend, and he in his turn had acquired
a sense of his responsibilities to her which would have
done credit to a boy three times his age. That was one of
the reasons I found it hard to win him round, particularly
as Mary and I decided that after my initial bribes of gold
and moccasins I should win or lose him without material
inducements. But once we trusted each other—I think I
was jealous of him, too, at first—the adulthood he had acquired alone with Mary turned to new purposes. Since he
had realised he was not like other children, he had set
himself to find out why. Whether he was digging for sea-
squirts on the beach or discussing the reasons why seal
pups had to be taught to swim by their mothers, he was
always working out patterns. Mary accepted this without
question, because she lived as part of the great deep pattern that was her Scilly. But I had seen the fungoid sprawl
of the gold fever in the valleys of North Carolina, a can-
cerous growth with no pattern but greed. And I found in
the calm acceptance of it all a great peace.

There was a part of the summer that was not so idyllic.
There was a custom of long standing that on a farmer's
death, his land was divided equally between his sons.
Smith was determined to change this. He had decreed
that only one son should inherit the land; which, given the
exiguous size of the subdivided holdings, seemed to make
good sense. Until the day I met Mordecai Ellis down by
the quay. Usually, Mordecai was a cheerful soul, dedi-
cated to doing his bumbling best to brighten up the lives
of his fellow-men. But on this day, despite the fineness of

the morning, he was surrounded by an aura of gloom thick as fog.

When I asked him why, he told me that Agent Johns had told him he would not be able to farm the Ellis land with his brother. And when he had asked Johns what he was supposed to do with himself, Johns had told him he could find employment elsewhere, and failing that he would as a special favour find him a berth in His Majesty's Navy. There had been Ellises on their land since memory began, said Mordy. He weren't going to work for no other bugger. And as for the Navy—you'd as well be a bloody convict as go in the Navy. So what was he going to do? Was it human justice? I agreed that it was not, but felt that I might be allowing my friendship with Mordy to colour my judgement. I was disabused of these doubts later in the week, when I saw men building a stone hedge round the good south-facing land on Abbey Hill. Mary, with whom I was walking, said that this was to be the Proprietor's demesne, and told me further that the same fate lay in store for large expanses of Middle Downs. At which point, I became angry. Why, I asked her, should Smith be allowed to throw good men off the island so he could indulge his whims? She only shrugged and said that it was his island now, to do as he liked with.

"So you didn't mind him moving you out of your house," I said.

"Of course I minded," she said. "Don't be ridiculous. But things change, and you have to change with them." She took my arm. "Do you remember that you told me you'd rather live in a cottage with me than in a palace with anyone else?"

I did. "It's true."

She smiled at me, tilting her head. "There's more to living in a cottage than small rooms," she said. "You have to do what them in the palaces tells you."

I knew she was right. When I was with her, the cottager's life was easy. I was ridiculously in love, and ridiculously proud of our son, and that was enough. But when I was on my own or talking to the other islanders, the changes were always with me. The summer wore on, hot and bright, but always I felt there was a shadow over the doings of the island. Once, the islanders had said what they thought, or been devious for their own good reasons. Now people hesitated before they spoke, while they calcu-

lated whether you were Smith's man or a neutral or one
of the shadowy band of malcontents who prowled at night,
recognising none of the Proprietor's myriad rules. And
more and more, when I was away from Mary and the boy,
I found myself identifying with the last group. That made
me profoundly uneasy. I had struck a bargain with myself; after the horrors, a quiet life. New Botallack had
given me bad habits, I told myself. I was only feeling my
oats.

But sometimes I found myself walking down Palace
Row to the old dispensary, now used for storing nets, wishing for a sight of Little John's lowering glare as he wove
lobster pots on the beach, the sound of Charity's voice
chiding my patients on the benches under the granite
walls. The old, hard times.

It was a hot day in early September when Aunt Ellis
came to see me. I was sitting in the little garden at the
back of the house, attempting with young Nick to deter-
mine the half-digested contents of a conger eel's stomach,
spread before us on a board. We had caught the beast on
a line of our mutual devising the day before, and the intense heat had done nothing to sweeten it. So it was with
considerable relief that I heard the gate open, saw the
Aunt's thin, bent figure hobbling up the path. "Good day
to you," I said.

"Doctor," said the Aunt. "I wants to talk to you."

I sat her down in a driftwood chair, and offered her tea.
She shook her head firmly, cocking a bright eye at the
house. Mary's voice came from the open window, humming one of her strange pentatonic tunes. Aunt Ellis, like
most of the Tresco folk, retained her mistrust of Mary.
Young Nick removed the horrid remains, leaving us alone.
I said, "Fire away."

"It's like this," said the Aunt gravely. It was not like
her, this gravity. "We's faced with trouble. And I was
talking with Aunt Woodcock, and we was remembering
how you did help us out. For which we be most thankful."

"Is it Mordecai?" I said.

She nodded. " 'Tis so. After I'm gone, which won't be
long—"

"You're strong as a tree. But he told me. What can I do
about it?"

"We was remembering how you did speak up at the
Council on St. Mary's that time. 'Tis a tremendous tongue

you have, Doctor. And you a gentleman too. If you could speak for Mordy to the Emperor . . . Smith, that is. . . ."

"Yes," I said. "Yes, I see." I stirred my toe in the grass. "Of course I'd be pleased to help. But. . . ." My mind went back to the scene in Star Castle, the purple face of John Johns and the rest of them, and Maltby, the Preventive with the eyes that took notes and filed them away. Maltby was gone, and so was the Council. But from then on I would be a marked man. No more peace.

Aunt Ellis had not lived eighty years without learning what went on in men's minds. She heaved her tiny body out of the chair. " 'Twas wrong in me to ask," she said. "You done enough, Doctor. We'm grateful for it." She smiled at me, encouragingly. But she did not look happy. Mary had stopped singing. I breathed the chamomyle-scented air, heard the still noises of the evening. And I knew I was a coward. I might not be the wild-eyed Power who had played advocate in Council, but there were other ways. "Wait a minute, Aunt," I said. "There's no need for Mordecai to go." I might live in one of Smith's houses, but I was a free man. He had no hold on me. "Would he fish, if he had a boat?"

"Always did. But where'd he sell 'em? And he ain't a licensed pilot."

"Penzance?"

She shook her head. "How'd he get there?"

"A big boat."

"We'm poor folks."

"But I'm not. I'll advance him the money for a boat. He can pay me back out of what he catches."

She shook her head again. "Cost fifty pound, a boat like that. We don't see that in five year. Let alone pay you back."

"We'll see," I said. If she thought I was offering charity, she would turn me down flat. "You send Mordecai down here and I'll go over it with him. I don't care if it takes him fifty years to pay it back. I did well enough in America, and I don't want the money to lie idle. You'd be doing me a favour."

After she had gone on her way and young Nick was in bed, I sat at the back of the house with Mary, in silence. It was not her usual sort of silence. There was something edgy about it. After a while she said, "I heard what you told the Aunt. Nick, I wish you hadn't."

A mosquito settled on my hand. I let it drink. "Why not, for the love of God?"

"I don't think it's right."

"What isn't right?"

"You buying Mordecai a boat."

"You'd see him thrown off the island?"

"It's not Mordecai Ellis. Not only him. You're always trying to change things you can't change. You think you're doing good, but you're sand in the machinery. No. Not machinery. In the animal. This place is like an animal. It works its own way, and you don't know the way. Hundreds of men—thousands—have drowned or died or gone away. Now you're only one of those. They're not your islands. You must admit that to yourself."

"Is it Smith that's worrying you?" I said, to hide a new emotion that felt like jealousy.

She sighed. "I don't know. Yes, partly. He won't take kindly to it. He's Scilly now."

"And what about us? Are we only figments of the imperial imagination?"

She hesitated a moment, then smiled. "No," she said, "Never. But we live in a cottage. Together. That's what's important."

"But I can't let Mordecai down."

"No," she said. "You wouldn't be comfortable with yourself. I know that."

And there we left it.

Later that night we walked to the north and watched phosphorescent creatures blaze and die and made love in the flowering heather and the dull boom of the sea on granite, and I thought she had forgotten. But later, as we lay in bed, I could feel her awake and worrying.

Next day Mordecai came and we discussed the question of his boat. He seemed almost hangdog at first; but when he lumbered off for St. Mary's, he was puce with delight and there were rough sketches for a thirty-two foot gunter yawl in his pocket. On his return, he described with huge glee the look on Mr. Mumford's face when he had plonked down his deposit, and we wetted the plans with brandy. I had enjoined him to strict secrecy, knowing the power of gossip; but my injunctions proved unnecessary. There was an item of news going the rounds that would have eclipsed the descent from heaven of a Blackwall frigate. Emperor Smith and his retinue had arrived at the

Hugh House on St. Mary's. The Lord Protector was in our midst.

Mary and I and young Nick were eating dinner at the kitchen table. While I admired Nick's patience in his pursuit of knowledge, I found it somewhat exasperating at mealtimes. I was trying to convince him of the importance of a balanced diet in attaining a size and strength appropriate to sturdy manhood, Mary looking on with the amused tolerance of one who had fought the same losing battle at every meal for the past five years. Nick was seeking a diversionary tactic. He had failed to foist his cabbage on the parrot, and was gloomily settling down to the final horrible mouthfuls when there came the clip-clip of hooves from the road. Hoofbeats were a rarity in themselves, and these, hard and purposeful, were so unusual as to be astonishing. He dropped his knife and fork and ran to the window. The door flew open. A voice said, "Good evening, Mistress Prideaux." A man walked in.

He was of middle height, straight up and down, dressed in a blue coat vaguely nautical in cut, with a telescope clipped under his right arm like a field-marshal's baton. There was something of the field-marshal, too, in the way he swept the room with cold, grey eyes above long, clean-shaven cheeks and a prim, set mouth. Mary said, "Good evening, Mister Smith, Sir." I found that I did not like the 'sir' part of it.

"I want a word with this gentleman," said Smith. "Alone. If you would be so good as to step outside?"

"We were just going," said Mary in a strange voice. It was almost a mumble. She took young Nick by the hand and led him quickly out of the room, eyes lowered. She was blushing. I had never seen her blush before. I did not like it any more than the 'sir.'

"Please sit down," I said, when she had gone. He ignored me, looking round the room as if checking that nothing had been stolen. I sat, and said, "A cup of coffee?"

"No," he said, appearing to remember that I was among those present.

I gave myself one, and said, "What can I do for you?"

He turned to face me. He was younger than I had expected. About the same age as me. "I am very displeased," he said.

I said, "Dear me. Could one help?"

"I want to know what you mean by sneaking behind my back on my island. What d'ye mean by it, Sir?"

I sipped coffee. "I think I should tell you that I find you somewhat impertinent, Sir." I was beginning to understand the islanders' awe. Out of a clear sky, Mr. Smith would have been daunting as a runaway ore-truck. But I had had some experience of runaway ore-trucks. "You burst in unannounced while I and Mistress Prideaux are dining. Could one ask for an explanation?"

"Don't you bully me," he said. "I will not be bullied."

I could well believe it. "I should have thought the boot was usually on the other foot," I said.

His neck swelled. "You can keep your opinions to yourself," he boomed. "I should like to know by whose authority you are lending vast sums to the miserable Ellis. Speak, man!"

I finished my coffee. "I was not aware that I needed any authority other than my own."

"When you are on my islands you will do as you are told, God damn and blast you!"

"I was under the impression that slavery was abolished the year before last," I said.

Suddenly, he smiled. It was a pleasant smile, and I realised that it was just possible that he had a sense of humour. "Perhaps I misjudged you," he said. "Perhaps you are neither a fool nor a rogue." He sat down in Mary's chair, with his back to the window. "Or perhaps you do not realise your abysmal folly."

"Please enlighten me," I said.

"They tell me you are a scientist, and you seem to be a gentleman," he said. "You will understand my position if I explain it to you as a proposition in . . . sound management. I came to Scilly and found it a perfectly lovely place, administered and inhabited by some of the hungriest ragamuffins since errant Israel. By none of their fault. I intend to put matters to rights. But I cannot possibly—not *possibly*—listen to each individual tale of woe. I base my principles of management on the greatest good of the greatest number. And I tell you here and now that I intend to see them carried out." He looked at me from under level black brows, very portentous.

"I am sure that you will see them carried out," I said, and meant it. "I, myself, am by training a Doctor of Medicine, and I am afraid I have no time for such luxuries as philosophy. I am bound, when I observe symptoms, to attempt a cure. As in the case of Mordecai Ellis. With whom, I may say, I have undertaken a business venture. No more."

"So you refuse to reconsider."

"I hardly see how I could. I have given my word."

He rose to his feet. "Well, I shall make it easier for you. No shipbuilder on St. Mary's will fill Ellis's order. I shall see to it." No more sweet reason. Now his voice was cold and sharp.

"It seems a pity to take the business away from St. Mary's and give it to a Falmouth yard," I said. "Which is what I suppose Mr. Ellis will be forced to do."

"As I said to you before, the greatest good of the greatest number is paramount."

"I find your interpretation of the case curious. But so be it. Falmouth it is."

He walked slowly to the door, tucking his telescope more firmly under his arm. "I do not think I know your name," he said. "What is it?"

"Nicholls," I said. I had given him the weapon. He would try to use it.

"Well, Doctor Nicholls, I shall take my leave of you. It seems we are both stubborn men. But you will find that in the end I am the stubborner. I should be very careful, if I were you."

"Thank you for your good advice." I walked him to the gate in silence. It was rather like walking next to a steam boiler with the safety valve screwed down. A boy was holding a thickset white cob. Smith mounted and rode away. He was no horseman. But my mind was not on equestrianism. One day soon, Scilly was going to be too small for the two of us. It was going to be a hard game. And I had no illusions as to who held the strong cards.

Mordecai accepted the interdiction with considerable philosophy, and a week later he and I took advantage of a fresh, westerly breeze to sail over to Penzance. I wanted to see Mrs. Pembarra, who had written to me before I had left America with the news that she had bought the Trengwainton Arms, a public house on the Bodmin road not far from the scene of our flight. There were certain facts I wanted clear before Augustus Smith started trying to get me off the island.

We arrived in Falmouth after one of the less pleasant
voyages of my experience, me dressed as an invalid, muffled in a great-coat with a sealskin cap pulled down well
over the eyes. Not that I had much fear of being recognised; but Mordecai, who in common with most of the
other islanders believed the Proprietor's influence to ex-
tend far beyond the shores of Scilly, was in mortal terror
of Smith and his agents. Once in Falmouth we took ourselves to Gurney's shipyard, a branch of the great Norfolk
concern. There a bullet-headed Scots gentleman by the
name of McIver debated with Mordecai the mysteries of
rake, sheer, and tumblehome; when Mordecai had spoken
his mind on these subjects, Mr. McIver cast himself into
deep thought and said he thought he could help us, and
quicker than we expected. There was a boat just off the
slips and fitted-out, thirty-five foot ketch, oak on oak,
grand piece of ship, no expense spared, man who had ordered it had died sudden like. Mr. McIver needed the
mooring, and though he could sell it any day it was a bit
of luck we had arrived in his office the day he had heard
the sad news, 'twas a boat to be proud of though he said
it himself, Mordecai could put a price on her. . . .

It took me back to the horse fairs of my youth, and I
did not know how Mordecai would react. Faced with the
ketch, gleaming black hull and varnish that made her
look as if she had just been dipped in honey, I expected
him to give way to his delight. I need not have worried.
He became scornful, clumped about kicking lockers and
making insulting remarks about cutting corners, and eventually outed with a huge knife and stabbed her in the hull
several times, wondering aloud if 'twas oak or match-
board Mr. McIver was using. If I had been Mr. McIver I
should have taken this to heart, rather; but he turned not
a hair. And eventually, after much bargaining, I handed
over to Mordecai the sum of forty-three pounds and ten
shillings, receiving in return a note for the amount, at one
per cent per year; which sum Mordecai exchanged for the
ketch, remarking that it was the dearest load of firewood
he had bought in his life. After which we sailed, carrying
as crew a small, active boy who rejoiced in the name of
the Bear, because, McIver informed us, he was always
Russian about. We put in at Mullion, and I set off for the
Widow Pembarra's.

The Trengwainton Arms was sited at the crest of a hill

dotted with engine-houses. By the look of the long grey
rows of stables and the press of carriages in the yard, it
was a popular staging-post. I found Mrs. Pembarra in the
kitchen, supervising the construction of an elaborate dinner. She received me with considerable emotion and
rushed me into her private parlour, where a serving-maid
brought tea and heavy cake. Inn-keeping seemed to suit
her. She wore a gown of black silk which did little to hide
her matronly charms, and we talked long and, after some
sad reminiscences, cheerfully. Over the chimney-piece
there hung a stiff portrait of Joby, looking, I thought,
slightly surprised at the solid comfort of his surroundings.
Mrs. Pembarra's bright blue eyes turned to it often; but
she seemed to have found consolation.

"It was a funny thing," she said. "When we come back
the rest of them moved up Somerset way. I went there for
a while but somehow I didn't take to it. Too soft. I said as
I never wanted to see a mine again, but then I had a
cousin told me this place was being sold, and I thought
well, I'd have a look. Next thing I knew, I'd bought it."

"You look as if you're not regretting it."

"Bless you no," she said. " 'Tis a reminder of Joby, and
besides they're such a lot of savages in Penzance that we
do get a lot of the gentry putting up here. We had Mr.
Smith not six weeks back. Him as went to Scilly."

I told her of my dealings with Smith. She said, "Well I
am sure I am sorry to hear that. You did deserve to get
the place. Still, we all has our crosses." Her eyes went
again to the portrait above the mantel. "I was a bit nervous myself when I come, with the Preventives and all. But
they didn't pay me no mind, not so long as I runs an honest house. Which I do, barring a drop of this and that."
She smiled. "We'll have an ask about it, though. Liza."
The serving-maid came into the room. "Be so good as to
ask Squire Trengwainton to step by, would you?" The
maid curtseyed and left. "Squire knows what the Preventives is up to," she said.

Heavy boots sounded on the stairs, and a voice said,
"The inner sanctum, by God!" The door opened.
"Tamzin," said the voice. "Honoured, damn if I ain't—
Oh. Didn't know you had company."

"Doctor Power," said Mrs. Pembarra.

Squire Trengwainton, a horsy-looking gentleman with
high, red cheekbones and narrow, black eyes, grinned at

me like a lurcher. "Lucky man," he said. "Tamzin's not so free with her invitations to the *sanctum sanctorum*. Been tryin' for years."

"Ah, go on with you," said Mrs. Pembarra, blushing like a schoolgirl. "Terrible rake, the Squire. The doctor came to us just before we . . . left. You remember Captain Bolitho?"

"Do I," said the Squire. "Do I.'"

"I wanted to thank you for the loan of a horse," I said. "And some clothes, which I fear I was never able to return."

He looked at me hard. Then he slapped the knee of his riding-breeches and let out a raucous bellow of laughter. "You're the priest!" he said. "By God, but I never thought I'd see the day. Let me shake you by the hand, Father!"

When his mirth had subsided, I told him the circumstances of my living at Scilly and asked him how the case against me stood.

"Never you fear," he said. "I made damned sure all those soldier-boys were out of the county a month later. Your only problem would be that maniac Woodcock. I heard he was dead."

I told him the circumstances of Little John's death, and he wagged his head. "Well, blow me. Old Horace Bolitho always was a damned Mohawk, but I never would have thought it. Never would. Sounds as if you're all right, then."

"I very much hope so."

"But you want to watch that Smith. Met him at an Electors' dinner. Worst kind of Liberal. Always sticking his nose where it doesn't concern him."

"As long as there's no chance of a prosecution, I can manage him."

"They'll never prosecute. No shred of evidence." He shook his head, and suffered a return of the raucous laughter. "They told me you were a mad Irishman with an ashplant and a beard like a Devil himself. If I didn't know it was true I'd never have believed it, lookin' at you. Eh, Tamzin?"

"We've all become respectable," said Mrs. Pembarra, winking at me.

"More's the pity," said Trengwainton. "Now. Mrs. Pembarra. Your holiness. Dinner?"

The following morning I breakfasted with Mrs. Pembarra and made affectionate farewells. Then she drove me to Mullion in the gig, to find Mordecai chafing to catch the tide. We dropped anchor in New Grimsby Harbour on Sunday morning. As I walked down the road with the distant sound of the church bells in my ears I felt I could deal with three of Smith. I greeted Mary and young Nick. Mary hardly looked up. She was at her embroidery again, silvering the crest of a breaking wave with white silk. Nick said, "There's a letter. Can I open it?" He broke the wafer and unfolded it. "What does it say?"

The hand was small, neat and firm, with a strong forward slope. The writing of a man quite at ease with himself. On the outside of the packet was one word. Nicholls. No more.

> *The Hugh House,*
> *St. Mary's*
> *27th October.*

Nicholls,
I have made enquiries about you. I do not like what I hear, but I and my fellow Magistrates are in agreement that there are no grounds for proceedings against you. From now on, you will behave yourself.
> *A. Smith, Lord Proprietor.*

I showed it to Mary.

"So that's that," she said.

"Rather mild, I think. I should have expected more of him."

"He had a lot on his mind. He sent a man to look for you with the letter. Said he needed a doctor."

"When was this?"

"The day before yesterday. He had a young lady staying with him. She was ill."

"Why won't Doctor Blewett see her?"

"He has. No result."

I said, "I'd better go." I picked up my bag and ran out to where an ebullient if rather intoxicated Mordecai was holding court to an admiring crowd. There was just enough water for us to make it down-channel.

When I rang the bell of the big grey granite Hugh House, a maid answered. It was the same woman who had once worked for John Johns. She had spread a little since then. Her face was pale and frightened. "Who shall I say?"

"Doctor Nicholls." I went in. The blinds were drawn. It was dark. "Where's Mr. Smith?"

"Who is it?" said a voice from the murky back of the hall. I could hardly see Smith. His face was a pale mask in the gloom. He was holding something in his hand.

"Doctor Nicholls. You sent for me."

"I am afraid you are too late," he said. His voice was quiet, with a catch in it. "She is dead."

"My condolences," I said.

He jerked his eyes up from the object in his hand. I saw it was a leghorn hat trimmed with fronds of fern. "Where the hell were you? Buying a boat for that damnable rogue Ellis, no doubt. You had no business to be there."

"I deeply regret that I was too late to be of assistance," I said. I could understand why he was feeling so savage. "I hope that in the future—"

He made a sound between his teeth. "Don't count on your future," he said. "I am going to give you some rope, Doctor. And I confidently expect you to hang yourself with it." He turned on his heel and walked away.

When I returned to the quay, my cheerfulness had left me. Mordecai lumbered into step at my side. "Pore young thing," he said, heavily. "Come down for a 'oliday with 'er uncle. Pewmonia. Stayed up to watch one of Mumford's ships into the water, cold got to 'er, they was saying in the Anchor. Only fifteen, and pretty as a picture. I seen 'er once or twice." He brightened. "Still, maybe it'll get the Hemperor off of our backs for a while. Maybe 'e'll decided Scilly's bad luck and not come back.

I found his brightness rather offensive, and I told him so. I had no affection for Smith. Still, I wished I had not been on the mainland. Doctor Blewett was by all accounts a decent enough man, but he was no means *au fait* with recent developments. There was no guarantee that I would have succeeded any better. But it would have eased my conscience to try.

Feeling ran very high in the islands after Smith had left. Winter was coming in fast and hard. The harvest had been poor. Smith's walls laced the hillsides, and the roof was going on the great house on Abbey Hill; but the islanders had nothing. Nothing except the new leases his tenants had been forced to sign or quit. Under the new leases, the Lord Proprietor's authority became law. No tenant was to cut turf for fuel, on pain of eviction. No tenant was to keep a dog or a gun without the Lord Proprietor's express permission, on pain of eviction. All wreck was the Lord Proprietor's automatic property; nothing was to be kept back, on pain of eviction. All walls, houses, buildings were to be kept up, on pain of eviction. Harry Jack summed it up one grey, drizzling afternoon, when I met him carting bladder-wrack for manure. We started out talking English politics, which he loved; but his heart was not in it, and as always nowadays the grievances broke through. "We ain't got no food, and no money," he said. "Even if we had got food, we ain't allowed to get the fuel to cook it. And how does he think we're going to keep the houses and the walls in, ahem, substantial repair if we got no food in our bellies? I say bugger that and bugger the Emperor. If he wants to throw me off, he can try. I'd like to see him do it."

Harry Jack was not the only one who thought like that; it was only that he was the most articulate. Even the Emperor's men, those hopeful souls who still treasured in their hearts bright visions of plenty, were shaken in their faith.

In late November, Aunt Ellis died. Indirectly, it was Mordecai's new boat that killed her. Her visit to me, I heard later, had been the culmination of months of worry. Once there was nothing left to fight for, the light in her dwindled. I saw her on the afternoon she died. She was lying in her bed with her eyes closed; already the flesh of her face had fallen back on the bones, the skull showing clear beneath the ancient skin. It was a dirty day, the tide whipped to evil grey waves in the harbour as it neared the flood. Harry and Mordecai and Aunt Woodcock were there watching, in the little bedroom where draughts blew long, candlelit shadows across the board ceiling. Mordecai raised his eyebrows at me. I shook my head. I had seen many faces with those blue-grey hollows. It was a matter of hours.

The Aunt's eyes opened. "Well, it's the doctor," she whispered. "Not much for you to do."

"Come now," I said. "You'll be up like a lark soon."

She smiled her cheerful smile. "Not me." The voice was
the merest sigh. "I'm going with the ebb. I be ready."

There was no point in arguing. I said, "Goodbye,
Aunt."

She smiled again and closed her eyes. Two hours later,
when the angry waves began to retreat on the rain-grey
sand, she died. It was a peaceful death. Most old people
at Scilly died with the first of the ebb, their deaths running like their lives, in time with the vast, slow rhythms
of the ocean.

What followed was not so peaceful.

The Ellises were Bryanites, of the sect led by a woman
preacher from Agnes called Ann Guest. I had met her
once or twice, a dark-haired woman, slow of speech with
the enthusiast's fire lurking at the back of her brown eyes.
The Lord Proprietor did not approve of the Bryanites, for
they kept no parish registers, leaving their births and
deaths unrecorded; so he had told Johns to do his damnd-
est to make them keep the law, and he did it. But they
clung doggedly to their ways. Doggedness was one of their
chief characteristics. Little John Woodcock had been a
Bryanite.

We buried Aunt Ellis with no parson but Ann Guest.
She said the service, and delivered an address full of fire
and poetry. Then we went back to New Grimsby in a
blustering west wind that blew grit and rain in our faces.

There was a boat by New Grimsby quay. Mary took
my arm. "It's Johns," she said. "Keep back."

"Why?" I said.

"There'll be trouble."

I put my hand on young Nick's shoulder, and we stood
watching as the funeral crowd walked on down the hill.

A man in a brown coat had come from behind the
houses on the road leading to the quay. Johns. He stopped
Harry Ellis, and said something to him. Harry's shoulders
hunched forward, and he seemed to stiffen. A bluster of
wind brought the noise of shouting. The main body of the
party caught up. Johns' face was white and scared. There
was more shouting, and Johns' voice said, "Heathen!" An
arm went up and down, Johns flung his hand in front of
his face, turned and ran. The crowd went after him, but
he was fast. I saw him tumble into his boat and cast off
and his two men jump in after him. The sail filled and

they shot under the snub end of the quay, out into the white horses of the channel.

That night, all the windows in Smith's new house were smashed. The message got through, and the Proprietor in his wisdom must have ordered concessions to be made. Two weeks later, word came from St. Mary's that the Proprietor would have no objection to the burning of wreck-wood for fuel, provided only broken lengths were used. A notice appeared at the quay, offering a ten pounds reward for information about what it called malicious hooliganism.

But nobody paid any attention to the Proprietor's proclamations. The Atlantic had taken matters into its own hands, with a screaming gale from the west that drove ship after ship scampering for shelter among the islands. And Scilly, as it often had before, began to fatten itself off the leavings of the hungry ocean. In the process, it became once again a place I recognised. And once again I found myself useful. Mary had a share in one of the gigs, and many a time I took an oar; but better than that, I was impartial in the question of shares, and there was a lot of sharing out to do. So once again I held court, delving into the mysteries of the division of the spoils. And I was busy. I was at sea a good deal of the time; the foul weather was knocking the older people down like ninepins, and I found myself constantly at bedsides and funerals.

There was something else, too.

On Christmas Eve, Mary and I were sitting over the fire. Outside, the wind hammered at the windows; but the fire, coal off a Sunderland brig broken up on the Crow Bar a week since, threw out a great heat from its red heart. We were talking, but not much. Mary looked rather tired, I thought. But young Nick had been plaguing her all day, vastly over-excited by the idea of Christmas. Mary stitched away at her embroidery for a while. Then quite suddenly her face turned white, and she got up and went out into the garden. I picked up my book, but I could not read. When she came back she drank a glass of water and sat down again. She looked better. In fact, she looked more beautiful than I had ever seen her. There was a bloom to her skin, a soft shine to her eye. And a complete tranquility to her, a turning away from the world to something within. I had never seen anyone look less ill.

I said, "Mary. . . ."

Her night-blue eyes held the dancing gleam of the fire. "You guessed," she said. "Clever old Nick. I'm pregnant."

XII

ONCE THE WINTER had the bit firmly between its teeth, there was no stopping it. The gales that began before Christmas howled a welcome to the New Year and raged and battered their way far into Scilly's early spring.

Like limpets in heavy weather, the islanders clung close to their homes, living almost in suspended animation, waiting for the storms to roll away. No-one stayed closer to home than Mary.

She was not having an easy pregnancy. It was difficult for her to eat, and on some days the slightest movement brought on vertigo and nausea. All through the first bad months she kept to her bed, working at her tapestry and her books. Often she was too low to talk; and often I found myself talking to her as doctor to patient, not as lover to lover. It was not only the illness; she always seemed to be listening for the life growing in her belly, and I had seen her when she thought I was not watching, stroking her stomach and crooning her strange tunes. Though I knew it was ridiculous, I could not help feeling a little jealous of that embryo, sightless in the warm dark. Once I admitted it to her and she laughed at my stupidity, and after that I know she made an effort to talk. But I could always tell she was trying, and that made it worse, as if in some obscure way she was sliding out of my arms with each beat of the embryo's tiny heart.

Of course, there were distractions in work. There was

doctoring and writing to be done. Young Nick, who was at
Smith's school plumbing the mysteries of arithmetic and
the alphabet, had discovered the joy of asking questions
which were susceptible to answers, and before I knew it I
was teaching him geography and Latin.

Even with Mary silent in the upstairs room, the days
were full; but I was surprised to find that life seemed
empty.

At first, I could not put my thumb on it. Before, when I
had been at Scilly, I had never been bored. Now, after
Nick was in bed, I often found myself sitting by the hissing fire, staring at the embers and wondering why there
was nothing I wanted to do but talk to Mary. I put it
down to love; and during January and February I lived
through pangs of separation worse than any I had felt at
New Botallack.

It would not have been like Mary not to notice. In early
March, on a raw day when the wind was squeezing rain
through the window-sashes, I had finished examining her.
She was lying on the pillows, I thought asleep, and I went
softly to the door.

She said, "Nick. Why are you unhappy?"

"I'm not. Perfectly cheerful."

"You are. Are you getting bored with living in a cottage?" She gave me a sad, knowledgeable smile. "It's not
very exciting, is it? Since Smith."

"Exciting enough."

"Ach, but you're so good," she said. "You really are
trying, aren't you? You could be a Smith in your own
right, but you're content to live in a little house with a sick
woman and a small boy."

"With the woman I love and our son."

Again the sad smile. "You're a sentimentalist, Nick.
And I love you for it. Do you know, I sometimes—Oh!"
She put her hand to her belly and said, "You kicked. You
did, you clever little thing. Now, baby, sleep. Sleep and
let the mother rest." When she looked up, it was as if she
were looking at a stranger. Her smile was perfunctory and
it did not touch her eyes. "I'm tired," she said. "I must . . .
oh, I'm sorry, I don't want to drive you away, but I must
get some rest."

All that evening, I sat by the fire. Now I knew why I
was bored. The reason was called Smith. To be fair, it was
no fault of his. But I was used to making things happen;

and all I was doing here, while the gales blustered, was waiting for things to happen to me. That was the price I paid for living with Mary. And cheap enough, in all conscience; but to pay and yet to feel her slipping away was very hard. I felt a moment of fierce anger. Mary had not been like this before he had come. In the old days I had mixed with whom I liked, said what I liked. It was Smith who had me trapped.

But even as the anger flared, I knew that it was a lie. I was here of my own choosing, and here I must stay. If Mary's pregnancy was difficult for me, it was ten times as difficult for her. At the end of it all we could go back and everything would be as before. Or so I told myself, and so I hoped; but I was never quite sure if I believed it.

My fireside vigils always produced more questions than answers, and not all the questions were about Scilly. Principal among them was the question of Michael Fitzpatrick. He would be back in Ireland now, far beyond my retribution, even if I had any proof against him. Sometimes I entertained wild fantasies in which I confronted him, made him admit his guilt, saw myself vindicated in the eyes of Dublin and Drumcarty. They were ridiculous, of course; but they planted in me the seeds of a wish to set foot once again on Irish soil. My agreement with Mary meant that quixotic deeds at Scilly were out of the question; and I supposed I must have had in me a quantum of quixotry which would not be denied. Whatever the case, the wish sprouted into a desire, and the desire became a craving; and finally, to put off the evil day. I had to make a bargain with myself that if I yielded to the craving it would be after the baby was born. Until then I had no right to put myself in jeopardy.

But luck beat my resolution down, and in the end the craving got the better of me.

One evening at the Ship Inn, I was talking to John Sinclair and another man I knew, a pilot by the name of Harry Hicks. Harry had had a man washed overboard from his cutter in a gale the week before, and he wanted another. And I, on impulse, said I would go.

It could be argued that the Western Atlantic, at the tail end of one of the worst winters in human memory, is not the place to get a grounding in elementary seamanship. Whether or not this is true, there is one thing to be said for it; you learn fast or not at all. And I learnt.

The *Shearwater* was out in all weathers, the worse the better, cruising the Atlantic far to the west, looking for ships homeward bound. She started out crammed with pilots; one by one she dropped them off, and they took the ships up-channel and straggled back to Scilly from as far away as Flushing. I suppose there was a certain absurdity in a millionaire employed as a common deck-hand on a pilot cutter. But the absurdities tend to slide into the background when you are two men and a pilot in a gig, coming alongside a tall ship in a blizzard a hundred miles from land.

When I was ashore I spent most of my time with Mary and the boy, in whose eyes I could do no wrong since I had begun to go to sea. The pilots might be earning a good living, but the island was full of sourness. There were some wrecks—enough to keep starvation at bay; but the winter was cold and hard.

All good things, as Harry observed with no great originality, must come to an end. The weather gradually improved, and the crops came on, and there were no more wrecks. The bad winter had made the early potatoes late, and at the end of April there was a rush of panic that had some of the younger men at Smith's new house, breaking more windows and smashing down walls. Smith had still not returned, and there was a school of thought which maintained that after the death of his niece he never would.

Mordecai Ellis began to do pretty well at the fishing, swore off drink and paid me back five guineas in the middle of April, much to his satisfaction and mine. And Mary grew very large and placid, and laughed at herself for being so like a cow. She did not look like a cow to me. The flawless bloom of her cheeks had intensified, and her face had a new gentleness. She carried her great belly like a banner. Somehow, we had fallen into an agreement. She never discussed the baby with me, except as patient to physician; and I never spoke of Mordecai or Smith or any of the other new island things with her. She was happiest that way, it seemed. I cannot say I felt the same. I was always filled with the sensation that something was driving a wedge between us. So, as much to keep my mind off the pain as anything else, I continued to sail with Harry Hicks, as spring drew on into summer and her time came near.

We were playing cribbage, Harry and I, when it really began, and I was beating the hell out of him. I always had the edge on him; whereas I could give my whole attention to the cards, Harry was always half-squinting at the horizon. His concentration thus suffered severely.

On this particular day, my splinter sat maybe forty holes ahead of his. Normally this would have been cause for satisfaction; not so this day. We had been cruising a week, a hundred miles west of the Bishop Rock. It had been a fine week for a yachtsman, but a lousy one for a pilot. The sou'west breezes had blown force two and three from the deeps of a royal-blue Atlantic, and what ships we saw were taking good advantage of them. The distant pyramids of canvas slid by hull-down to the south. We could not even sell them the fresh vegetables we had brought with us; a captain making a good passage is not inclined to wait for a pilot-cutter to come alongside for the sake of a few spuds and cabbages. After the winter, it was all very tame and tedious.

"And one for his nob," said Harry. He moved his pin by touch, gazing over the stern to the southward. "Dirty weather down there."

I looked aft, as much to give him a chance to cheat as because I was interested in weather, dirty or otherwise. The horizon was a clear blue curve, except for one five-degree quadrant where it was dulled with a haze faint as breath on a windowpane.

"She'll be blowing in a couple of hours," said Harry. "Your deal."

We played on for half an hour. Harry never liked to abandon hope, but he continued to lose. Finally the man at the tiller said, "What about it, Harry?"

Harry said to me, "We'll chalk'er up, then. One and eight-pence, I make it." Then he got to his feet with an agility surprising in a man of sixty, and said to the helmsman, "How's your barley lasting, Thos?"

The helmsman showed teeth very white in the brown of his face. "Could do with another ten winchester."

"Yes," said Harry. "Can't make Scilly in a storm, can we? Black as a Turk, too."

"Oh dear me no," said Thos, shaking his head and tut-tutting. "Waterford?"

"I think we might," said Harry, and went to look over the after-rail.

This exchange had left me mystified. I joined Harry at the rail and said, "Ireland?"

"Quite so," said Harry, staring on.

"Why're you after barley? You'll get all you need on St. Mary's."

"So we would, God knows."

"So why go to Ireland? It'll be no cheaper."

His sharp blue eyes were innocent. "Like to give the poor Irish a chance. Wouldn't want word to get around Scilly."

Light began to dawn. "Would it have anything to do with the fact that Smith will grind it for you cheap?"

"What an astonishin' idea," said Harry, blank-faced. "Though now you come to mention it, 'twould be an advantage. If I had more meal 'n I could use, I could sell it on to them as hadn't. On the mainland, you mean?"

"Poor bloody Smith," I said. "Robbing him blind. I could almost be sorry for him."

Harry shook his head. "So could I," he said. "Almost." He looked ruminatively astern. "But I'm an old man, and I must have my consolations." He turned those bright young eyes of his back on me. "'Tis what I always do say. What's the use of being old if you don't be artful?"

Which, finally, was logic unassailable. But Waterford. . . .

"I'm not so sure," I said. "I'm none too popular in that quarter." But I could feel the craving rising in me.

"Lord bless you," said Harry. "They'd never know as you was there. All we'll do is sit in Waterford Harbour while I sees a man I knows, and then we'll be off." A gust of wind howled in the shrouds, and the deck heeled away. Harry cocked an eye at the belly of the mainsail. "You could stay below hatches if you was worried. We won't let on."

I stood in the lee shrouds as the wind blew on up, heedless of the whips of spray cracking back from the cutter's bow. Harry was at the tiller now, leaning with the timber in the small of his back against the long boom's weather helm. Up from the south came the cloud, white edges first against the milky blue, then huge muscular rolls of purple-grey that pressed onto the sea and licked at it with stinging tongues of rain. And after the grey came the night, shoving the sky down onto the ship's masts and hiding her wet canvas. I heard Harry yell once, felt her come head to wind, felt the thunderous flogging as we beat down the mainsail and made fast the reef-points. Then there was a roll and a glimpse of a great shining trough, and the next wave lifted the stern and we plunged on to the northward with the gale singing warsongs at our backs.

Sometimes I caught the yellow shine of Harry's oilskins in the dim light of the binnacle, but mostly it was only blackness and sheets of spray. And sure as the needle of the ship's compass held to the north, my thoughts held to Ireland, to the heavy grey walls of Drumcarty sweeping down to the muddy waters of the Barrow. I did not remember it as I remembered Scilly, as a home where I had lived. It had a glaze to it like the glaze one sometimes feels when dreaming; as if I could float round the crumbling towers without being seen, only seeing.

When my watch was over I stamped my boots to get the circulation going, shook myself and went below. As I rolled into my damp bunk, I told myself that I would stay aboard, out of sight, and take myself back to Scilly in due course. The roll and pitch of the ship battered me like a loose barrel in a tumbril, and I dozed, seeing once again the grey walls and the brown mirror of water. I knew then that there was no more chance of my staying aboard *Shearwater* than of my climbing over the side and walking back to Scilly. I fought it, though; and still fighting, I slept.

My resolution had returned the next afternoon as we came into Waterford Harbour. The land was low and green, edged with a tumble of dark rock and white water. The sky was ribbed with long squalls of cloud, and a gleam of sun turned the patchwork of little fields behind the ruins of Duncannon Fort to cloth of gold. But ahead, where the hills steepened into the grey-blue chop, the clouds hung low and dark and full of enigmas. At Cheekpoint, where the Barrow and the Suir mingle their waters, we took the westward fork. It was raining, a warm, light rain driven on a wind that hardly filled the cutter's sails. On the last of the flood we anchored.

Next morning we moved up towards the city of Waterford, sprawled up its hills from the quays. The clouds were high now, washed with a cold dawn like blood in water. One or two chimneys spouted smoke into the breeze. Harry flung a line to a sleepy-eyed man in boots and a blue jersey and a tasselled night-cap sitting on a bollard. I stood behind the crumpled folds of the mainsail, watching as the strip of water narrowed. There was potato-peel floating in it, and something that might once have been a dead dog. With a tiny, prosaic bump, *Shearwater*'s strake touched the shores of Ireland.

Harry went ashore about his business. I stayed aboard with a couple of comatose pilots, all of us sick and ill for our different reasons. They had last night's drinking to thank for it. I had only myself. The touch of that edge of dirty coping-stones twenty feet away might be the kiss of death. But as the morning wore on and the sun rose in the now cloudless sky, I craved it like opium. The dark mouth of an alley pressed up against the round stone flank of Reginald's Tower. Bridie Slattery's was up there, only a step. I had not shaved for three days. I was wearing seaboots, filthy canvas trousers, a dark blue jersey of oiled wool and a stocking cap. My face was beaten and burned a reddish mahogany by wind and sun, my hair cut ragged round my collar. Nobody would recognise me.

I turned to Thos and said, "I'll be back."

He looked at me without curiosity and said, "Mind you catch the tide."

I nodded, pulled my stocking cap down, and stepped ashore.

Mistress Slattery's was the same as ever, jammed to the doors with hard-drinking humanity. Bridie sat among the barrels behind the bar of coffin-planks, her face folded in half over her gums, yelling advice at her tapboy. I elbowed my way up and got my tall pewter of stout. With the dark, sour taste of it, the noise and confusion began to take meaning. Over in the corner there was a man wearing a collar and cravat and drinking madeira, with a line of carters before him. The agent's clerk. Inside in the private parlour would be the agent, drinking sherry with his ledgers. Beside me, two gentlemen of ragged appearance were drinking whisky and arguing about a horse.

"Sure and he could run the legs offa the mare over a fence," one of them was saying. "Did you not see him go above at Punchestown the last year."

"Ah," said his companion, having drunk deep. "True enough. But 'twas the last year, and he's an old horse."

"Old horse or no, he'll bate them all," said the first

man, polishing off glass and mouth. "Them's fierce big fences above at Carthystown, and him with the wisdom of his age on him." At this they left, hastily. By their accents they were Corkmen. By the fact that they had not gone through the formality of settling their account before leaving the hostelry, they were embarrassed for petty cash. By the speed with which Bridie's tapboy vaulted the bar and precipitated himself after them into the street, they were not trusted regulars. By the language he used as he returned, they were damned souls and Bridie was about a quart of whisky the poorer. But most of this went over my head; for I was reading the poster nailed to the smoke-varnished pine panelling behind the bar.

GRAND STEEPLECHASE

By Kind Permission of

THE EARL OF DRUMCARTY

at CARTHYSTOWN

for a prize of

FIFTY GUINEAS

and a

HANDSOME ARTICLE OF PLATE

I knew the "handsome article of plate" well. For a whole year, thanks to the endeavours of my father's horse, Union Jack, it had sat on the sideboard in the dining-room of the Steward's House. It was a silver rose-bowl with a scalloped rim and legs heavily gadrooned. The memory of my father's nose reflected in it was a symphony in maroon flesh and white metal. I called for another pint of stout.

Carthystown Races came but once a year, and if you lived within fifty miles of the town you did not miss them. As well as the races there were booths, every tinker in Leinster, a lot of drinking and considerable fighting. To keep the peace there were usually a couple of squadrons of dragoons, who contributed little either to the maintaining of order or the general level of sobriety. All in all, it was an event which no red-blooded Carthystown man could afford to miss. And with the second pint, it was borne upon me that nor could I.

I walked along the quays, passed over the toll-bridge and got a lift on a cart heading north over the hills that swell in the angle between the rivers Barrow and Suir. The road was draped with the dust from hundreds of wheels and hooves and feet, for the sun had sucked yesterday's wet from the mud. There was every kind of conveyance, from a donkey tiptoeing under the weight of a gaunt farmer to a big, flash coach and four covered with drunken swells from the new villas at Tramore. And all of us jogged up the crooked white road under the blue sky, sweating, skins caked then eroded into flesh-coloured rivulets that took the dust under the collar and into the back and itched.

I shared the cart with a Waterford greengrocer called Sheehan and his fat wife. Mr. Sheehan kept up a low, monotonous stream of oaths at his horse and the pedestrians who darted round its hooves, while his wife fanned herself with a playbill in which, by the smell of it, a cauliflower had once been wrapped and said, "O Gods. The hate." The public houses on the road were the centres of swirling knots of thirsty men and lathered horses. Only by dint of hard shoving and shouting and fierce applications of the lash did we get through, and then so slowly as to cause Mr. Sheehan intense pain. So we had to pause often for refreshment, which abated the pain but caused further congestion of the road. We crossed the river and started downstream again. Here the crowd lapped the banks of the narrow lane and spilled over into fields on either side. Mr. Sheehan, his eye fixed and glassy, held dead centre and flogged on like Culchulainn riding down Queen Maeve's armies.

At the crest of the hill over into Carthystown, there was a clamour in the road behind us, a great tooting of horns and a shouting of pedestrians and guffaws of bibulous laughter. Mr. Sheehan continued on his inflexible way down the middle of the road. There was a roar of abuse, a thunder of hooves, and a team of four frightened bays shot between our off wheel and the hedge. I looked up and saw a fat-cheeked coachman white with terror, the pistol of a red-faced youth of about eighteen jammed in his ear. The youth was well-dressed, very drunk, and grinning a wide grin. He was yelling, "Ride 'em down! Three minutes is all!" Then the coach drew level.

Someone inside was singing *Croppies lie down*. The window slid down and a claret-jug, glittering in the sun, sailed out and over the hedge. I heard the sound of its smashing, and the grind of the coach's hub against the

wheel of the cart. Then there was an outraged squeal from
the far side of the hedge and something big and dirty and
pink crashed through the briers and under the feet of the
coach's leaders. I have never seen such a jump by horses
in harness. Both of them stood up on their hing legs and
made for the moon. And they came down safe, too, but
across the road, in front of Sheehan. He would have
driven straight through if he could, but his horse had other
ideas. It ran into the hedge, the near-side wheel went up
the bank, the cart came down with a tearing crash, and I
was spinning through space, firmly clutched by Mrs.
Sheehan. I landed on top of her with a *whump* that raised
dust twenty feet in the air.

Down the road the coach was still going strong, by the
roars of its passengers. Someone was firing pistols in the
air. At least I hoped it was in the air, and not at the poor
coachee. Mrs. Sheehan's face was the colour of a ripe
raspberry as I crawled off her, and she was making curious
whooping sounds. I took her pulse, examined her as best I
could. At first I thought she was in hysterics. Then I realised she was laughing. Quite a crowd had gathered, with
she and I as the centre of attention. Mr. Sheehan, face
like thunder, crawled out of the ruins of the cart and began abusing all coaches, horses, wild young rips, and pigs.
I slid into the crowd. Soon there was the long, grey wall to
the right. I found a place where it was broken down,
slipped through and cut myself a walking-stick. There was
a certain satisfaction in it. For the wall was the wall of
Drumcarty park, and the ash one of the Earl's. I thought
he probably owed me that much.

Carthystown Races were held inside the park, over a
course of about four miles embracing several fallen trees
and some vicious open ditches. As I walked between the
lodges the dreamlike sensation of last night had gone. The
ground was solid under my feet. To my left, pasture
scarcely visible under clumps of dying ragwort trended
down to the reed-fringed river. Ahead, the weedy drive
stretched between ancient oaks out of sight into a copse.
Beyond the copse rose the Lady Tower of Drumcarty
Castle, hoary with lichen. The ivy on the trees had grown;
otherwise it was just as I remembered. I pushed my way
through the crowd surrounding the group of red-and-white
striped tents where the hucksters were plying their trade,

my eyes fixed on that distant finger of masonry. And before I properly knew what I was doing, I was walking under the green tunnel of the copse where moss grew all year round on the hardcore.

After a mile, the drive came out into the open and ran down to the river. My heart was beating so hard it nearly choked me. I had forgotten about the races. At the bottom of the drive on the left was the grove of pines that sheltered the grey house Drumcarty had given me for life. The pines were higher than I remembered. Beyond it the drive ran on to its end, the bridge and the sprawling curtain-wall and keep of Drumcarty Castle. I walked on down the drive, forked off, and climbed over the wall surrounding the Steward's House. The gravel sweep in front bore a dense crop of grass and dandelions. The front door hung by one hinge, and four of the windows were jammed half-open, the frames rotting away from the glass. When I pushed the door the hinge gave way, and the crash of it sent a couple of blackbirds chattering out of the drawingroom.

I walked down the gloomy hall. There were the same brownish pictures of overweight fatstock, the pegs where my father's coats and whips had hung. But there were no coats now, and cobwebs lay dense over the gooseberry-eyed bullocks. Even the spiders had left. I opened the door of my father's office slowly, half-expecting to see his fierce eyes and whisky nose level at me from behind the desk. But the Virginia creeper had levered the glass out of the window and covered walls and desk, pale-leaved in the green gloom. I stood for a while looking at the worn patch in the carpet before the tangled mass covering my father's desk. Then I turned and went out of the house, quickly, the hair on my neck prickling with the sense of being followed. But only the dead inhabited the Steward's House now.

The day after St. Stephen's Day it was raining and Katie still had not appeared, so I rode up to New Ross to visit Doctor Connolly.

Connolly was sitting by his fire, looking hale as ever but protesting about his gout, which he was doing no good with a huge jar of whisky punch. After a few congratulations on my progress—Duquesne and he kept up a regular correspondence—I mentioned the sorry condition of the Drumcarty lands.

He sighed gustily. "I know," he said. "But what can ye do?"

I was surprised to hear fiery Connolly so despondent, and I told him so.

"Ah, you're young yet," he said. "You'll find that patience is the only way, at last. Now if Drumcarty didn't have his pride, he'd tear up all them papers and get out and do something. But since your father went, he never stirs beyond his walls. He wouldn't recognise half his tenants if he met 'em in the courtyard."

"He won't listen to anybody?"

"Nobody but his lawyers. Dublin blackguards. Sure if they told him the truth they'd be taking the bread out of their own mouths. I heard he offered you the Steward's House."

"I've enough to do in Dublin."

"Quite right, quite right. Duquesne was telling me. There's nothing you could be doing at Drumcarty. Nothing anyone can do, till the old man dies."

"He's young enough yet."

"What d'you think?"

"Consumption. Do you see him?"

Connolly laughed. "Drumcarty see a doctor? He wouldn't listen to any man told him he wasn't immortal. No, he'll go soon. And God knows what happens then. That Katie'll get the lot."

"Yes." Katie's absence was puzzling me badly. I could not think of anything I had done to upset her; but upset she certainly seemed.

"Maybe she'll marry well," said Connolly.

"Maybe," I said. "I wouldn't bet on it."

"Nor would I," said Connolly, blowing out his cheeks. "I get the Dublin papers." He stared into his glass, and we were quiet. Finally he said, "God damn all proud fools. Maybe you can do something with them, Nick. The old man likes you, and I hear you can control Herself."

"I wouldn't be so sure."

"Well, just you convince yourself and stop looking like a drowned rat, and for the love of God fill your glass and we'll talk about horses."

It was late when I left Connolly's and took the road for Drumcarty. Luckily, the horse knew its way.

Next morning, I was sitting over my porridge with a bad headache when Katie appeared. She bade me a friendly good morning and said, "Shall we walk? It's a lovely day."

It was. Katie walked beside me with her arm in mine, chatting away as if we had parted the best of friends. She took me to the theatre her great-grandfather had built on the steep northern bank of the island, now overgrown with briers and nettles. Young sycamores and ash-saplings had forced aside the marble flags, and the columns of the proscenium lay tumbled in the rank grass. It was a sad place. I said as much to Katie.

"Don't be said," she said. Behind the stage there was an arbour with a porphyry bench overlooking the smooth brown river. "Shall we sit down?"

We sat and watched the river for a time. Then she said, "Perhaps it is a sad place, after all." She took my hand. "I'm sorry I went off in a huff. You have the power to hurt me, Nick."

"You know I would never do that," I said.

"I know." She rested her head against my shoulder. "Do you ever wish you were fifteen again?"

I laughed and shook my head.

"I do," she said. "Fifteen and able to see the future. There are so many things I'd change." She lifted her head and looked at me. There were two tiny Nick Powers in the centre of the emerald-green irses. Her lips were parted, trembling. I moved my mouth down to hers and kissed her. There was nothing else I could do.

When I looked up, the first thing that caught my eye was the black winter shadow of Drumcarty keep. I said, "No," and got up. Katie's eyes were dazed and vague. She said, "Come back."

Drumcarty keep was a giant chord of harsh music that drowned softness and pleasure. The Earl had laid his charge on me. My job was to look after Katie, not allow myself to be seduced by her.

Her eyes cleared, began to glitter. She said, "Are you frightened of my father, Nicholas? You are, aren't you?"

"Not frightened," I said. But I knew she would not listen. She ran away to the stage, and I heard her voice through the leafless saplings.

Oh, how wretched
is the poor man that hangs on prince's favours

> *There is betwixt that smile we would aspire to*
> *more pangs and fears than wars or women have*
> *and when he falls, he falls like Lucifer*
> *never to rise again."*

Next morning we returned to Dublin, in silence.

I started out of the gate and up the hill the way I had
come. After I had gone twenty yards, I stopped. Behind
me the reflection of Drumcarty wobbled in the mirror of
the Barrow. The Lady Tower was a huge beckoning finger lying across the water. Weeds grew up between the
wheel-ruts of the bridge, but the ruts themselves were
clearer, as they were still travelled, if only infrequently. I
stood indecisive. Then I went back into the garden of the
Steward's House.

At some time in the distant past, one of the Earls of
Drumcarty had had a liaison with someone who lived in
the Steward's House. Nobody would ever say for sure
what kind of liaison it was, but presumably the Earl had
not wished it made public, for on the southern side of the
bridge, eight feet below the parapet, there ran a little catwalk. It was hidden from the bridge by the overhang of
the coping, and none of the castle windows overlooked it.
Legend connected it with the tides of blood which had
ebbed and flowed against the castle walls in the middle
ages. Myself, I had always thought it looked more recent.

The tangles of ivy that grew out from the bank were
thick, and they filled my eyes and mouth with bitter dust.
After thirty feet it died out in a few ambitious tendrils.
The paving of the catwalk was green and slippery, but I
had walked along it many times before. I passed the key-
stone and paused. Little whirlpools hovered downstream
of the piers. I could hear the minute gurgling of them, and
the distant clamour of rooks in the tall elms of the park.
Behind that was a murmur of voices from the racecourses,
and once a bugle-call. The castle sat at the end of the
catwalk, weighing the earth down with its silence. Not a
flower waved on the battlements. Not a jackdaw clacked
above the courtyard. Not a wheel crunched the deep
gravel of the carriage-drive. Only a quiet-like death. I
walked on, choosing my steps carefully, into the oblique-
walled arch at the end of the catwalk. Once arrived, I
looked back. The last Earl had stuccoed the stern stone of

the Steward's House in imitation of an Italian villa. Now it was crumbling away like paint from the face of an old countrywoman. I turned away into the echoing stone staircase that led up into the walls.

I knew the passageways of old. The steps opened into a hall, lit by a high window piercing deep stone. Out of it there led a spiral staircase which passed into the machine-house for the drawbridge, and on again into the battlements. The wall was fifteen feet thick. I kept to the centre. Here, too, grass grew. Great chunks of stone had fallen away from the inner edge into the courtyard below. I arrived at the point where the roof of the guardroom connected with the huge stone cylinder of the keep. I dropped down and went carefully on my hands and knees to the ragged hole at the far end.

Nobody knew how the hole had arrived; like most things at Drumcarty, it had always been there. I passed through it, up the granite treads of the staircase, until I came to the long, curving gallery built into the thickness of the wall. It was quite dark, but for the two beams of light, one blue, one red, shining on the motes of dust my progress raised. The eyeholes of the mask. I waited a moment, to catch my breath. I filled my lungs twice. Then I leaned forward and put my eyes to the eyeholes.

My eyes were accustomed to the black of the passage. At first I could see nothing but a dazzle of many-coloured lights. Gradually, it swam clear. The stained glass of the huge window flooded the room with light, ghastly and cheerful in incongruous blotches on the carpeted flags. The Gothic hunting scenes on the walls looked dull and faded by comparison. Below the window sat the Earl. It was seven years since I had last seen him; but I had the impression that he had not moved since then. Only the red-taped piles of paper had grown taller. I could not see his face, only the bony silhouette of his head against the rouge and gules of a sunlit heraldic shield behind him. The stone smelt old and musty. I sat watching him, waiting for something to happen. Nothing did.

On the right of his desk, hung in the thickness of the wall, was the Lawrence portrait of Katie. At last he turned his head to look at it, a weary, absent-minded movement with the restlessness of an insomniac's head rolling on the pillow. It was a picture of Katie at her most glittering, virginal and cool, in white muslin and diamonds. The painter had caught both her beauty and, in his treatment of the eyes and mouth, something of the devil of her. Drumcarty kept his eyes on it for a long time. Then he put his hands on the arms of his chair and heaved himself to his feet. It was slow and painful, the movement of a very old man. For a time he stood before the portrait, supporting himself with one hand on the desk. The window splashed red across Katie's white bosom, and pale purple across her face.

Drumcarty turned and looked at something hung opposite, on the side of the window I could not see. He shook his head and walked slowly and stiffly down the two steps of the dais and lowered himself into the sofa before the fire. Then he coughed for nearly five minutes, a low, exhausted hacking that shook his shoulders and doubled him over and crawled round the fan-vaulting. The bony hollows at temples and cheeks were dark with shadow, the lips thin and bluish. All that remained of the red hair were a few copper-coloured curls at the nape of his neck and behind his ears. The fingers that brought the dirty silk handkerchief to his mouth were clawed and shaking.

The Earl in his pride. Walls broken down, farms gone to ruin, tenants starving, kitchens empty, windows smashed. An empire crumbling under creeping acres of ivy, squeezed dry. And over it all, death hovered like a kite.

The Earl began coughing again.

I turned away into the darkness, walking slowly. The mask had been a symbol, as well as a convenience. Never again could I look at the country where I had been born, except through a disguise. When I had thought I was invisible, in the dream-world, I had been right. But my invisibility cut both ways. Nothing I could do would have any effect on the lives of these people. Of course, I told myself as I crossed the catwalk under the bridge-coping, I had known this for years. That was why I had made a new life for myself at Scilly, with Mary and the boy. Then I saw the cold, grey eyes of Augustus Smith, and I became suddenly unsure. I came out of the tunnel of trees and plunged into the noisy crowd milling over the racecourse.

I saw a lot of faces I recognised, most of them people I had known at school. No one recognised me, though I got some strange looks. Although Carthystown is only fifte miles from the sea, it is very unusual to see a man in sea-boots and stocking-cap. I pushed through thickets of bodies to one of the booths selling drink. Sipping, I looked about me. The revels were in full swing. I could hear three separate fiddlers above the din of voices and laughter. I sipped again. It was not the best whisky I had ever tasted. I said to the man next to me, "Did they run the first race yet?"

He turned round, and I knew why his back had looked familiar. He had sat at the front of Maconochie's class. Jer Murphy was his name. He was not the quickest thing in God's creation at the best of times, and now, luckily, he was pixillated to the wide. "The first," he said, half-focusing on me with one red eye. "An' the second. But not the third yet." He wagged his head. He was six months older than me, but he was bald and he looked sixty. "Not yet the third. 'Tis the Plunderer thass runnin', and 'tis hardly worth the others' while. He'll bate them all."

"He will so," I said, gulped back the rest of my vitriol and dived into the crowd before he could recognise me. While I was here, I thought, I would see horses run. So I made for where the crowd was thickest and elbowed my way through to the paddock rails.

There were five horses inside; but in comparison with the Plunderer, the others scarcely deserved the name. He was a huge bay, standing some eighteen hands. The muscles bunched and shifted under his glossy coat, and the eye he rolled back from the skinny groom leading him was soft and intelligent. "Sure and he's a cat at the fences," said a man with a greyhound on a short lead. "He has my money."

"And everyone else's."

"There's some wouldn't dirty it, win or no," said the man with the greyhound. "The horse is owned by the Major beyond."

The Plunderer walked away from my line of sight. On the far side of the paddock I saw his owner, a stocky individual with a dense moustache in the scarlet and sabre-tasche of the Dragoons, talking to a little wizened man in breeches and tops who must be the jockey. The groom stopped the Plunderer and the boy twitched the blanket off the shining tawny hide. The jockey stepped over to check the girths. The Major ran a haughty eye over the crowd and applied himself to earnest sucking of the handle of his whip. Someone barged into my back and said, "Will you get out of my way, be damned to you?"

I turned round fast, and said, "Watch your manners, you—" Then I stopped. All I could see above the crowd was a pair of shoulders in a good black coat, black whiskers shiny with macassar, and a jolly red face with calculating eyes. Michael Fitzpatrick.

I said, "Sorry, Sir, your honour," and coughed, hiding my face behind my hand. Michael paused for a moment. Then he said, "Watch how you talk to your betters," and ducked under the rail into the paddock. The man with the greyhound spat at the retreating heels of his patent-leather boots. I stood rigid. My stomach felt as if I had swallowed a live pigeon.

Michael strolled across to the Major and said something to him in a low voice. The Major laughed a hard laugh and clapped him on the shoulder. But his eyes flicked across to me, and I saw him beckon with one white-gloved hand for the cornet hovering at a discreet distance. The crowd pressed in on me from behind. Michael looked across, straight into my eyes, and bowed gravely. The cornet shouted something in a high, squeaky voice. I tried to get back, but the bodies hemmed me in and a low growl went up from the crowd behind. The Plunderer was coming round, saddled, his groom on the inside, away from me. Above the heads of the crowd I saw the helmets of a squadron of dragoons begin to push towards the ring. The cornet lifted his hand and pointed at me. I swallowed. There was nothing to swallow. Then I got one foot on the paddock rail, one hand on the shoulder of the man with the greyhound, and jumped. I landed across the Plunderer's saddle with a whack that drove the breath out of me. The groom's eyes rolled at me, startled, and he began to jag down at the bit. I swung at him with the big end of my stick and felt the smash of his collar-bone. Then I put my left leg across and dug in my knees as the great horse plunged. My right foot found the stirrup, then my left. I pointed the Plunderer at what looked like the thinnest bit of the crowd and let in my heels. There was a sensation as of the uncoiling of a tremendous spring. Then I was clinging to the mane, looking down on open mouths a long way below, hearing confused shouts. Up and over rail and crowd we floated, and landed without a false step in a space that magically cleared in the press. I crouched firmly in the saddle, laid my cheek alongside the Plunderer's neck, and made for the arch of the park gate.

When there were only a hundred shrinking yards of turf between me and the lodges, a red mass of dragoons came though at the trot. I pulled the horse's head round. There were dragoons behind me, too, and the roar of an angry crowd. It took me perhaps ten seconds to decide. I put the Plunderer's head down the hill towards the river, and shouted, "Go!"

We went. Christ, how we went. Down the slope through the ragwort and up to the screen of neglected withies that separated the reedbeds from the dry land. The hooves made a double thump and we were up and over with a sting of willow on my cheek, and the Plunderer put his four feet goat-like on the only clump of hard ground for a hundred yards, and I found myself with my face between his ears with the suddenness of his stopping. I slithered out of the saddle and dragged him through the reeds. My feet sank into the first of the mud. I dragged on until the Plunderer was rearing fetlock-deep in the river. I pulled him down and he plunged forward and began to swim.

Then and only then I looked back into the pandemonium flowing down the hillside. The red coats were cut off from the riverbank by a seething grey mass of running figures. I heard a dull, angry roar. One red-coated man broke clear and galloped down at the withies, but the hill ran his horse too hard and it missed its footing and jumped too early. The last I saw of them was the horse plunging in the reeds, riderless, and the red coat struggling in the branches of a grown-out pollard.

The tide took us upriver until I saw the west wall of Drumcarty past the bend. The Plunderer's shoulders worked powerfully by my head, and we drew across, trailing a vee of ripples. I looked back again. There was another dragoon by the water now, far down beyond the ledges. I caught the sun's wink on epaulettes. The Major.

Across from Drumcarty the road runs straight under trees for perhaps two miles until it joins the river. I saw it as a long snake of black shadow and white dust, rolling under the Plunderer's hooves. The clenching and unclenching of his muscles underneath me was as regular as a metronome, his breathing easy. I looked back. The Major was flittering from shadow into light and back into

shadow, about two hundred yards behind and gaining
fast. I did not want to push the horse any further. His
head was steady and high. Between his cars the road
stretched away, undulating gently. At the limit of vision
the light blurred and diffused on a cloud of dust. My heart
rolled over in my chest. At the base of the cloud, red
coats and bright metal glittered.

The Major, riding in my dust, did not see them. He
was only a hundred yards behind me now. I could see
him as a dim shape, veiled in dense, white billows.

By the time the Major got enough dust out of his eyes
to see what was ahead, I could see the braid on the troop
sergeant's tunic. I rode straight at the red wall blocking
the road. Behind me, the Major started shouting. I began
to sing, to drown him.

> *"Oh love is the soul of the Irish Dragoon,*
> *In battle, in bivouac, or in saloon—*
> *From the tip of his spur to his bright sabertasche—"*

and then I roared, "Stand away, boys, 'tis a match for
fifty guineas!"

The troop-sergeant looked at me, then at the dust-
caked Major. He barked an order and the dragoons drew
to the side of the road and I thundered past, standing in
the stirrups, bowing and waving to their cheers. Then I
was away and the Major got in among them and the
cheering stopped, and I heard him barking orders. And
twenty seconds later, the road behind me was wall to wall
pounding hooves and red tunics and polished steel. I
heard the bang of a pistol and a ball whizzed through the
air by my head. "You bloody idiot!" roared the Major's
voice. "Kill the man, not the horse!" I tapped the Plunderer's ribs with my heels until we were out of shot.

After its run along the river the road curved back on
itself, uphill. There were dense woods to my right and I
did not remember any short cut through. To my horror I
saw, as I galloped into the approach to the bend, the yellow stumps and dust-piles of recent timber-cutting and a
boreen heading uphill to intercept the road at its return.
But it was too late to turn round; and by the time the
dragoons were up with the boreen I was round the corner. So I let in the Latchfords and started on the curve.

At the top of the hill, I reversed my ashplant, and began looking for the mouth of the boreen. It was easy to

spot. It came out as a raw new hole in the bank where the road began to level off, and even if I had not seen the hole I would have known it easily because, when I was twenty yards away, the Major came blazing out of it and pulled up in a shower of sparks. I had no time to rein in. He gave one startled look behind him, saw me. His right hand was down by his side, but as I came past him he brought it up and round in a flat sweep and I slammed my face into the Plunderer's mane and the sabre sang six inches over my back. The Plunderer stumbled for a sickening moment and I thought I was done, but he bunched up and pulled himself out. The Major was three feet away on the right, his coat flecked with the white foam the steep boreen had brought to his charger's nostrils. His helmet was knocked to one side and the snarl on his face was enough to curdle hot lead. One look was enough. Michael had told him to kill me. No doubt about that. I could hear the bellows-to-mend of his horse as he brought his sabre hand back for another chop. I looked quickly ahead and gave a nasty twitch to my right rein. The Plunderer swerved and met the Major's charger shoulder to shoulder. The charger stood seventeen hands, but next to the Plunderer it was a pony. Its right forefoot went forward to steady up, but instead of the road it met ditch, and the last I saw of the Major was his sabre arching through the air, sun flashing on steel, and a young fountain of dirty water.

Twenty minutes later I was looking at Waterford sprawled on the far bank of the Suir. The Plunderer had cast a shoe a mile back, poor beast, and was badly lame in his near fore. His chest and flanks were lathered white, and his head had a weary droop. I walked him down, keeping an ear open for the dragoons. They did not come. Two hundred yards before the bridge I hailed a man leaning by the doorway of a mouldy-thatched cottage and slid off. His eyes near fell out of the head when he saw the guinea in my hand. I pressed it into his palm and said, "Keep this. There'll be an English Major after the horse." Then I walked down the road and across the bridge. High water. The merest suspicion of the ebb's beginning. Down the quay I could see the *Shearwater*'s mast. I pushed through the crowd, fast, jumped aboard. "Are you loaded?" I said.

Harry Hicks directed a sardonic eye at me. "Yes, thanks," he said. "In a hurry, are you?"

"Yes," I said.

Harry began calling orders. The jib went up, backed. *Shearwater*'s nose came off the quay. Thos held her by the after warp as she caught the tide under her stern.

"Glad you could come," said Harry, following my eyes. "Looks like your friends missed you. Sad."

High on the slopes where the road from New Ross threaded over the horizon, a red centipede trailed a long feather of dust. "Oh, I don't know," I said. "I'm not sure I wanted to see them anyway."

The mainsail rumpled and filled, and Harry walked the tiller to port. Water began to gurgle at the counter and the low, green downstream hills folded us safely in.

I knew Smith was back before we landed. Normally, there would have been men out among the rocks, scouring the shores for wreck. Now there were only the gulls. I landed at the quay, leaving Harry and the other men to unload *Shearwater*'s bulging holds under cover of darkness, when Smith was safely off the island. It was early evening, the light low and seeming to re-invent everything it touched.

I walked round the harbour to the house, greeted Nick and Mary, and ate a large dinner. I did not tell Mary I had landed in Ireland, or the purpose of Harry's errand. Now Smith was in residence it would only have worried her, and although we had come through the nausea she was still easily upset. So we talked to Nick, and I think she was almost relieved he was there so she did not have to talk to me. After dinner she went to lie down and I with her, her dark head on my shoulder, smelling the warm smell of her hair and trying to feel close to her and to keep my mind away from Drumcarty.

After a while she said, "There's something wrong."

"Nothing," I said. "Nothing you'd want to know about."

Once that would have not have been enough. Now, she smiled and burrowed her great belly up against me for warmth. I dozed. In my dream I heard the Earl's phthisic cough, and walked through the vari-coloured pools of light in Drumcarty solar and stood before Katie's picture again. And the Earl once again turned to look at the wall facing the picture, and I turned with him, but before I could see what he was looking at, the great door boomed open and Michael Fitzpatrick's voice was shouting, "Keep away! Keep away!"

It must have been a couple of hours later when I awoke. It was dark. Mary was sleeping by my side. I felt the push of the baby's foot in the firm mound below her swollen breasts. I lay gathering my senses for a moment, wiping away the shreds of the dream. Then I made myself a cup of coffee, stuck my head in on Nick, and went for a walk.

I bent my footsteps towards the Palace. There was a new moon crooked over Samson, floating among big battleship clouds. What wind there was came from the west, bringing low voices from the quay, where Harry Hicks would be unloading his sacks. They would be nearly finished by now. I thought I might have a glass and talk big talk with Harry Jack. Harry Jack would want cheering up. Nowadays, he always wanted cheering up.

The barley-bags were coming ashore in *Shearwater's* punt, up onto the quay where four or five men were carrying them into what had once been the taproom of the Palace, but which now did duty as a barn. I took a hand. After my fifth bag, I heard an unusual sound. There were the usual night-noises—the lap of the waves, the distant calling of oystercatchers, the slap of halyard on mast from the anchorage. But there was something else. I stood listening, and Thos cannoned into me, laden with a bag. I moved out of the way. It came again. The sound of a horse's hooves on road metal.

There were not many horses on Tresco, and I could think of no reason for them to be out at this time of night. I said as much to Thos. He listened too, then said, "I did hear Smith was on the island."

"He'd be over to St. Mary's by now."

The dark silhouette of Thos' head wagged side to side. "He does have a little room all a-fitted out up at the Abbey." We walked down the quay. The hooves were louder now, coming past Mary's house. A fitful gleam of moonlight shone white on a stocky cob. "Bugger me it is him," said Thos. He exchanged low words with the men in the boat. They pulled away, drifting into the dark shadow of the rocks. I picked up the last of the sacks, ran back to the barn, and dumped it on the pile. Then I went round the back of the house, away from the quay, into the safe shadows.

The hoofbeats turned down Palace Row. There were footsteps as well. Two voices. One of them Smith's, the other Johns'. Otherwise, silence. No light showed from *Shearwater*. Her boat had disappeared. Thos and the other men were somewhere in the black rocks. The window of the Palace was a cheerful orange. I sat down and chewed a bit of grass, waiting for Smith and his agent to go.

Smith's voice said, "Well, goodnight, Johns. Tomorrow at nine."

"Tomorrow at nine," said Johns, "Goodnight, Mr. Smith." I heard his boots on the rough granite of the quay. Then they stopped. "Hullo," he said. "What's this?" A pause. "Barley," he said. "Wonder who's been throwing it about? Oh, well. Goodnight."

"Wait a minute, would you?" said Smith. I heard him dismount. "Shall we have a look?" The clang of a lantern-shutter. I spat out my grass-stalk. I remembered a trickling sensation when I had been carrying the last sack. My hand went to the collar of my jersey. The fingers encountered a grain of corn.

"Well, well," Smith's voice again. "Who'd be shipping barley at this time of year?"

"Can't think," said John's voice, puzzled now. "Little enough of it in the islands."

"Then perhaps it was going in, not out," said Smith. "Something smells, Johns. Look here." Again the crunch of his feet. Patches of lanternlight swung on the rocks. I began to move quietly backwards, through Harry Jack's garden towards the cairn behind. Johns said, "Good God," his voice echoing hollowly in the barn.

"Very smelly," said Smith. "Perhaps we'll have a word with the enterprising Mr. Jenkins." More footsteps, and a hammering on Harry Jack's door. I kept moving until I reached the cairn, the voices muffling with distance until all I could hear was Harry Jack's indignant tenor. Then the Lord Proprietor's voice, raised and booming. "God damn and blast you, you bloody little man!" it said. "Tell me the truth!" More yelps. Then Smith again. "We'll see about that. Mr. Johns! Take this man's name. And if he hasn't found his memory by next rent-day, off he goes." The slam of a door. A hiss, as of escaping breath from

Smith. Then his voice again, booming round the rocks. "And if there are any more of you skulking out there, ask Jenkins what I said to him." Then the clip-clop of hooves back up the road to the Abbey, and the sound of Johns' gaff going up, and the creak of the shrouds as his sail caught the wind and he was away down-channel.

Later, there were a lot of people in Harry Jack's house. Word had got round fast. Whatever had happened to Harry Jack could happen to them. They all knew it. There was the sniff of something raw and ugly brewing. I was one of the first in, with the other men who had been unloading the barley. I said, "There's no law against bringing in a little corn from Ireland. No harm in the truth."

Paradoxically, Harry Jack seemed to have experienced a return of his old resolute dignity. He shook his head. "I'm going anyway. I can't stand no more like this. Not being able to call your soul your own no more."

"It's a shame," said Mrs. Harry Jack. "A crying shame." Normally, she was a meek, greyish woman, who left the hard words to her husband. But tonight she was walking a keen edge of desperation. Her greying hair stuck out in spikes, and her eyes were red-rimmed from crying. "He can't do it to me and Harry."

There was a murmur of agreement. The place was filling up. There was a sour smell of bodies and drink. "Forty year," said Mrs. Harry Jack. "Forty year we slave to keep decent and look after our young 'uns, sea beef and all. And now this Smith come and take it all away because we won't keep to his rules. Do he think we're children? Or crazy folks?"

The murmur was a low growl, this time. The crowd pressed forward round her. Harry Jack, looking pained, put a hand on her shoulder. She shrugged it away fiercely. "What do he think we're made of?" she screeched. "How can he sit up there in his bloody big house on what was Tresco farms? How can he sleep safe at night?" She rounded on Harry Jack. "Because the menfolks won't do anything about it. 'Tis all 'Yes, Governor, no, Hemperor, three bags full, Mister Smith.' And meanwhile he's throwing honest folks out of their homes. Men? Sheep!" She collapsed, sobbing.

Some of the men looked embarrassed. A woman's voice

said, "Burn him out." The cry was taken up by another voice, then another. The men joined in.

Mrs. Harry Jack, recovering, said, "Give 'im a taste of his own! Pull his 'ouse down round his ears. Burn him out!"

There was an ugly roar and a rush for the door. I stood in front of it. The crowd halted, piled up, baying like hounds. I said, "Wait a minute."

"Get out of the bloody way, Doctor," shouted a woman.

"Not until I've said my piece. If you burn Smith's house he'll have you all off the island, and he'll see you hang. That's the kind of man he is. He hasn't put Harry Jack off. Harry Jack is leaving of his own free will. Not so, Harry?"

"Quite right, Doctor," said Harry Jack.

"So before you burn anything, think. Hard. Mrs. Harry Jack's upset."

There were jeers. But I saw Mordecai, towering over Harry Hicks. They were not jeering. Their faces were serious, but not sceptical.

"Suppose you burnt him out," I said. "Killed him. That's what you'd have to do to get rid of him. Well, the lease is on three lives. That means that when you'd buried him, you'd have two more like him to deal with. They might be better, they might be worse. But you wouldn't know about it. You'd be hanged."

Now there was silence. Mrs. Harry Jack broke it. "You're a friend of his, are you, Doctor? All cosy with the gentlefolk, is it?"

"He's no friend of mine. You know that well enough." She knew, and so did everyone else. "There are better ways than killing and burning. That's all."

"Ways such as what?" said Mordecai.

"Pay no attention. Do your duty by him, nothing more. Outside the terms of the lease, he can't touch you. He's only a landlord. A tenant farmer. Not a king or a god. So why encourage him to believe he is?"

"He's right," said Harry Jack, firmly.

"He is," said Mordecai, and blushed scarlet at his boldness.

Mrs. Harry Jack shrieked, "Cowards!"

"Shut up, Emily," said Harry. "You said enough."

And the cruel tension went out of the people. The

younger ones left; evidently, some of them were still unhappy. Six or seven of us stayed behind, talking. I found I
was wet with sweat, my hands trembling. I was sure I had
acted right by my conscience; but I was not so confident
that I had done right by the people of Scilly.

XIII

NEXT DAY Mary looked tired, so I told her to
keep to her bed. I did not tell her about Harry Jack. She
had enough to think about already.

I left her with her embroidery and set off in the punt
with young Nick. We spent the morning trolling atherines
for pollack to the west of Samson, and in the early afternoon went ashore with a full basket on Samson itself. Nick
cherished a special affection for Samson. On the South
Hill, above the seven houses clustered by the sandbar that
joins it to its rocky twin, there is a nest of tumuli. We often went there, to sit a hundred feet in the sky among the
bones of ancient kings, watching the sea roar and spume
in the ledges that spike its bed between Mincarlo and
Minalto.

Nick lay back on the west-facing slope of a tumulus,
pushed the black hair back from his ear and applied it to
the wiry turf. He always claimed he could hear the old
ones talking to him; now, having listened, he said,
"They're hot. They were cold in the winter, but they say
its pretty tolerable now. It's the gold. Once it gets
warmed up, they're all snug."

"What gold?" I said.

"Oh, crowns and things. Knives. Teapots." He rolled
over again, listening. Like Mary, Nick had the idea that
the dead of Scilly were only sleeping, waiting for a great
resurrection. He spoke to them not only about their personal comfort, but about the daily life of the islands, the

farming, the fishing, what he knew of the gossip. Which was a surprising amount; he was big for his age, in mind as well as body.

I lay watching the long, slow topple of the waves. My back and arms were aching from the morning's rowing, a pleasant, satisfying ache. Bees hummed in the heather, and there was the thick hint of honeysuckle from the tangled slopes. The ugliness of last night faded into a warm peace. It had a strange reputation, this island. The people who dwelt here were poor even by Scillonian standards, but they clung to it with a fierce, irrational strength. It was said that there were other things here beyond reason. There was no church, no burying-ground but the kings' tombs on their cyric. At low spring tides, walls of cyclopean masonry could be seen, reaching across the barren sea-sand towards Tresco. Scillonians did not lightly walk on the South Hill at the new or the full of the moon—except the Webbers. And curious things were said about the Webbers. Once I had seen an Italian seaman, filling water-barrels at Southward Well, make a sign at her with horned fingers. *Mal'occhio,* he had said to his mate. But this June afternoon, lying on the scented ground lulled by the soft booming of the sea, that was hard to believe. And the Widow Webber was a friend of mine. She lived in the uppermost of the cottages, with her two sons, a chair, a plank bed and three black pigs. When she laughed it was not always easy to see what amused her, but she had a deep fund of stories that she loved telling, and she knew the plants and herbs of the islands as well as she knew the greasy old pack of cards with which she told her fortunes. I resolved to take her a couple of pollack from the fern-shaded basket in the boat. Then I fell into a doze.

I was woken by a hand shaking my shoulder. Nick was kneeling at my side. His eyes were wide and terrified, and tears were running down his broad brown cheeks. "What is it?" I said. "Here." I gave him my handkerchief. He shook his head, speechless with sobs. After a while, he quietened down. "What is it?" I said again.

He got up. "I want to go," he said. His eyes were still frightened. "Come on."

"Tell me first."

"I was talking to Og. He's the King. I was telling him what I could see. He likes to know. Then he said. . . ." He shook his head violently. "No. I can't."

"You had a beastly bad dream," I said. "Tell me about it. That's the way to make it go away."

"He asked me if I wanted to go down there with him. Under the ground. Soon. Then he put up his hand. It was cold. Only bones. I could feel the bones." He shuddered.

I put my arm round his small shoulders. "We'll go," I said. "But we'll have a look first." I bent to where his head had lain. "Look. No bones. Only grass." . .

He said, "Yes." But he did not sound convinced. In his eyes was the fey look I sometimes saw in Mary's, as if he was watching something a long way away in time.

"We'll go and see Mrs. Webber," I said. As we walked down the bracken of the hillside, he took my hand. And I forgot about the dream.

The Widow was sitting on a boulder in front of her house, spinning. When she heard us, she hauled herself up on her stick and said, "But 'tis the Doctor and little Nicholas. Good day to 'ee, sirs." The words sounded as if they had been ground by worn millstones. It must have been twenty years since she lost her last tooth. Her skin was blackish-brown with sun and dirt, drawn over nose and chin in wrinkles tributary to the deep furrows in her shrunken lips. Her eyebrows were surprisingly black and hairy, and her ancient eyes dodged brightly in and out of the foliage, giving her a slightly furtive look. But the Widow was anything but furtive. The bent remains of big bones knobbed the brown wool of her shapeless dress. Her twisted feet were bare.

Nick had got over his dream enough to be disgruntled by her calling him 'little,' so I sent him off to get the pollack from the boat. The Widow and I talked about the winter. Since I had come ashore under Shag Point with Little John and the wreck of the *Maracaibo* she had me posted as a useful man in a gig, so we talked mostly about wrecks, and the perpetual quarrels over the division of the spoils. I got the impression that there was something troubling her, but it would have been the height of bad manners to ask her what it was. Nick came back with the fish, for which he seemed duly grateful. Then he went back down to the beach to play, and we talked on. Eventually the conversation, like all island conversations nowadays, came round to Smith. The Widow's agitation increased as I told her about last night's doing with Harry Jack.

"Ah," she said. "That man Johns. All winter 'e was at me."

"At you?" Even by Smith's somewhat bizarre lights, the Widow was a law-abiding creature. "What for?"

"Said as 'ow I was too old to be 'ere no more. Nosey bugger. I soon sent 'e on 'is way. Trying to move me to St. Mary's, 'e was."

I nodded. Several old women on Tresco had been moved across the water, and several more were resisting still.

"What's the use?" said the Widow. "They 'ont want me on St. Mary's. I don't want they neither. I likes my peace." She laughed, a deep croak. "They'll never shift me."

"Did they give up?" I said. We were getting close to the heart of the matter.

"Look you over by Puffin Isle," said the Widow, pointing with a finger like a brier-root.

My eye went out across the silver beach and the turquoise shallows to where the water blued with depth. Beyond and to the right of the green topknot of Puffin Island was the dot of a boat, with oars that dipped and rose.

" 'Tis Smith," she said. "I was told as he was coming to reason with I."

"Bully you," I said. "I think I'll stay."

"No you don't," she said, to my surprise. "He won't get far with me. Gale and calm I lived here, and no man'll move me if I don't want to go."

"He's worse than a gale," I said.

"You get along. He can't be worse than the Widder," she said, and laughed again, that weird raven's croak of hers.

"I'll stay."

She turned to look at me. The eyes were suddenly opaque under the wild brows. "Just you get down to the beach and watch," she said. "It'll be him as needs you. Not me." She hobbled into the house and slammed the door. I stood for a moment staring at the horseshoe nailed to the rotting boards, hearing her mumbling inside. Then I went down to the beach. It was a hot summer's afternoon. But for some reason I could feel every hair on my body standing on end, prickling, as if I were naked in a cold wind.

Augustus Smith was standing in the stern of his private gig, hands behind his back, telescope under arm, jaw thrust out. He looked solid as a rock. I heard him bark an order. The rowers skied oars. Bow jumped out as the stem touched the steeply shelving sand, and the boat came alongside as if to a quay. Smith went over the side without looking at the duckboard laid for his Imperial boots. He was staring ferociously up the hill at the cottages huddled like dirty sheep in the bracken. On the beach he stopped, feet firmly planted in the sand, glaring.

The door of the topmost house opened and the Widow came out. Nick was digging in the sand by the water's edge. The same thing that was freezing my spine made him look up at that bent brown figure framed in the doorway of the miserable turf cottage. He forgot his game, ran over to me, and took my hand. The chill was running in waves up my back. Gulls swooped and shrieked in the clear blue sky above the catspawed green glass of the channel, cursing and fighting over a lump of offal. The terror had no effect on them. It was something invented by the mind of man, in the dark places where horrible things wallowed and sucked.

I had the extraordinary sensation that I was no longer there. There was only an inky void humming with a beastly whistling drone like the sound of an ocean and its weather heard from a distant planet. And suspended in that void, two figures. Smith, planted on the beach with his head thrust forward from his shoulders. And the Widow, a brown glyph of rag and bone high on the hill. The deep cleft of her gums was moving. Slowly, her left arm rose from her side, the knotted index finger stretched sinew-cracking tight. It came up until it pointed direct at Smith. Then it stopped.

Smith fell forward on his face.

The Widow's door slammed.

The darkness cleared, with an indescribable twisting in the brain. And once again I felt Nick's hand in mine. I looked down at him and said, "Are you all right?" in a voice that shook.

"Of course I am," he said. "Why's Mr. Smith fallen down?" His small face was red and brown from the sun, the black hair shaggy, the long eyes frankly curious.

I stood as if in a trance. "You didn't feel anything?"

"A bit," he said. "Mrs. Webber witched him, didn't she?"

"How do you know that?"

"The other boys said, at school. Is that what witching means?"

"I suppose so," I said. Then I remembered Smith.

All I could see of him was his back, blue coat and serge trousers. His face was pressed down into the sand. The sound of muffled bellowing came from the mouth regions. As I walked across to him, I thought he looked sunk further into the beach than he should be. His back heaved with his struggles. I crouched beside his head, caught him by his curly black hair and tried to put his face on one side so he could breathe.

I could not move it.

I tried again. Muffled roars of agony from down in the sand. But still no movement. I began to scrape the sand from under his nose and mouth. I said, "Can you hear?"

"Of course I can hear you, God damn you!" he roared. "I'm not deaf."

"And how are we feeling?" I said, with my best bedside manner.

"Can't move," he said.

"Any sensations in the head? Like the tap of a hamer?" I wondered for a moment if he had had an apoplexy. It seemed most unlikely. Anything further from unconsciousness than his present state I could not imagine.

"Will you stop babbling and get me up!" he roared.

I beckoned to his boatmen. They were young men, and strong. Under the tan they were the colour of wet flour. They took him one on each arm. I said, "One, two. Heave." They heaved.

At harvest-time last year, I had seen one of those men run up Abbey Hill with a hundredweight sack of barley on each shoulder, for a bet. He had won the bet, and I knew he was no weaker now. But strain as they would, they could not raise Smith from the ground.

"Christ," said the man who had run with the sacks.

"It ain't. . . ." He looked up the hill. "It ain't in nature." He licked his lips.

"Hold your tongue, man!" said Smith's voice, muffled. "Get some oars under me and get me off this damned island." There was no fear in his voice. Only rage.

Nick was finding the whole thing extremely amusing, though he was politely holding his nose and mouth to stop the sound of his laughter reaching the Lord Proprietor. "She said. . . ." He paused to cover his snorts. "She said,

'Let bones be lead.' And they are." He laughed outrageously. "Oh my eye, don't he look silly, pa!"

I knelt down and took Smith's pulse. It was full, a little frequent, but that was to be expected. What surprised me was the weight of his arm. It was not like a thing of flesh and bone. Weight for weight, it was like a chunk of lead drainpipe.

They got the oars under him, but it did them no good. All six oarsmen heaved and strained; but they could not lift him an inch. He had stopped bellowing now, and lay still and dark and weighty. I sat by his head, making soothing noises, and told his men to go back to Tresco and get more men and blocks and tackles if necessary. The fear had left me. Instead, there was the feeling that this could only be a dream. My mind, faced with the impossible, continued to work clearly and lucidly; but every time I approached the problem, my carefully trained intellect told me that it was not possible for such a problem to exist, thereby confounding the evidence of my own eyes. I had read of Doctor Mesmer's work in magnetism, however, and I concluded that this must be something similar.

The boat returned from Tresco full of men, some of whom had been at Harry Jack's last night, and there was a good deal of laughter once the first fear had worn off. The Widow did not reappear. Four of the new men caught Smith under the arms and heaved. He came up like a feather, his face and waistcoat and trousers covered with sand. Under the veil of quartz and mica, his face was the colour of ripe figs. The laughter stopped. The helpers set him on his feet. He fell flat on his face again, roaring.

I said, "Put him in the boat."

They took him by his arms and his legs and swung him onto the bottom-boards. For a second, the boat sank deep in the water. Then it rose again. Smith scrambled to his feet. He did not look at the Widow Webber's cottage. His face had lost its colour. In a voice strangely quiet, he said, "New Grimsby." The rowers took their places. Oars dipped, and the boat glided away over the translucent blue.

I looked up at the Widow's cottage. The door was still closed, the windows empty and silent. One of the Samson men, a half-wit, limped along the sandbar dragging a long strand of weed, singing, "Oo. Oo. Oo. Oo," like a cretinous owl. Cold touched me again. I said, "Come on, Nick. Let's be off."

When we went up the quay steps, Smith was talking to one of his oarsmen. His colour was returning. They were discussing the building of a wall. From the look on the seaman's face, it was something they had gone over before. I guessed that Smith was trying to reassure himself that he was still the Emperor. Against my will, I rather sympathised with him.

Nick caught sight of some of his friends playing in an old boat down on the beach, and ran off to join them, jumping across the sand-pools like a thin, brown shore bird. I started down Palace Row. A tendril of smoke was rising from Jimmy Pender's chimney, so I thought I would go and see him. As I was opening his gate, hooves sounded on the road behind me and Smith's voice said, "Nicholls. A word, if you would be so good."

For a split second his voice held something that took me back to Carthystown school, Maconochie singling me out from the rabble for an interview with the strap. He looked up and down the row of cottages and said, "I'll walk up the road with you." He slid off his horse, which surprised me. Normally he liked to conduct his interviews from a suitably imperial height. I gathered that we were to talk as equals.

I said, "Rum business."

He looked at me blankly, eyebrows raised. "What are you talking about?"

"On Samson."

He snorted. "Superstitous old fool." He had an astonishing capacity for putting everyone but himself in the wrong. Now I realised that it did not only apply to people; the forces of nature, ancient gods, hallowed custom—all were merely petty obstacles, to be surmounted. And if the only way to surmount them was to ignore their existence —well, said his cold grey eye; so be it. "I hear I should be grateful to you."

"On what account?"

"The silly doings at the Palace."

He had picked his boatmen with an unerring instinct for the stool-pigeon. "Don't thank me," I said. "I didn't say what I said for your sake. It was the islanders I was concerned about."

"I am sure," said Smith. "Very well."

We walked on in silence. When we came to Mary's gate, he said, "Walk on a little, if you would be so good."

We passed beyond the houses to where the road ran along the north-western end of the Pool, Smith talking about birds. He was certainly a fair ornithologist. We stopped to look at the fleets of mallard cruising the brown water. He said, "Johns was telling me we had a purple gallinule the other day. Did you see it?"

"Yes. A male."

"Wonderful, these migrants and accidentals. Don't you think, Nicholls?"

"Yes," I said, wondering what he was driving at.

"Interesting to know where they come from. The gallinule, for instance. All the way from America, it seems. And you, Nicholls." He turned his eyes on me below the Imperial brows. "I've been making inquiries about your flight-path."

So that was it. "I hope you found it as interesting as the gallinule's."

"More so, I am happy to say. The gallinule's life is a simple and straightforward matter. It has a genus and a species. It merely happens to have landed in unusual quarters. But in the course of your migrations you have managed to change your name and even your species. You are a rum bird, Nicholls. A very rum bird."

"I think you will find it difficult to support your allegations."

"I haven't made any yet," he said brusquely. Then he cocked an eyebrow at me. "I was in Ireland during the winter," he said. "Staying with some . . . ornithological friends. And some of the things I heard . . . they made me wonder. That is all. They made me wonder."

I felt giddy. My knees tried to knock together. "I am afraid I don't understand you," I said.

"No. Probably not." Smith pulled out his spyglass, focussed it on the knot of mallard. "Couple of teal with them," he said. "In case understanding should come on the wings of midnight, consider this." He folded the glass with a snap. "I feel very strongly that a man should exert himself to the limit of his abilities. This you are not doing. Last night, you averted a most unpleasant and silly interlude. I owe you something for it. But do not count on me. If you want to make yourself useful, well and good. If not. . . ." He put his boot in the stirrup and swung himself clumsily into the saddle. "I shall tell nobody what has passed between us. You will also keep your mouth shut. When I find out more about you, I shall tell you, and we shall see what we shall see." The cob took a couple of steps. He dragged back on the reins with heavy hands, "I am not entirely unsympathetic, you see. I am something of a bird of passage myself. But I intend to make my home here. You are too strong-minded for comfort." His face relaxed into his sudden attractive smile. "One might say that the islands can only contain so much power." He spurred his horse away up the road.

I stood looking over the reddening pool. I had noticed that English gentlemen, however grave and heavy, shared one weakness. They loved puns, the worse the better. "The islands can only contain so much power." Or was it Power?

I do not know where I walked that night. I suppose I must have covered the whole island, head down, pondering. The sense of unreality left over from the extraordinary events on Samson was still with me, strengthened by my conversation with Smith. Perhaps it made me more objective; perhaps it detached me from myself to a point where I became slightly mad. Whatever the truth, the questions came very clear to my mind.

How much could Smith know? He would know that I had arrived at Scilly in a gale six years ago, sole survivor of the wreck of a nameless ship. He would know the gale had been from the North. He could even have checked the Register for ships lost at that time. He would have to be thorough; but Smith was nothing if not thorough.

He knew I was a doctor. My accent had been educated out of me, so that would give him no clues. My appearance was not particularly distinguished; my limp, having been acquired *en route* for Scilly, would serve to mislead. There was the grave in Tresco churchyard with my name on the headstone. And even if he had got past that, New Botallack had changed me. He had been in Ireland. He would have stayed in great houses, met ladies and gentlemen who might have been my patients. Would the story still be alive? Six years was a long time. But assuming that he had checked the Register, he would have been asking questions. Discreet, but specific. And the drawingrooms of Ireland were as full of gossip as the tap-rooms of Scilly. It would not have taken some poor relation, flattered by the attention, much time to pour the whole story into his ear, wih embroideries. And Michael Fitzpatrick would have featured in the story. It would not have taken him long to find Michael, my friend and confidant. The friend and confidant who had tried to have me murdered at New Botallack, and again at Carthystown Races. If Smith had talked to him, Michael would have told him what he wanted to know. It was pretty plain that to Michael my presence on the face of the earth was nothing but an embarrassment. I was in the way of one of his schemes. But what scheme, I did not know.

However, Smith was the immediate problem. If he had found out as much as I suspected he was capable of, he knew it all.

So what could he do about it? I was a thorn in his flesh. I might have prevented the mob burning his house round his ears last night; but his practicality would not let him put too high a premium on that. He would want me off the islands. That was plain enough. He had failed to collect enough evidence on the smuggling charge; but if he had talked to Michael he had enough to ship me back to Ireland tomorrow, in irons. All he had to do, as magistrate, was to secure the agreement of the Bench. And everyone knew who the Bench paid its rent to.

So why was he hesitating? He was not returning a favour. That I had already concluded. Could it be that he did not believe the stories against me? Michael Fitzpatrick was as slippery as an eel. Smith had the Imperial gift of seeing through a cunningly-woven story. But Michael was a master tangler. And my flight was hardly the act of an innocent man. No, I was sure that in Smith's mind I already stood convicted. There was no sense in wondering any more about that. It could only be that he felt either that the evidence against me was incomplete, or that my presence on the island served some hidden purpose. For a moment, I flirted with the idea that it might be a whim of kindness or cruelty. But Smith was not the kind of man given to whims. He ran his life by reasons.

So what could I do about it? The options were quite simple. I could run away. There would be no difficulty in asking Mordecai or Harry Hicks to take me to England or France, and then taking passage to America or Australia. But running away meant leaving young Nick. And

Mary, with the baby due any day now. Leaving a home and a family, trying to start again from scratch. I had the money to do it. Money was no object. But I did not have the heart. So I would have to stay.

1828 began badly. When I returned to Dublin, I found Mercy Hall full of typhus cases for whom there was no room in the fever hospitals. For two months it was there I spent my waking moments and there I slept. The Merrion Square practice we closed, for the time being, and Duquesne came out of his semi-retirement to do what he could. So day after day the sick came in and lay raving in the straw, while outside the rain fell and the filth in the gutters overflowed into the wells and the hearses rattled endlessly to the cemeteries. Finally, as the weather began to improve and the streets to dry out, the patients became fewer. But by that time Duquesne had fallen sick, and, despite all I could do for him, he died. I missed him worse thant I had missed by father.

I returned to Merrion Square, which by the terms of Duquesne's Will was now mine, in a state of complete exhaustion. I had to employ two other doctors to look after Mercy Hall; and by May, when I was again on my feet, they were making such a good job of it that I decided I would devote all my time to the fashionable side of the practice, in an attempt to refill the dwindling coffers.

It was not as easy as that. The epidemic, like all epidemics, had not been a respector of rank. Three of my smart patients had died of the fever, and the gossips had gone to work. My connections with Mercy Hall had become known, and pretty soon the word was out that I had carried the infection from my vile den of paupers to Merrion Square. Several of my fellow physicians made it clear to an avid public that they considered—had always considered—me criminally irresponsible. The crowds in my consulting-rooms dwindled overnight.

In mid-May I dined with Michael at his splendid new house in York Street, and I could tell that I was in for one of his lectures by the fact that, while he pressed me to drink hard, he himself drank little. Finally he said, "Nick, you're in a mess."

"What makes you say that?" I was in no mood for listening to confirmation of the evidence of my emptying appointment-book.

"You've been foolish. Killing your patients. How can you expect to keep 'em if you're infecting them with paupers' diseases?"

"I didn't infect anybody. Besides, I had the foolish idea that it was more important to save lives than pander to a lot of fashionable hypochondriacs."

"It was foolish," said Michael, grinning. "That is to say, you can have your motives admired without neglecting your bread and butter."

"Very sensible," I said, with bitterness.

"Damn it, man, you're my oldest friend," said Michael, looking wounded. "I'm a professional advice-giver. I'm giving you the benefit of it free."

I nodded. Michael was always ready to put himself out to help. And he often did help, despite his distinctly venal approach. "You're probably right," I said. "But I think there's something else."

"There is," he said. "Lady Katherine. She's not helping you."

"I haven't seen her for two months."

"Maybe not," said Michael. "But she never stops talking about you. If you stay mixed up with her you don't look . . . solid. And if there's one thing you have to do, to get your patients back, it's look solid. I should know."

"Then damn you and damn the rest of them."

"Ah, well. I only thought I'd tell you what was being said." He poured himself a glass, a full one this time, and drank it off. The homilies were at an end.

"Thank you."

"Great days in store," said Michael. "They've given me Drumcarty."

"What do you mean?"

"From today on, I have charge of the Drumcarty estates. The partners were asked to recommend a man. They recommended me. I'm told there's a mort of law, all of it tangled to hell."

"There is," I said. "Better than a pension for you. Congratulations."

Michael nodded. "Soon have 'em sorted out."

"I wouldn't bet on it," I said. I remembered Doctor Connolly's remarks about lawyers. "It could be a great estate. But you'd have to cut rents to put it back on its feet."

Michael's eyes went blank. "We'll see," he said. "I'll do as I'm told. I'm in no position."

"But you'll try."

"I'll make that place pay," said Michael. "You see if I don't."

I found myself at the garden gate of Mary's house. It was late. There were no lights in the windows. I put my hand to the latch. There was another option. Smith had said that our conversation would go no further. He and I were the only ones who possessed the link which would complete the chain that could drag me away from the things I loved, back to Ireland and my enemies. If one of us died, the chain would be broken. He was up in the Abbey, camping in the half-finished house with one old servant. My hand went to the pommel of the knife at my belt. Four inches of steel between the ribs. A fire. Nobody would suspect me. Had I not argued against exactly that last night? But even as the thought grew and brought the hot sweat to my forehead, it faded. I could not, in fairness, do that to him. They were my crimes; if anyone should suffer for them, it must be me.

But much later, after what was going to happen had happened, I wished I had killed him there and then.

The fire in the living-room was banked to a dull red glow. I lit a lamp and sat down, listening to the hiss of the coals, Nick murmuring in his sleep upstairs. But I was too restless to sit. I got up and took down the big calf-bound catalogue of the sea-life of the islands and leafed through the pages, looking for a memory that would take me away from the answerless questions. All I found was the mass of entries in my own small handwriting, with here and there a notation in Mary's Italianate scrawl. It brought back the memories all right, but it was a record of easier, peaceful days. It hurt. So I put it back on the shelf and walked over to the fire. Mary's embroidery frame caught my eye. I rested my hand on the worn brocade cover. My life, she had said. She would never finish it. I never looked at it unless she invited me to. Lately, she had not asked. I took off the cover, brought over the lamp.

The scene had changed. The background was still a sunset: but the apocalypse had turned into a pastoral. The light on the sea, done with wonderful skill in stitches too small for my eye to see in the lamplight, was a soft pink glow. There were ships at anchor, small and tubby, like toys, and in the middleground, houses, neat and square. There were four figures now. In the right foreground stood young Nick, brown and smiling, beside Mary in a dark blue dress, turned half away from the boy, huge and gravid. Flanking them on one side was a figure in a black coat astride a white horse with a crown on his head and a telescope under his arm. Smith. He was looking over the heads of Mary and Nick, at a figure set a little back to the left, among some rocks. The figure wore a jersey and sea-boots, and leaned for support on a white caduceus. It stared out of the frame beyond the horizon, beyond Scilly at a point doomed forever to recede. The eyes were blue, and they looked straight into mine, haunted. The face was my own.

I sat looking at the embroidery until the yellow leaf of lamp-flame died to a red worm of smouldering wick. After that, I sat in the dark, dozing, dreaming I was being chased by things I could not see for reasons I did not understand. The singing of dawn birds woke me. I went outside. The grass of the new lawn was wet with dew, the air fresh and full of the salt of the virgin morning. In the sky, lemon strands of cirrus floated against the blue of a Madonna's robe. It was going to be a beautiful day.

I made coffee and swallowed some bread and bacon. When the sun was well up Nick came down the stairs and took a lump of bread and a mug of milk. He was very excited. Mordecai Ellis had told him he could come out in his boat. I told him he could cut a few cabbages and see what the chickens had left in the way of eggs. There was always the chance they would run across a ship homeward bound and get a good price for fresh food. When I had helped him fill his sack, we shook hands, according to established ritual, and I watched him running off down the road, hopping clownishly over a cowpat in the white gravel. At the corner he turned and waved. I waved back, kept waving until after he was out of sight. I wished he was not going with Mordecai, today of all days. I needed his simple faith as an anodyne against the tangle of my life. But it was a self-indulgent need. I stuck my hands in the pockets of my serge trousers and went in to Mary.

She was asleep, but her eyes opened at the sound of my feet on the boards. She smiled. "I didn't hear you get up." She looked across at my undinted pillow.

"I wasn't tired." I sat down beside her. "How are you?"

"I feel like an egg about to hatch." She put her hand on my cheek. "You look ill, Nick."

"No." Her fingers were warm from the bed. "I couldn't sleep. I worked, instead. That's all."

She looked at me in the old way, with the eyes that burrowed into the soul. "And what else?"

For a moment I thought I would tell her everything. Then I saw again the tapestry figure with the white caduceus and the haunted eyes. I could not show her what was in my mind. There was the baby to think of. She needed safe, solid things. A future beyond the ordeal of childbirth. So I said, "Something that happened yesterday. On Samson. I was going to tell you last night, but there were . . . matters to attend to."

She nodded. Nowadays, what I did held little interest for her.

I told her about the Widow Webber and Smith's collapse. When I had finished, she laughed, the old mocking laugh, and my heart warmed to her. Then she said, "Stupid old woman."

I was taken aback. I had expected her to take pleasure in the old ways winning over the new. "Ach, Nick. Will you never learn? Moth-eaten superstitions. Rubbish."

"But I saw it happen. With my own eyes."

"I'm sure you did. They run deep, the old ways. They were useful, once. But their time is gone."

I stared at her. "But that was the Scilly you loved. That was what kept you here when I asked you to come to America."

She turned her face away, towards the sunny window. "It was Scilly kept me. No particular Scilly. Just Scilly. And the Widow Webber and her tricks aren't Scilly. Not any more."

"It isn't the same place. It could be anywhere. A rich man's estate anywhere."

"You're wrong. No one man can change this place. It may alter on the surface. But past, present and future all live together. I love them all."

"And so do I," I said. "Because it's my home. For Smith it's a toy."

"Oh, Nick." Her voice was very quiet. "I love it, but

I'm not sentimental about it. Smith's the driving force. You must be able to see that."

"And I'm a sentimental cottager."

"You try, but I think you might be pretending to be something you aren't." She took the sting out of it with her smile.

I said, "That's for me to decide." But I knew she was right, and the knowledge sharpened the feeling of loss.

Later in the morning, I made a brief examination. By my count Mary was about a week from her time. The foetus' head was not yet engaged in the pelvic bones, but in a second pregnancy that was to be expected. I patted the tiny posterior I could feel under the smooth bulge of brown flesh below the xiphisternum and said, "We'll be seeing him soon."

"Thank God for that," said Mary. As I left the room, she was singing to the baby in a low croon, locked once again in her shell.

I called in on Aunt Woodcock, who despite her age still clung jealously to her role as midwife to Tresco, and we discussed the case. She professed herself quite confident, it being a second child. She had had some trouble with Nick, for Mary's bones were small; but she held up her brawny forearms for my inspection, and said, "If there's a way through at all, these 'ere can stretch 'er." Having drunk the cup of tea she pressed on me, I went on my way. The Aunt was a skilful midwife by any standards; she had lost mothers and babies, but not, she claimed with pride, more than two in ten. And that was good practice by any standards.

The technicalities of the morning had prevented me from brooding, but as I walked back to New Grimsby, the apprehension returned. The day was blue and clear, with a south wind blowing warm up-channel. I could see Jimmy Pender carrying a length of new timber into the workshop behind his house, so I went down to pass the time of day with him. When I went in he was bent over the vice on the side of his bench, planing, a short pipe protruding from his long yellow moustache. He looked up, gave me a shy nod and carried on with his work. I leaned against the wall, watching his old shoulders seeing as he drove the blade along with the grain of the yellow pine. The resinous smell of the shavings took me back to the mountain clearings behind New Botallack. He checked the plank with his square, unclamped it and stacked it in a corner with others like it. "Kitchen table for the Emperor," he said, his enthusiasm getting the better of his awkwardness. "Four by eight. Wood brought in special. Lovely job."

I asked after his rheumatism. He said, "Twice the man. Sun does take the ache out of it. Fine thing to have some real work. Before the Emperor came, all I ever made was coffins." He hobbled to the door and stuck his head out. "Two o'clock," he said. "Done enough for the day." Stooping laboriously, he pulled a black bottle from the dusty recess under the bench. "Doctor?"

"Thank you."

We drank. Then we talked for a while. Working for Smith had given Jimmy a new lease of life. He was making much of the furniture for the new house, and Smith had presented him with a foot-lathe which was his pride and joy. Having demonstrated its working, he passed on to the gossip. As I well knew, his house was best placed to observe comings and goings to the quay, and he treated me to a full catalogue. There was Mordecai's boat, Charlie Jenkins from Bryher, Tom Sinclair with sheep for St. Mary's, and the mail. Busier than Penzance, Jimmy reckoned. I nodded and got up and made my farewells. Mention of the mail had set my uneasiness going again.

Beyond the quay I saw the yellow-varnished masts of Mordecai's ketch, sails descending in billows of clean white canvas. Mary was on the quay, her black hair blowing in the breeze. She would have seen the boat come in, walked down to meet Nick. She was standing with her back to me, talking to someone hidden round the corner of the shed that had been my dispensary. As I drew nearer, I saw that it was Smith. His face wore an expression I had not seen before. It was amused, without hardness. The face of an ordinary man talking to a pretty woman.

When he saw me the face changed, became aloof and imperial. I heard him say, "Good. Capital." He made a cold inclination of the head. Mary turned with a ponderous swing of her belly and said, "I was just taking my constitutional. Mr. Smith was inquiring about the new house." Her voice was curiously stilted. Smith settled his telescope under his arm, clasped his hands behind his back and strode to the seaward end of the quay, martinet's eyes flicking about him. Nick's voice came across the water. "Mama! Papa! Look at me!"

Nick often went and watched Mordecai at work on the boat. For his benefit, Mordecai had stepped a mast in the tender, a ten-foot pram dinghy, and cut a lugsail from an old jib. There was rather too much sail on the dinghy, but Nick was only allowed out in light airs in the company of an adult. Now, he was coming close-hauled in from the ketch's anchorage, a little white bone of water at the pram's snub bow. He was sitting very straight at the tiller, squinting up at the luff in fine seamanlike style. Mordecai was on the centre thwart with his knees round his ears. He looked round, saw Smith, ignored him, and called to me, "He'll be a captain afore you know it." His voice sounded a little blurred. Then, to Nick, "Tiller away from you. Up into the wind alongside." The dinghy's nose came round, sail flapping, and her paint ground against the quay. "Va-ary good," said Mordecai, belching. "A little rough, but va-ary good." Nick beamed at me and looked across at Mary, who smiled, and then back at Smith. Smith nodded indulgently. Nick's face turned bright red, and he dropped his eyes.

Mordecai stepped on to the quay with the painter, rather clumsily. I was about six feet away, but even at that range I could smell the drink on him. He said, "Never mind about the sail. Come and show your Dad how not to tie a slippery hitch."

Nick picked his vegetable sack up from the bottom-boards. He had gone out with it full. Now it was empty, except for a heavy object about the size of a man's head. Mordecai said, "Give up your hand," and reached down and pulled him onto the quay with a mighty heave. Nick came flying out of the boat and landed on his feet. The sack swung down and hit rock. There was the sound of breaking glass. Brown liquid seeped over the grey stones.

Nick said, "Oh blast," and peered into the sack. "It's broken. I got it for the eggs. It was a present for you, Pa." The smell of cognac rose powerfully from the remains.

I said, "Bad luck, old fella. It's the thought that counts."

Heavy steps ground on the quay. Smith said, "Brandy, eh?" A look of terror came over Nick's small face. The Proprietor's voice was heavily jocose. "Smuggling. Serious business."

Nick looked at me, then at Smith. His eyes were like a frightened animal's, his bare legs trembling. Then he made a sudden dive for the painter, snatched it out of Mordecai's hand and jumped into the dinghy, pushing away from the quay with his foot and pulling the tiller towards him. The sail filled. He let out the sheet, and the dinghy skimmed away to northward.

I shouted, "Come back!" He could sail well enough, but he was too young to be in a boat on his own. "Where are you going?"

He looked round. He was a hundred yards off now, his face white and scared. Smith chose the moment to boom, "Come back, sir! Come back, I say!" The little head, black-topped below the sail, turned away, hunched down into the shoulders.

"He'll be all right," said Mordecai. "Good in a boat, Nick."

"Not when he's frightened out of his wits and he doesn't know where he's going. We'll get after him."

"And when you catch him you can tell him what I think about bringing spirits ashore," said Smith.

"I should think he already knows," I said, furious. "You must have better things to do than frightening children."

As I turned to follow Mordecai, Smith said, "I want to talk to you when you come back."

There were no punts tied up at the quay. Mordecai and I dragged a dinghy down the beach and took Jasper Bond's fishing-boat off its moorings, hauled up the lugsail and made chase. When we came under the head of the quay, Mordecai said, "Bugger to go, that dinghy." I followed his pointing finger. To the north, Nick's sail was a dirty white trapezium against the green lichens of Hangman's Island. Beyond, a lift of swell whitened the black glacis of Shipman's Head. "Wonder where he's off to?" mused Mordecai. "Ain't right to frighten the boy like that."

Jasper Bond's boat was old and heavy, very slow. Nick was gaining on us, running up to Hangman's Island as we cleared the Palace to starboard. A hard gust of wind stiffened our sail and heeled us over until our boom skimmed the water. Ahead the gust raced on, darkening the turquoise sea. Nick was close in under Hangman's Island. I saw him stand up, peer over the side for rocks. The shadow of the gust bore down. Mordecai said, "Sit

down, Nick boy," in a quiet voice. I glanced at his face.
It was set hard and tight and sober. Then I looked ahead.

The patch of dark water hit the face of Hangman's Island. Nick was looking over the starboard side, half-
standing, when the gust swerved across the granite face
and caught the back of his sail and gibed him all standing.
The boom, out to port at right angles to the boat's centre
line, swept across like a flail. I heard the crack as it hit
the base of Nick's skull. He went into the sea, smooth as
a seal off a rock. The boat slewed and capsized. I was
standing up, roaring without words, eyes searching the
blue water. He did not come up.

After the gust, the wind died. The heavy boat wallowed
through the water like a derelict. Mordecai, cursing under
his breath, got out the oars. Very slowly, we moved up-
channel.

Someone was talking in my head. Please wait, Nick.
Hold on. We're coming. We'll pick you up and dry you
down, and take you home and put you in a blanket in
front of the fire, and you can have tea with sugar in it and
then I'll read to you before you go to bed. And tomorrow
we'll go over to Beady Pool and look for beads . . . Hold
on. Five more minutes. Only five. A very little time.

The dinghy was drifting towards the blue open sea. The
reflection of Hangman's Island wavered on the glassy surface. A little puff of wind. The sail filled. Water gurgled
past the rudder. A drift of gulls rose screaming from the
rocks. No head broke the sea.

Please, Nick. Please hold on. Such a little time. I love
you. God, how I love you. Your mother loves you. We
mustn't lose you. We've lost too much already. You're all
we've got. You'll have a little brother. Or would you prefer a sister? One or the other. If you just hold on. . . .

Hangman's Island loomed high to port. I had my boots
and trousers off, pulled my jersey over my head. Mordecai
said, "Here. 'Twas here. He won't be with the boat."

The high rocks reeled about my head. I drew a long
breath that shuddered, tasting salt. In the shadow of the
boat's side, the bottom crawled twenty feet below, brown
weed and dark rock.

"There," said Mordecai.

Wavering in the slow bend of the ripple, a black cross,
the horizontals thin and crooked.

Air whooped into my lungs and I crashed through the

surface and into the fuzzy green sting of the water on my
eye-balls. Legs kicked. The cross grew, sprawled over the
brown tendrils on the bottom. It became a jersey, arms
and legs, black hair waving with the weed. My finger
closed on rough wool and I pulled up. Nick was light in
my arms, the same weight as the water. Above, the long
dark oval of the boat.

My head broke surface. "Take him."

Mordecai's hands reached down, lifted Nick up and in.
I put my foot in the loop of rope, climbed over the side,
gasping for breath. Mordecai had the little boy over his
shoulder, head down. The face was blue. Water ran from
the nose and the mouth.

We laid him on the bottom-boards and Mordecai began
rowing again. I tilted the head back, brushed the wet hair
from the small features. The long eyes were half open.
Only the whites showed. There was no pulse, no breathing. I cleared the air passages, began to blow air into the
lungs. His skin was cool to the touch.

We landed at the little cove under Cromwell's Castle. I
carried him out onto the beach and laid him in the sand
and knelt over him, breathing warm life into his lungs.
Someone brought blankets and chafed his limbs, and I
breathed on, the tears running from my eyes over the
blue-white face.

Come back. Don't go away. I'll hold you back. Try. Try
to breathe. The warm red muscle can throb and pump yet.
Not gone. Try, Nick. Try. Please.

The shadows on the sand under my eyes grew long and
black and covered the beach. The skin of his face was
cold, smooth and cold. But still I went on.

There was an angry red light across the sky. The murmur of the sea was far away. The knowledge bloomed like
an icy flower. My son Nicholas had sailed on the ebb tide
to join the legions of the dead.

I gathered the small husk of him in my arms and went
up over the rocks. His white cheek rested lightly against
my chest. He could have been asleep.

I was blind. The tears fell down my face, and I stumbled in a maze of uncaring rock. A hand took my elbow
and steered me. I did not care where I went. Nick was
gone. There was nothing left. The red ruin of the sun's
setting blazed in my eyes.

Someone said, "We'd best get you home."

There was whispering. Smooth grit under my feet. A gate opening. A door closing. Many voices, soft and hushed. The smell of steam. Lamplight glowing on the child's dead cheeks. Home.

I carried him up the stairs and laid him on his bed. The room was as he had left it, book open on the floor, the wooden soldiers I had carved for him drawn up in ambush behind his sea-chest. I folded his hands on his breast and knelt beside him and tried to pray. All I could find in my heart was bitterness. And after a while even that passed and I was cold and empty, empty as the white thing on the counterpane.

I heard the door open. Skirts brushed my shoulder. Silence, with the sound of harsh breathing. Then Aunt Woodcock's voice. "I beg your pardon, Doctor. But you'd better come and see to Mary."

I raised my head from my clasped hands. "Mary," I said shakily. "Where was she? Where is she?"

"She is in her bed," said Aunt Woodcock. "And her time is upon her. You'd better come."

I took a deep breath and struggled to my feet. Then I kissed Nick's forehead and left him in the light of the watch-candles.

Through the door of our room I heard a quick, violent gasping. "Does she know?"

"She saw it all," said Aunt Woodcock. "'Twas on the quay she started. Coming powerful fast."

"So much the better," I said harshly. "We'll have a look at her now."

Mary was lying on her back, long lashes shading the purple hollows under her eyes. I took her wrist. Pulse firm and steady, not too fast. The eyes opened. The whites were crossed with red veins. She had been crying, and her face looked young and naked, too young for all the pain. I said, "Do you want me to stay?"

She said, "Poor little Nick."

I nodded, swallowing the lump that rose in my throat. "Try to keep it for later," I said. "You've got this one to think about."

"I want to talk to you about . . . later. . . ." Her lip went between her teeth and her eyes hazed back as she felt the next pain coming. I sponged her forehead with cool water, watching her jaw tremble with the agony of it, trying to keep my mind with her, away from the candlelit room across the landing. When it was over she lay resting with her eyes closed. At last she said, "That was a bad one. Nick, there's something I had to tell you."

"Now you stay quiet," said Aunt Woodcock. "Don't you be troubling yourself."

The muscles in Mary's wrist tensed, and I pulled out my watch. When it was over I said, "Ninety seconds. When did you last examine?"

"Just before . . . you come in. Four fingers dilated." The Aunt's red face creased in an encouraging smile. "Soon be over." She went and threw another shovelful of coal on the fire. "Can't have the little mite taking cold, can we?"

Mary said, "Nick. You—" The pain came again.

After that, they came thick and fast. I stood by with my watch and the sponge, and between contractions Mary lay quiet, very pale, gathering herself for the next. She did not try to talk again.

Half an hour later, she was fully dilated, in transition. After that there was no talking. Only my soothing murmurs and the Aunt's grunts as she pressed down on the hipbones with her great red hands, and Mary's screams, finally, bursting through her clenched teeth and ringing round the ceiling. Then a head and two shoulders and a little body sliding out into the hot redlit room, and the herring-gull wail of the tiny frog-like creature with a mop of wet black hair hanging upside-down from the Aunt's hand, and her saying, "It's a boy. Well done the both of you. Fine big lad." But my thoughts were swimming down through twenty feet of stinging salt water, towards the spindly cross of a blue jersey on the waving brown weed. As Aunt Woodcock cleaned the child and wrapped him in a white shawl, I could only see the fiery sunset dazzling my misted eyes, a dead white cheek resting confidingly against my shoulder.

The Aunt carried the squalling bundle across to the bed, and gave it to Mary. She opened her nightgown and the little mouth gaped and began to suck. Her eyes were fixed on the crumpled face. There was nobody in the world but the two of them.

"Aren't you going to introduce yourself to the little one?" said the Aunt. "Go on, Doctor. 'E won't bite you."

I moved to the chair beside the bed. The Aunt clattered buckets and bowls and said, "I'll be downstairs if you want me." Her face grew grave. "I'll get the women in for the . . . for Master Nicholas."

I could not look at the new baby. I put my face in my hands and said, "Yes. Yes. Do that, if you would be so kind."

She paused with her hand on the latch. When she spoke, her voice had lost its professional briskness. "The Lord giveth and the Lord taketh away," she said. Then she went out. I looked at Mary.

"Well done," I said.

The tears were dropping onto her bared breast. "Yes," she said, choking. "But there is something I must tell you."

"Not yet. Not about Nick."

"It's not about Nick. Look at the child."

I looked. At first, with hope. Many things hung on that wrinkled apple crowned with ragged black hair. Whatever future I had, with Mary and with the other matters that pressed in from the hostile world outside this hot little room with its smell of blood and pain. Now Mary would be free again. The child would be with us, not between us. Perhaps one day he would fill the raw wound Nick had left. If I was still alive, unhung. But I could not convince myself. Grief weighed on my soul like lead, and I found I could only see that poor greedy scrap of humanity as an intruder. I wanted to be alone with Mary and our sorrow. God knew, there was little enough time.

The infant detached itself from Mary's nipple, drooling. She cooed at him. Then she held him up so I could see him full face and said, quietly, "Well?"

There is an old wives' tale about newborn babies that I have often found to be true. It is said that for the first hour of life, the child may bear a striking resemblance to one or other of its parents. The crumpled face had nothing of Mary in it. Perhaps it looked a little like me; I did not think so. The tumblers of a huge lock clashed and fell deep in my brain. The midget red face, with its creases, the tiny drooling mouth, the eyes taking their first contentment after the struggle of birth, reminded me of somebody. But it was not the face I saw in the shaving-mirror every morning. It was a face that liked to be watched from below, frowning out at the disorderly world like an emperor on a Roman coin. The face of Augustus Smith.

Mary put the baby to her breast again. When she was sure he was sucking properly, she said, "Yes."

I stared at her without speaking. It was as if I had been standing on a dry rock above a howling sea, and the rock had crumbled under my feet.

"It was while you were at sea. And since then. I love him, Nick."

"You love him?" I could not think about myself. The waves were beating me numb, too numb to swim. I was sinking. "How?"

She was looking down at the baby, her black hair falling across her pale cheeks. "It was the first time I saw him. He talked to me, and I knew. He was so . . . sharp. He moved through the people like a knife. He was lonely, too. I asked him to tea, and, . . ."

"He found he had a new toy." I got up. "Another one for his collection. Another little joke for himself." I went to the door. "Like the joke that killed Nick."

I slammed it behind me. There was the low sound of women's voices from Nick's room. I went downstairs, taking the steps four at a time. Now there was nothing between me and the darkness. No Nick. No Mary. I slammed the door behind me, and vaulted the gate. Mars hung in the sky, burning red into my brain.

Smith. Sharp Smith. Philanthropist Smith. I'll-play-you-fair-if-you-play-me-fair Smith. Actor Smith. Seducer Smith. Selfish, stubborn, pig-minded Smith.

Smith the killer.

His last words to me rang in my ears.

"I want a word with you when you get ashore."

He would have his word. And it was not only me he would talk to. He relied on me. He had information against me. I was a gentleman. Gentlemen didn't do the sort of thing I was going to do to Smith. But gentlemen didn't do what Smith had done to me. Or Nick. Or Mary.

I went to five houses. When I started back up the Abbey Road, there were ten men behind me, torches flaring under the stars. Our boots hammered the road, the hot beating echoing the fury that drove the blood blazing through my veins. I could feel the huge flat sea stretching into night all around the crumbs of granite on which we crawled like ants. The sea where the islands had floated like black jewels at the setting of the blood-red sun. And the serpent of fire crawled with deadly speed under the

winking stars, up to the crest of Abbey Hill and the dev-
astation of the hub of the Proprietor's realm. It swung
through the piles of stone and timber and into the courtyard. Tall windows of shaped granite with the torch-flame
dancing in the panes, the faces of the men who carried
them red demon-masks with black holes for eyes. I said,
"Wait here." Then I went in.

Smith was writing at a table in the window of the half-
finished drawingroom. The lamp threw a pool of light
over the papers before him. When he heard me he looked
up and said, "Is that you, Batchelor?"

I walked forward. The brows were furrowed with impatience, the right hand holding the steel pen poised over
his writing. When he saw me he wiped the pen and put it
in a silver tray and said, "Nicholls. What is the meaning
of this?"

"You wanted a word."

"Do you know what time it is?"

"I do." I waited. He searched my face with his eyes.
Some of the confidence went out of him.

He said, "About your son. I am desolated—"

"You are. Thank you for your condolences. My congratulations to you."

"What are you talking about?"

"You have a son. By Mary Prideaux. Your mistress.
The woman I loved."

His eyes softened for a moment. "Is she well?"

"As well as can be expected. As the midwife said, the
Lord giveth and the Lord taketh away. Admittedly, she
was referring to God, not to Smith who sits at his right
hand."

He stood up. "I understand your feelings, so I shall forget that remark."

"Then forget it quickly. You have very little time."

"Go home, Nicholls. I am becoming angry."

There was the sound of breaking glass from the hall.

Smith said, "What is this outrage? Damn and blast you,
I'll—"

A stone whizzed out of the darkness by the door. It
caught him on the temple and he clapped his hand to his
head and fell back onto the writing-table. The lamp went
over. Blazing oil spilled through the papers and dripped
to the floorboards.

Mordecai Ellis and Eddie Jenkins came out of the

shadows and took him one under each arm. His eyes were vague and glassy, the head rolling forwards over his collar. Mordecai said, "Appletree." Flames were swallowing the table, licking up the panelling to the unpainted ceiling.

"Put out that fire," I said. I wanted to be sure there would be no traces.

We walked down the rocks to the south, striking off across the flat grazing by the pool to the fringe of dunes above the beach. There was no haste now, no torches. When I looked back, the red glow in the Abbey windows had died. Smith was beginning to recover. He said, "Where are you taking me?"

Mordecai's voice said, "To the beach. Very pretty under the stars."

Silence. Only the thump of our boots on the turf. After a while Smith said, "Power."

"Are you addressing me?"

"It is your name, is it not?"

"Yes," I said. "It is. You have your evidence to hang me, if you like."

"If you like."

We were crossing the dunes now. I had come this same way with Mary once, on the night of the Jenkins kelping. Below us was the beach and a sea of dark iron and the far-off glow of Agnes light. The tide was two hours into the flood. We slid down the seaward face of the dunes, Smith stumbling. Eddie Jenkins lashed out with his boot. I said, "Enough of that."

We walked past the highwater mark, onto the firm sand the tide would cover in an hour. "Far enough," I said. John Sinclair dropped the bundle on his shoulder with a thump. The canvas of the big sail gleamed grey in the starlight.

"Augustus Smith," I said. "You came to these islands to change them into your plaything. You have used the inhabitants without regard for anything but your own convenience. You have perverted natural justice to your pleasure. You have debauched a woman of this island. By your officiousness you caused the death of my son. You have turned a haven of liberty into a prison of your own design. What have you to say for yourself?"

Smith looked at the sail spread on the sand, then at the sea lapping twenty yards down the beach. "Only that I expected better of you, Doctor Power." He walked to the middle of the sail. "Do I lie down here?"

He looked almost amused. His face was grey in the starlight, a trickle of blood black in front of the left ear.

"If you please."

He lay down and composed his hands on his breast. Two dark figures rolled him into a sausage of canvas and hammered the ends into the sand with long stakes. Then we went up the beach. There was no talking. I could feel the wires of tension along the frieze of watchers. I said, "There's no need to stay. I'll do what's necessary. Thank you for your help."

Mordecai said heavily, "We came of our own free will. If it wasn't for you we'd have done it long ago."

One by one they melted away into the dark.

I sat down to watch. Wavelets broke with a puny roar on the sand. Already the sea was creeping up on the long bundle of canvas. Once, I saw it bulge. Then it lay still again, almost as if he had found his position uncomfortable and had rolled to shift his weight. He was a brave man. I pushed the thought aside. The night was warm, the sigh of the wind in the bent-grasses lulling. I thought of Mary and Smith's baby, Nick cold on his bed with the old women muttering over him. Of the stone walls, the evictions, the sundered families. My anger flared again. It was fitting. He had earned it three times over, from me. Let alone the islanders. A life for a life. God knew how many lives he had ruined.

The waves lapped to within three yards of the bundle. He must be able to hear them now, in his dark, mildewy shroud. He would know he was finished.

Still the bundle did not move.

I heard a sound behind me, a faint rustle above the sigh of the wind. I looked round, heart hammering. It was a woman in a hooded cloak. As I watched her, frozen, she swayed. I caught her as she fell, laid her on the sand. I said, "Mary."

Her voice sounded very far away. "I came to watch. I had to be here."

"You've no business. You should be in bed."

She laughed, brittle and harsh. "I had to come."

"Why don't you save him?"

She shrugged her shoulders. "If he is meant to die, he will die. I may not like it, but I can't stop it."

"You love him."

"And others hate him."

"So Scilly's will be done."

"Quite so."

I got up. "Then damn Scilly," I said.

When I reached Smith, the first wave had wetted the canvas. I heaved at the first peg. It was hammered deep and hard. I pulled it from side to side. As I felt the first hint of its loosening, a wave came over my feet, splashing up from the body in the canvas. I pulled again. Again the peg gave, but I could feel the suction keeping it back. Another wave. No sound from Smith. Again I pulled. This time the peg came out clean. I dragged the end of the bundle round until it was facing up the beach. By the time I finished the second peg the water was up to my knees. I pulled the canvas up out of the way of the waves. Then I began to unroll it.

Smith stood up and said, "My feet are wet," in a voice full of wonder. Then he seemed to recollect himself. "I suppose I should thank you, Doctor Power. Or was the idea only to put a scare into me?"

"The idea was to kill you," I said.

He looked at me for a long time. Then he said, "We had better go back to the Abbey and talk about it."

"I have nothing to say to you," I said. "But Mary Prideaux is above in the dunes. She should be got to shelter."

"Then she can use my bed." He gave a short laugh. "I suppose it is only appropriate."

"I suggest you keep your jokes to yourself." I walked up the beach. He paused a moment, bundling up the sail.

"I think I shall claim this as salvage," he said.

I was beginning to wonder whether it would have been possible to drown this man. He had the hide of a hippopotamus. Perhaps he had the lungs as well.

I carried Mary back to the Abbey. She was white and faint, and I could feel wet blood on her dress. She was very agitated, too, laughing and weeping by turns. I looked her over, changed her dressing and put her to bed.

From the door, Smith said, "There are some explanations due, I think."

I shook my head. "No explanations." I started for the door.

He barred my way. "One moment." He pointed across

the room to a glass-fronted cabinet. "Take a gun. You will find powder and shot in the drawer. Load it."

I opened the cabinet, took down a fowling-piece. Then I said, "Why?"

"Tonight you set out to murder me, and you changed your mind. I want you to hear what I have to say to you. Then if you still want to kill me, you can. I should not like to think of you as having been defeated by . . . flexibility of purpose."

I poured in powder, rammed the wad, shot, and another wad. Then I primed the pan.

"Good," he said. "Now, please sit down."

I sat.

I was reaching the point where nothing was real anymore. Not Nick, not the baby, not Mary in bed next door. And certainly not the man sitting in a deep chair with a glass of brandy in his hand, the blood washed away from the graze in his forehead, as urbane as if he was in his London club. The man I had watched cold-bloodedly as the tide crept up the beach not half an hour ago.

He crossed his rather plump legs, took a sip of his drink, and fixed his cold grey eyes on the join of the wall and ceiling. "Well, Power," he said. "I think I shall have to tell you a story."

XIV

"I TOLD YOU that over the winter months I spent some time with friends in Ireland." Smith began. "By making the appropriate leading remarks, I heard of a fashionable Dublin doctor answering your description who had disappeared in suspicious circumstances. The stories circulating about him were most unpleasant. But I was told that he had paid the penalty for his supposed crimes, the ship on which he was discovered to have sailed having been lost between Kingstown and the Cove, supposedly with all hands, position unknown. On pursuing my inquiries based on certain facts of which I had apprised myself at Scilly, I deduced that this was not the case. You will have concluded as much already."

"I have."

"I could have acted on that evidence. I decided, however, that I would continue my inquiries. I like to follow such matters through to their conclusions. The gossip I heard dwelt rather on the sensational aspects of the case. So I did a little more research. This led me to a hypothesis based on the fact that the evidence against you was more circumstantial than conclusive without the testimony of another person, a lawyer by the name of Michael Fitzpatrick." He sipped his brandy. "I see you are with me in this.

"I therefore visited Mr. Fitzpatrick in Dublin. I once considered purchasing an estate in the West of Ireland, and had conincidentally made some inquiries in this respect with Mr. Fitzpatrick's partners, before he joined the firm." He frowned. "I should not, I think, care to deal with them now. I did not form a very high opinion of that gentleman. But I flatter myself I made a strong impression upon him.

"I then let slip that I had taken on Scilly. He accepted the news calmly enough, but I rather think it shook him. At that point we were close to the termination of our interview, he having some appointment that would take him out of town. But quite suddenly he cancelled his appointment and asked me to dine with him. And a capital dinner it was. Unfortunately, I did not enjoy it as I should have. He was trying to make me drunk. I may say that he did not succeed, though that was not his belief at the time. He flattered me abysmally, pried into my personal affairs, and finally, when he thought my defences were drowned in his excellent port, began to pump me. He had noticed my interest in your case, he said. He had known you well, once. He thought it was as well you had died, rather than face the consequences of your crime. I asked him why; he, cool as you please, gave me his version of your life history. It was not a pretty picture.

"As you know, I like to make two and two equal to four. I was beginning to believe that you might after all be nothing but a turbulent rogue. But so black was the portrait Fitzpatrick gave, so complete the reversal of the friendship he claimed with you, that I began to think he did protest too much. I had heard no very good account of you previously; but there was a consensus that, however reprehensible the consequences of your actions, the motives were usually worthy. A conclusion which my experience of you has reinforced, I may say. So I began to ask myself why this man Fitzpatrick could not use you more kindly. And none of the answers satisfied me.

"I then told him that I had met you at Scilly and that I found you a malcontent and a troublemaker, and I wanted to get rid of you. That holds good, still. I asked him if he thought I had grounds to put you in irons and send you back to Ireland. At this, he went exceedingly pale. And then he damned himself. He said that he thought it best that I did no such thing. You had blackened the name of a great family: it would only reopen old wounds; he had known you were alive, he frankly confessed, but he was the only man who did. Out of regard for this great family he had held his peace, provided only that you stayed away. I demurred, on the grounds of danger to the public if you remained at liberty. He then suggested, in view of certain remarks of mine, that I have you tried and transported for some non-capital offence, next time you showed your face in my islands. He seemed under the impression that I could make and break the law as I pleased." Smith glared at me from under black brows. I kept my mouth shut. "I did not disabuse him of this notion. In fact, I believe I gave him ground to think I would do as he had suggested. It is one of the advantages of being descended from a Nottingham mercer, that there is a large section of the fashionable world ready to believe one will do almost anything to spare the aristocracy pain. Except appropriate a coat of arms and try to pass oneself off as one of its members, like my cousins, the Carringtons.

"Upon this, Mr. Fitzpatrick looked most relieved and assured me that I was doing the Irish nobility signal service, and I took my leave. I confess I was not sorry to go. Next day I made further inquiries. I had heard that Mr. Fitzpatrick had taken into his hands the running of the estates of a certain Earl. I thought it would be interesting to find out this Earl's opinion of you, in view of your con-

nections with him. I therefore went down to Carthystown
—you are familiar with the place?"

"I am," I said. "Continue, if you please."

"There is not much more to say. When I reached
Carthystown, a domestic informed me that the Earl was a
sick man with an infirmity of mind as well as body. Under
no circumstances did he receive any visitors but his legal
advisers and his chaplain. I tried to reason with the fellow,
but he was adamant, and finished by slamming the door
in my face. I set off for Dublin, wondering how next to
proceed in view of the fact that urgent business made it
necessary for me to return to England forthwith. As we
drove through the park—sadly run down, I fear—I had
the good fortune to meet the Earl's chaplain, and fell into
conversation with him. He was a sorry fellow, I think
drunk. We parted friends, however; and as soon as I was
in England, I wrote to him inquiring in a veiled manner
about the Earl's state of mind. I regret that he may have
been under the impression that a better post awaited him
with a rich and elderly relation of mine, and that my inquiries about His Lordship were effected with a view to
comparison with the foibles of my supposed Aunt. I received his reply by the mail today." He paused, frowning. "It was among the papers burned by your folly. Your
inexcusable folly. I shall give you a digest, however.

"The Earl, he says, is a man devastated by consumption. His end is anticipated in short order. He spends his
days and nights in the castle solar, apparently brooding
over the loss of his daughter and another person. His affairs are entirely in the hands of one Michael Fitzpatrick.
I rather gathered from the letter that Mr. Fitzpatrick had
drawn up a will for the Earl in his own favour, thereby
disappointing the Chaplain's expectations. The Earl is
now Fitzpatrick's creature. He is deeply melancholic, and
has allowed his estates to go to ruin about his head. One
can only suppose that Fitzpatrick, in his anxiety to have
the Earl to himself, has dispensed with any other advisers
who might interfere with his purpose. But that is by the
by. The part of the Chaplain's letter that interested me
more than Fitzpatrick's grubby machinations is that in
which he speaks of the loss the Earl sustained. One can
understand his grief over an only daughter, the last of his
ancient line. But why should he so mourn the Dublin doc-

tor who was by all accounts responsible for her untimely death?"

There was a terrible silence in the room.

I blew the priming from the pan of the fowling-piece, rose, and put it back in the rack. Then I said, "I think I shall take some brandy."

Soon after my dinner with Michael, I went to see Katie. I had heard that she was living pretty hard, but that did not prepare me. Her butler was drunk, the footmen had made off with the silver, and there were two of the young gentlemen from the garrison asleep on the stairs. I kicked the officers out of the house, engaged new servants, and set to work on Katie. She had been drinking a lot and eating not at all. She should have gone out of Dublin, but she said she would only go if I accompanied her, and I had not yet got enough of my patients back to be able to leave. She did not mention Drumcarty; and as she improved, we became good friends once more. There were times, since Drumcarty, when I wished we could be more than that, and in retrospect she must have wished it too. But I kept the Earl's charge.

We passed a happy summer. When I could get away from my patients we went to the theatre or walked in the Park or rode in the Wicklow Mountains. She seemed to trust me as she trusted no-one else; and I trusted her in return. I should have known better.

Katie called on me one evening in October and told me that she had to go to spend a few days with Lord Ballysaggart at his house near Malahide.

"God they're so tedious," she said. "Would you come with me, Nick?"

"But I haven't been invited."

"Oh, they won't mind. You can be my personal physician. Do come. I must have someone I can talk to."

The green eyes had the old devil in them. I knew I would have to go, or there would be trouble. So I cancelled my appointments, packed a valise, and off we went with our respective servants.

The Ballysaggarts had four stout daughters, all of whom had been my patients, none of them married despite *their* mother's untiring efforts. As soon as we arrived, I realised that this must be one of these efforts, and they would have invited Katie in the hope that her wildness would show off the daughters' solid manners and orthodoxy to good advantage. Certainly the house-party was well seasoned with marriageable young men of suitable wealth and breeding.

Katie did not disappoint. The candlelight flashed in the wild green eyes. She stayed sober, but teased the gentlemen half out of their minds and ignored the daughters. The Ballysaggarts were staunch Orangemen, so Katie naturally crowed over the Clare election in July, where O'Connell, the founder of the Catholic Association and the Orangemen's arch-demon, had beaten the candidate approved by the county gentry. At first she was treated with tolerant amusement, but by the evening of the second day she had got well under their Protestant skins and the house-party was not so much a social gathering as a hostile mob. I suppose it was my fault, to a certain extent, for not restraining her before it was too late. But I did not like the Ballysaggarts and their friends, and when she sensed my approval there was no holding her.

There was to be a ball on the evening of the second day. Before it we dined thirty-two round the table. I was sent to a sort of conversational Connacht between a couple of maiden ladies far down the table from Katie, who had been set to frighten a couple of Ballysaggart suitors. As I chattered mechanically to my elderly partners, I could hear Katie's scornful laugh and the awkward silences that followed it. So far, the evening was not being a success.

When the ladies left the gentlemen to their port, there was the usual conversation about corn and rents and fish-eating Catholics. I managed to excuse myself before the inevitable toasts to King William and No Popery. The footman at the drawingroom door told me there was a lady sick upstairs. As I climbed, I reflected that baiting the Ballysaggarts was one thing; open warfare was quite another and that was the way Katie was heading.

To arrive at my room I had to pass Katie's door. It was half-open, with a dim glow of candlelight reflected in the dark wood of the jamb. "God damn them all," said Katie's voice. It sounded as if she had a pebble in her mouth. I hesitated a moment. But the voice was too strange to ignore. I went in.

She was sprawled on the bed, the white satin train of her gown flowing like a waterfall to the carpet. The diamonds in her hair flung split light across the wallpaper.

"Come in," she said in that same blurred voice. "Come in and sit down, old Nicko." Her white hand reached for the bedside table, poured from a decanter into a glass. She drank. The decanter was nearly empty. The room was full of the smell of brandy. I sat down and took her long, pale fingers. She pulled her hand away.

"Don't use your quack's tricks on me, Nick Power," she said. "The draught as prescribed. Nothing to worry about. Fill you with hope. Be right as rain, by the time you die."

"Come along, Katie," I said. I had got used to this kind of performance. "You must compose yourself. The guests will be arriving soon. And there is a lady sick."

"That's me," she said. "Oh, the guests! Lord and Lady Linendraper and all the other Linendrapers, of Castle Rackrent, County Squeezem."

"Drink some water. I'll ring for your maid."

"You will not," she said. "Water and maids. Gruel. Slop. I want filling up with red meat and hope. Not this wet muck." She laughed, harshly. "Get the carriage, Nick. I can't stand it. I can't do any more of this." She buried her face in the pillow.

Twenty minutes later I led her down the stairs in her travelling-cloak. She leaned heavily on my arm. The hall was blazing with candles and full of Dublin notables. From the ballroom came the sound of an orchestra sawing through a quadrille, and under the drawingroom arch Lord and Lady Ballysaggart were receiving their guests. I heard Lady Ballysaggart say, "How *simply lovely.*" Then her eyes caught Katie, and went quite round.

"I fear Lady Katherine is indisposed," I said. Lady Ballysaggart took in the cloaked figure leaning at my shoulder, and sniffed. She could not have failed to smell the brandy.

"Oh my *dear,*" she said with a bright, false smile. "Oh I am *so* sorry."

"I'm not," mumbled Katie, apparently to herself. "Damned prosy old bitch. Of all the tedious—"

"A minor indisposition," I said loudly, feeling the eyes of the reception line homing like pigeons. Lady Ballysaggart was clutching at her husband's arm for support. "The coldness of the season—the change of air. . . ." I began edging Katie towards the door, trying to bow without dropping her on the Carrara marble tiles.

"Hideous!" yelled Katie. "Bloodsucking hideous old fools! O'Connell would eat the lot of you."

I dragged her out into the rain, away from the shocked O of Lady Ballysaggart's mouth and into the carriage, and shouted, "Drive, damn you!" at the coachman, muffling Katie's mouth with the collar of her cloak. We started with a lurch. The lights of the house faded behind, and we rattled into the safe blanket of the night.

"Phew," said Katie. "Thank God for that."

I felt my mouth fall open. "My God," I said. "You—you—"

"Oh, monstrous, wasn't it," she said. "Still, desperate straits, desperate measures. Cuddle up and let's get warm." She wriggled across the seat. "Calm down, Nick. You're stiff as a board. You did very well, I thought."

I began to laugh. I could not stop myself, and Katie laughed too, until the carriage swayed and the coachman yelled at his horses and the tears ran down my face. All the pompous hypochondriacs who trooped through my consulting-rooms, all the God-fearing rackrenters, all the idiot eldest sons were in that last horrified O of Lady Ballysaggart's mouth. I was still laughing as her arms went about me, her fingers in the hair at my nape, and in the dark I knew her face was very close to mine. She kissed me, and I could feel the warm push of her breasts and she lifted her hips and her skirts came up, and I was gone. Her fingers fought with the buttons of my breeches and the carriage lamps shone cool on her white thighs above the stockings, and then the warmth of her and she moaning in my ear, and the carriage jounced and bumped and the matched black horses galloped on with a rattle and a roar down the black tunnel of the night.

When it was over she rubbed her cheek against my shirt front and said, "Oh. Oh, Nick, darling. You're good at that."

I said, "You seduced me."

I saw her smile flash in the dark of the cushions. "I always get what I want," she said. "That was clever, wasn't it?"

"Very." The laughter had gone. In its place there was something like shame.

It must have come through into my voice. She said, "Do you regret it?"

I could not answer.

I slept in my own bed that night, alone. When I went to call on her the next day, the butler said she was not at home. It was the same every day for the next week, and the week after that. And the word was going round Dublin that she was back in her old courses.

Smith said, "I should very much like to hear your side of the story."

I told him. It took a long time, and when it was over I was exhausted. I said, "Well? Do you believe that? Not very likely, is it?"

He was looking into the depths of his brandy-glass, lips pursed. "Likely enough," he said. He looked like a man who had lit the fuse of a bomb which may or may not explode.

I said, "Why did you do all this?"

"Two reasons. First, I want you off the island. Second, I don't like lawyers' tricks."

"I tried to kill you tonight." Still I did not trust him. He could be trying to deliver me to the Dublin hangman. "Why do you not give me in charge? You could easily have me hanged or transported. That would suit your book."

"It would," he said. "But I can see disadvantages. As an Irishman, you should be aware of the folly of making martyrs. I have a pretty good idea who your accomplices were in tonight's idiocy. With guidance, they could be good men. If I let you stay, they would have a leader. If I handed you over to the justice you richly deserve, they would have a martyr."

"So it's Ireland or nothing."

He leaned forward in his chair. "Now listen to me, Power. I have told you before that you have great possibilities. Despite your idiotic behaviour I am still sure. There is nothing for you here."

"Not since you killed my son and debauched the woman I loved."

A look of pain crossed his face. "I am very sorry about the boy. I would not have had it happen . . . I shall never cease to reproach myself with it. You have my sincere sympathy. More than that I cannot say."

"And Mary Prideaux? You expect me to leave her here as your plaything?"

"I think you would be happier if she stayed. It is up to her whether or not she remains my . . . plaything."

I leaped to my feet. "It seems to me that you consider you have a monopoly of insight into the happiness of others."

"Very well," said Smith. "Shall we ask her?"

"I heard," said Mary. She was clinging to the door post. Her face was the colour of paper. "You know what I want, Nick. I'll never leave. And you can't stay." I caught her as she slumped to the ground.

"Harness your cart," I said to Smith. "I'm taking her home."

We walked down the Abbey Road. Mary was wrapped in blankets. It was exhaustion that had laid her low, not loss of blood. The exhaustion was just as dangerous, though. It would lower her resistance. Puerperal fever was a terrible scourge in the islands.

Smith had come with us. He began talking again. I wanted to tell him to shut his mouth, but I was too tired for that.

"You were saying that I considered I had a monopoly over the happiness of others. All I can say is that you are misled. As you have seen, I like to pursue my objects to the uttermost end. It will be so with Scilly. In your efforts for the good of the place—and I respect your intentions, if not the results—you have treated the symptoms and ignored the causes. I intend to proceed differently. You accuse me of treating the islands as a toy. Nothing could be further from the truth. It is only that there is good and evil here as everywhere else. I intend to weight that evil and sink it without trace. To do so, I must live here. I will not be an absentee. But I must live in a style which will make people respect me, and behave accordingly. I do not enjoy moving old women out of their homes. I would rather be admired than feared. But I will not sacrifice the principles on which I intend to base my administration in order to curry favour with those who will take advantage of me as soon as I turn my back. The greatest good of the greatest number, Doctor Power. It is not a maxim that admits of sentiment. But it is a splendid cure for sentimentality."

"You would drive out terror with terror," I said.

"If you want to see it like that. I should like to hear your views in a year's time."

"If I am alive in a year's time."

"I have a feeling that you will be. But there is always a chance, of course." He pulled up the horse. We carried Mary into the house. Aunt Woodcock was dozing by the fire. She woke and curtsied to Smith, and me as an afterthought. Then she followed us upstairs.

We put Mary to bed, and I told the Aunt to give her a draught of port wine and catechu, the wine to renew the blood and the catechu as an astringent for the vessels in the uterus. Smith stood looking down at her circled eyes and the white face with the lashes impossibly black and long. Then he bent over the wicker crib in the corner. I remembered the embroidery on the frame. I knew my eyes would be as lost as Mary had painted them. I turned and left the room.

Nick was lying on his bed. They had dressed him in a white nightgown, brushed his unruly black hair flat. Already he looked older, farther away. The candles were paling with the light coming through the window.

I heard a noise in the doorway. It was Smith. I turned away to hide my tears. He said, "A final word. Outside."

I followed him down the stairs. I said, "Make it quick, if you please. I would like to be with my son."

"You will leave after the funeral. I hope one day we shall perhaps meet again, in happier times." He frowned. Then he put out his hand. "Goodbye, Power. You may be interested to know that you are the only person on Scilly who has given me cause to think." I looked at his hand for what seemed like a long time. Then I grasped it and shook.

"You will please think about Mary, from now on," I said. He nodded and turned away, head bowed. I went into the house to watch over my son.

I left Scilly four days later, in the early afternoon. That morning I had heard the clods rattle on the lid of Nick's coffin; afterwards I had made my farewells and gone aboard the *Shearwater*, which was to take me to Waterford. I had dreaded the farewells; I had not needed to. Already I was passing out of the people's consciousness. True, they had been warm enough, and some of the women had cried. But they were tears at the passing of a chance visitor. I had watched them mourn the departure of islanders evicted by Smith. That was different; deeper, with real pain; a mourning for a friend who might never return, not sorrow over parting with an agreeable companion. My accomplices of four days ago avoided me. They had made their bargains with Smith. I had had my chance with the fowling-piece, and I had let it pass. It was no place of mine to interfere.

I stood by the boom watching the shore slide by. There were men working in the poor fields running down to the rocks and the rippled blue water. Then there was Cromwell's Castle, its sullen granite cylinder a miniature of Drumcarty keep, and after that Castle Down, purple with flowering heather, running up to the crags of Gimble Point. On the rough crags crowning the point there stood the figure of a woman, the wind plucking at her long cloak, pulling her black hair out in a banner that caught blue glints from the sun. In her arms she held a bundle muffled in shawls. *Shearwater*'s mainsail filled with the west wind from Hell Bay. I stood motionless, watching. She raised a hand, let it fall. I waved back. The wind lulled, and I heard the child's thin yell coming across the water. She did not look at me again, but pulled hr cloak aside and began to feed the child. That was my last sight of her, eyes bent to look at Smith's infant, adoring as the Madonna with the infant Christ.

Two days later, I landed at the Customs Quay in Waterford.

I took a room and ordered a chaise. While I was waiting I shaved and changed out of my seaman's gear into white cravat, black coat and trousers and polished black boots. The clothes had been made by my Charlotte tailor. They had a hungry American look to them. I studied myself in the cheval-glass. I was not the Power who had left Kingstown seven years ago. I looked wide and solid, the gold watch-chain gleaming across a broad expanse of waistcoat still not convex. The hair was long and black, pepper-and-salt at the temples. The face was sad, the eyes long above the lines where the pouches would soon form. It was brown and lean. There was none of the fat of easy living that had given me my supposed look of Napoleon Bonaparte. The cheeks ran hollow to the jawline, eroded by suffering. Sad as it was, there was no weakness in it. And whatever the uncertainty hidden beneath the grey kerseymere of the waistcoat, no trace of it showed in the face.

The boots' knock came on the door. I picked up my hat and went down to the waiting chaise.

It was raining as the horses clattered over the bridge and up the hill. Trees and cottages loomed out of the soft drizzle as if in a Chinese painting. As we crossed the hills the mists thickened, and I gave myself over to my preparations. They had been extensive. I was conscious of a slight quickening of the pulse, a nervous difficulty in controlling my hands. If Smith was right, and I had to believe he was, Michael Fitzpatrick had systematically concealed my existence from the Earl for seven years, in pursuit of his own ends. Seen in the proper light, that was evidence enough of Michael's duplicity. But it left unresolved the question of my guilt or innocence in the matter of Katie. It would be my word against Michael's; and I had few illusions about the sort of hold that Michael might come to exert on an ailing melancholic over such a span of time. He had deceived me for long enough, in all conscience.

My entire future depended upon my getting redress. There was nothing to fall back on. True, that had been the case before; but then there had always been the sense that I might be in the wrong. Now, I knew I was in the right. And if I could not convince from a position of strength, then I deserved whatever might befall. This time there were no sentimental attachments, no over-dramatic gestures. It would be quick and clean and precise, or I would perish.

We rumbled and jingled across the river and through New Ross. Then we were on the last lap. The clouds were thinning and a gleam of sun lay across the fields. As the grey mists rolled off the sky I caught a glimpse of the rearing green summit of Barrow Hill. Many was the day I had spent riding to hounds on its shoulders. I took it as a good omen.

A quarter of an hour later, we were driving past the Drumcarty demesne wall. I knocked on the shutter and told the coachman to stop. Then I climbed down into the mud of the road and said, "That's as far as we go. Thank you."

The coachman looked puzzled. "Will you not be going back?"

I shook my head. It was not a question I wanted to answer, even to myself. He cursed his horses round, and away they clattered, the carriage swaying on the potholed surface. When it was out of sight I walked down the road to the first hole in the wall. I took a deep breath. Then I stepped into the park.

The woods were a tangle of briers and wet ivy, the paths of my childhood long overgrown. When I reached the drive I struck off to the right. There were the marks of carriages in the mud and grass that covered the hardcore. Company at the Castle. The woods were overgrown, the fields rank with weeds. Above the trees the empty eyes of the Lady Tower wept jackdaws. I turned down the last hill to the river. The roof of the Steward's House showed rafters like ribs through holes in the tiles. And beyond, the grey curtain wall sweeping down to the muddy waters of the river, the keep a jagged-topped drum of stone towering above the steep roofs of the Jacobean part of the castle.

Drumcarty.

"Here's to tomorrow," said Michael.

"Tomorrow," said I, and gulped back the whisky. "Fifteen miles straight across country, and devil take the tailer."

We were at the end of a little supper, Michael and I. Christmas was nearly upon us again, and the jollities were moving into full swing. Hounds were meeting at Naas the following morning with a hunt breakfast and all the trimmings, and Michael and I had resolved to approach the day well primed. There was to be no Drumcarty this Christmas or any other. Even if Katie had wanted me there, I could not have faced it. I had not seen her for three months. I had not seen anybody much for three months, except Michael. Seeing people got between me and my drinking.

I reached for the half-gallon bottle, mixed and stirred. "Here's to us," I said.

"Us," said Michael, and knocked it back. "And goodnight. I'll have the hacks round at four. Wish you the best two hours' sleep you ever had."

"And you," I said, weaving after him to the door. When he had gone I sat down and mixed myself a final glass. But I fell asleep in my chair before I could drink it.

It seemed only a minute later that the slow hammering came. I clambered to my feet, my head splitting, and lit a candle. I had told the servants not to trouble themselves with the first knock.

I fumbled with the latch. The door began to open. I said, "Jasus, Michael, I think I'm dying, come in—"

It was not Michael. It was a woman, tall and slender, bonnetless, grey and haggard of face. "Katie," I said. "What—"

She took one staggering step and fell at my feet.

I went down on my knees at her side. Her face and hands were cold. The pulse was thready, barely perceptible, her breathing shallow. I picked her up and took her into the consulting-room, laid her on the couch. As I lifted her, a great mass of cloth fell to the floor. With shaking hands I lit the oil-lamp under the reflector. The cloth shone bright red with new blood. I took a huge breath to steady myself. Then, with fingers still numbed with sleep and alcohol, I examined her. It was as if a stranger was doing the work. My mind blundered in the fogs of my awakening as the blood ran out of her in a stream, and I groped for the useless pressure-point, tore linen to stauch the remorseless flow.

Until a very short time ago, Katie had been pregnant. Someone—some butcher—had tried a curettage. They had slashed her to ribbons, and she had gone out into the street. That she had got this far was a miracle. Now she needed another.

Her eyes fluttered open, blinked at the glare of the lamp. "Nick," she said. "I was going to have a baby. Oh, you do look worried." She gave me a weak, grey smile. I tore up more linen. "Could you light a fire?"

"Not yet. You be quiet. We'll have you right in a trice."

"Oh, you are worried," she whispered. "You needn't be. It wasn't yours." A long pause. Only her shallow breathing, the new drip of blood from the saturated linen. "I wish it had been. I missed you."

Five minutes later, she died.

I sat looking at her. The pale lips held the old smile, proud and mocking. All around me I could feel the familiar pictures and furniture of the consulting-room, the silent small-hours street beyond the red velvet curtains. Oh, Katie. You a stranger in the midst of it. A stranger in the world, too wild, too proud. And now taken out of it by a sordid back-street butcher. Poor, poor Katie.

Hoofbeats rang on the pavement in front of the house.

I got up, slowly, walked across the hall and opened up.
Michael was big and breezy in a heavy riding-coat.
"Grand morning for it," he said. "You'd best be getting
yourself ready—what's that?" He was staring at my
hands. I looked down. It was as if I were wearing crimson
gauntlets. "Have you got a patient in there?"

I began to shake uncontrollably, leaning against the
doorpost to stop myself falling. "You'd better come in," I
said. "Have you brought the groom?"

"He's coming on later." He hitched the hacks to the
rail. "What's the matter, man?" His eyes travelled to my
bloody footprints across the white tile of the hall. "Nick.
What have you been doing?"

I showed him.

He looked at the face. "Oh my God," he said. "Sweet
Jesus. It's Katie. Katie Drumcarty." He swung round on
me. "You bloody idiot. Haven't you enough sense to—"

"She came to me. Like that. I tried . . . she was too far
gone."

Michael was very pale, but the shock was fading from
his eyes. They were turned inward, calculating. "She
didn't say who . . . operated on her?"

"No."

"You're sure you didn't do it?"

"Would I?" I sat down and held my throbbing head in
my hands.

"Was it your child?"

"She said not."

"But you were known to be pretty thick with her.
Christ, Nick. Oh, Christ."

"I'll find out who did it. I'll see them hang—"

"Nick. You're the one that'll hang. The way it looks."
He paced up and down, worrying his fleshly chin between
thumb and forefinger. Finally, he stopped and said, "Wait.
Unless you go away. Now."

I was beyond thinking. "Go away?" There were slow
footsteps high in the house. The butler.

"There's a fellow I saw today. Emigrant ship. He's sailing from Kingstown to pick up a load from the Cove.
Then to America."

"America?" I said stupidly.

"I'll do what I can here. But it'll take time. And when
Drumcarty hears about this he'll—well, you know what
he'll do."

"He wouldn't believe. He couldn't—"

"He could. He would. Nick, time's running out. Trust me."

"But if I run it's as good as admitting it." The footsteps were tramping down the stairs, very slow.

"And if you don't you'll hang. The mob'd get you if Drumcarty didn't. Now get your bloody boots on." I took one last look at Katie. Michael shook me by the hand and said, "Good luck, boy." He held the hack for me as I swung into the saddle. Then I pounded away down the Kingstown road.

When the emigrant ship *Castletown* sailed at dawn, I was on her, watching the mountains slip away. Thick black cloud was pouring down from the north, and the wind was rising.

As I walked across the bridge in the new wheel-ruts, the westering sun glowed scarlet on the stained-glass of the solar window. Then the gatehouse cut it from my view.

The wheel-ruts ran through the clumps of dandelion and elder sprouting from the paving and under the sound of raucous male laughter. The nailed oak doors in the base of the keep were closed. I tried the heavy iron handle. Locked. I hesitated a moment, grasped the bell-pull. I heard it ring, far away. I waited. Slow, shuffling feet dragged across the flags inside. There was a little hatch in the door at about head height. I did not remember having seen it before. It slid back, and an old, rheumy eye peered out. An eye I knew.

"Good day to you, Kelly," I said. "Is His Lordship inside in the house?"

The eye blinked. "He don't see nobody."

"Is it you don't remember me?" I said. "Not Nick Power?"

The ancient pupil dilated sharply. "Master Nicholas. By Jesus is it yourself?"

"It is. Now would you open?"

There was a silence. Again the distant raucous laughter. Jackdaws quarrelling in the holes and crevices above. The door swung open slowly.

"By God it is," said Kelly. "Sure and it's a fine thing to see you after all these years." His old white head looked nervously over his crooked shoulder.

"Is His Lordship above?" I said.

"He is, poor man," said Kelly, dragging me across the flags. "They said you was dead." His withered fingers squeezed my arm, as if he was reassuring himself that I was no ghost.

"So I heard." I walked across to the stone staircase curving in a spiral up the cylindrical walls. "Don't tell Michael Fitzpatrick I'm here."

"I wouldn't." Relief broke his cheeks into a broad grin. "He'll have heard nothing. Him and the others is at their dinner. They won't be out till morning."

"We'll see about that," I said.

The stairs were as I remembered them, treads worn by the feet of ages. The threadbare hangings that clothed the naked stone rippled in the wind of my passing. I went through the muniments room, pile upon pile of papers and ledgers in a compost of spider web and dust. I paused in front of the door of the solar. From within, there came a long bubbling cough. Very gently, I lifted the latch.

The room was flooded with sunlight from the huge Gothic window, lying in brilliant splashes of aquamarine and crimson and amethyst across the worn Turkey carpets that clothed the floor. Round the walls marched faded horses and huntsmen, tiercels on gauntlets, endlessly pursuing their stately prey. A great fire of logs blazed in the open hearth. It was stiflingly hot with a smell of sickness and age-old dirt.

He had heard me come in. He was sitting with his back to me at the desk on the dais before the great south-facing window. The towers of paper before him teetered higher than his naked scalp. He coughed again, thin shoulders heaving under the red brocade dressing-gown. When it was over, he spat into a handkerchief, laboriously, as if even spitting was too much trouble. Then he turned his head to look at the two portraits that hung in the window-niche, one on either side, invisible against the sun's dazzle.

I said, "My Lord?"

Very slowly, he turned. I could not see his face against the glare from the huge window, but I saw his cheekbones silhouetted against the light. There was no flesh, nothing but the bones. He said in a voice not much more than a whisper, "What do you want?"

I stepped closer. "To make my peace with you."

He unhooked a stick from the back of his chair, pulled

himself to his feet, and struggled with tiny steps down from the dais.

"There are a lot of people who want to do that," he whispered peevishly. "Who are you? I can't see you."

"Nicholas Power," I said.

He was shuffling past me as I spoke. He stopped dead in his tracks, standing on the tripod of his two legs and his stick, and thrust his face into mine. The skin was white and dense as a baby's but for the nose and the cheek-bones. The nose was red and blue and sharply pointed; at each cheekbone there burned the hectic scarlet spot of his disease. "So you are," he said between his thin blue lips. "So you are." Very slowly he shuffled over to the sofa pulled close up to the roaring fire and lowered himself into it. "Come and sit down."

I sat. The sofa was too deep, too soft. I could feel myself beginning to sweat.

He turned to look at me. "Nicholas Power," he said, musingly. "You were supposed to be dead."

"So I believe." His face displayed no emotion stronger than mild curiosity. I had expected anger, at least.

"You want to make your peace, do you?"

"I should be grateful if you would give me a hearing."

Papery eyelids came down. He inclined his head, very slightly. And I told him. I told him that I was innocent of the murder of his daughter, but that the case against me had seemed insurmountably strong. That I had left Ireland and attempted to make a life elsewhere; that I had succeeded, if money was any token of success. And that finally—I did not spell out the exact circumstances—I had been induced to return, to try to make what amends I could. It had sounded convincing when I had rehearsed it in the chaise. Now, it sounded very lame. If the Earl had retained any of his old acuity, he could not but have noticed the lameness.

The silence went on and on, for so long that I thought he must have fallen asleep. I said, "My Lord?"

"Yes, yes." He lifted a hand, let it fall wearily on the handle of his cane. "So you stayed away all this time. Could you not have come before?"

"I was advised against it."

"I seem to remember that in earlier days you were deuced unamenable to advice." The pepperiness in his tone made me feel more at home. "Was it not cowardice, Sir?"

I waited for the coughing to die away. "It came from a source I trusted implicitly. The man who was the only friend I had."

"Oh? And who was this plausible fellow?"

"Michael Fitzpatrick."

The pink-rimmed eyes became perfectly circular. "Sir! Do you seek to drag that estimable man into your web of deceit? How dare you!"

"It is true," I said. "When all Ireland thought I was dead, he alone knew I was alive. I can give you an account of his visits. I have kept his letters. I have them here." I took out my pocketbook. "Read them, if you will."

"I will not!" he said. But there was less conviction in the reedy voice. "I remember you were friends. And most unsuitable companions. Good enough one at a time, but bad together. Very bad. And now you seek to blacken his name with this scandalous imposture. Damn me, Sir, I will not have it."

"I beg you, read these letters."

"I will not. Fitzpatrick has been a faithful friend and companion. I will hear no word against him. Not a word." Another fit of coughing took him. I caught a glimpse of bright blood on the handkerchief.

"Not even from his own pen?"

A long pause. I was almost sure he would refuse. But, finally, he gave me a strange look, almost of fear, and said, "Very well. My spectacles." As I went to fetch them from the clutter of the desk, I knew I had seen that look before, and recently. He balanced the glasses on his nose and smoothed the paper with his ruined scholar's fingers. Kelly. It was the same look Kelly had had when he let me into the keep against Michael Fitzpatrick's orders. My old friend Michael must rule this ancient tower and its senile inhabitants with a firm hand. It did not dispose me any the more kindly towards him.

At last, the Earl said, "So that proves Michael knew you were alive. What else, though?"

"His tone is hardly what you have a right to expect from him."

"I do not seek to rule his life. I merely place my faith in him as administrator of my affairs."

I thought for a second. Then I said, "There is one thing. May I ask if you were . . . sorry to hear I had died?"

He watched the fire. "I was," he said. "Very sorry."

"Even after what I had done?"

"Even after what you had . . . done." A look of pain crossed his face.

"And you confided in Michael Fitzpatrick to this effect."

He looked surprised. "Of course. I have no secrets from him."

"Then why do you suppose he instructed a Major of Dragoons to assassinate me?"

"What are you saying, Sir?"

I told him of my flight from Carthystown Races. "You must have heard about it."

He nodded. "I did. But Michael would have it that you were John Foley, a known insurrectionist, and that it was the Major of Dragoons that noticed you."

"I am positive there are witnesses no further away than Carthystown who will confound him."

He looked thoughtful. I could hear the breath rattling in his throat. There was a bell-push at his elbow. Beside it, a curious funnel-shaped object protruded from the wall. He said, "Pull the bell." I rose and pulled. The Earl flicked back the lid of the funnel. After a couple of minutes Kelly's voice said, "My Lord?" thin and tinny.

"Would you desire Mr. Fitzpatrick to step up?"

"He is dining, Sir."

"I don't care if he's dying," snapped the Earl, his voice almost its former self. "Send him up." Kelly said, "Very good, My Lord." Even through the voice-tube he sounded shocked. The Earl snapped the lid back and gave himself over to his cough. He was tiring visibly. I hoped he would last.

When the spasms had subsided, he said, "Go and open the bottom right-hand drawer of the desk. You will find a deed-box and an envelope. We shall have them out. You might stay in the alcove, behind the curtain, while I chat to Michael. While you are there, you may care to examine the portraits."

I went to the desk and took out deed-box and envelope and tucked them under the sofa. Then I pulled the heavy velvet curtain a couple of feet and stepped behind it. The

sun was lower now, and it threw the Lawrence portrait of
Katie into deep shadow. Her green eyes mocked me from
beyond the grave.

I had thought that the portrait opposite was a pair to the
one of Katie. But it was not. It showed a young man of
dandified appearance. The left hand rested on a human
skull set on a truncated Ionian column; the right held an
open book, as if the sitter had been surprised while reading. The face was young, perhaps a little fleshy, with long
eyes and high cheekbones. The cropped black hair gave it
a superficial resemblance to Napoleon Bonaparte.

*Why should the Earl of Drumcarty hang opposite the
likeness of his daughter the likeness of her murderer?*

The door opened. Footsteps sounded on the floor, muffled by the thick carpets. I drew further into the shelter of
the curtain. The Earl's voice said, "Ah, Michael, dear boy.
So sorry to take you from your dinner."

"By no means." Michael's voice was a little thick.
"What can I do for you?"

"I fear I am sinking," said the Earl. His voice was a
whisper, scarcely audible. "I wished once more . . . before
the end . . . to remember poor Nick with you."

Michael sighed gustily. I thought I detected in it more
impatience than regret for a departed friend. "Poor fellow," he said. "We shall never see his face again, more
sorrow to us."

"More sorrow to us," echoed the Earl. "And so the
Name dies. It is a long passing, and a sad one."

Michael's voice became low and reassuring. "The Name
may pass. But the lands will be in safe hands. You may
rest easy on that."

"Rest. The long sleep in the cold, narrow bed." The
Earl coughed, long and nasty. He had willed his estates to
Michael. That made clear his wish to have me considered
dead. The business about the Name, however, defeated
me. I found my eyes again on the portrait.

"It was a sore blow," said the Earl. "A sore blow. Perhaps it is a judgement."

"Never say that," said Michael. "You did nothing to
earn such ingratitude."

"Only to look on his dear face once again."

Michael cleared his throat and said, "Don't upset yourself, now. It does you no good." His patience was obvi-

ously waning. "Are you sure you're quite comfortable? Only I should see to my guests."

"Oh, quite comfortable." I could imagine the papery lids fallen over the eyes, the tiny inclination of the sick face. "Go to your friends." The door opened. "One moment," said the Earl. "One small thing?"

"What is it?" said Michael. Now he barely troubled to hide the impatience in his voice.

"I find myself indisposed. Would you . . . draw back the curtain a little further. So I can see him?"

The footsteps came towards me. Thick fingers gripped the velvet and pulled it back. I stood still, smiling.

His face was its usual hearty red between the oily black whiskers. I said, "How d'ye do, Michael?" The skin paled through pink to white, from white the grey of old wood-ash.

"Holy Jesus," he whispered.

I took his arm and led him down from the dais. "Please be seated," I said. "It will help restore the blood to the brain."

He was regaining control of himself. "Nick," he said. "By God but when I saw you standing there—by God I thought you were a ghost. How is it, old friend?" He jumped to his feet and grasped my hand. "Oh but it's grand—we thought you was dead."

I detached myself. "I nearly was. Several times. But not nearly enough."

"But that's grand. Oh, that's grand." The Earl coughed. Michael looked down at him, turned back to me, but not all the way, so the Earl could still see his left profile. Had he been a professional actor he could not have done the change in his face more perfectly. The broad grin of the long-lost friend was crossed, as if by a shadow, with the recollection of Duty. Innocent delight made a counter-attack, got a foot over the battlements. Then Duty sallied forth and swept it aside. He ducked his head and brought it up again, eyes levelled frowning at my own. "For myself, I confess I am delighted. But His Lordship—that was rash, Nick. I find it most rash in you." He took my arm. "Come away, Nick. Your presence can only cause pain to the one you so shamefully wronged."

I said, "Take your hands off me."

The Earl said, "I should be pleased if you would offer me an explanation."

There was a new expression dawning on Michael's face, like a fox with hounds at his brush finding a paving-stone stopping his earth. "Your Lordship is tired," he said. "In the morning we'll have a long talk. Look, now, the sun's nearly set. Take your sleeping-draught and old Nick will take his bottle and tomorrow——"

"I am at the stage where tomorrow is more a possibility than a probability," said the Earl. "If you would be so kind as to explain yourself."

"Explain?"

"I think we should both like to know why I am thought to be dead," I said.

"For your own damned good," said Michael.

"And for mine?" said the Earl. "The thought has caused me nothing but pain and grief. And if I am not mistaken, you have derived some considerable advantage from it yourself."

"I acted from a sense of my duty," Michael said.

The Earl took the envelope from under the sofa. He passed me a fat packet of paper. "Let us allow Nicholas to draw his own conclusions," he said.

It was a Will. By its terms, the Drumcarty estates in Ireland and England were to pass, by default of legitimate succession, to Michael Francis Fitzpatrick, Esquire, of St. Stephen's Green, Dublin. It was dated January, 1831, signed, and duly witnessed. I had expected no less.

"I'll look after that," said Michael. "It should be filed. Put in a place of safety."

The Earl said, "You have looked after me for a long time. All I have has been in your hands. And now I find you have betrayed my trust."

"For your own good," said Michael. "Protecting you."

"From what, may I ask?"

Michael clasped his hands behind his back and walked away, head bowed. "I would rather not say."

"I'm sure you would," I said.

"Very well," he said, pivoting on his heel. "It concerns that night in Dublin. The night you fled. I had evidence —I had evidence that would have damned you, Nicholas. Proof of your folly. Oh, I hoped that the doubts as to your guilt would persist. They have persisted, elsewhere. But I know, Nicholas. I know."

"What, precisely?" said the Earl.

"A letter. I have it at my office. From Nicholas to the

Lady Katie, arranging time and place, with some . . . intimate details."

"That's a lie," I said. "It'll be a forgery."

"His Lordship will decide that for himself," said Michael. "I shall send to Dublin for it straight away."

"His Lordship has already decided." The Earl's face was stretched in a dreadful skull-like grin. "I received a letter myself some weeks after poor Katie died. She had left instructions that it should be posted in the event of her death. There was delay, I do not know why. In it she explained her . . . predicament and the rash means by which she hoped to extricate herself. She cast the blame squarely on a Dublin midwife, a Mrs. Egan. Mrs. Egan has, I believe, long passed to her reward."

"Why did you not tell me?" said Michael, cheeks grey and ghastly.

"Some things are best kept to oneself," said the Earl.

"But why did you not blame Mrs. Egan publicly?" said I.

"Because she might have . . . made fuss. I thought you dead, Nicholas. And whatever that drunken fool of a chaplain may say, the dead are beyond harm. There was enough scandal . . . at the time. I could bear no more. I suppressed the letter to avoid further pain to myself." He paused to cough. "I am more inclined to believe Katie than you, Michael. I wish I had time to do you justice. Unfortunately, I have not. Nicholas. You may throw that piece of paper on the fire."

Michael's head moved into a patch of blue light that gave him the colour of an old corpse. "Reflect," he said, and moved forward, turning green and red by turns. "Hastiness you will regret." As he passed me his hand shot out and made a grab for the paper. He caught me off guard, and I felt the heavy seal slide away between my fingers.

The Earl said, "Michael! What——"

"His Lordship has only to make a new Will," I said.

"Right, so," said Michael. His smile was very jolly. The black eyes held a hard, triumphant glitter.

"You will please burn that document," said the Earl.

Michael bowed. Slowly he bent down to the fire, the paper in his left hand. He crouched in front of the flames, his broad back bent, oily black ringlets curling down from the white bald patch. The Earl said urgently, "Nicholas—" Then he started to cough.

I looked down at him. He was bending forward, handkerchief to his lips. His eyes were bulging towards the fire, round and horror-struck. For a split second I heard a vicious hum in my right ear. My head exploded with pain. The blue arabesques of the carpet looped up and dragged me down, rolling away from the agony in my skull. The humming was very loud. I saw Michael, poker in hand, lever blazing logs onto the carpet and the sofa. Thick smoke rose between me and the Earl. Michael's lips moved, but I could not hear what he was saying. He tucked the long packet with its red seal into his breast pocket, and walked out of my vision. I clawed at the curtains of pain and smoke that tried to pull me down into the dark. The sofa cushions took fire with a dusty *whoosh*. Dimly, above the ringing in my ears, I heard the Earl coughing. He was bending forward, struggling with the tin deed-box. I got on my hands and knees and began crawling. Michael bowed, slow and respectful, his back to the door. In his left hand he held up a long, slender wedge. The latch was on the outside. It was a good latch, of stout iron, I remembered. Above the coughing I heard Michael say, "Goodbye." There was no pretence left on his face. It was sharp and smug. I remembered the face from Carthystown school, when I had been smaller than him and I had been beating him in a fight and he had driven my kidney against a door-handle. Win at any cost, said the face.

I crawled on across acres of undulating carpet, a red sea with snaking bands of green and muted blues, towards his feet. The door opened. I felt the draught on my face, heard the flames behind roar. Still he stood there. He was laughing now. My eyes travelled up from his shining brown boots to the check trousers, the green waistcoat with hunt buttons, the wide cruel mouth between jolly red cheeks, the eyes glittering with the tiny flames dancing in the pupils.

From behind me there came the boom of an explosion. The door behind his head turned scarlet and shiny and slammed open and was empty. I heard a heavy thump, a rustling of paper. I climbed slowly to my feet and went back to the blazing sofa.

The Earl of Drumcarty was lying back. But for the coughing, he looked very comfortable. The flames were licking at his right sleeve, caressing the long, scholarly fingers loosely wrapped round the horse-pistol. I pulled his left arm round my neck and heaved him up. Then we struggled for the door, his long legs trailing behind like the legs of a mounted skeleton. The coughing was an earthquake. Great spasms tore him, his fleshless ribs jumping under my fingers. On the landing I kicked the door shut. The air was better here. I tore off his blazing dressing-gown and flung it away. It went over the railings billowing with the air trapped inside it. For a moment it hung over the stacks of paper like a fiery butterfly hovering over a field of daisies. Then it sank over the face of the fallen scarecrow in the green waistcoat, hiding the poppy-red pool spreading from among the oily Medusa hair.

By the time I staggered into the courtyard, the coughing had stopped. I laid the Earl down on a tuft of rank grass. His face was quite white now, the hectic spots gone. A red river of blood stained his chin. Above, a pillar of black smoke was rushing into the blue. The jackdaws had left their holes, cawing and shrieking. There was a dull rumble. A fountain of black paper-ash belched from the ragged battlements, swooping and fluttering with the birds. After that, there were only the flames.

The walls of the keep were twelve feet thick. It burned like a furnace, the air roaring in through doors and arrow-slits and belching up in smoke and flame from the ruins of the roof. There was only one door leading to the Jacobean part of the house. We kept it closed, piled earth from the weed-covered garden against it. I put two servants on the roof with buckets against flying sparks, arranged for them to be kept supplied. Then I carried the Earl up into one of the bedrooms on the first boor.

With Kelly's help, I got him into the bed. He had stopped coughing, now. His hands and feet were cold, the pulse frequent and thready. The rattle of his breathing was very loud. Kelly made a fire. It had been a woman's room, the bed-hangings pink, the carpet deep Aubusson blue with flowers. There was a hint of very old powder in the still, musty air. I went to open the windows. Kelly said, "The doctor did insist he was to be kept warm and close."

"The doctor's a murderer," I said.

"What . . . what am I doing here?" said the Earl's voice from the bed.

"The keep's burnt out. You are to lie still, not to talk."

"No. Come over here, Nicholas."

"You keep yourself quiet," I said. "Time enough for talking later."

"There is no later," said the Earl. Again he coughed, struggled to reach handkerchief to mouth. He was too weak. I wiped away the fresh blood. He was right.

"You will have been wondering. . . ." said the Earl.

"Quiet, now."

"Keep your advice to yourself, damn you!" He closed his eyes, opened them again. Even the fever was going. "You will have been wondering why I kept your portrait by me. After what happened."

"Yes."

"It is quite simple. I should have told you long ago. I should never have tried to hide it. It was what . . . people would say. I was most scrupulous about that, once." He paused, chest heaving for air. "Do you remember your mother?"

"I do not."

"No. Of course not. How should you?" He sighed. "She was a beautiful woman. This was her room, once."

I stared at him. "Her room? I don't understand."

"She was the daughter of a Limerick horse-dealer. When I married her I had never seen anyone like her. She had your eyes, Nicholas. Every time I saw you I saw her. I think it was that that made me ill, first. The knowledge like a disease. No cure—"

"What of my mother?" I said.

"She was living here. I was drunk. There was a parson here, desperate soak. He married us. And a month later she told me she was pregnant. With you . . . I found I could not countenance it . . . . my pride . . . God, she was beautiful—but a child . . . You have known me for a long time, Nicholas."

"Not as well as I thought."

He raised a hand on the coverlet. "I put her out of the house. Power—the man you thought was your father . . . I knew he wanted her. He had no pride. None. He took her. I suppose he loved her. Then she died when you

were born. I thought I could forget about it. I married
again. Then after Katie had come I was drunk and I told
. . . I told my wife about you. She was a woman who
could not live with that sort of truth. The right woman for
me, I suppose. She killed herself. And I was left with
Katie. Katie was going to be everything. And then, . . ."

"And then Katie died."

"And I knew I was being punished. But still I could not
own you, Nicholas. The disgrace would have been too
much. God help me, I was glad you were dead. Everything would blow over. . . ." He turned an agonised face
to me. "Do you understand, Nicholas? Do you understand?"

"I think so," I said.

Nicholas Power. No. Not Power. Browne-Ormonde.
Fifteenth Earl of Drumcarty. Incestuous lover of Lady
Katherine, his half-sister, deceased. Patient of Charity
Pender of Scilly, deceased. Supposed rival of Little John
Woodcock of Scilly, deceased. Lover of Mary Prideaux,
father of Nicholas Prideaux, deceased. Rival of Augustus
Smith of Berkhamstead and Scilly, but for the grace of
God and a tender conscience deceased. Champion of the
weak. Scourge of the pitiless. Son of the Fourteenth Earl
of Drumcarty, who had caused all the death and flight
and pain by his pride in his name.

"You will wear the name well," said the Earl. "With
pride."

"I shall try to," I said. But I was humouring the dying
man. Pride had undone him. Pride had undone me.

Outside the window, black birds reeled against the sky
like the fragments of a burned banner. The Earl said,
"In the pocket of my waistcoat. My marriage certificate
to your mother. The certificate of your birth. Get pens
and paper."

I rang for Kelly and the chaplain. Then Drumcarty—
my father—dictated and signed his new Will. Afterwards
he lay very still on the pillow, refusing food and drugs,
eyes sunk far back into the sockets. His breathing was
fast and stertorous. Half an hour later he sat up, his
mouth hanging open. I went and put my arm round his
shoulders as the coughing tore him, holding the handkerchief to his blue lips. The fit passed, and he said, "I am
proud—" and it began again. This time it did not stop.

The blood poured into the handkerchief and down onto the white sheets. One convulsion took him halfway to the floor. Then he fell slack in my arms.

I laid his head on the pillow. The chaplain turned frightened eyes on me. "He's dead," I said. "Leave us, now."

After he had gone I remained by the bed looking down at the pinched face. In death there was no pride. Only the ravaged flesh that pride had gnawed away from within. Only the desperate meanness of a life spent hoarding secrets. And for what purpose?

I walked across the blue carpet to the window. Beyond the curtain wall, the river, ebbing brown towards the sea. And beyond the river the shambles of Drumcarty park, ruined houses, dead trees, ivy and decay poking skinny fingers to tear it down. At the far end of the bridge there stood a ragged crowd. Tenants, drawn by the smoke of the keep trailing black into the reddening sun. Perhaps they were full of hope. The Earl might be burned, rebellion in the land, freedom close. They would be disappointed when they heard they had a new landlord. As the men of Scilly had been disappointed. It was my job to see that their disappointment did not last. Those tenants were mine. I could use them as I wished.

I thought again of Scilly. There, the sea would be muttering in the rocks as it always had and always would. And on the rocks, people. Not people as I had known them seven years ago, struggling through their ancient world, free to wreck or starve. People living in a new world of straight roads, full bellies, roofless houses, hard laws. And the legion of the dead standing behind Mary, those dark blue eyes that had once had no focus but infinity now caught on Smith's child at her breast. The world had changed.

And I had changed too. Scilly, New Botallack. It had been a hard course to follow. But I had followed it, and it had given me the wherewithal to mend roofs, improve farms, put new heart into Drumcarty's mouldering acres. If I wanted to.

The house was like a great tomb. Katie, my mother, her mother. My friend Michael Fitzpatrick, his ashes mixed with endless law in the glowing ruins of the keep. The ghosts came around me as I stood by the window, looking out at the green slopes and the distant blue mountains. But they went by me, fled across the land and away. The sun shone clear through them; ghosts cast no shadows. The only shadows were in the pinched faces of my tenants, waiting at the bridge.

I went and rang for Kelly, to send for my boxes from the Bell.

Acknowledgments

I SHOULD LIKE to express my gratitude to my cousin Robert Dorrien Smith, who lent me one of his extraordinarily beautiful cottages on Tresco and gave me the run of Tresco Abbey's splendid, curious and picturesque library. I should also like to thank Roy Cooper, of whose researches I have taken shameless advantage; and Johnny Barbadoes, Martin Shrub and their friends and wives, without whom none of this would have been possible.

Finally my thanks to Karen and Bill Llewellyn for their meticulous editing and advice; and to Annie Murley and Jane Wingfield, for endless nights crouched over a hot typewriter.

Bestsellers
from
BALLANTINE BOOKS